Follow the bestselling adventures of

STAR WARS
YOUNG JEDI KNIGHTS

HEIRS OF THE FORCE
The *New York Times* bestselling debut of the young Jedi Knights! Their training begins . . .

SHADOW ACADEMY
The dark side of the Force has a new training ground: the Shadow Academy!

THE LOST ONES
An old friend of the twins could be the perfect candidate for the Shadow Academy!

LIGHTSABERS
At last, the time has come for the young Jedi Knights to build their weapons . . .

DARKEST KNIGHT
The Dark Jedi student Zekk must face his old friends Jacen and Jaina—once and for all.

JEDI UNDER SIEGE
The final battle between Luke Skywalker's Jedi academy and the evil Shadow Academy . . .

And don't miss the new dangers, new enemies,
and new adventures in . . .

SHARDS OF ALDERAAN
While visiting the remains of their mother's home, Jacen and Jaina encounter a long-lost enemy of the Solo family . . .

DIVERSITY ALLIANCE
Everyone is searching for Bornan Thul, but the young Jedi Knights may be too late—for their true enemy is about to show his shockingly familiar face . . .

ABOUT THE AUTHORS

KEVIN J. ANDERSON and his wife, **REBECCA MOESTA**, have been involved in many STAR WARS projects. Together, they are writing the eleven volumes of the YOUNG JEDI KNIGHTS saga for young adults, as well as creating the JUNIOR JEDI KNIGHTS series for younger readers. Rebecca Moesta is also writing the second trilogy of JUNIOR JEDI KNIGHTS adventures.

Kevin J. Anderson is the author of the STAR WARS: JEDI ACADEMY TRILOGY, the novel *Darksaber*, and the comic series THE SITH WAR and THE GOLDEN AGE OF THE SITH for Dark Horse comics. He has written many other novels, including two based on *The X-Files* television show. He has edited three STAR WARS anthologies: *Tales from the Mos Eisley Cantina*, in which Rebecca Moesta has a story; *Tales from Jabba's Palace*; and *Tales of the Bounty Hunters*.

For more information about the authors, visit their Web site at
http://www.wordfire.com

STAR WARS

YOUNG JEDI KNIGHTS

DELUSIONS OF GRANDEUR

KEVIN J. ANDERSON
and REBECCA MOESTA

BOULEVARD BOOKS, NEW YORK

STAR WARS: YOUNG JEDI KNIGHTS:
DELUSIONS OF GRANDEUR

A Boulevard Book / published by arrangement with
Lucasfilm Ltd.

PRINTING HISTORY
Boulevard edition / July 1997

The Putnam Berkley World Wide Web site address is
http://www.berkley.com

ISBN: 1-57297-272-6

BOULEVARD
Boulevard Books are published by The Berkley Publishing Group,
200 Madison Avenue, New York, New York 10016.
BOULEVARD and its logo are trademarks
belonging to Berkley Publishing Corporation.

PRINTED IN THE UNITED STATES OF AMERICA

10 9 8 7 6 5 4 3 2

acknowledgments

Writing each volume of the Young Jedi Knights requires the help of many different people—Sue Rostoni, Allan Kausch, and Lucy Wilson at Lucasfilm Licensing; Ginjer Buchanan and Jessica Faust at Boulevard Books; Dave Dorman, cover artist extraordinaire; Vonda McIntrye (who created the character Lusa); Mike Stackpole for his help with Evir Derricote and the plague; A. C. Crispin for her help with Aryn Dro and Bornan Thul; Kaisa Wuorinen for her beautiful name and for being a faithful fan; Nick Peterson for the joke; Lillie E. Mitchell, Catherine Ulatowski, and Angela Kato at WordFire, Inc.; and Jonathan Cowan, our first test-reader.

A special thanks to all of the fans and devoted readers whose enthusiasm and support gave us the energy and encouragement we needed to keep writing.

STAR WARS

YOUNG JEDI KNIGHTS

WARS ®

DELUSIONS OF GRANDEUR

1

A KNOCK AT the wooden door startled Jaina Solo out of her reverie. She had to blink a few times to orient herself as she shook off memories of recent events.

Her gaze swept around her stone-walled room, across the sleeping pallet and the small work desk by the window slit. Against one wall, neatly stacked containers of spare cyberfuses, salvaged circuit loops, and miniature gears gave evidence of her love for electronics and tinkering.

When Jaina heard the second knock, she glanced toward the arched doorway. "Oh—come in!" she called, and her twin brother pushed open the newly repaired door.

Jacen's eyes, the same brandy-brown color as her own, shone with barely contained excitement. "Hey, guess what? My gort egg is finally about to hatch! It's making weird noises and rocking around. Wanna come watch?"

It took a moment for Jacen's news to sink in. "Sure," she said, proud to know that the incubator she had built for Jacen's gort egg—a gift from their father, Han Solo—had worked so well. "I'll be right there. I'm just finishing up something. Give me five minutes."

Jacen gave her a curious look. The room held no obvious projects that could not wait until after the hatching. "Okay, but hurry—that egg could hatch anytime now. I'm going to get Tenel Ka." He raced out of the room.

Jaina smoothed her straight brown hair back behind her ears and turned to face the tiny holocam that sat in front of her on her desk almost hidden by a mound of spare parts. "Let's try this one *more* time, from the top," she muttered. Then, taking a deep breath, she switched on the holocam.

"Hello, Zekk. Things are pretty quiet here on Yavin 4. I really miss—well, we *all* miss you. I wish you'd reconsider and come back to the Jedi academy. Uh-oh. That's no good." She flicked the tiny holocam off, erased her message, and flicked it on again. She cleared her throat and started over.

"How are you, Zekk? I realize you didn't stay here for very long, but things at the academy just haven't been the same since you left. It seems like such a long time since we last saw you."

Jaina switched off the recorder again. "Oh, great. *That* was cheery," she scolded herself. "Guaranteed to send him running to the Outer Rim Territories and beyond."

She closed her eyes and imagined Zekk was right here in front of her . . . his emerald eyes alive with intelligence, his almost-black hair tied back at the nape of his neck. . . .

Opening her eyes again, she reset the recorder to the beginning and readjusted her features to look more happy and relaxed. She actually felt calmer then, and switched the holocam back on. One more time. Forcing a twinkle into her eye, she flashed him the same lopsided grin that she and Jacen had inherited from their father.

"Hi, Zekk. Hope you get this hololetter soon. I recorded a few others and gave them to old Peckhum. He said he'd send the messages to you, but he couldn't guarantee *when* you would get them." She cleared her throat and kept talking.

"We're all busy as ever, still at work rebuilding the temples." She winced at the memory of the Shadow Academy attack Zekk himself had helped to engineer, but plunged ahead and steered her thoughts toward safer topics. "Seems like each time we get settled in, something comes up and I'm off with Jacen, Tenel Ka, and Lowie on some new adventure. Not as exciting as the life of a bounty hunter trainee, maybe, but it keeps us on our toes."

She bit her lower lip and thought for a second. "By the way, nothing fresh to report about Bornan Thul's disappearance yet. In fact, things only seem to be getting worse. We went to a planet called Kuar to look for clues and wound up tangling with a batch of combat arachnids instead. You should've seen the battle! Anyway, Thul's brother Tyko showed up afterward to help us search. That night we were attacked by assassin droids led by IG-88! We fought in the catacombs, but there were so many droids *and* combat arachnids! IG-88 snatched Tyko Thul right in front of our eyes—and there was nothing we could do to stop it. Now both Raynar's father *and* his uncle Tyko are missing."

Jaina shook her head. "I know you're looking for Bornan Thul, too. Have you caught any news on your end?" she added hopefully. "Wish we could find something good to tell Raynar when we see him next. Last we heard, he was still in hiding with the Bornaryn fleet—the trading ships his parents own. We tried to send messages, but we can't tell if word got through." She sighed. "Course, I have no idea if this letter'll get through to *you*, either.

"Anyhow, if you run into the fleet or get any word about Bornan or Tyko Thul, we'd sure like to hear from you." Jaina stopped, blushed slightly. "Well, we'd like to hear from you *anyway,* if you get the chance. I'm rambling, so I guess I should sign off now. Peckhum will encrypt this message and send it out to all the bars, cantinas, smuggler's dens . . ." She grinned. "You know, all those places where scoundrels and *bounty hunters* hang out. I'll send another hololetter when I have time. Until then, may the Force be with you." She smiled one more time. "Bye, Zekk."

Jaina stopped recording and nodded. "That ought to do it—not too gushy or emotional." She really hated having to walk on eggshells when she spoke to an old friend.

Eggshells. Egg!

She had completely forgotten about Jacen's gort egg hatching! Slipping the hololetter into a pocket of her flight suit, she dashed for Jacen's room.

Only one room of the Great Temple boasted an entire wall of terrariums, incubators, cages, and aquariums on sturdy stone shelves: the room occupied by Jacen Solo. On most days at the Jedi academy, Jacen spent an hour, or sometimes two, feeding and caring for his various pets, using the Force to send them pleasant thoughts and to sense anything they needed.

Today, however, he was interested in only one creature—one he had never seen before.

"The shell appears . . . flawless," Tenel Ka said, holding her hand above the spheroid egg.

Under the light of the incubator, the pearly pink shell gleamed softly. Jacen glanced at the warrior girl who crouched beside him watching the egg. The egg made a sudden rocking movement, but Tenel Ka didn't flinch.

"Pretty neat, huh?" Jacen said.

"A beautiful color," she remarked.

"Uh-huh," Jacen said, though at the moment he was admiring the red-gold of Tenel Ka's hair, some of which was loose and flowing, the rest caught up in braids that fell forward over the shoulders of her green lizard-hide armor.

"May I touch your egg?" Tenel Ka asked. She nodded toward the object, which had once again begun to rock and emit clicking noises.

"Uh . . . sure," Jacen said.

"Did I miss it?" Jaina burst into the room. "Did it hatch yet?" The pearly egg gave a soft *thump-thump* and rolled up against one wall of the incubator.

"Looks like you're right on time." Jacen moved a bit closer to Tenel Ka, ostensibly to give his sister a better view of the incubator's front panel.

Jaina glanced around the room before plopping herself on the floor beside him. "Where's Lowie?" she asked.

"He has not yet arrived," Tenel Ka said.

"I told him about the hatching," Jacen added. "He said he needed to stretch his legs, but he should be here any minute." The pearl-pink sphere in the incubator bounced a few times and made a louder ticking noise.

"Come on, little one," Jacen coaxed, leaning closer to the incubator. "You can do it."

A moment later, a warbling bellow could be heard just outside the smashed window opening in Jacen's room. All three young Jedi turned just in time to see Lowie swing through the opening in an uncharacteristic display of swashbuckling bravado.

Part of the window area had been demolished during the Shadow Academy attack, but since there was no major structural damage, Jacen was in no hurry to get it repaired. He liked the fresh air.

Now the lanky, ginger-furred Lowbacca landed neatly on the flagstones, smoothed a large hand over the black streak of fur that ran up over his head above the left eye and down his back, and roared a Wookiee greeting.

Tenel Ka raised an eyebrow and glanced at Lowie. "A fine entrance, friend Lowbacca," she observed. "I will remember it."

"Dear me, I do hope we haven't arrived too late," Em Teedee said. The little silver translating droid was clipped to his usual place on Lowie's syren-fiber belt. "I've never had the opportunity to witness a gort hatching before."

As if on cue, the gort egg made a sharp clacking noise. Lowie crossed the room in three long strides and crowded between Jacen and Jaina on the floor.

The gort egg knocked loudly, bounced, and rolled

until it rested against the front panel of the incubator.

"Good," Jacen said softly. "That's it—you've almost got it. A few more times now."

Click-click. Thunk. Clack.

Jacen touched his fingers to the transparisteel. "There's a warm, friendly place waiting for you," he whispered. With one more click and another thunk, a tiny fissure appeared in the surface of the shell.

Lowie gave a thoughtful rumble. Jaina drew in a sharp breath and bit her lower lip. Tenel Ka reached out and placed her hand just next to Jacen's on the clear front panel, her fingers barely touching his. Jacen felt soothing, welcoming thoughts join his own and flow toward the egg.

The egg tapped and bounced. Another crack appeared.

A loud noise at the doorway interrupted them as one of the New Republic soldiers stationed on the jungle moon during the reconstruction activities stuck his helmeted head into the room. He blinked, looking somewhat confused. "Excuse me, I was trying to find a refresher unit." The soldier made a hasty retreat and continued urgently down the hall.

The young Jedi Knights turned their attention back to the hatching egg.

"Oh, I can scarcely bear the suspense!" Em Teedee said in a hushed voice. "Master Lowbacca, if I might impose on you for just a moment? I should like to get a closer look."

Lowie unclipped the little droid from his belt and held him up to the incubator for an unobstructed view. The gort egg bounced and rocked, bumping itself repeatedly against the clear front panel.

"Come on, you can do it," Jacen whispered.

Crack. A piece of shell, perfectly triangular in shape, fell away from the side of the egg. Then the egg jumped and rolled until the triangular opening was on top. Suddenly a downy ball of blue fluff poked through the hole. The fluff parted, like two halves of a curtain pulling aside, to reveal an inquisitive sapphire-blue eye.

"Hey! Hello there," Jacen said gently.

The sapphire eye went wide, then nictated a few times, as if it could not believe what it saw. It swiveled on its down-covered eyestalk for a complete view of its surroundings. Another ball of fluff appeared through the hole in the egg, and a second sapphire-blue eye blinked furiously at them. The two fluffy eye-balls bobbed up and down on their stalks, looking first at each other, then around the incubator. When the two eye-balls were joined by a third puff of downy blue that blinked sleepily at them, Jaina giggled.

"Oh my!" Em Teedee said. "How many ocular appendages does this creature possess?"

Jacen shrugged. "Just three . . . I think." Tenel

Ka's hand dropped away from the incubator, and she looked at Jacen in surprise.

The eye-balls bobbed wildly. A hollow tapping sound came from inside the remaining eggshell. Finally the shell broke apart into a dozen pieces, revealing the tiny gort hatchling.

Blue fluff clothed every square centimeter of the creature, except for the wide, flat beak set a third of the way down its little body. The rounded body, as large as Jacen's fist, perched atop a pair of short legs, supported by broad, flat feet. The three toes were splayed for balance, and the gort's thin prehensile tail curled into the air behind it. The tip of the tail reached forward to scratch one of the gort's eyestalks, as if it were confused.

"Hello, little girl," Jacen said. He turned to the others. "Don't ask me how I know it's a girl. I just do."

Lowie gave an urf of laughter, and tapped one finger against the incubator's front panel. All three of the gort's eyestalks retracted into its body, and the eyes nictated shut, so that the creature looked like a lump of blue down.

"What is her name?" Tenel Ka asked.

All three eyestalks extended again and the sapphire eyes blinked open.

"She blinks a lot," Jacen said. "I think I'll call her Nicta."

Jacen slid open the feeding chute in the incubator; several insects and grubs he had collected cascaded into the feeding dish. "There you go, Nicta. Morning meal."

With a warbling sound, Artoo-Detoo entered Jacen's student quarters. "Artoo, what brings you here?" Jaina said.

The silver, blue, and white barrel-shaped droid beeped and twittered a rather long explanation.

"Uh, Em Teedee?" Jacen said, still preoccupied with his new pet. "Would you mind translating on this one?"

"Why, certainly, Master Jacen. How could I mind? After all, translating has always been my primary function, though it's seldom used these days. I am fluent in over six forms of communication. Why, in my prime, I—"

"Em Teedee," Jaina cut in.

"Yes, Mistress Jaina?"

"The translation please?"

"Oh, yes. My associate, Artoo-Detoo, was sent by Master Luke to request that you report to the landing field to assist Master Peckhum in unloading supplies for the Jedi academy and for the New Republic defensive forces. He is due to arrive in just over four standard minutes."

"Old Peckhum's coming here?" Jaina asked.

"Hey, that's great," Jacen said. Lowie jumped to his feet.

"Perhaps Peckhum will bring news of Zekk," Tenel Ka said.

Jaina blushed slightly and looked away, and Jacen knew the same thought had occurred to her. "Well, what are we waiting for?" she asked.

Jacen turned back to the incubator. He picked up the perfect, triangular shard of eggshell, put it in his pocket, and crooned to the little hatchling. "Don't worry, Nicta. We won't be away long." Then he and his companions raced together out to the landing field.

Though they'd seen it twice before, Jacen found it hard to get used to Peckhum's new ship, the *Thunderbolt*. It still seemed strange to see the old spacer flying the modern midsized cargo hauler. The gleaming entry ramp extended, and several more New Republic soldiers accompanied Peckhum down to the ground.

"Hope you don't mind some company," Peckhum said as the guards headed for their briefing rooms. "Had to drop off supplies with the ships up in orbit, and these five needed shore leave somethin' fierce. I also brought someone else with me. Chief of State Organa Solo wanted to make sure he got here safely."

Jaina's eyes lit up. "Zekk?"

Peckhum sighed. "Naw—wish it were. I *have* been gettin' messages from Zekk fairly regular, though. Doesn't say much, 'cept that he's learnin' a lot about bounty huntin'."

Jaina slipped the holorecording out of her pocket and pressed it into Peckhum's hand. "Will you get this message to Zekk for me?"

"Sure will," Peckhum said. "Least we know the people we love are safe," he added. "Which is more than my passenger can say."

"Raynar?" Jacen guessed.

Peckhum nodded. "I'm afraid that boy could use a good deal of cheerin' up right now."

Lowie rumbled his willingness to help and headed up the ramp.

"Don't worry, we'll take good care of him," Jaina assured the old spacer.

"This is a fact," Tenel Ka said. "We will remain close to him while we unload supplies."

"We'll find a way to get his mind off his worries," Jacen said, following Lowie up the ramp. "I'll even tell him some of my best jokes."

"Uh-oh," Jaina said as she and Tenel Ka hurried on board. "We're all in trouble now."

2

A SHOOTING STAR streaked across the velvety blackness of the night. From his safe perch in the treetops, Lowbacca looked up hopefully, wondering if it was a ship arriving unannounced. Perhaps a stranger, perhaps another addition to the New Republic defense fleet . . . perhaps his friend Raaba.

His golden eyes studied the trail of light—but it dwindled to a fiery sparkle. Just a small meteor. The complex gravitational paths in the Yavin system sent many fragments of rock and dust into the fourth moon's orbit.

It wasn't Raaba, then. Not yet.

With a grumbling sigh, Lowie leaned back against the cushioning branches of the Massassi tree. *Another false alarm.* Returning to his routine of scouting the night sky, he let his thoughts and his memories drift again. . . .

He had come here alone after dark, disregarding

the dangers of Yavin 4's wilderness. Lowbacca was a powerful Wookiee, and he could take care of himself. The jungle moon's predators couldn't hold a candle to the nightmares he'd already encountered in the lower forest levels on Kashyyyk.

Trying to hide his inner turmoil from his friends Jacen, Jaina, and Tenel Ka, Lowie had climbed out of the partially rebuilt Great Temple in the middle of the sleeping period. Lowie had hauled himself along the dew-slick stone blocks until he reached the place from which he could spring across to the wide boughs of the nearest Massassi tree. From there, he climbed higher until he reached the treetop canopy. He spread the shiny leaves and found himself a spot where he could sit back and look up into the vastness of stars. Where he could keep watch.

His friend Raaba was out there . . . somewhere.

Lowie touched his syren-fiber belt where Em Teedee normally hung. He had left the little droid switched to recharge mode on a shelf in his quarters. Em Teedee would have scolded him for going out alone at night, and undoubtedly would have talked too much when Lowbacca simply wanted peace and quiet.

Below, he heard a large animal crashing through vines and underbrush. Plant-eating creatures chittered through the leaves, searching for tender night-blooming flowers. He heard the howls and snarls and snapping twigs of some violent struggle, but the commotion was far away. A nocturnal stalker had found its food for another day.

It seemed long ago that Lowie had undergone his ordeal, risking his life in the lower Wookiee forests. It had been an important rite of passage to secure the gossamer fibers from the jaws of the carnivorous syren plant. And he had done it alone.

Lowie had been cocky, so foolishly brave, but he had come back a hero, earning new respect from his fellow Wookiees. That newfound standing had won him the freedom to choose what he wished to do with his life. More than anything else, Lowie had wanted to be a Jedi Knight. . . .

He hadn't dreamed, though, that his bravado might prove deadly for his friend Raabakyysh, a chocolate-furred Wookiee female who was a close companion of Lowie's sister Sirrakuk.

Normally, comrades would accompany Wookiees during this coming-of-age ritual. But Raaba had been so impressed by Lowie's solo feat that she had attempted to duplicate it. If Lowbacca could do it alone, Raaba reasoned, then *she* needed no assistance either.

Raabakyysh had vanished that night, leaving behind only a bloodied backpack. Lowie and Sirra had mourned the loss of their friend. Everyone had presumed her dead.

But on Kuar, while Lowie and the other young

Jedi Knights were searching for Bornan Thul in the ancient ruins, Rabba suddenly reappeared. She had been hiding all this time, trying to find her own way in life.

During her long absence, Raaba had joined the Diversity Alliance, a political movement she believed in fervently. Its leader, a Twi'lek woman named Nolaa Tarkona, demanded restitution for all the damage inflicted by humans upon alien species. When Tyko Thul offhandedly insulted Tarkona in conversation, Raaba had taken offense and departed from Kuar.

Now Lowie feared his long-lost Wookiee friend might not come back—at least not anytime soon. But he still held out hope.

From his perch in the trees he perked up again as he saw another flaming streak cross the sky. The burning white line sliced the night. But it was just another shooting star.

He sighed again and settled back to wait. It would be a long night.

The next morning, his body aching from his long vigil, Lowie went to the comm center and requested permission to send a message to his family. The request was quickly granted. All Jedi trainees had the freedom to communicate home whenever they wished.

While Lowie secured a transmission link back to

Kashyyyk, he checked the chronometers on the wall and calculated the time shift, hoping he wouldn't wake his family in the middle of the night. He saw that it was early morning back on the forest world; both of his parents would be at work in the high-tech computer fabrication facility.

Lowie's sister Sirra answered the call; her image glowed brightly before him. She stood back in surprise, opening her mouth in a wide grin as she recognized her brother. Thanks to her radical trimming and cutting, Sirra's fur stood up in bristly shocks. She shaved it in various patterns at the wrists, ankles, knees, and elbows to give herself a distinctive look, an individuality that many younger Wookiees preferred. They each designed their own fur patterns, trying to establish a new identity for the youth of their species in this time of prosperity after years of Imperial oppression.

No one else in the comm center had any idea what the two barking, growling Wookiees were saying to each other, so Lowie did not worry about eavesdroppers. He had wanted to let Raaba keep her secret, give her time to deliver the news herself, but he needed to talk to *someone*—someone who understood.

Warning Sirra to keep his words in strictest confidence, he told her he had good news and bad news. Lowie stumbled around at first, unsure of how to begin. Finally, he blurted out that Raaba was alive, then breathlessly summarized how the chocolate-furred Wookiee had shown up on Kuar.

Sirra was overjoyed to hear the news and voiced a yelp of ecstatic surprise. She followed with several minutes of joyous questions and demands for details, interspersed with low crooning and cries of delight.

When Lowie explained how Raaba had vanished again, though, Sirra gave a concerned growl. But even that sad note was not enough to diminish her joy at learning that Raaba still lived.

Lowie's own thoughts remained in turmoil. No matter how often he contemplated Raaba, he still couldn't make up his mind how he really felt about her, what he hoped might happen between them, or what he expected her to do.

After leaving appropriate greetings for his parents, Lowie signed off. He shuffled down winding stone corridors on the way back to his quarters. With a long, throaty sigh, Lowie picked up the translating droid and switched it on, finally ready to face the day's training activities.

Em Teedee bubbled happily. "Ah, Master Lowbacca, good morning to you! I must say, I feel thoroughly recharged. How utterly restful it is when we're not out having dangerous adventures."

With a click, Lowie attached the little droid to the glossy fibers of his belt.

"I trust you slept well yourself, Master Low-bacca?" the droid asked.

Lowie gave a noncommittal grunt, which Em Teedee took as a yes.

3

INSIDE THE BUSTLING, hollow asteroid of Borgo Prime, signs along the walkway fluoresced and flickered, leading Zekk back to Shanko's Hive. The dark-haired young man had received his first bounty assignment inside that popular cantina—and he had come back empty-handed.

Zekk rehearsed various explanations. The blue-skinned bartender, Droq'l, had hired him to find a scavenger and his cargo, but Fonterrat, the missing scavenger, was dead and his cargo of precious ronik shells destroyed. He had no idea how his employer would react to the bad news.

How would Boba Fett have handled this situation? Zekk asked himself. Fett, one of the most respected (and feared) bounty hunters in the galaxy, would waste no energy on lengthy explanations or excuses. Fett would come straight to the point. Zekk decided he would have to do the same.

Tossing his ponytail over his shoulder, Zekk stopped before the entrance to an enormous cone-shaped building with horizontal ridges like smooth circular waves up its sides. He took a brief moment to perform a Jedi relaxation technique, something Master Skywalker had taught him—*not* Brakiss of the Shadow Academy.

Then, projecting all of the confidence a professional bounty hunter ought to feel, Zekk strode into Shanko's Hive.

Air clouded with exotic scents and flavors enveloped him in a pale gray haze. Though the interior of the hive cantina had no flat edges, the contrasting islands of sound and silence, of light and dimness, gave the illusion of dozens of shadowy corners. A quick glance at the bar told Zekk that the insectoid proprietor Shanko had emerged from hibernation and was in no mood to humor fools.

Brief, confident, professional, Zekk reminded himself. His steps did not falter as he walked toward the bar and tossed a credit chit on it. "Osskorn Stout," he said without preamble. "I have business with your bartender."

Dark, foamy ale sloshed onto the counter from the flagon Shanko thunked down in front of him. As Zekk scooped up the tankard to take a gulp, one of Shanko's many glossy arms roughly swept out to mop up the spill while another gave an abrupt jerk, indicating an area to Zekk's right.

Still drinking thirstily, he looked over to see Droq'l in conversation with a patron who stood just outside the circle of light cast by the bar's globe-lamps. Zekk nodded his thanks, and with renewed confidence strode toward the three-armed bartender. As if he had an extra eye in the back of his head—which he did, Zekk now recalled—Droq'l turned just as the young bounty hunter approached, tankard in hand.

"Did you find what I sent you for?" the bartender asked, his blue face eager.

"Fonterrat is dead. On Gammalin."

Droq'l grimaced, showing his shiny black teeth. "Gammalin, huh?"

Zekk shrugged. "Fonterrat accidently exposed the colony to a plaque. He was imprisoned after the plague hit. The frightened colonists destroyed his ship and burned his cargo, but the sickness swept through the colony anyway. It killed every human."

"And Fonterrat wasn't human," the bartender mused, "so he starved alone in prison after those colonists ruined my shipment of shells." A glint of pleasure replaced the disappointment in his eyes. "At least it was a slow, lingering death."

Zekk nodded warily. He reached into his vest pocket and produced the holocube that contained the scavenger's final message.

Droq'l watched the entire holomessage, sighed, and spread all three hands in a gesture of resigned acceptance. "Just as well. I might've been tempted to terminate Fonterrat myself for his incompetence."

Then, to Zekk's pleasant surprise, the bartender paid him in full.

"Glad to see a young trainee with some presence of mind," he said. "You finished what I sent you to do, and you had the good sense to bring back proof of it. That's more than I could say for some bounty hunters two or three times your age."

A thoughtful look crept over the bartender's blue-skinned face, and he drummed the fingers of two hands on the bartop. "Come to think of it, I may have another job for you, if you're interested. Got a client who's looking for a bounty hunter. Wants someone resourceful and trustworthy—but unknown. That might just be you."

"You seem to be a good enough judge of character," Zekk said, crossing his arms over his chest. "After all, you've judged *me* correctly."

The bartender chuckled at his bravado. "You'll take the job, then?"

Zekk didn't dare let his excitement show. "Of course. May I speak to him?" He felt a sense of exhilaration. He'd fully expected to come away in disgrace, without pay, after reporting his failure . . . but now, because of his sense of honor—something he'd feared the dark side had stolen from him forever—a new job had dropped right in his lap!

The bartender grinned. "He's pretty particular, even a little skittish—I think he'll want to talk to you himself before you're hired."

Zekk could learn nothing for certain about his prospective employer. Sitting at a low table in the shadow of a staircase that spiraled up the inner wall of Shanko's Hive, Zekk stared at the . . . *creature* in front of him.

"My name is Zekk," he offered. "I hear you need a bounty hunter."

"Yes. You come well recommended," the creature replied. "Call me . . . Wary. Master Wary. Yes, that will do."

Zekk shrugged in amusement. "Whatever."

Wary's voice was masculine, but synthesized. His body and arms were engulfed in gray robes and furs that made it impossible even to guess the creature's species or probable shape. He wore a holographic mask set to randomize so that his features changed constantly. A reptilian tail coiled out from beneath the robes and furs, but this could have been part of a disguise. For all Zekk knew, he could have been talking to a female Wookiee, a Jawa on stilts, or even his friend Jaina Solo.

The thought of Jaina made him smile again, and he patted his vest pocket, in which rested two message packets—one from Jaina and one from old Peckhum; the bartender had found them for Zekk in the general-delivery message area behind the bar.

"And who exactly do you want me to find, Master Wary?" Zekk asked, deciding on a direct approach.

Wary looked around, as if to be sure no one was listening in. Zekk glanced unobtrusively toward the nearby tables. A Devaronian played Sabacc with a pair of disreputable-looking spacers; a Ranat consulted a Hutt information broker; a furry white Talz and a hammerheaded Ithorian drank colorful intoxicants and sang duets to the accompaniment of a nine-stringed wrist harp. No one paid any particular attention to Wary.

"I want you to find a man who's been kidnapped," Wary said, though the mouth of his disguise mask did not move. "His name is Tyko Thul."

Zekk's entire attention snapped back to the creature in front of him. "Did you say *Tyko* Thul?"

The holomask blurred and shifted. "Yes, Tyko Thul," Wary repeated. "He was recently abducted by several assassin droids. I want you to find him."

"Every other bounty hunter in the galaxy is out looking for *Bornan* Thul," Zekk pointed out. "Are you sure it's Tyko you want?"

Wary nodded. "The two are brothers. I have

reason to believe the disappearances are . . . related—just as the two men are."

An interesting twist, Zekk thought. Finding one brother might lead to information about the other. After failing to find Fonterrat, Zekk had intended just to strike out on his own, looking for clues to Bornan Thul, hoping to repair his reputation. But this direct commission was a much better prospect.

"I'll take the assignment," Zekk said. "How much are you paying?"

Wary quoted him a generous figure. "But only if you find him."

Zekk tried not to show his surprise at the high amount. But then, Wary stood to make a lot more credits than that if Zekk retrieved information that led him to Bornan Thul.

"But that is not all there is to the task," Master Wary cautioned. "I also need you to send a message for me. I have other urgent business to attend to that prevents me from sending it myself. I will give you instructions on how to transmit it." He slid a hololetter packet across the table toward Zekk. "Do not try to listen to the message. It would mean nothing to you."

"That's it?" Zekk accepted the packet and slid it into his vest pocket.

"Not as simple as it would seem," Wary said.

"The message is for the Bornaryn fleet. All the ships went into hiding shortly after Bornan Thul's disappearance, and they are impossible to locate."

"Then how do you expect me to get the message to them?" Zekk asked, instantly suspicious.

"I ask only that you broadcast the message to the following locations." He listed several sites along major trading routes, many of which Zekk was already familiar with from his days with the old spacer Peckhum. "I will meet you here again in ten days to learn of your progress—and to pay you if you have already achieved both of your goals."

Zekk relaxed again. He still wasn't sure why Wary would want to send a message to the Bornaryn fleet, though. Did he hope to flush them out of hiding? To question Thul's employees and family members in hopes of locating him?

Just as Zekk opened his mouth to ask, an explosion erupted at a nearby table. Zekk blinked, trying to see what had happened as a cloud of white smoke billowed outward from where the Talz and the Ithorian had been sitting.

Droq'l bustled up with a disgusted snort to sweep the broken and steaming glasses away. "I *told* you two not to let your drinks come into contact with each other," he growled in exasperation. "You should know they're chemically incompatible!" With a big paw, the Talz batted at a smoldering patch of its white fur.

Amused, Zekk turned back to the conversation with his new employer—only to find Master Wary gone.

Apparently the assignment was made and the interview had ended. Zekk shrugged. He had his commission, and he knew what to do. He might as well stay to view the new hololetters from Jaina and Peckhum.

Calling Droq'l over, Zekk ordered another Osskorn Stout, drew one of the message packets from his pocket, and slid it into the reader slot on the table in front of him. He waited eagerly for the image of Jaina to appear—then blinked in disappointment.

ENCRYPTION PROPRIETARY
MESSAGE UNREADABLE

Why would Jaina or Peckhum have sent him a message in code that no standard reader could decipher? He realized his mistake as he pulled a second hololetter from the pocket of his vest and then a third.

He had accidentally tried to view the message from Master Wary.

But how could the disguised man expect an encrypted message to get through to the Bornaryn fleet? And how would the fleet read it unless *they* already knew the key?

Perhaps they did, Zekk mused. Maybe this was a code that belonged to the Bornaryn trading company. Wary might be a former employee . . . or even Bornan Thul himself!

As the thought occurred to Zekk, he suddenly saw the truth of it. He felt it in his bones, in the background music of the Force that sang through all things. Master Wary's synthesized voice had held an urgency when he spoke of the need to find Tyko Thul, and a tender quality when he spoke about the fleet.

Zekk shook his head to clear it. Bornan Thul had been here, right in front of him!

He jammed the message packets back into his pocket and jumped to his feet just as Droq'l approached carrying a fresh tankard of ale in his middle hand.

"Which way?" Zekk asked, breathless. "Where did he go?"

The bartender didn't pretend he had no idea what Zekk meant. He jerked his head toward a small door in the wall to the other side of the stairway.

Dashing out into a tiny alleyway, Zekk looked left and right, but saw no sign of his new employer. His heart raced with the realization that he had been less than a meter away from the most sought after bounty in the galaxy! Although he knew Thul was probably far away by now, he kept looking.

Farther down the alley, Zekk was not surprised to find a pile of gray robes and furs along with a prosthetic reptilian tail. Bornan Thul had shed his disguise. . . .

4

THE T-23 HAD never been so crowded, but Lowie was proud of the way his skyhopper handled the load.

While other engineers continued to repair the ancient pyramid, he and Jaina had fixed the damage the skyhopper had sustained in the Shadow Academy attack, then augmented the T-23's engines and stabilizers. Eager to test the improved craft, Lowie offered to take his friends out for a spin.

Because Raynar was so downcast about the disappearance of both his father and his uncle, none of the Jedi trainees had the heart to exclude him. The young man had appeared in the hangar bay wearing a plain brown jumpsuit, instead of his usual robes of garish purple, scarlet, yellow, and orange.

Now, as they soared above the canopy of Massassi trees, the skyhopper's performance was flaw-

35

less, even with so many extra passengers. Lowie roared a question back to his friends.

"I think my foot's asleep," Jaina answered from the cargo well, where she had volunteered to sit. "But other than that, I've probably got the most comfortable spot on board."

"Hey, I'm fine," Jacen said. He and Tenel Ka were jammed together on the passenger seat.

"I am experiencing no discomfort," Tenel Ka reported.

"Uh, this is fun," Raynar said stoically. He was wedged sideways in the passenger footspace with his knees drawn up to his chest. One of his elbows rested on the few remaining square centimeters on the passenger seat.

"Indeed, Master Lowbacca, I am also quite comfortable. Thank you for inquiring," Em Teedee answered last of all.

Once he'd traveled far enough from the Jedi academy's traffic of transport ships, construction crews, and military vessels, Lowie decided there was little danger in a bit of creative flying. With Raaba gone, he'd been feeling restless for days and needed a safe way to release his pent-up frustration.

Lowie woofed a warning for everyone to secure their crash webbing so he could test the T-23's maneuverability. He zigged and zagged across the treetops, eliciting squeals and laughter from his passengers, though he did detect one or two of them applying their Jedi relaxation techniques.

He brought the T-23 about in a tight curve above the trees, spiraling in until everyone on board was thoroughly dizzy. Then, amidst giggles and applause, he took the skyhopper into a steep climb. After pausing in midair, he put the craft into a steep dive toward the Massassi trees. Lowie pulled up just before crashing, then leveled out to skim across the treetops.

Jacen whooped, and Jaina shrieked with the thrill. Raynar spoke in a rather timid voice. "I've never done that before. It was fun."

"This is a fact," Tenel Ka said.

"Quite exhilarating, I'd say," Em Teedee put in, "so long as the appropriate safety factors are applied."

"We'd better be getting back," Jaina yelled from the cargo well. "Tionne asked us to help her out with lessons this morning."

"Yeah, it wouldn't be fair to leave her alone with all the new trainees, since Uncle Luke is off on an adventure again," Jacen said. "Besides, I want to check on Nicta—I'm not sure how much care a baby gort needs."

Lowie turned the skyhopper back toward the Great Temple, feeling some of his tension relieved at last.

• • •

The Jedi instructor Tionne asked all students to gather in the practice courtyard just outside the temple. With Master Skywalker off on another mission for the New Republic, she had taken over the lessons. Above, workers continued to repair the roof platform on the damaged pyramid.

Joined by his friends, Lowie climbed up one of the courtyard's retaining walls. Though the afternoon was warm and humid, a light breeze rustled the jungle leaves, and Lowie could almost imagine he was alone in the treetops—or perhaps with Raaba—listening to the tales of heroes who fought to defend what they believed in.

Tionne sang an ancient ballad—one of her favorite methods of teaching—about young Gav and Jori Daragon, a Force-talented brother and sister who had given up on their Jedi training. They'd tried to make their fortune by exploring the galaxy, but instead stumbled upon the ancient Sith Empire and sparked a war that nearly toppled the Old Republic.

Lowie closed his eyes and let the story grow like a secret garden around him. Tendrils of tale and melody twined together in his mind, blooming with ancient splendor. He wondered if Raaba would enjoy this tale, too. He might tell it to her . . . if he ever saw her again.

Then, all too soon, the music ended. A murmur of

appreciation rippled through the crowd of Jedi trainees and the few New Republic guards who had stopped to listen. Reluctantly, Lowie opened his eyes and looked up at the Jedi teacher and historian.

"Gav and Jori had meant to discover many things—but not what they actually found," Tionne said in her melodious voice. "Remember that what you look for and what you find may be two different things." Her fine silvery hair floated on the breeze, and her enormous mother-of-pearl eyes seemed to look directly at Lowie.

"As your Jedi training progresses, many causes will call for you to use your powers on their behalf. But how can you know if the cause is one you should champion? You must learn to listen to the Force, and the Force will guide you. Hate and mistrust, domination, revenge—even glory—these are *not* the things a Jedi fights for.

"A Jedi defends justice, protects the weak from tyranny, and rescues those in harm's way—but *always* with the guidance of the Force. If you do not believe this in your heart, you are not ready to become a full Jedi." Tionne's delicate face dimpled into a smile. "But do not despair: there is time. Time to learn. And that's why we are all here: to learn together."

The Jedi instructor then dismissed them all to continue their independent lessons.

Jaina's mind was completely exhausted after hours of practice sessions with various Jedi techniques. As always, she had made sure the subtle exercises strained her abilities to the limit—that was the best way to learn and grow in the Force.

Tenel Ka rolled both shoulders to stretch the kinks out of her muscles. Perspiration from the late afternoon heat glistened on her face and neck. "Very satisfying effort," she said, "but I believe I could use a swim in the river."

"Hey, great idea!" Jacen said. Raynar hesitated, then agreed.

Jaina nodded. The suggestion brought back memories of the last time she and Zekk had gone to the wide greenish-brown river that ran through the jungles. "Sure, it'd be refreshing."

At the river's edge, Jacen, Jaina, and Raynar all stripped down to their minimal exercise gear. While Tenel Ka peeled off her boots and her lizard-hide armor, Lowie unfastened the syren-fiber belt from his waist, with Em Teedee still attached, and set it aside.

The little droid gave what sounded like an aggrieved sigh. "So, I'm simply to be left behind. Unwanted. Unneeded."

"We could try to float you on the water, Em Teedee," Jacen said with a roguish grin.

"Oh my, no, Master Jacen!" the little translator

cried. "I'm certain I should sink and be lost forever."

Jaina cast the droid an apologetic glance. "If you want, I could figure out a way to waterproof you. A few gaskets, some aquasealant . . ."

"I should like that very much, Mistress Jaina!" Em Teedee said. "It's a wonder I hadn't thought of it before."

Tenel Ka, already poised on a rock, dove into deep water, and Jacen immediately followed her. Raynar waded through the shallows, while Lowie climbed a boulder and leapt into the water with a Wookiee bellow.

Taking up the challenge, Jaina plunged in after him. Soon all of them were splashing and enjoying themselves. Jaina, Lowie, and Tenel Ka took turns diving to the bottom of the river to bring back interesting water creatures for Jacen to examine.

Even Raynar seemed to release his worries. After the boy had been humiliated in the river during the battle with the Shadow Academy, Tionne had taken it upon herself to teach him how to swim better. Now he enjoyed spending time in the river.

While the Wookiee was on one of his dives, Jaina surfaced and heard the sound of a ship's engines. Looking toward the landing field, she saw a small two-passenger star skimmer circle in front of the temple and then head straight for the river. Jaina recognized the *Rising Star*, Raaba's ship! Jaina gave a tentative wave as the skimmer sped toward them, no more than two meters above the water's surface.

Lowie burst up from the river bottom holding a six-clawed crustacean. With a speed and precision that Jaina had to admire, the *Rising Star* spun once, zipped up the riverbank, and came to a neat landing just clear of the mud. Jaina stifled a giggle at her friend's roar of surprise and recognition.

Before Lowie could recover from his shock and make his way to shore, the chocolate-furred Wookiee woman had climbed out of her skimmer. Shedding unnecessary pieces of equipment with each running stride, she headed directly for Lowie.

"Oh, do be careful," Em Teedee exclaimed as Raaba's foot narrowly missed him on her way into the river. The two Wookiees swam toward each other, bellowing and growling and barking at each other like a pair of nek battle dogs.

Jaina chuckled as she picked out a few of the guttural phrases—things like "I thought I'd never see you again" and "I told you I'd find you"—but most of the interchange was too fast for her to follow. Watching the two splash and frolic in the water, she felt a pang. Jaina couldn't help but wish that Zekk was here, too. She had so much to say to the young man who kept trying to find a way to erase his dark side past.

She realized that Raaba and Lowie must also have a lot of things they wanted to say to each other.

Chiding herself, she said, "Jacen, Raynar, Tenel Ka—I think we need to get back to the Great Temple now. Lowie can come back whenever he's ready."

Tenel Ka, treading water beside Jacen, caught on quickly. "This is a fact," she said.

Jacen shrugged. "Okay." He swam with the warrior girl back to shore. Raynar gave Jaina a questioning look, but did not argue. Turning back toward the river, Jaina yelled, "Hey, Lowie, will you be needing Em Teedee for anything?"

He rumbled a negative and cocked his head, as if to inquire why two Wookiees would need a translating droid.

"Okay, I'll take him to my room, give him a tune-up, maybe figure out how to waterproof him."

But the two Wookiees didn't hear her. Lowie and Raaba were already splashing together toward the far side of the river. . . .

For the next two days, the Wookiees were completely absorbed in each other as they went for climbs in the jungle and flew around the small moon in the *Rising Star* or in Lowie's T-23.

Jaina found it sweet to see Lowie so smitten, but disturbing as well. Aside from perfunctory greetings, Raaba made no effort whatsoever to converse with anyone but Lowie and one or two alien Jedi trainees. She seemed to find humans not worth the bother.

Jaina knew, of course, that Raaba was angry at Tyko Thul for insulting Nolaa Tarkona and the Diversity Alliance just before she'd left Kuar, but Jaina had hoped the chocolate-furred Wookiee would want to get better acquainted with Lowie's friends. That did not prove to be the case.

It came as an even greater shock, then, when Lowie announced that he was leaving the Jedi academy, at least for a while.

Raaba intended to return to Kashyyyk for a reunion with her best friend, Sirra, and to announce to her family that she was still alive. She had invited Lowie to come along so that he could visit his own family and so that she could spend more time talking with him about the Diversity Alliance on the way there and back.

He would be gone with Raaba for no more than a few weeks, Lowie assured them all. Then, without ceremony, he packed a small satchel of belongings and necessities for the trip and clipped his lightsaber to the glossy, woven belt. Since he would have no need for a translator among Wookiees, he asked Jaina to take care of Em Teedee for him while he was gone.

"Do be careful, Master Lowbacca," Em Teedee called forlornly from Jaina's hand. "I shall await your return with great anticipation."

Lowie made his goodbyes and climbed into the *Rising Star*. Jaina, Jacen, Raynar, and Tenel Ka stood back, and Raaba's little skimmer took off. Tucking the translating droid under one arm, Jaina watched the ship dwindle into the distance and vanish into the cloud-streaked skies.

Lowie was gone.

5

THE DAYS ON the jungle moon seemed longer and emptier.

Jacen *missed* Lowbacca. It wasn't as if the young Wookiee had never gone away before, but this was different—unplanned, an interruption of their normal Jedi training schedule. It also hurt that Lowie had so easily chosen other priorities and left his friends behind.

Jacen felt uncomfortable not knowing exactly when his friend would return to them. He had no logical reason to worry, but the situation was disquieting all the same. His sister had seemed upset as well. She and Lowie had been planning some modifications to Tenel Ka's ship, the *Rock Dragon*. But without the ginger-furred Wookiee to assist her, Jaina made excuses to put off the project, even though Jacen, Tenel Ka, Raynar, and even Em

Teedee had offered to help. Jacen hoped she would perk up soon and change her mind.

Luckily, the antics of his little gort hatchling often cheered Jacen. "Here, Raynar. You hold her," he said, handing the long-tailed ball of blue fluff to the other boy.

Raynar pushed back the sleeves of his plain brown Jedi robe. A bit gingerly, but with obvious pleasure, the young man held Nicta in the palm of his hand and stroked her with a forefinger. The little creature wound her tail around the Alderaanian boy's forearm and trilled happily. Raynar was beginning to show a genuine, though timid, interest in Jacen's numerous pets.

Nicta chose that moment to leap from Raynar's palm with her tail still wrapped around his wrist. She dangled upside down, clacking her wide, flat beak. Raynar laughed. "She'll probably be a good tree climber like Lowie. Too bad he can't be here to see this. I think he'd enjoy it."

"Yeah," Jacen agreed. "I was just thinking the same thing."

A knock sounded at the door and, without waiting for a reply, his sister popped her head in.

"Hi, Jaina," Jacen said. "Need us to work on those sublight engines yet?"

She shook her head. "Comm center just received a message from Uncle Luke. Said he's coming back with a surprise and wants the two of us to meet the

Shadow Chaser out on the landing field. No idea what it's all about."

"Well, well, well," Raynar said, standing up and putting Nicta back in her terrarium. He had been careful not to intrude too much on the activities of the other young Jedi Knights. "I've got some studying to do back in my room. I'll catch up with you later."

Luke Skywalker's surprise, as it turned out, was a visitor. "Lusa!" Jaina exclaimed. Her mouth opened and closed a few times in amazement as she looked at the beautiful alien girl who stood before her—a Centauriform, with the lower body and four legs of a horse and the upper torso of a humanoid.

Jaina reached out to hug the girl. Just seeing Lusa again brought back a flood of memories of when she, Jacen, their brother Anakin, and the Centaur girl had all been kidnapped by power-hungry Hethrir, nearly ten years before. To increase his own power in the Force, Hethrir had hoped to sacrifice a Force-talented child to a being named Waru near the Crystal Star. Jaina and the centaur girl had formed a bond during their captivity and had helped each other resist Hethrir's attempts to control them. Though all the children had been rescued, Jaina still had occasional nightmares about the ordeal.

As she pulled back to look at her old friend, though, she saw torment in Lusa's wide, round eyes.

She wondered if their past experience had scarred the Centaur girl more deeply than it had the Solo children.

A bit shyly, Jacen extended his arms to squeeze Lusa's hands in greeting. "Hey, you've . . . um, changed." He stumbled a bit over his words. "What've you been doing all these years?"

The red-gold Centaur child had grown into a beautiful young woman. The color of her mane and flanks had deepened from a coppery color that nearly matched Tenel Ka's hair to a rich reddish-brown like polished cinnamon. The dapple markings were gone from her flanks now, and her curly mane fell down her bare torso nearly to her waist. Transparent horns with smooth ridges like carved ice grew through the cinnamon curls on Lusa's forehead.

"It's good to see you again," Jaina said. "Have you come to study at the Jedi academy?"

Luke Skywalker had been watching the reunion with sober interest. Now he spoke up as the Centaur girl shifted uncomfortably from hoof to hoof and flicked her long tail. "Lusa has a lot she wants to tell you, but let's get her settled first."

Jaina invited her to join them for the midday meal, and Lusa accepted in a husky voice, her eyes not quite meeting Jaina's. Then she followed Master Skywalker quietly into the Great Temple, her hooves clopping on the flagstone floor.

• • •

At mealtime, Jaina was surprised to find that her uncle had arranged for the young Jedi Knights, as well as Raynar, to eat with him in his private quarters rather than in the large dining hall. She soon understood why.

"Lusa has a painful story to tell us. I felt it might be easier if she started with a very small group," Luke said. "A group of friends."

The meal was already on the table, and the companions seated themselves. When Lusa folded her horselike legs beneath her and sat up at the table, her head rose to the same height as Luke's. After introductions, Tenel Ka immediately offered a toast of friendship to the new arrival, while Raynar stared tongue-tied at the beautiful Centaur girl. Luke scanned the tiny group for a moment, as if searching for Lowie.

Jaina watched her old friend Lusa glance nervously around the table, then look down for several seconds. "Master Skywalker thinks it's important that you all hear this," Lusa said. "And I agree." Her voice, though barely audible at first, carried a husky, mesmerizing quality.

"Ever since we were kidnapped . . . when we were children"—she looked at Jacen and Jaina—"I've had an angry place inside of me. Even when I returned to my family, they never understood that anger. Maybe I didn't either. As I grew up, I had a hard time making friends, a hard time trusting anyone . . . until two years ago.

"I met others who knew what it was like to have their lives disrupted, how it *felt* to be violated. They understood my anger—and shared it. They had dedicated themselves to making life better for the downtrodden of the galaxy. They offered me a place working for justice and fair treatment of nonhuman species. They were fervent and idealistic. And so was I. I admired what they stood for.

"For the first time in many years, I felt accepted and needed. Not only did I have a place where I felt I belonged, but I was doing good for others. With each individual I helped, I saw a pattern emerging. In one way or another, they all had been taken advantage of or harmed by humans . . . like *Hethrir*." She spat the name.

Jaina blinked in surprise, leaving her food untouched. She wasn't sure what she had expected of Lusa's story, but it hadn't been this. The tone reminded her of some of the things Raaba had told Lowie back on Kuar.

"My new friends showed me how human domination had caused our problems. It was so clear, I wondered why I hadn't seen it before," Lusa continued. She seemed distant, as if talking in a dream.

Jaina felt her stomach tie itself into a knot, and she exchanged glances with her brother. Certainly Hethrir had been human . . . but so was Jaina, and so were the people who had rescued the children from him. How could the Centaur girl have blindly accepted such a pernicious generalization about humans? With a sinking heart, Jaina waited to hear what Lusa would say next.

"The more I understood how humans had trampled my species and the other aliens I was helping, the greater responsibilities I was given in our group. Our leader began sending me on covert missions. I saved alien lives, rescued slaves, helped to overthrow tyrants. I knew I was doing good work, and for a good reason.

"Then, about ten days ago, our leader gave me an assignment to wipe the navicomputers of a geological survey ship. Through carelessness and neglect, its crew had destroyed a forest on the planet Kaisa and had caused the extinction of the Buro, a species of ethereally beautiful sentient insects. My job was to make sure that the survey ship's navicomputer would never again guide its geologists to a new world they could destroy.

"I eagerly took the assignment. I had been so indoctrinated by the group that I cringed at the very *sight* of the humans whose computer I had been sent to sabotage. But for some reason—maybe because one of the geologists had a daughter who was the same age as you were when I knew you, Jaina . . . I—"

Lusa's voice broke, and she paused before going

on. "As I watched the geologists boarding their craft, whose computer I had just sabotaged, I realized that after their very first hyperspace jump no one aboard would have any idea where they were. When they emerged from hyperspace it was entirely possible that they would be lost in uncharted territory—or worse yet, that they might come out at the center of a star or at the edge of a black hole. I could be responsible for killing all of them."

Lusa's body went rigid, and she shuddered at the memory. "I had never stopped to think exactly what I was willing to do for the cause I believed in. Was I willing to kill? And if so, what must the victim's crime *be* to deserve that death? Should I judge each one, or could I trust my leader to judge them for me?" She shuddered again and tossed her mane of glossy cinnamon curls. Her crystal horns glinted in the light.

"I couldn't go through with it. I stopped the geologists and told them what I had done. I planned to surrender myself to the proper authorities. I was shocked when, instead of hating me, they were grateful. After their navicomputer was repaired, the geologists offered to take me anywhere I needed to go. I went with them to Coruscant. I was afraid to contact the Chief of State of the New Republic—or you—directly, but I recalled that Master Skywalker had suggested that I consider studying at the Jedi academy someday. I sent him an urgent message, and he came to Coruscant to get me." Lusa fell silent.

Luke Skywalker nodded. "I think Yavin 4 will be a good place for you to recover and to get a sense of perspective, to let your mind heal."

"You are welcome among us," Tenel Ka said.

Jaina reached out to touch her friend's arm. "I'm glad you remembered we're your *friends,* Lusa," she said. "I'm happy you're here."

Raynar said in a bemused voice, "I never knew anyone could hate us so much . . . just because we're humans."

Jaina bit her lower lip. A memory tickled at the edges of her mind and she asked, "This group that you were a part of, Lusa—did it have a name?"

The Centaur girl sighed. "A silly, idealistic name. One that sounds like it includes everyone. But that would be a false assumption." She shook her mane. "We called ourselves the Diversity Alliance."

Jacen yelped. "Hey, Lowie's friend Raaba is part of the Diversity Alliance."

Luke Skywalker looked at them in alarm.

Jaina swallowed hard. "And Lowie left here with her. Alone."

6

ZEKK BROUGHT THE *Lightning Rod* down through the atmosphere, confident that no one would disturb him . . . at least not here. This planet was the farthest place from *anywhere* he could possibly find.

The charts called the bleak world Ziost. Glaciers covered much of what had once been a towering outpost of the fallen Sith Empire, so that only a few broken turrets still protruded from the landscape of ice. Frozen tundra crackled blue under the shimmering auroras dancing above in the sky.

Ziost was too inhospitable to harbor any sort of colony and the Sith ruins too decayed to shelter pirates or other refugees who might seek to hide from the scrutiny of authorities.

It was, however, a good place for Zekk to do his work, undisturbed and alone. Without risk of detection.

The disguised man on Borgo Prime—whom Zekk was certain must be Bornan Thul himself—had commissioned him to transmit a coded message to the Bornaryn merchant fleet. In the wake of Thul's disappearance and the kidnapping of his brother Tyko, the fleet had gone into hiding and now hopped at random through hyperspace to keep from being found.

Zekk had to communicate with them somehow. His bounty depended on it. "Master Wary" had offered suggestions, places from which he might attempt to send his message—and Zekk intended to try them all. He would not give up easily.

The *Lightning Rod* headed toward a broad shelf of ice under a twilit sky. Fissures ran across the frozen plain, and slushy water burst through the cracks, propelled by tidal pressure. Trusting his instincts, Zekk found a safe place to land and shut down all systems: he would leave no bright sensor traces for spying eyes, however unlikely their presence might be.

Working in silence, he rigged up his transmitter, fed in power from the engines to give his signal a spectacular boost—and began sending Bornan Thul's message.

Zekk wasn't sure what the coded burst said, but now he could hazard a guess: Thul would most likely explain his disappearance, announce that he was still alive, or perhaps estimate when he expected to come home.

He first sent the signal to the Bornaryn headquarters on Coruscant, on the chance that Aryn Dro Thul might check in for urgent news. It only made sense that she would have made arrangements to learn if her missing husband reappeared.

Zekk didn't know why the man was so desperately hiding, but Thul was obviously frightened. He did understand why Thul might go to Shanko's Hive in disguise to hire a bounty hunter—a *little known* bounty hunter like Zekk. Since Thul had such a high price on his own head, he would be foolish to send the message himself. Any glory-seeking bounty hunter might spot the signal and race to its source fast enough to capture him.

Being a bounty hunter himself, Zekk was paid to assume such risks. Even so, he did not intend to be easy prey for his competitors.

Everyone in the galaxy seemed to be looking for Bornan Thul—including Zekk . . . until he had unwittingly been hired by the very quarry he sought. On the other hand, Thul had already set up another meeting with him, so perhaps when the time came, Zekk could capture the wanted man after all and take the whole bounty. Then he would prove himself a bounty hunter to be reckoned with.

The ethical question was a hindrance, of course.

Next he sent a duplicate message to other places

where "Master Wary" thought the merchant fleet might pick up transmissions. Zekk couldn't be certain exactly how Thul's scheme worked, but the merchant might well have made plans for such a contingency. Their business had boomed, and successful traders always lived with the threat of being held for ransom.

Leaning back in his creaking cockpit seat, Zekk transmitted the message to a fourth and final set of coordinates. He had fulfilled his obligation, everything "Master Wary" had asked him to do. Time to go.

As he reached forward to power up the *Lightning Rod,* he felt suddenly uneasy in the cockpit. Were his rarely used Jedi senses sending him a warning? Or was his imagination just running away with him?

He decided to leave Ziost as quickly as the battered old ship could carry him. Repulsorlifts blasted, melting a crater into the plain of ice. Zekk let the ship hover as he contemplated his course. Next, he would begin his search for the abducted brother, Tyko Thul.

The ship's rear sensors sounded an alarm. Zekk's hand flew over the control panels and spotted another ship fast approaching—a souped-up hunting craft made from new and old components pieced together.

The intruder soared out of hyperspace without

slowing, barreling directly toward the *Lightning Rod*. A warning tingle along Zekk's spine supplemented the flashing red lights on the control panels. The newcomer had already powered up his weapons systems—and Zekk was in his sights.

A gruff, phlegmy voice came over the comm system. "I have my targeting computer locked in on you, Bornan Thul. Surrender—or I'll simply destroy your ship and take your remains for the bounty."

The *Lightning Rod* protested as Zekk flew a rapid evasive maneuver. He shouted into the voice transmitter. "Wait, who is this? I'm not Thul, I'm a bounty hunter, just like you are! My name is Zekk!"

After a pause, the bounty hunter's voice came over the speakers again. "Never heard of you, Zekk . . . but you've no doubt heard of me. I am Dengar. Now surrender your ship. I must interrogate you regarding Bornan Thul."

Zekk streaked across the glacial plain, pushing the *Lightning Rod*'s engines to greater speed. He certainly knew of Dengar, one of the most fearsome hunters in the galaxy.

Shadowy circles surrounded deep-set eyes on Dengar's pasty face, giving him a skull-like visage. His head was wrapped in bandages to cover the scars and perpetually seeping wounds from a hideous injury long ago. Once a crack flier in a swoop gang, he had suffered a severe accident caused by a young Han Solo, and later his brain had been cybernetically enhanced by the Empire. Dengar was also one of the elite hunters Darth Vader had hired to track down the *Millennium Falcon* after the battle of Hoth.

This was indeed a man Zekk did not want to cross—but neither did he want to surrender for a long and intense conversation with the bounty hunter.

"I can't tell you anything about Bornan Thul," Zekk said, still flying at breakneck speed. "By the Creed you can't fire on another bounty hunter unless I am obstructing your own target."

Dengar replied, "I interpret your resistance as such an obstruction. You transmitted a coded communication for the Bornaryn fleet through relays to known rendezvous points. I planted numerous drone buoys to intercept any suspicious signals, then waited. You triggered my alarms; therefore, I intend to seize your data banks and study them for myself."

Any other person might have laughed, but Dengar simply let the pregnant silence extend for several seconds. At last he said, "I *will* have that information, whether you give it willingly—or force me to rip it from you."

Without waiting for a reply, the veteran bounty hunter fired a pulsed ion cannon, a disrupter that was as high-powered as it was illegal to own. Zekk had not imagined the device could be made with such devastating output.

The ion blast brought down all of Zekk's shields. Luckily, the *Lightning Rod*'s life-support and engine systems ran off of a separate protected power array and survived. The *Lightning Rod* was now defenseless, however. One more shot would cripple it completely.

Zekk swerved upward from the base of a sheer cliff of ice that bristled with rock outcroppings. Dengar's ship howled close behind, demonstrating the bounty hunter's cybernetic reflexes. Zekk leveled off at the top of another frozen plateau and streaked along, low to the ground.

Dengar launched a small concussion grenade, and Zekk braced himself for impact, knowing his disabled shields could offer no protection against the explosive. The detonation would destroy his rear engines and send him to crash and burn on this abandoned ice-age world.

The grenade struck his starboard hull . . . but no explosion followed. He heard only a dull metallic *thud,* as if a hammer had smacked his cruiser. He breathed a huge sigh of relief at this incredible stroke of luck—Dengar had fired a dud!

Master Skywalker at the Jedi academy had said there was no such thing as luck or coincidence. There was only the Force, which moved in mysterious ways . . . and Zekk wondered if he could subconsciously have used a trace of Jedi powers to deactivate the explosive.

Before the bandaged bounty hunter could launch another attack, though, Zekk gritted his teeth and threw every possible ounce of his piloting skills into getting away. Right then.

Dengar fired laser cannons, but Zekk intuitively knew what to do, *knew* how to react. He jinked the *Lightning Rod* to the left, then curved up in a loop, elbowing back to the right, zooming in a serpentine maneuver that neatly avoided the bounty hunter's pattern of strikes.

Zekk felt the fluid instincts move through him, like a Jedi Knight using his lightsaber to deflect blaster bolts. The entire ship seemed a part of Zekk. He dodged and hopped, ducked and swerved, perfectly avoiding the rapid-fire attack. Like a Jedi. It simultaneously frightened and exhilarated him.

"You may not have heard of me, Dengar," Zekk said, "but you *will*. One of these days, I'll rival even Boba Fett."

In an uncharacteristic display of emotion, Dengar roared at him over the comm systems.

The ice-bound plain swept beneath him, reflecting the booms from his high-powered engines. Zekk got an inspiration—a desperate idea that just might allow him to escape. . . .

He powered up his forward laser cannons and

deployed them in a wide arc, firing low and directly ahead. Using all of his weapons without slowing for an instant, Zekk strafed the frozen glacier field.

His superhot lasers bombarded the snow and ice, slicing open a molten wound as he flew onward. The meltwater flashed into steam that billowed up in huge evaporating clouds and froze again into icy mist crystals. Fog swelled to fill the air behind him like an ever-expanding smoke screen. The cloud slammed into Dengar's ship, blinding him.

Zekk pulled the *Lightning Rod* up, rocketing straight toward the edge of the atmosphere. Below, he left the befuddled bounty hunter's ship enveloped in condensing steam.

Knowing he had only a few seconds, he let the Force flow through him and punched numbers at random into the navicomputer. He'd have to trust in his inordinate "luck" to select a course by chance that wouldn't take him through the core of a star or down the gullet of a black hole.

As soon as he escaped the gravitational pull of the planet, the starlines of night elongated to welcome the *Lightning Rod* as it shot forward. The entire planet of Ziost shrank to a tiny pinprick behind him as the nothingness of hyperspace swallowed him up.

Dengar would never know what had hit him or where Zekk had gone.

7

ARYN DRO THUL stood on the busy bridge of the flagship *Tradewyn,* gazing out into space. She turned slowly to get the full 360-degree view of her fugitive fleet. A simple gown of midnight blue shot with silver draped around her like the star-dusted vista of space. Her fingers plucked absently at the material of her garment.

Even surrounded by the entire Bornaryn fleet, she felt alone. Her husband was missing, her brother-in-law kidnapped, her son Raynar returned to the Jedi academy.

The merchant fleet looked to her for guidance and reassurance, but Aryn had no one to rely on but herself. As the wife of Bornan Thul, she was their leader, and she could not let them—or herself—down. She *would not* let them down.

Aryn forced herself to stop fiddling with her gown. She excused the communications officer from his post. Sitting down at the station, she quickly calculated the coordinates for sending a routine message to her staff on Coruscant, composed a dispatch, and set the message pod's origin memory to scramble as soon as it left the *Tradewyn*. Taking care of business details like these kept her busy, kept her mind off her own troubles.

Aryn sent a similar message pod every few days to corporate headquarters on Coruscant. The reports were encrypted with a proprietary code, based on a complex combination of music, light, and speech, which Aryn and Bornan had devised together while they were still students at the university on Alderaan, a long time ago.

In this way, she managed to communicate with the fleet's administrative staff, who also sent out regular messages in encrypted scattershot packets, hoping that the fleet would intercept at least some of them. So far, Aryn had only obtained the messages numbered two, seven, and fifteen. She took a deep breath, straightened her shoulders, and launched the new packet with its instructions for the staff and a special note to her son Raynar.

Then Aryn scanned the hyperwave frequency bands in hopes of finding one of the message bursts sent from Coruscant. A minute later, her efforts were rewarded when she located a transmission packet carrying a Thul family identifier. Grateful to finally have some news from headquarters, Aryn quickly retrieved and decoded the message while her navigators and helmsmen calculated a new jump through hyperspace.

Staring off through the viewports while she waited for the usual audio message to begin, Aryn Dro Thul was astonished to see a tiny hologram appear in the air above the comm console.

Bornan Thul, himself.

It was her husband, alive and well! The image of his face seemed thinner, and he wore the rough-woven garb of a Randoni trader, but he seemed healthy.

The figure seemed to stare directly at her as it spoke. "My dear wife and son, I've been hiding for so long now that you may have feared me dead. But I am very much alive—for the moment at least. In my tradings I learned of a conspiracy so powerful, so . . . *evil,* that the fate of all humanity may depend on its prevention. I can tell you no more without placing your lives in great danger. I will not contact you again until I'm certain this threat is no longer to be feared. I hope I can survive long enough to do it. My thoughts are, as always, only with you."

The tiny figure raised its hand as if to turn off a recording device, then seemed to think better of it. In a low voice, Bornan Thul added, "Perhaps I have too rarely told you in the past, but I love you both."

The image dissolved into static.

Silent tears of relief, joy, and loneliness ran in rivulets down Aryn Dro Thul's face. She reset the holomessage and played it again from the beginning. Lifting a finger to touch the tiny image in front of her, she listened.

Again. And again.

8

FOR THE TENTH time Lowie adjusted his crash webbing and rearranged his limbs in the *Rising Star*'s cramped copilot area—but his fidgeting was due more to nervousness than discomfort. In contrast, Raaba's movements were spare and confident, like a well-rehearsed dance. Her deft fingers punched in coordinates and flicked switches, preparing for the skimmer's jump to hyperspace.

Away from Yavin 4, away from his friends at the Jedi academy.

Lowie's fingers tapped restlessly against one hairy knee, until Raaba told him to relax. He tried folding his hands and leaning back in the seat, but that felt too stiff and awkward. He reached down to check Em Teedee, only to remember that he had left the little droid behind with Jaina on the jungle moon. The tension inside Lowie just had to get out. He jiggled one leg but decided it might irritate

Raaba, and so he stopped. He settled for simply crossing his arms over his chest.

It was ironic that Lowie should feel so self-conscious alone with Raaba. She had been his sister Sirra's friend, but Raaba had always admired *him* when they were growing up—had even attempted her rite of passage alone because that was the way Lowie had done it.

But now . . . the chocolate-furred Wookiee seemed different. Poised, independent, self-assured. He was not sure what to make of her anymore. Even the freshly washed strip of red cloth she wore cinched above her ears as a headband made him wonder how well he knew her—or had ever known her. She carried an energy and a sense of direction that he couldn't help but admire. Lowie supposed anyone would find those qualities attractive.

A tunnel lined with star streaks dilated in front of them as Raaba launched the *Rising Star* into hyperspace. Lowie shifted his weight and began to assess his agitation and restlessness with detached interest. He had always been confident, too, priding himself on being a deep thinker; he knew he could figure this out. Reason and logic came naturally to him— and he had no rational cause to be nervous, just because Raaba had changed.

In the past, however, deep thought and discussion had not really been something that he and Raaba had shared. Lowie wondered if she had changed in that respect, too. Well, they were going to be in hyperspace for quite a while, so there was no better time to find out. He started the conversation by telling Raaba that it seemed she had done a lot of growing up since they'd known each other on Kashyyyk.

The Wookiee woman found grim amusement in his observation and answered with a bitter growl of laughter. It would have been hard *not* to grow up after the atrocities she had heard of and witnessed firsthand. She and Lowie had both led sheltered lives in their beautiful tree city on Kashyyyk, she explained. Even the dangers of the lowest forest levels were nothing compared to the barbarous cruelties the alien species of the galaxy had suffered. *This* was what the Diversity Alliance had taught her. And most of those atrocities had been committed by humans.

That was why the Diversity Alliance was so important as a political force for change, Raaba went on, the passion in her voice rising. The Alliance accepted and championed the rights of all the species who had suffered indignities at human hands. For example, the Empire had never been punished for its enslavement of Wookiees. The Diversity Alliance vowed never to allow such a thing to happen again. All species had been affected by the human-loving Empire's repression and prejudice, in fact.

Raaba spoke with fire in her voice. Her eyes flashed, and Lowie couldn't help but realize how large and beautiful those eyes were—or how the shaved patches at her wrists, elbows, and neck contrasted with her luxurious dark fur.

Clearly, Raaba had given some thought to the Diversity Alliance and what it stood for. Lowie was impressed by her spirit and enthusiasm . . . but also disturbed by the conclusions she drew. Humans were not the only species that had ever mistreated another, he pointed out. Surely she couldn't believe that *all* of the ills of the galaxy were the sole responsibility of human beings?

Raaba pondered for a moment. No, she admitted that other species had also mistreated one another. The Diversity Alliance abhorred any abuse of alien species—even by each other.

Lowie rumbled thoughtfully, then asked if the Diversity Alliance also abhorred the mistreatment of *humans* by other species.

Raaba looked uncomfortable at the turnabout. For now, the Diversity Alliance did not have the resources to concern itself with the treatment humans received. The subject simply did not come up. Raaba shrugged. Besides, such situations were anomalies, a minor swing of the pendulum. It was the *alien* species who needed protection from abuse; humans could take care of themselves. With the Diversity Alliance, Nolaa Tarkona was searching for the answer to all of *their* problems, and as soon as they found the long-awaited solution, the galaxy would be free again.

In a consoling tone, Raaba asked Lowie not to make up his mind in advance. She wanted him to meet her friends and listen to what they had to say. The Diversity Alliance was a place where she felt she belonged. If Lowie kept an open mind, he might find that he belonged there, too. It would be so nice to have him with her.

The Diversity Alliance could very much use the help of someone special like a Force-talented Wookiee. Perhaps his sister Sirra would want to join, as well. Even if Sirra wasn't interested, though, Raaba asked Lowie to think about how much time the two of them could spend together if they were both part of the Diversity Alliance. . . .

Lowie thought about it. A lot.

9

"YES, I *DO* have a plan," Nolaa Tarkona said. "And I don't think the humans will enjoy it very much." When she smiled, her sharply filed teeth glinted like daggers in the dim light.

"All the better then," remarked Adjutant Advisor Hovrak, a bristly faced wolfman who growled under his breath. He used a long claw to pick shreds of meat from along his gumline. A few fresh blood spatters on his otherwise neat uniform indicated that Hovrak must have eaten recently.

Nolaa glided past the long black table in her private chambers. "Are the other representatives here in the caves? The three Diversity Alliance soldiers who have recruited the greatest number of new members?"

"Yes, they just arrived on Ryloth." The wolfman shuffled his feet, uncertain. "I agree they deserve induction into our inner circle as a reward for their efforts. But are you sure that it's wise to use our last sample of the plague for so small a demonstration?"

"It isn't a *small* demonstration, Adjutant Advisor," she said. Her remaining head-tail twitched with agitation, making her tattoos ripple. From the folds of her black robes she withdrew a vial that contained the deadly solution. "This spark will ignite the fire of utter loyalty we require."

Two decades earlier a rebellious nonhuman group, the Alien Combine, had attempted to accomplish goals similar to Nolaa Tarkona's. But the Alien Combine had been unwilling to take sufficiently extreme actions. Nolaa knew how to learn from mistakes, though, and she vowed that her Diversity Alliance would succeed . . . no matter what it took.

With the wolfman beside her, she walked into the echoing main grotto to receive her newly promoted followers. The chamber was cool and dim, just the way she liked it. The light was a deep red, as if filtered through panes of bloodstained glass.

Three important Diversity Alliance soldiers stood waiting for her, puffed with pride. Out of all the thousands of members in her political movement, Nolaa had chosen *them* for this private meeting.

She studied Rullak first, a tentacle-faced Quarren from the ocean world of Calamari. Decades ago, the amphibious Quarren species had collaborated with the Empire to protect their underwater cities, while the more peaceful Mon Calamari were enslaved, their floating cities blasted to ruins. Now, Rullak stood basking in the shadows, rubbing his clammy hands together to distribute the bodily excretions that prevented his skin from drying out.

In the middle, a reptilian Trandoshan named Corrsk loomed silent and ominous, sluggish but powerful. His breath came out in a rasping gargle. The Trandoshans had a long-standing blood feud against Wookiees, and their bounty hunters made a habit of collecting Wookiee pelts. But in uniting alien species to fight the common enemy—humans—Nolaa had managed to secure concessions even from the vicious reptiles. Corrsk had sworn to ignore his natural bloodlust for any Wookiee who adopted the cause of the Diversity Alliance. All others were, of course, fair game.

Finally, on the right stood a wily Devaronian female, Kambrea, whose curving horns, hooded eyes, and pointed fangs gave her narrow face the appearance of a she-devil.

"You three have heard me speak before great crowds, but this demonstration is for your eyes alone," Nolaa said, and sat down easily in the massive stone chair. On a low pedestal at her left she kept a rough file for sharpening her teeth during idle moments. She toyed with the tool now, running its pointed end under her fingernails.

"This is a private ceremony—a reward for your

unwavering service." Her breath came out in a hiss of anticipation. "What I am about to show you will convince you more than any words I can say."

"You don't need to convince us, Esteemed Tarkona," said Kambrea. The Devaronian female's bright eyes darted from side to side, as if probing for assassins in the shadows. "We know our cause is just. The weight of human domination has crushed the galaxy for too long. We will follow you wherever the fight may take us."

"Kill humans!" said Corrsk in a rough voice. Even with this brief statement, the towering reptilian seemed to feel he had said too much.

"*I* wish to see this demonstration," the Quarren countered, the tentacles around his mouth quivering. Rullak's voice bubbled up like words spoken through a drinking tube into polluted water. "I harbor no doubts, Honored Tarkona . . . but I am certain it will be entertaining."

Nolaa laughed. "Yes, it will be very entertaining." She held up the glimmering vial so that reddish light twinkled from its crystal sides. "This vial contains more destructive power than the Death Star—than even the Sun Crusher. *Selective* destruction."

The Quarren and the Devaronian sat in anticipation. Nolaa did not know how to interpret Corrsk's breathy snort.

"You see, the Emperor did more than just create

weapons of mass destruction. He had an entire cadre of his finest scientists—*humans,* but talented nonetheless—working on more insidious schemes. The great biological engineer Evir Derricote created numerous diseases that spread like wildfire through some species, *particular* species. Recall how non-human peoples suffered during the unleashing of the Krytos plague on Coruscant during the Rebel takeover."

The three representatives all nodded gravely, remembering the death and terror shortly after the fall of the Emperor.

"I have learned that Derricote also developed an organism more deadly than Krytos, perhaps even as bad as the Death Seed plague. A virus so horrible that Emperor Palpatine himself feared to use it." She held the vial out toward them. "This contains a sample of that plague."

The three Diversity Alliance soldiers shifted uneasily and took an instinctive step backward.

Nolaa restrained her smile of self-satisfaction. Good, she had impressed them—but not nearly enough. Her slick robes draped themselves regally around her as she stood, then she took two steps down to the floor of the grotto. The three representatives flicked nervous glances at each other.

Clutching the vial, Nolaa snapped at her Adjutant Advisor. "Hovrak, bring out the prisoner." Her tattooed head-tail thrashed in anticipation, while the optical sensor implanted in her other tentacle stump gleamed, recording all the details around her.

The wolfman barked a command, and two lumbering Gamorrean guards strode in from a side tunnel, bearing between them the cloaked form of an Imperial guard. Limp scarlet robes hung around him. His bullet-shaped helmet was an impenetrable red mask with only a black vee-slit over his eyes.

"An Imperial guard!" Rullak said, raising his moist hands. "I thought they had all been destroyed."

"This one had schemes of his own," Nolaa said. "He and several partners concocted a fake Emperor in hopes that they could rule a Second Imperium in his name, like a gang of thugs—but their plans fell apart when the new Jedi Knights defeated the Shadow Academy. He was the only one to escape."

The captive struggled, but the piglike Gamorrean security escorts held firm, paying no heed to the Red Guard's resistance.

Kambrea, the Devaronian, leaned forward and cackled. "Yes, I remember how powerful the Red Guards were. They used to bully us."

"Kill humans," Corrsk growled, as if the comment were somehow relevant.

Nolaa stood in front of the scarlet-robed man. "This Red Guard continued to wear this uniform, this mask, to bank on his intimate connections with the former Empire. He went to the fringes of the underworld, hoping to ingratiate himself with certain . . . criminal elements." Her head-tail twitched. "For some reason he apparently considered the Diversity Alliance a 'criminal element.' He didn't realize just how much hatred alien species still hold against the Empire. And now the tables have turned on him."

Nolaa leaned closer to the guard, who stood rigidly at attention. "We can still make use of his Imperial knowledge, however."

"But what about the plague?" the Quarren asked. "When will we see the demonstration you promised?"

Nolaa wrinkled her brow. "Though the Emperor had no intention of ever unleashing it, he could not bring himself to destroy such an efficient, *useful* tool. So he ordered it stored in a hidden weapons depot on a small asteroid station. Then he erased the depot's coordinates from Imperial archives, so that no one knew where the stockpile of his terrible virus lay hidden.

"Most of the surviving Imperials have been scattered by now, but this one ranked high, close to Palpatine himself. I presume he knows the location of the plague storehouse. I have asked him to direct me there so that the Diversity Alliance may commandeer these valuable resources. . . ." Nolaa ran her clawed hand along the polished plasteel of the Red Guard's helmet. He flinched. "But he has declined our offer." She flicked a glance back at the three spectators. "So far."

She held up the tiny vial in front of the Red Guard's eye slit. "Tell me where the rest is stored. This is your final chance."

The Red Guard's helmet swung from side to side in mute defiance.

Nolaa heaved a sigh. "Very well, then, face the consequences." She dropped the crystalline vial to the stone floor of the cave. With barely disguised relish, Nolaa stamped down and crushed it with her booted foot, exposing the viral solution to the open air.

The three spectators staggered backward. Gasping in horror, they scrambled to cover their mouths and nostrils and tried—unsuccessfully—not to breathe. Confused, the Gamorrean guards blinked stupidly down at the broken vial, wondering if they should clean it up.

Nolaa Tarkona merely watched.

The Red Guard lunged and writhed in a violent attempt to escape the Gamorreans' grasp—but the seizure rapidly became something else entirely. His body trembled. He bucked convulsively.

"You may release him," Nolaa said. "There's no longer any danger." The piglike guards looked at each other, shrugged, then stomped away.

The captive sank to his knees, shaking. His gloved hands pawed at his chest, his stomach. The three honored Diversity Alliance soldiers stood back against the wall of the grotto, staring in fascinated horror.

The Imperial guard's chest heaved. Gurgling sounds came from beneath the scarlet helmet, as if he were trying to suck in lungfuls of air but only managed to inhale viscous saliva.

His gloved hands reached up to grasp his smooth helmet, fumbled with the hidden catch. His arms shook and his feet tapped against the floor as the plague flowed like molten lead through every nerve in his body.

Above the noise of his rasping and retching for breath, Nolaa could hear the clasp of the helmet come loose. The Red Guard's hands clutched the glossy plasteel and pulled. His body arched. The helmet lifted just a little, not quite revealing the guard's face—then he sagged into a limp pile of scarlet cloth.

"Impressive," Hovrak said with a growl, his long tongue licking the points of his canine teeth.

"Even better than I had hoped." Nolaa turned to the three still-frightened Diversity Alliance observers. "You see, the plague was developed to be DNA-specific. It affects only victims with a *human* genetic structure. Aliens are immune. All of us here are breathing the same air, moving in the same room—yet the disease struck down only this pitiful

Red Guard, while the rest of us went about our business unaffected."

"But," Kambrea said, gradually inching forward, "why would the Emperor develop such a thing? Humans were his subjects."

"True," Nolaa answered, "but many were also Rebels. Palpatine intended to unleash this plague to quash insurrections on colony worlds—until he realized how easily it could spread. One carrier from world to world might break a quarantine—and within weeks this disease could have made his Empire a galaxy-wide charnel house."

At Nolaa's gesture of dismissal the Gamorreans came forward, grabbed the Red Guard's body, and dragged him by his scarlet sleeves across the stone floor. Once they turned down a side passage and out of sight, Nolaa heard the Red Guard's helmet clatter to the flagstones. The Gamorreans grumbled and snorted, blaming each other for the accident, then one apparently snatched up the helmet again. They continued dragging their victim away to where he could be disposed of.

"You mean to spread this plague?" Corrsk asked. "Kill all the humans?"

Nolaa crossed her arms over her chest. "Wouldn't that be the proper work of the Diversity Alliance?"

Rullak leaned forward, facial tentacles quivering. "How did you obtain this sample, Esteemed Tarkona? And where may we get more?"

She stepped up onto the dais, where she slumped back into her stone chair. Hovrak stood quietly beside her, letting Nolaa do the talking.

"A scavenger named Fonterrat stumbled upon the secret depot where this plague is stored. He stole two small samples, not entirely realizing what he had found, and brought the vials to me, along with a description of the facility. But Fonterrat was suspicious and greedy. He cited an outrageous price. I quibbled with him.

"Because only Fonterrat knew the location of the depot, he was afraid I might torture him for the information. Of course, the Diversity Alliance would never harm a fellow alien." She smiled sweetly. "Humans are our only targets.

"Fonterrat requested that I send an emissary to a neutral location. There, my emissary would hand him a time-locked container holding his enormous fee. He, in turn, would deliver his entire navicomputer module, the only repository of the plague depot's coordinates."

She tapped her long fingernails on the arm of her chair. "It seemed a safe enough arrangement for all concerned. It amused me to enlist a human emissary to do my dirty work. Such delicious irony. I chose Bornan Thul, an arrogant merchant, who seemed to think he owned the galaxy.

"Thul met with Fonterrat on the ancient world of Kuar. They presumably made the exchange and went their separate ways—but Bornan Thul never delivered the navicomputer to me. He must have figured out what he had been given, what the module contained, and so he chose to disappear. Thul never arrived at the Shumavar trade conference where we were to have consummated our deal."

Nolaa folded her hands together, wearing a perplexed expression. "Oddly, he hasn't gone to the New Republic either. Perhaps he assumes that the Diversity Alliance has infiltrated the government on Coruscant. And of course we have."

She tapped her other fingers on the opposite arm of her chair. "Unfortunately, since Fonterrat didn't trust me enough to make the deal directly, and since my human go-between betrayed me, I still haven't retrieved the information I paid for. I had my joke on Fonterrat, though. In the sealed locker containing his fee, I placed one of his plague samples. As soon as he unsealed the time-locked box to study his reward, a device secretly cracked open the vial. Since Fonterrat was immune to the disease, he didn't even know that his ship was full of the plague organism when he landed on the isolated human colony of Gammalin."

Nolaa smiled, looking up at Hovrak with her rose-quartz eyes. "Everyone on Gammalin is now dead. Unfortunately, no one managed to leave the colony to spread the virus. The plague organism doesn't survive long in open air without a host, and so Gammalin did not prove to be a proper flash point for the plague. Regrettable . . ."

The three spectators now came forward, eyes gleaming. The Trandoshan scooped up a few broken shards from the plague vial. He brought them to his blunt nose and sniffed with great interest.

"So how are we to obtain an adequate stockpile of this weapon to aid us in our fight against oppression?" Kambrea asked, brushing a hand across her smooth horns. "This was your last sample, and Bornan Thul has disappeared with the knowledge of where the rest is stored."

"It is merely a setback," Nolaa said. "I have offered a large enough reward that every bounty hunter in the galaxy is trying to bring Thul to me. He won't be able to move anywhere without someone capturing him."

She stroked her tattooed head-tail, feeling the tingle of response from her sensitive nerve endings. "It's only a matter of time."

10

IN FLIGHT, ZEKK spent days studying the Bounty Hunter's Creed, memorizing its rules and practices as he wrestled with conflicting thoughts. He had so many questions, and so much to learn.

It seemed impossible to reconcile the desire to capture Bornan Thul with the fact that he had accepted an assignment from him, regardless of the fact that Thul had been disguised at the time. Zekk also remembered that in the rubble field of Alderaan he had promised to give Jaina any news of the missing man who was Raynar's father. . . .

Of all the hunters in the galaxy—Dengar and Boba Fett and a thousand others who were scouring the starlanes—*he* alone knew where Bornan Thul could be found. He had a meeting scheduled with his mysterious employer in less than a week, to tell him of his progress. At that rendezvous, Zekk could easily set a trap, deliver Thul to Nolaa Tarkona, and reap the fame and extravagant reward. How could he pass up such an opportunity?

But betraying his own employer would forever blacklist Zekk among bounty hunters. No one would trust him for the rest of his life. Jaina and Jacen would be angry with him, too. His situation seemed untenable.

He pondered the question while mulling over where to begin searching for Tyko Thul, the other half of the assignment he had accepted. Could he somehow take both bounty hunting assignments— find and bring back both brothers? Or would he have to make a choice? No matter how long he drifted in the *Lightning Rod*, he wouldn't resolve his dilemma by himself.

He remembered hearing that Boba Fett had recently turned up on Tatooine in his own relentless search for Bornan Thul, and came to a decision. Since he was in the same sector, Zekk would go to meet the fearsome hunter who had proved an uneasy ally on the plague-ridden colony of Gammalin. . . .

Fighting thermal updrafts, Zekk cruised under the harsh double suns down to the broiling city of Mos Eisley, the hub of civilization (such as it was) on this backwater world. Below him, the space-port's towers and low adobe structures shimmered in the afternoon haze.

Zekk requested clearance and transferred credits for a temporary berth in one of the low-rent docking stalls in the busy traders' district. After he landed, he shut down his ship's systems and activated the theft-prevention devices old Peckhum had installed . . . though the best deterrent had always been the *Lightning Rod*'s own battered appearance, which did not speak well for the fortunes of its owner.

Zekk stepped out of the dock only to slam into a wall of heat rising from the dusty streets. He tied his dark hair back in a sweaty ponytail and kept to the shadows of low buildings, seeking relief from the harsh sunlight as he staggered along. He breathed through his sleeve to filter out the worst dust as he looked for the infamous cantina.

The other creatures stirring in Mos Eisley's afternoon seemed either stunned and lethargic or hurried and anxious to get into the shaded coolness indoors. Zekk, his green eyes stinging, wanted to do the same.

After making his way down narrow back alleys, he entered the noise and smells and blessed air-conditioning of the spaceport bar. The Mos Eisley cantina had a long history and quite a reputation, but little cleanliness or fresh air. In this dark and seedy bar, Luke Skywalker and Obi-Wan Kenobi had first hired Han Solo and Chewbacca for their legendary run to Alderaan.

Boba Fett himself had come here in search of clues to help him ferret out Bornan Thul.

Behind the bar stood a grizzled old Wookiee named Chalmun, who owned the cantina. Other bartenders often took care of the actual work so that Chalmun would not have to mingle with his own disreputable clientele.

Zekk strode up to the bar, trying to look surly and tough, just like everyone else in the place. The old Wookiee snorted, seeing right through the young man's act, as if he had witnessed these shows of bravado so many times that they no longer impressed him.

Zekk ordered a cold fizzy drink, then lowered his voice. "I'm looking for Boba Fett."

The furry bartender chuffed with surly laughter. Zekk didn't understand the Wookiee language very well, and Chalmun gestured toward a small hairy creature propped up on one of the stools.

The creature blinked its huge black eyes and spoke in a squeaking voice. "He laughs at your request," the creature said. "Boba Fett always looks for other people. No one looks for *him*."

"He and I have met before. I need to speak with him, and in return"—Zekk swallowed hard—"I can provide information that may assist him in his current assignment."

"Boba Fett will be here," the furry creature said. "Just drink and wait." The creature took a long snort from a foaming green beaker, swallowed noisily, and said, "But you'd better keep drinking or Chalmun may throw you out into the streets. Hot out there."

Eavesdropping, the Wookiee laughed and went off to serve other customers. . . .

Zekk waited. The hours passed at a crawl, and he drank as slowly as he could get away with, ordering another beverage only when he saw the old Wookiee scowling at him.

On the bandstand a group of soft-skinned amphibious musicians with multicolored neck frills auditioned for a job. The song sounded like echoing belches made into a sensitive microphone, while "musicians" jangled high-pitched bells at random. On the cramped and dirty dance floor, two aliens that looked like sea urchins with far too many eyes rolled around locked in an embrace—whether dancing or brawling, Zekk couldn't decide.

He continued waiting. Another hour dragged by.

Boba Fett did not enter the cantina until the light had begun to fade during the first of Tatooine's twin sunsets.

The band stopped playing, and most of the background noise in the bar dwindled to murmurs. The masked bounty hunter paused in the dimness, swiveling his head back and forth, exuding confidence. Zekk could feel Fett's gaze burning through the black slit in his Mandalorian helmet.

The bounty hunter saw Zekk and froze, suspicious.

The moment of silence ended, and the band began playing again. Through his peripheral vision Zekk noticed several patrons wince at the resumption of the noise. The two sea-urchin aliens on the dance floor continued tumbling about; they had not stopped even during the brief silence.

The bounty hunter strode up to the bar beside Zekk. Zekk momentarily wondered if the Wookiee bartender would require *Fett* to buy a drink as well, but Chalmun pointedly remained at the other side of the bar, serving customers who watched the masked hunter with unconcealed anxiety.

Zekk could feel the power, the spring-tight rage and dark energy in this man. Fett had killed an uncounted number of enemies, served no cause, and had at one time worn Wookiee scalps at his belt. Zekk could imagine no glimmer of friendship from this vicious man—but Boba Fett was one of the best bounty hunters in existence. And Zekk needed to learn from him.

Zekk turned, but the bounty hunter spoke first. "What do you want from me? And what do you offer in exchange?"

The young man gathered his courage. "I need advice. If I'm going to be the best bounty hunter, I had better ask questions of the best."

"Advice?" Fett said dubiously, scornfully. "Nothing is free."

Zekk sat up straighter. "I have information that may help you find Bornan Thul." He certainly wouldn't give away the knowledge of his scheduled rendezvous on Borgo Prime . . . but he had less-important details to offer. He let the words hang in the air, then added, "I know where another bounty hunter was searching for him. It may give you a clue."

Boba Fett said, "Many are searching for Thul. Most of them are fools. The value of your information depends on how much I can trust this lead."

"It's Dengar," Zekk said, then squared his shoulders. "I know where Dengar went looking for Bornan Thul."

Fett paused, as silent as a statue. "Dengar is . . . not a fool." The bandage-wrapped hunter had rescued a grievously injured Boba Fett after he blasted his way free from the sarlacc in the Pit of Carkoon. "What do you need?"

"Listen to this problem," Zekk said. "I'm new to being a bounty hunter, and this is a hypothetical situation that any of us might run into."

Fett waited. The alien musicians croaked an announcement that they were taking a break but would be back with more music before long. Only a few inebriated patrons clapped.

"Suppose I accept an assignment—say, to find a

lost treasure or a missing document—and in the course of my hunt I stumble upon completely unrelated information that reveals the location of a much larger bounty."

Fett said, "Then secure both. Keep your honor and make a greater profit."

Zekk arched his eyebrows. "But what if chasing after the second bounty puts my first employer at risk? In fact, if I find the larger bounty, my original employer will certainly come to great harm." He paused, hoping he wasn't giving too much away.

The bounty hunter pondered in silence. "You must not betray your employer. That is one of the worst crimes a bounty hunter can commit."

"So I just have to give up the second bounty?" Zekk said, somewhat disheartened, though a bit relieved.

"No," Fett said. "Deliver the first bounty, take payment, and terminate your service with that employer. *Then* pursue the second bounty with a clear conscience, since you no longer work for the employer who might be harmed."

Zekk mulled over this answer. He had already discharged half of his assignment by sending the coded message to the Bornaryn merchant fleet. Now, if he could just find Tyko Thul, he would be under no further obligation. From that point on, Zekk would be free to do as he pleased.

Zekk had no idea what Thul had done to warrant

such a manhunt or why Nolaa Tarkona wanted him so desperately—but it was clear she primarily wanted his *cargo,* some mysterious navicomputer module.

Zekk smiled. He could do it. He could do both.

"Now," Boba Fett said, "tell me where you saw Dengar."

Zekk told him about Ziost, but gave few other details. Then the two of them hurried away from the Mos Eisley cantina, parting without any word of farewell to return to their respective ships.

11

TWO CRACKLING STUN-RODS crashed against each other in a shower of sparks. Jacen descended a few steps on the temple's rugged stairway and went on the attack. Below him, Raynar backed down two stairs as he deflected the next several blows with his own stun-rod.

With the sleeve of his jumpsuit, Jacen blotted away the sweat running into his eyes, then swept the training weapon in a counterstrike. The sun that beat down outside the Great Temple already seemed unbearably hot for this time of morning.

He pressed downward another step, raising his glowing pewter-colored staff. Raynar spun out of the way and danced along the wide stone ledge, dodging some scaffolding that had been erected by the repair crew, then rapped the stun-rod against Jacen's wrist.

Jacen howled at the sudden tingling zap. "Ow!" he said, then, "Nice move, Raynar!" He hopped down to the ledge and continued the sparring match, bringing up his own staff. The pewter rods clashed again. "Pretty soon you'll be ready to fight against a real lightsaber."

Raynar's sweat-soaked training robe clung to him but did not hamper his movements. "Thanks," he said, catching the next blow against his stun-rod. "That's why I asked for your help during practice. You're one of the best here at the academy."

Jacen fell back a step. "Jaina's as good as I am." Raynar swung low, and Jacen blocked again.

"She takes it too easy on me," Raynar panted. "Feels sorry for me, I guess."

Jacen gave a wicked grin. "How about Tenel Ka, then?" He nodded toward the base of the ancient pyramid to where the warrior girl and Lusa were setting out for a morning run. The two exercised together because no one else could keep up with them.

Raynar shook his head, and droplets of sweat flew from side to side. "Just the opposite—no mercy whatsoever." He turned to stare at the two runners with great interest. "Can we take a breather for a minute?"

"Sure," Jacen said, ready for a break himself.

Powering down the stun-rod, Raynar sank to the ledge and dangled his feet over the side. Jacen followed suit, and the two watched Lusa and Tenel Ka race each other across the landing field, cinnamon mane and red-gold braids streaming out behind them.

"Amazing, isn't she?" Raynar said, still breathless from their workout.

Jacen watched Tenel Ka's easy long-legged strides with admiration. He felt a brief flash of jealousy at Raynar's comment, but it was gone as quickly as it came. "I've always thought so," he said. "You mean you *just* noticed her?"

"I, uh . . . not exactly." Raynar blushed a deep red. "I thought so from the moment we met, but I've only known her for a few days."

Jacen suddenly realized that Raynar was talking about the sleek Centaur girl, not Tenel Ka. A slow smile spread across his face. "Yeah," he said. "I know just what you mean."

Holding a pair of delicate wires with two fingers, Jaina stuck her other hand out from beneath the *Rock Dragon*'s sensor array panel. "Could you hand me that circuit fuser please?"

An electronic sigh answered her. "I should very much *like* to accommodate your request, Mistress Jaina," Em Teedee said morosely, "but I'm afraid I'm completely useless to you in that respect— useless in almost *every* respect at the moment, I should say. I can't move about on my own, I am no longer needed for my translation functions—"

Jaina groaned and dropped the wires. For a second she had forgotten that Lowie was not here working beside her, and now she had hurt the miniaturized translating droid's feelings. She scrambled out from under the control panel and grabbed the circuit fuser herself. "Sorry, Em Teedee, I didn't mean—"

"Oh, it's quite all right, Mistress Jaina," the little droid said. "I'm resigned to the possibility that being wired to a diagnostic panel may be my only beneficial purpose. And even that is nonessential, since you have such an excellent ability to diagnose malfunctions on your own." He gave an electronic moan. "Why, I shouldn't be at all surprised if one morning I reactivated from my shutdown cycle only to find myself in one of those electronics bins in your chambers, ready to be disassembled for spare parts."

Now it was Jaina's turn to sigh. She closed the access panel under the sensor array she'd been adjusting and then heaved herself up into the copilot's seat. Lowbacca's former seat. "I miss Lowie, too, you know."

"I'm certain Master Lowbacca misses all of his friends here at the academy as well." Em Teedee's electronic voice quavered. "I'm the only one he hasn't any use for anymore."

Jaina reached out and disconnected the silvery

droid's leads from the *Rock Dragon*'s diagnostic panels and tucked them back into his case. Carrying Em Teedee under one arm, Jaina went to the rear compartment where she stored maintenance supplies.

"You know, Em Teedee," she said, "you'll feel much better after a lubricant bath. Then I'm going to do that waterproofing I promised you."

She placed a small bucket on the floor and opened the valve above it, letting an iridescent blue liquid flow into the pail.

"But, Mistress Jaina," Em Teedee protested, "unlike my predecessor, See-Threepio, I have almost no moving parts. My continuous function does not rely on lubricant baths. Why, I've never even experienced one—"

"There's a first time for everything," Jaina said, shutting off the lubricant valve. She held Em Teedee above the full bucket and gave him a little pat. "Enjoy it. You'd be surprised what a good bath can do to change your outlook on things." She lowered the little droid into the iridescent fluid.

Em Teedee had just enough time to say, "Indeed?" before his speaker grille was completely submerged.

Walking along beside Lusa after the midday meal, Raynar clasped his hands behind his back to keep himself from fidgeting. He had hardly expected the Centaur girl to agree when he'd offered to show her his favorite waterfall.

Well, she hadn't actually *agreed*. Upon overhearing Lusa shyly turn down Raynar's invitation, Master Skywalker had stepped in and encouraged her to reconsider. The Jedi teacher quietly reminded Lusa that as part of her healing she needed to learn to make new human friends. With obvious trepidation, Lusa had relented.

Now, alone with the cinnamon-maned Centaur girl, Raynar came to a belated realization. He had never really learned to make conversation with people whom he did not know, since people usually came to *him* to talk. Raynar had begun to learn negotiation techniques from his father—Bornan Thul could wield words much as Master Skywalker wielded his lightsaber—but he had unfortunately learned most of his conversational skills from his uncle Tyko's proud boasts and blunt observations. Though his mother possessed grace and social skills in abundance, she had not yet managed to pass them on to her son.

Frantically trying to remember what Aryn had taught him about polite conversation, Raynar walked faster along the jungle path. A multicolored swarm of button beetles buzzed up from a nebula orchid where they had been feeding. Lusa let out a small gasp of delight at the shower of color.

Raynar held aside a branch that had grown across

the path so that Lusa could pass without being scratched. He wondered whether his action would be seen as kind or merely insulting. She edged past him, nodding to Raynar in silent thanks. The tips of her crystal horns sparkled, and the tense rippling muscles in her cinnamon flanks seemed to relax a bit.

Encouraged, Raynar asked her a question. "What do you *admire* in . . ." He searched for a suitably neutral word. "I mean—what is it you look for in a friend, exactly?" He hoped that her answer would not be something simple and abrupt like, "I look for *nonhumans* as friends." He didn't want to remind her of the Diversity Alliance. Then again, he thought, perhaps he should consider it progress if she answered him at all.

At first Lusa said nothing. They continued in silence through a thicket of blueleaf until they emerged beside a chattering stream in a small clearing. Raynar turned and headed upstream.

Lusa finally answered him. "Loyalty. Commitment. Deep beliefs and a willingness to act on those beliefs. I look for an openness to finding new solutions to old problems." She paused. "I guess those are some of the things that drew me to the Diversity Alliance."

Raynar tensed at her mention of the political group. Before Lusa, he'd never been aware that he could be hated—not because he was proud and boastful, or because of the tough trading deals his family negotiated . . . but for no other reason than his species.

"Um, the waterfall's just a little farther that way." He raised his arm to point higher along their route and accidentally brushed against Lusa. She instinctively recoiled from him and took off at a gallop upstream.

Startled, Raynar ran after her. He caught up with the Centaur girl beside the sparkling green pool at the base of the waterfall. She stood on the bank with her front hooves in the water, staring at her own reflection and shuddering.

"I . . . I'm really sorry," Raynar blurted. "I didn't mean to—"

"No," she answered. "You did nothing wrong. Master Skywalker was correct: I let the Diversity Alliance poison my mind against humans, and now I must *unlearn* the hate they taught." She tossed her head and sent him an apologetic smile. "Please be patient. It may take me a while." She looked longingly at the waterfall, then back at Raynar. "Would you mind if I went in?"

Feeling humiliated that a brush of his arm had been so revolting to the beautiful girl, Raynar decided they could both use time to collect themselves. He climbed up onto a round boulder beside the stream. "Go ahead," he said. "I'll wait for you here."

Lusa plunged into the pool and made straight for the deeper water beneath the surging waterfall. Watching the silvery liquid cascade over her, Raynar wondered if she would ever consider him her friend. Loyalty, she had said. Deep beliefs. . . . She looked for these things in her friends.

What exactly *did* he believe in, though? He believed in his training as a Jedi, he supposed. And when he finished that training he would go out on an assignment to defend the New Republic before taking his place as heir to the Bornaryn fleet.

But what about *now*? He believed in his family. How had he acted on that belief?

Raynar could go out to search for his father and his uncle, he mused, but as only one of many, many searchers. He would probably make no difference to the final outcome.

He could do nothing to protect his mother that she could not do for herself.

Bornaryn Trading headquarters on Coruscant did not need him.

So what could he do?

Lusa submerged herself completely in the water and then surfaced again, letting the rushing stream beat down on her head and shoulders, as if its flow could cleanse her inside and out.

Raynar smiled. He loved waterfalls. They reminded him of fountains like the ones used in the Alderaanian ceremony of waters. He and his mother and Uncle Tyko shared a love for that ceremony. . . .

Raynar sat up straight. Uncle Tyko. There *was* something he could do for his uncle. With Tyko kidnapped, all the systems on Mechis III would be running unsupervised. He could go to the droid world and see that the manufacturing facilities there did not fall into disrepair while his uncle was absent.

Raynar's excitement grew as the idea caught hold in his mind. When Lusa cantered up onto the soft riverbank, he jumped down from the boulder to share his news. Before he could approach, she stretched luxuriously and then shook herself dry, sending glistening droplets of water in every direction.

Raynar didn't mind getting wet. He waited to make sure Lusa saw him and would not get spooked. She met his eyes tentatively, smiling. This time she did not recoil as he came closer.

Eyes bright, Raynar told Lusa of his new plan to go to Mechis III. "It's the least I can do for my family."

She looked surprised, supportive, and—Raynar hoped he sensed it correctly—slightly disappointed. "Will you be going alone?" she asked. "Do you have your own ship?"

The question brought Raynar up short. He had not thought of how he would actually get to the droid world. "Well, if I have to find my way there alone, I will," he said firmly. He was surprised as he spoke the next words and realized they were true: "But I have some friends—I think they'll volunteer to go with me."

And he was right.

12

AFTER HIS DISCUSSION with Boba Fett, Zekk plunged into the search for Bornan Thul's brother. According to Jaina's recent hololetter, Tyko had been kidnapped by the assassin droid IG-88 during a battle in the lost city on Kuar.

Jaina sent Zekk news-filled messages to reassure him of her friendship. Someday he intended to respond, when he felt confident enough in his new life that he could rise above the dark things he had done to her and her friends when he was part of the Shadow Academy.

Zekk missed Jaina more than he could admit—even to himself—but he couldn't face her until he redefined who he was. First, he had to make his name as a bounty hunter. At the moment, an important part of his quest was to find Tyko Thul.

By tapping into galactic information databases, Zekk compiled a dossier of background information on Raynar's uncle. After the destruction of Alderaan, Bornan and Aryn Dro Thul had transformed their remaining family wealth into a profitable merchant fleet. Tyko, on the other hand, had invested his fortune in rebuilding the droid manufacturing facilities on Mechis III.

Next Zekk reviewed Jaina's hololetters and quickly summed up the details. When his brother became a fugitive, Tyko had retreated briefly to the safety of the Bornaryn fleet, and then joined Jaina, Jacen, and their friends to search for clues on Kuar. In the ruins, the group ran afoul of IG-88 and his squad of assassin droids, and the other Thul had been abducted during the battle.

Zekk found it astonishing that IG-88 had so far made no ransom demands. The assassin droid seemed to be waiting for Bornan Thul to reappear from hiding and ask for his brother's release. But Zekk alone knew that the wanted man had other plans. Zekk would have to find Tyko himself.

He searched through the *Lightning Rod*'s navigational files until he found a minor notation on the ancient world of Kuar—enough to help him plan his route. Kuar was a faint clue at best, but at the moment he had no better leads. The ship launched into hyperspace.

All civilization on the planet had turned to dust, leaving only skeletal cities poking out of craters and cliffsides. Archaeological evidence from long-ago expeditions suggested that this place had once served as a gladiatorial training ground for the fearsome Mandalorian warriors. Now, only ruined cities remained, like scars gradually fading with time.

It didn't take his sensors long to locate residual traces of the young Jedi Knights' encampment and the site of their fateful battle. At least now he had a place to start.

He set the *Lightning Rod* down on the crater rim where Jacen and Jaina, Tenel Ka, and Lowie had begun exploring the ruins. Standing beside his ship, which ticked and hissed and clanked as it settled on its landing pads, he stared into the immense bowl-shaped crater. These ruins were older than even the Mandalorian conquests. Towering skyscrapers had fallen apart, leaving only girder superstructures that protruded from the floor of the crater and rose nearly to its rim.

The crater's sheer walls were riddled with tunnels and catacombs, like worm-infested wood. He let his imagination wander. On the balcony seats below, spectators had once watched life-and-death struggles inside the arena.

Zekk surveyed the crater, pondering his next step. In order to search for any clues, he would need to find the exact site of the battle with the combat arachnids and the assassin droids.

He armed himself with two blasters, knowing that the catacombs might still be swarming with the ferocious spider-monsters. Zekk wanted to make his inspection and get out before he attracted the attention of the arachnids.

Keeping his weapons handy and his Jedi senses alert, Zekk followed ramps, crumbling stairs, and interlocked balconies down the crater wall. When he discovered scuffed footprints in the dust where his friends had walked, he did his best to retrace their steps. Perhaps in the aftermath of battle, some clue had been left unnoticed by one of IG-88's droid henchmen.

It was a slim chance, though, and he didn't hold out much hope.

Zekk followed the trail until he came upon recent blaster scars. Zekk reconstructed the details of the battle from what he saw. IG-88 and his cohorts had pulverized part of the crater wall to get into the catacombs. Under attack, Jacen and Jaina had fled downward, hauling Tenel Ka, Lowie, and Tyko Thul after them. They had rushed into the dark passageways, hoping to escape. But the assassin droids had found them anyway—and so had the combat arachnids.

Zekk sniffed the metallic tang in the air, the mustiness, the sharp odor of dust and long-dried blood. Yes, this was the place.

He listened intently for the tapping of jagged

feet on stone, large bodies stirring, mandibles clacking . . . but the tunnels were filled with only the sifting of dust, the whispers of shadows.

He switched on a glowrod, keeping the light down low. Then he advanced deeper inside.

Within the chamber he saw numerous dark tunnels in the cliffside, probably the dank lairs of surviving combat arachnids. Zekk tried to keep his light from dancing inside the protective darkness of those passages. He was not afraid to fight, but he didn't want to.

He thought he heard a sound. Pausing in midstep, he waited to hear it repeated. A trickle of sweat crept down his back. Silence, punctuated by his own pounding heartbeat and the roar of his own breathing. He continued his inspection, trying to maintain his concentration. He didn't want to miss a thing.

On the ceiling and walls of the grotto Zekk saw pitted impact points where energy bolts had struck. The floor itself was stained, discolored, tacky with dried ichor from the slaughtered creatures.

Like discarded garbage, the torn and blasted remains of slain assassin droids were scattered everywhere. Durasteel arms, torsos, central processors, built-in weapons systems, and metallic skull-heads lay where they had fallen. Either the combat arachnids had no interest in the spare parts, or they had intentionally left the fallen enemies to show their scorn.

"Must have been a titanic battle," Zekk muttered.

He picked up the twisted remnant of a tubular durasteel torso from one of the powerful assassin droids. Such merciless killing machines were illegal and kept under tight security even during Imperial days. He found it incredible to discover so many here, in one place.

Zekk reached in, fiddled with the wreckage, and finally pulled out the central processing unit from the metal body core. He studied the serial number on the CPU, frowning deeply.

This was not at all what he had expected.

Zekk had assumed that IG-88, an old-model semi-sentient assassin droid, had gathered a cadre of discontinued machines that were still deadly, still functional. In theory, at least, assassin droids had not been constructed for decades—not since the fall of the Empire.

But this chip was new. The date-coded serial number and designators suggested that its programming was less than two months old. This assassin droid had been manufactured *recently*!

Zekk held up the chip, shining his glowrod onto its surface again to double-check its markings. Something was terribly wrong here. This was a mystery he had not anticipated.

He heard a stirring noise, clear and definite this

time: the cautiously approaching footsteps of a creature that had far too many legs.

Zekk stood up straight, gripping a blaster in one hand and his glowrod in the other. He dimmed the light even further when he heard clacking noises and skittering footsteps from other catacombs, coming closer, getting louder. The combat arachnids were alerted to his presence. They were nearby . . . and he had no doubt they intended to deal with another intruder swiftly and permanently.

Grabbing the CPU chip that held the information he needed—as well as another, deeper puzzle—he sprinted back out to the balconies and into the hazy sunlight of Kuar.

He didn't look behind him. His legs were strong and fit and carried him at full speed back to his ship. The combat arachnids could give chase if they wanted, but he sensed that they would be cautious, for a short time, at least—and he would get to safety first. He had left the *Lightning Rod* prepped for a fast getaway.

Sliding into the pilot's seat, Zekk activated the repulsorlifts and raised his ship off the dusty rim of the crater, taking time to fasten his crash restraints only after he had reached the air. Then he cruised away at a leisurely pace to give himself time to think.

Zekk held the chip in his hand, contemplating the inexplicably recent serial number. He ran a data check on the number using the *Lightning Rod*'s computers. The results verified his suspicions but raised many more questions than were answered.

The assassin droids that had accompanied IG-88 to kidnap Tyko Thul had been manufactured only a few weeks ago—*on Mechis III*.

In Tyko Thul's own droid factory.

As he reached the blackness of space, Zekk stared out at the cascade of stars . . . and decided that he had no choice but to follow the mystery where it led him. He was a bounty hunter, and he had an assignment to complete. He would go to Mechis III.

But first, he had one stop to make.

MECHIS III WAS a black world, its surface blanketed with slag and industrial debris, its continents covered with factories, processing centers, and automated assembly lines. It had originally been a lifeless planet with a breathable atmosphere, but ugly and barren—a place where huge factories could be set up without local inhabitants complaining about environmental damage. Better here, everyone agreed, than on some world worth saving.

Mechis III served its purpose, as evidenced by the proliferation of droids throughout the galaxy. Other planets, such as Telti, produced high-quality droids as well, but for generations this had been the center of the industry.

During the last days of the Empire, though, Mechis III had undergone a turbulent upheaval, which was largely undocumented. The supervisors of the automated assembly lines had been killed, but the mechanized, self-sufficient systems had continued regular production, unsupervised, for some time. In fact, several years had passed before anyone even noticed that the human attendants were no longer alive!

In the meantime, the systems had fallen into disarray. Programming glitches and minor breakdowns went unrepaired and gradually compounded themselves into worse disasters.

Thus, by the time Raynar's uncle took on the immense project of restoring Mechis III's former glory, entire sections of the factory had been blackened, burnt out, or shut down from lack of power. Much of the machinery lay in disrepair or total ruin. But Tyko Thul had promised to bring the place to peak production levels and had succeeded admirably—at least until he was kidnapped by an assassin droid.

Now Raynar vowed he would not let all of his uncle's work go to waste. . . .

As the *Rock Dragon* approached Mechis III, Jaina looked out the front windowports at the landscape far below. The lights of a thousand factories glittered like bright embroidery across the slag-covered surface. Beside her, Raynar sat in Lowbacca's accustomed copilot's seat, though the young man did not venture to help with the actual flying. Jaina did it all with only Em Teedee's assistance—which made her miss Lowie even more.

Jacen and Tenel Ka sat beside each other in the back, talking quietly. "Say," Jacen said, "what does an Imperial Star Destroyer wear to a formal occasion?"

"Why would Imperial Star Destroyers wear *anything*?" Tenel Ka asked. The warrior girl from Dathomir seemed to enjoy frustrating him, and Jacen never failed to rise to the challenge.

"Still don't quite have the hang of these jokes, do you?" he said in exasperation. "Come on, you know that's not the right response."

"Very well," Tenel Ka said with the barest smile, "what *does* an Imperial Star Destroyer wear to a formal occasion?"

"A bow TIE!"

Jaina groaned. "That one's bad even for you, Jacen. I think we may have to strand you here on Mechis III."

Raynar leaned forward in the copilot's seat to study the view, eager and nervous at the same time. "I've got coordinates for the administrative headquarters," he said. "My mother sent them. If Uncle Tyko left any messages, that's where they'll be."

"All right," Jaina said, thankful to turn back to flying the ship, "key the coordinates into the navicomputer and we'll be on our way." The blond young man blinked in surprise that she would have him do the work. Jaina raised her eyebrows. "Well, what are you waiting for?"

With obvious pleasure, Raynar quickly punched in the data and changed course down to the industrial planet. After cruising through thick clouds of obscuring smoke, Jaina brought the *Rock Dragon* down on the roof of the administration towers.

Raynar was the first to the hatch. Jaina picked up Em Teedee, tucked the little droid under one arm, and opened the passenger shuttle. Gusts of smoky air drifted in, smelling of burnt chemicals and ozone.

The companions stepped out and gazed around at the skyline. Lightning rods spiked upward from the corners of the tallest buildings, drawing down static in discharge blasts. Towering factories spewed exhaust into the air, and black clouds simmered just above the tops of smokestacks.

Tenel Ka drew a deep breath, scowled, then took a more cautious sniff. "The air is . . . brooding." She looked up at the blackness in the sky. In the distance lightning flickered. "Perhaps a storm is approaching."

"I think that's just the pollution, Tenel Ka," Jacen said.

A roof doorway opened, ratcheting on tracks that had not been lubricated in a long time. A platinum-colored protocol droid emerged, an older model that still managed to move with well-oiled grace.

"You are not authorized to be here. No visitors allowed." Its voice was harsher, less silken than

See-Threepio's. "You must depart immediately . . . or accept the consequences."

Em Teedee made a disbelieving sound that was muffled slightly by Jaina's arm. "Well, really! I am authorized translating droid Em Teedee, and my companions are students at the Jedi academy on Yavin 4. I can assure you we have every right to be here."

"I am Threedee-Fourex, official protocol droid and welcoming committee—and you are *not welcome*," the protocol droid snapped.

"Protocol droid, indeed!" Em Teedee scoffed. "I should say your programming requires significant adjustment, not to mention your manners."

Threedee-Fourex continued to block their path. "Go away. If you were the Emperor himself you would not be wanted here."

"The Emperor is dead," Jaina said, "and we have business on Mechis III." The protocol droid did not budge.

Finally Raynar stepped forward. "I am Raynar Thul, nephew of Tyko Thul, the administrator of this facility. In his absence, I have come to see that his business affairs run smoothly until he returns."

"You are not essential to this operation," Threedee-Fourex said. "Your presence will complicate matters unnecessarily."

Raynar drew himself up with all the dignity and determination his noble upbringing had given him.

"And a mere protocol droid is not authorized to make that decision. Now show me to my uncle's offices. We have work to do."

"I will do no such thing," Threedee-Fourex said, then swiveled about. "It would violate my current priority programming—which is to keep guests *away*. Depart immediately, or I shall be forced to take extreme measures."

Tenel Ka withdrew her lightsaber, but did not switch it on. "We are Jedi Knights, droid." She held the rancor-tooth handle with studied nonchalance. "Your 'extreme measures' would be useless against the Force."

After reconsidering the situation, the protocol droid scuttled away. The companions hurried after him, catching a lift platform that took them down several levels to the main administrative floors. But Threedee-Fourex had disappeared.

Raynar frowned. "Oh well, we don't really need him anyway. We can use one of these wall diagrams to find my uncle's office."

Jaina activated the computerized map and plotted the shortest route to Tyko Thul's suite of rooms. A few minutes later Raynar stood looking through the doorway in a heavy bulkhead that led into a spacious room. "Here's the head office," he said.

A desk, sitting area, and beverage center all sat carefully arranged in front of a wall of windows that provided a spectacular, if frightening, view of the grim industrial landscape. Computer screens lined a desktop piled high with old manifests, outdated production quotas, repair logs, and rebuilding plans. A set of holographic models shimmered on one corner of the desktop, showing projected upgrades to machinery and factory lines.

"My uncle told me he ran all of Mechis III from his office," Raynar said. "We can use this as our command center. Luckily, the systems are pretty well automated, so I should only have to keep an eye on the most important functions."

"Sounds like a big job, Raynar," Jacen said.

The young man nodded gravely. "Yes, but it's something I need to do . . . for my family. My mother would consider it great training." I hope Uncle Tyko would be proud of me." He sniffed. "One thing I intend to do is program *certain droids* to be more courteous!"

Raynar went to the desk console and checked the screens. He found a glowing icon that said "Current Operational Status," and touched it. The screen lit up.

Suddenly loud alarms blared throughout the room. A harsh mechanized voice bellowed from the speakers. "Intruder alert! Security lockdown initiated."

"Uh, wait!" Raynar said. "I didn't mean—"

The heavy bulkhead door to Tyko's office slammed shut with a thunderous clang, like an ore hauler crashing into a rock wall. Pneumatic locks hissed as the door sealed itself in place.

"Oh my!" Em Teedee wailed. "We're trapped!"

Drawing her lightsaber, Tenel Ka sprang to a fighting stance.

"Oh, blaster bolts. Now we're in for it," Jacen groaned, looking frantically around. "I'll bet Threedee-Fourex is laughing at us right now."

Jaina ran over to the computer console and nudged Raynar aside to see if she could deactivate the alarm. Glancing up, she suddenly noticed targeting lasers at the four corners of the ceiling. The weapons began to move, using motion sensors to acquire their marks.

"Laser cannons! Get them before they get us," she cried.

Jacen immediately saw the threat and drew his own lightsaber. Its emerald-green blade sprang out, ready for action. Needing neither explanation nor guidance, Tenel Ka streaked to the opposite side of the room, ready to do her part.

A brilliant laser danced out, leaving a black smoking crater in the floor at Raynar's feet. He yelped and lunged out of the way.

Jaina ducked, still hunched over the computer but with senses alert for any other blasts. She scrambled at the controls, working to open the heavy door. "Run for cover, Raynar," she called, and the blond-haired young man dove under the solid desk.

Feeling a warning through the Force, Jaina threw herself to one side as a laser bolt sizzled very close to where she had been standing. Then she leapt back to her work, trying to understand the ancient automated systems. "Come on," she muttered, "how does this work?" She fervently wished Lowie were there—*he* could always figure out strange computer systems.

Tenel Ka held her lightsaber in her hand, its deep turquoise throbbing with power as she slashed upward. The glowing blade severed the nearest targeting laser, leaving a stump of smoldering plasteel that sizzled and sparked.

Jacen chopped another of the weapons to pieces. "Two down," he said, "two to go." Instinctively working as a team, he and the warrior girl streaked toward opposite corners of the room.

The remaining weapons fired a dizzying web of laser bolts, which the young Jedi easily managed to dodge by letting the Force guide them. Jaina wondered if the targeting sensors had malfunctioned or if they were merely inaccurate. It seemed unlikely the powerful weapons would miss so many times. Perhaps office security upgrades were not among the high-priority repairs Tyko Thul had completed. She was thankful for that at least.

Jacen swiped with his lightsaber blade again, trashing the third of the weapons. Lasers burned scars into the walls like black bullet holes.

Jaina punched a final sequence into the computer, hoping she had guessed the proper string of commands—and heard a hissing *thunk* as the door unsealed. It didn't raise of its own accord, but at least the bulkhead was unlocked and they could lift it now. "To the door!"

Smashing the final laser cannon, Tenel Ka stood proudly under the rain of shrapnel. "We are safe," she announced. But loud alarms continued to blare.

Jaina still felt uneasy. "We don't know what other security forces might be coming," she said. "Better get out of these offices until the clamor dies down." She ran to the heavy metal bulkhead. "Help me with this. We'll need to lift it ourselves."

Together, the companions heaved, using their muscles and their Jedi strength. The heavy door reluctantly rolled up into its socket. . . .

And there, looming in the doorway, was the towering assassin droid IG-88, just waiting for them. Blinking red lights flared like the eruptions of miniature volcanoes in its conical head.

"Look out!" Jaina cried.

The assassin droid moved smoothly, relentlessly, raising both of its powerful metallic arms. IG-88 spoke no threat, but it clearly meant to take deadly action. In one arm its built-in blaster cannon powered up; in the other, a concussion grenade levered into place, ready for launch. The droid aimed its weapons and prepared to fire on the young Jedi Knights.

"Wait!" a man's voice shouted. "I command you to stop!"

A moment later, Tyko Thul himself appeared from the shadows! His face was flushed, and his eyes showed annoyance rather than fear. Raynar's supposedly kidnapped uncle, dressed in the garishly colored robes of the house of Thul, glared at the young Jedi Knights, then scowled directly at Raynar.

"Well, what are *you* doing here, boy?" Tyko demanded with a tremendous sigh. "Now you've ruined everything!"

14

THE *RISING STAR* dipped and looped and cavorted with its pilot's exuberance as Raaba flew across the jungle canopy of Kashyyyk. Lowie didn't have to use his Jedi senses to see how excited she was about coming back home.

He couldn't wait to see his sister's face when she saw her best friend again. Of all Raaba's friends and relations, Sirra alone knew that the long-lost Wookiee was actually alive. But even Sirra didn't know that Lowie and Raaba were coming for a visit.

He bared his teeth in a gleeful grin as Raaba accelerated, flipped the little star skimmer over, and flew briefly upside down just above the dense canopy. The branches were so thick and interlocked that thoroughfares as wide as highways had been chopped through the treetops so that beasts of burden could walk from place to place. Deep beneath the rooftop of branches lay the dark underworld where few Wookiees ever ventured.

Raaba flipped the *Rising Star* over again and waggled the tiny craft's airfoils back and forth so that the skimmer ruffled the leaves below it, like a Calamarian seaskitt dancing across the green waves. Then, finally, they headed toward the vast treetop city where they had both grown up.

The crowns of the tallest wroshyr trees rose above the level canopy like islands in an ocean; wooden platforms at various heights served as gathering areas and landing pads. High-tech facilities, such as computer fabrication labs and the planetary traffic control tower, had been erected in some of the larger trees, while more distant tree clusters served as dwellings for Wookiee families.

Raaba chose an open landing platform high on the outskirts of the city. Cinching the red band tight around her head, Raaba bounded out of the star skimmer, as full of cheerful energy as Lowie had ever seen her.

She made Lowie promise not to tell anyone, not even Sirra, of her presence. Instead, she planned to make her way unobtrusively to the Great Tree Arena, where she would register a request for an all-city meeting. She would let the Wookiee registry spread the word for her, and then make her surprise reappearance tonight with everyone present.

Raaba had much to do between now and then, and it had to be done just right. The sleek, dark Wookiee woman hurried off after Lowie agreed to urge his sister and family to attend the gathering.

It was a long way to Lowie's house yet, but he was in no hurry. His parents, Kallabow and Mahraccor, were probably still at work at the computer fabrication facility. After hours of cramped flight, he wanted to stretch his legs by striding along the spicy-smelling branchtop thoroughfare. The morning sun was warm, and the breeze fragrant. It felt good to be home.

He went to see his sister first.

A distinguished-looking older Wookiee with yellowing fur pointed Lowie toward the flight training area where Sirra took classes to become a star pilot. He leapt and climbed from branch to branch to reach the leafy field above which Sirra flew her training vessel.

He looked upward, watching her ship make one long dive and then another pass. With no slight amusement, he noted that Sirra's piloting style was very much like Raaba's. The two had been fast friends for years, after all.

The refurbished Y-wing had a cramped instructor's station built into the compartment where the gunner formerly sat. From the speed with which Sirra banked and looped, however, one would never have guessed that her practice vessel was a discontinued model now used primarily for training.

Sirra simulated a perfect reverse-throttle hop against an imaginary opponent, followed by an under split, then disengaged after performing a flawless Tallon roll. Her exhaust nacelles glowed orange-white as she roared back toward the treetop city.

With her lesson finished, Sirra brought the Y-wing to the landing platform low and fast, barely a meter above its polished surface. No doubt showing off, she pulled up into a steep climb, looped around, and landed with microcaliper precision directly in the center. Her ship's repulsorjets let out a hiss like a nervous sigh of relief.

Sirra popped the Y-wing's canopy and sprang out of the cockpit. Because she was pumped with adrenaline from her flying antics, she did not notice her brother at first, but Lowie had a front row seat for an amusing exchange.

Sirra raked long fingers through her ruffled patchwork fur, while her instructor, a portly human whom Lowie did not recognize, levered himself slowly and painfully out of the rear compartment. The man's face was flushed and indignant, and his voice shook when he spoke. "Why, in my day, young lady—" he began.

Wookiee, Sirra corrected him, growling in her own language.

"Yes, well, Wookiee then," the man said. "In my day, trainees understood how to follow instructions. And they did it politely with a 'Yes, Captain Thorn' or a salute. No grandstanding."

Sirra reminded Captain Thorn that she was not in the military, nor did she ever intend to be. Then, with sly deliberation, she pointed out that she had actually followed every one of his instructions. She had simply added a bit of . . . embellishment.

"Precisely," Thorn said, *"embellishment.* I did not tell you to embellish."

But he hadn't told her *not* to embellish, Sirra insisted in a mild voice, wrinkling her black nose.

Lowie, nearly shaking with laughter, chose this moment to heave himself up onto the landing platform where his sister could see him. Sirra uttered a yelp of happy surprise and crossed the platform in two long leaps. She threw herself into her brother's arms, and the two Wookiees set up a joyous interchange of growls, barks, and chuffing laughter.

Captain Thorn flushed a deep red all the way up to the scalp that showed through his thinning hair and stalked off the platform, mumbling something about needing a pay raise.

Sirra wanted to know why Lowie had come unannounced, when he had arrived, why his little translating droid had not accompanied him, how he had gotten to Kashyyyk . . . and whether or not he had heard anything from Raaba.

Lowie tried to explain without giving away Raaba's secret. Sirra gave a pleased growl, not noticing how he had evaded her questions. His timing was perfect, she assured him—though she cast an annoyed look in the direction of her departed instructor. She hoped that Lowie could stay a while and watch how well she had learned to fly since she, too, had completed her rite of passage down in the dangerous underworld.

She had so much to tell him, it might take days.

At early evening, Lowie and Sirra made their way to the amphitheater just outside the treetop city. Their parents were already there, along with half the city's inhabitants.

Sirra complained that they would have more fun staying home and playing combat-simulation games on their entertainment unit. Why in the sector would he want to attend an open city forum in the Great Tree Arena? Such meetings were always dull and never had any relevance to the younger members of society.

With a mysteriously cocked brow, Lowie hastened to assure his sister that she would find this particular meeting very interesting. Sirra threw him a doubtful glance, but did not argue further.

They chose seating branches high in the amphitheater, where they could get the best view. The sun sank below the horizon of the sprawling forest, and the sky grew rich and dark overhead. Lowie had a hard time distinguishing between the soft rustling of Wookiees finding their seats and the whisper of leaves in the evening wind.

Sirra grew restless for the meeting to start. Lowie began to worry that something had gone wrong or that Raaba had changed her mind. Maybe she had reconsidered her confession, and was ashamed after all to tell how she had staged her own death.

Then, just as the first few stars brightened in the sky, a shaft of blazing light stabbed upward from the center of the stage. In the center of the light stood a chocolate-furred female Wookiee—wearing her own dazzling belt made of syren fiber. *Fresh* syren fiber!

Sirra nearly fell backward off her branch in surprise, and Lowie fared no better. He had known Raaba set up this meeting, but the implications of her belt were enough to stun him as much as everyone else in the assembly. Surprised murmurs of recognition spread through the crowd, and Lowie heard Raaba's name repeated over and over. Sirra glared at her brother accusingly. He had kept this a secret from her!

Before Lowie could explain why he had kept silent about her friend's return, Raaba raised her arms to quiet the crowd. In a loud, clear voice she introduced herself, so that there could be no mistaking who she was.

Next, the beam of light in which Raaba stood split into a hundred smaller rays that opened and spread themselves flat on the stage, like the petals of some gigantic fiery flower with her at its center. She told everyone how she had been all but dead after attempting her rite of passage . . . and how the Diversity Alliance had given her back her life.

In much the same way, she said, the Empire's enslavement of Wookiees had taken the life of Kashyyyk. To a great extent, Wookiees still slaved for humankind, in one way or another. Lowie sat listening uneasily. He had not known Raaba was going to make this a political speech. Sirra, though, seemed thoroughly enthralled.

Raaba continued. Aliens of all species had suffered similar treatment since before the rise of Emperor Palpatine—all at the hands of humans. And the most shameful part, she said, spreading her arms to the crowd, was that *none* of it would have been possible if the nonhuman peoples hadn't allowed it to happen.

The Diversity Alliance and its visionary leader, Nolaa Tarkona, were ready to show the way. If Wookiees and Talz and Biths and Twi'leks and all other species would band together, unified under one leader, they would never need to fear the domination of humans again. She urged anyone who was willing to help to send a message to the Diversity Alliance, to go to Nolaa Tarkona herself on Ryloth, or to talk their friends into joining the cause as well.

Wookiee murmurs ran through the crowd again, this time sounds of approval. Raaba's voice grew no louder, but her words became more persuasive. Each of the glowing rays around her shattered into a million tiny shards of light, surrounding her like a swarm of phosfleas.

Individually, Raaba explained, each of them was no more than one of these tiny specks. Alone, they could do nothing. But *together*—she raised her arms high over her head and the phosflea-specks of light coalesced into a hundred dazzling rays—they could change the galaxy!

The rays snapped together again into a single brilliant beacon that speared upward toward the stars.

Then the stage went completely dark.

Wookiees on every side shook the branches to show their approval. Swept along by the emotion, Lowie and Sirra joined in.

Suddenly and without warning, Raaba stood there with them, out in the amphitheater seats. With a roar of joy, Sirra hurled herself upon her friend, pounding Raaba on the back and growling happily. Raaba chuffed her own delight to see Sirra again as she showed off her glossy new belt.

Unable to restrain his curiosity any longer, Lowie asked Raaba when and how she had gotten her trophy. The chocolate-furred Wookiee flashed her fangs in a wide grin, pleased by his surprise.

She had gone down to the world below only that afternoon, just before returning home to visit her stunned parents. Raaba had been hiding for almost a year, running away—and she wanted to have her trophy before she showed herself again. Completing the fateful mission that had been interrupted so long ago had made her return even more dramatic.

But then her expression grew serious again. Raaba looked shrewdly at her two friends. She needed to return to Ryloth that very night, she said; she had to report in to Nolaa Tarkona and the Diversity Alliance. There was no time to waste. Her eyes burned with an intensity Lowie could not entirely understand.

Then Raaba eagerly clasped both of their shoulders. If Lowie and Sirra would accompany her to

Ryloth, just for a few days, she would tell them all about her adventures in the lower levels and her battle with the syren plant.

Before Lowie could consider the question, Sirra enthusiastically agreed for both of them.

15

SPARKS FROM THE ruined targeting lasers continued to sputter into Tyko Thul's administrative office. The young Jedi Knights stood frozen in shock after hearing Raynar's uncle issue *orders* to the deadly assassin droid.

Perturbed, Tyko tried with little success to step around the metallic hulk of IG-88. "Out of the way, you big clod," he said as he pushed against the assassin droid's body core. The droid clanked dutifully sideways to give Raynar's uncle room to pass.

Tyko strode to the nearest of the wrecked automatic weapons in his office, grimaced, then turned to face Raynar and his friends. "You didn't need to destroy them all, did you? I specifically calibrated the targeters *not* to hit anybody," he said with a huff. "Now the entire defense grid in this room is ruined, and I'll have to have it replaced." He heaved a long-suffering sigh. "As if I didn't have enough to do already."

"But," Raynar spluttered, "Uncle Tyko, what's going on?"

Tyko rolled his eyes. "Isn't it obvious, my dear boy? I was trying to lure your irresponsible father out of hiding by making it look as if I were in incredible personal peril. I did it for all of us—so we can get everything back to normal working order again. But I see Bornan doesn't care a whit about me after all."

IG-88 stomped to the doorway and took up a position guarding the room's entrance. He held out his powerful upper limbs, high-energy armaments fully extended. Tyko flashed the droid a sidelong glance. "Oh, deactivate your weapons, you half-witted hunk of antiquated machinery! Can't you see you're not intimidating anyone anymore?" Tyko shook his head in disbelief. "Droids! No matter how sophisticated you make them, they still have no sense of propriety."

"I *beg* your pardon?" Em Teedee said.

Jaina shushed the little translating droid and turned to Tyko. "We could use some explanations, sir. This whole situation is pretty complicated, and we only came here to help. This isn't what we expected to find at all."

Tenel Ka's muscles tensed as she faced Tyko Thul, her voice gruff. "We believed you were in true danger. We risked much for you on Kuar—yet you say your entire abduction was a mere hoax?"

"I had to make the whole thing look believable, of course," Raynar's uncle said with a shrug. "But my droids were very careful."

Standing by the desktop computer pad, he punched in commands that shut off power to the security systems and stopped the flow of sparks from the broken targeting lasers. "Well, we'll have to fix that some other time. Come with me. I'm scheduled to check one of the assembly lines. We can discuss this as I go about my business." With that, Tyko turned and bustled out of the room, his bright robes swirling around him.

The young Jedi Knights followed, still perplexed. The assassin droid stood motionless and threatening, guarding the empty room.

"Well?" Tyko called over his shoulder. "Don't just stand there, IG-88. Come with us."

The droid strode after them, metallic feet pounding on the floor.

"I know my brother very well. Unfortunately— and I'm sorry you have to hear this, Raynar—" Tyko said, looking sympathetically at the young man, "your father has always tried to outsmart everyone in negotiations, relying on his wits . . . and that frequently gets him into trouble. I'm convinced he's on the run because some scam backfired on him—something too embarrassing to admit. And now he's simply hiding, without bothering to consider the incredible inconvenience he's causing the rest of us."

They stopped at a broad lift platform big enough for all of them to climb aboard. Tyko pushed a button, and the floor suddenly dropped out beneath them as the lift plunged down to the lower manufacturing levels.

"Bornan's dear wife Aryn is in constant torment," Tyko went on. "The trading fleet has stopped most of its work, subcontracted their primary merchandising accounts until further notice, and gone on the run from imaginary enemies. Poor Raynar here is worried sick about his father." He huffed.

"I decided I'd simply had enough of this charade, so I staged my own kidnapping, hoping that I could flush Bornan out. It was perfectly reasonable to suppose that if he thought his own brother was in danger, he would finally come out and set things to rights." Tyko sighed. "But instead of *him* coming to find me, you children arrived. Now he'll never show up."

The lift stopped, and they entered a tube shuttle that rocketed them to another factory complex. A symphony of industrial noises thundered all around them. Silvery pistons gleamed under harsh lights, whooshing up and down. Jets of superhot steam hissed, while pumps circulated supercold gases through cylinders of bubbling liquids.

Conveyor belts hummed as they hauled sparkling new parts to various assembly stations where meticulous multiarmed droids pieced the components together. Bulky worker droids thumped from one end of the cavernous room to another, using portable repulsorsleds to move completed machinery to the shipping areas.

"My, this *is* fascinating, isn't it?" Em Teedee said. "Look at all the activity."

Raynar's uncle stopped, distracted by one section of the line where droids were installing dozens of optical sensors like black blisters on a dome-shaped head assembly; farther down the same line, other droid workers attached the head assembly to a mobile torso equipped with small rocket engines. The entire unit was then installed in a self-contained hyperdrive pod.

"This is the production line once used to create the thousands of probe droids Darth Vader commissioned, back when he was hunting down Rebel bases like the one on Hoth," Tyko said. "Now we've retooled the probot apparatus and programming to produce these mapping and surveyor droids. They proved quite useful during the Black Fleet Crisis.

"The New Republic needs an accurate map of the galaxy, so that they won't be ignorant of lost colonies or uninhabited worlds rich in resources. The best surveys are centuries out of date, and many aren't up to the standards our modern technology will allow."

Proudly, Tyko rapped his knuckles on the hemispherical assembly, and spoke to the droids on the construction line. "Good work. Keep it up." Then he strode away. The droids took no notice of the compliment. IG-88 marched behind them like a bodyguard.

"But what about IG-88?" Jaina said, still more interested in Tyko Thul's explanations than in his tour. "The whole attack on Kuar? The assassin droids?"

Tyko clasped his hands behind his back and pressed his lips together. "The other assassin droids on IG-88's commando team were of . . . recent manufacture. I happened upon some old plans in the assembly facilities here on Mechis III, so I produced an extra dozen or so."

Raynar sounded indignant. "But it's illegal to manufacture assassin droids, Uncle Tyko! That was clearly stated in the New Republic charter when they turned this planet over to you. I just read all of those documents, because I was coming to help run this place while you were gone."

"Well, I suppose it's illegal . . . from a certain point of view," Tyko said, "*if* you're strictly literal about it. But they were just for show. All of my new assassin droids had explicit programming to prevent them from harming anyone. Rather disqualifies them as 'assassin' droids, wouldn't you say? Not terribly practical either, except that their other capabilities make them unusually versatile and powerful."

Tenel Ka's brows knitted together, and her storm-gray eyes flashed. "So. We were never in actual danger on Kuar?"

"Oh, you were in plenty of danger—but not from my droids," Tyko said. "The combat arachnids could have sliced you to pieces. I never anticipated *those* beasts." Tyko patted the gleaming durasteel arm of IG-88. "In fact, it's a good thing my droids were there, because I'm not sure you kids could have handled all those ferocious monsters."

Tenel Ka seemed somewhat mollified to know that at least *some* of the danger had been genuine.

Jaina looked the assassin droid up and down. "So, IG-88's just a replica, too? A copy of the original?"

"No, he's real enough," Tyko said. "I found him here when I took over Mechis III. This whole planet was such a mess!" He shook his head, and then moved on to inspect another station where motivators were being installed into the torsos of a new series of astromech droids.

"When I got here, all the systems were in a shambles. There was some sort of revolution here, and it took me a long time to uncover all the details. I was astonished to discover that the droids themselves had fostered this rebellion, killing their human masters as part of some grand plan to take over the galaxy. According to the records I was able to reconstruct, IG-88—the real assassin droid— was behind it somehow.

"Apparently, IG-88 had made several copies of himself, which went out to do the bounty-hunting work that made him so famous. Those copies were all destroyed in various escapades. This one, though, the primary one, had developed a scheme to upload his entire electronic consciousness, as it were, into the second Death Star computer core so that he could become the galaxy's most powerful weapon!"

"Not the best choice," Jacen said. "We all know what happened to the second Death Star."

Tyko smiled indulgently at him. "So IG-88 left behind the empty shell of his original body, which I found. I was careful to completely purge its systems, every memory bank. I replaced its central processing core, gave it new programming. This droid is now absolutely loyal to me, but still as capable as the old IG-88."

After completing the circuit of the manufacturing floor, Tyko took them back to the tube shuttle, which returned them to the main headquarters building.

"Well, well," Raynar said, his forehead creased with concern as he sorted out the details of Tyko's plan. "At least you've got IG-88 to protect you, if there's ever a real assault from the people who are after my father."

Tyko looked skeptically at his nephew. "My dear boy, I'm certain Bornan's gotten himself into some sort of trouble, but I doubt that there are really people chasing him who intend to harm him," he said as he led them to the broad lift platform again. "Mark my words—there's no danger here."

The lift platform lurched as it shot them skyward again, back up to the administration levels.

16

BEFORE HEADING OFF to Mechis III on his search for Tyko Thul, Zekk diverted the *Lightning Rod* to the asteroid station of Borgo Prime. He had no intention of missing the scheduled rendezvous with his mysterious employer.

Bornan Thul.

Zekk sat inside Shanko's Hive all alone at a table, wearing a scuffed flight suit, his long dark hair neatly tied back. While he waited, Zekk studied a datapad to which he had downloaded the shipping records and permits issued for legal droid commerce throughout the New Republic. All restrictions against constructing automated assassins remained in effect. According to public transaction records on file with the Department of Galactic Commerce, no droid construction facility— including Tyko's own operation on Mechis III— had a permit either to build or sell assassin droids.

IG-88 and his newly constructed companions remained a mystery to Zekk. Something just didn't fit. . . .

He had ordered a hot meal from the insectlike Shanko, but chewed without tasting, wrapped up in his own thoughts. Apprehending Bornan Thul for the famous bounty was not an option at the moment, since the contract with his employer was not yet complete. He still had to find Tyko.

Repeatedly glancing at his chronometer, he rehearsed what he intended to say to the man. Though Boba Fett had given him advice, questions remained at the back of Zekk's mind. This was a dangerous time for him. Less than an hour now until his meeting. . . .

Zekk slurped another mouthful of the spicy stew. His stomach roiled, but Shanko had assured him that this meal was human-compatible. His queasiness was due more to anxiety over the impending meeting than any lack of quality in the cooking.

Shanko's Hive was abustle with hundreds of patrons of all different species. The insectoid owner kept his crowded establishment clean and in excellent repair, much in contrast to the dingy Mos Eisley cantina. Zekk kept his eye on everyone, studying, searching.

Bornan Thul arrived in a new disguise this time,

but Zekk spotted him right away. His employer wore a maroon caftan, a brown turban around his head, and a metal breath mask that covered his nose and mouth, the type worn by inhabitants of heavily polluted worlds.

Thul didn't notice Zekk at first. The man's partially obscured gaze darted around the bar furtively, as if he were anxious about being among so many people. If Zekk had any lingering doubts about his employer's identity, they were dispelled the moment he sensed Thul's tension.

At his table Zekk sat back and wondered whether he should raise a hand to wave his employer over. He decided the attention might startle Bornan Thul, so he simply waited until the disguised man noticed him.

"I have only a few moments," Thul said without preamble when he finally located Zekk and slid into the seat next to him. The metallic breath mask filtered his voice. "Quickly—give me your report!"

Under the turban, Thul's gaze continued to dart warily around at the other patrons in Shanko's Hive. Zekk found this alertness ironic, since right now he himself was the bounty hunter Bornan Thul should have feared the most.

Zekk laced his fingers behind his head and feigned relaxation. "I've completed the first part of your task," he said. "I sent the message for the

Bornaryn fleet through all the communication nodes you suggested. I have, of course, received no word as to whether Aryn Dro Thul actually got the transmission . . . but it's likely."

Bornan Thul seemed to melt with relief, and instantly the lines around his shadowed eyes softened. Waves of long-repressed emotion flowed from him like a physical presence.

Zekk decided to tell the rest of his story. "Immediately after I transmitted your message, a bounty hunter attacked me. He'd been waiting for just such a signal. He pounced, but I managed to outwit him and escape."

The disguised man nodded gravely. "You see—I was right to be cautious."

"Yes. That bounty hunter thought he had found you . . . *Bornan Thul*." Zekk's voice was barely above a whisper.

The man stiffened and looked ready to leap away in panic. Zekk held up a hand. "If I had planned to capture you, I could have stunned you the moment you sat down. Relax." Zekk tossed his long dark hair, trying to unwind the tension in his neck. "How long did you think you could hide it? You were pretty obvious. I guessed your identity the first time we met, even in your disguise."

Bornan Thul swallowed so hard that Zekk could hear it through the metallic breath mask. Thul kept his voice low. "I was raised as a noble of Alderaan. I have been a successful merchant, a prominent trade negotiator—I have had little practice at hiding myself."

"That much is obvious," Zekk said with a thin smile. "I'm impressed that you've managed to elude capture so far. You know, I'd earn incredible fame and notoriety if I were to take you in now—but that wouldn't be honorable. The Bounty Hunter's Creed forbids me to work *against* my employer. I accepted your assignment, and I won't betray you. So you're safe—at least until I've fulfilled all my obligations to you.

"I still haven't found your brother, though I've got a lead on Tyko's kidnapping. I have quite a few questions that are still unanswered, so I'm on my way to Mechis III. I have a feeling I can learn more there about what's happened to him, maybe even find him."

"We cannot meet again," Bornan Thul said, his voice trembling. "Now that you know who I am."

Zekk's emerald eyes narrowed. "Then how can I be sure I'll get paid when I accomplish the task?"

"I'm an honorable man, too," Thul said. "When my brother is found, the credits will appear in your account. From that point on, I will consider you another enemy to be avoided at all cost."

He stood up, considered, then turned back to the

table. "Young man, you can't begin to understand the consequences if you delivered me to Nolaa Tarkona. Do you have any idea why she wants me so badly?"

Zekk shook his head. "A bounty hunter doesn't ask questions. My job is to complete the task. Politics, emotions, and legal nuances are better left to more complex entities."

Thul heaved a ponderous sigh. "Perhaps you would think differently if you knew all that I know," he said. "If Nolaa Tarkona were to get the information I am protecting, she would not hesitate to use it. It might result in the extinction of all humans. Consider how far you're willing to go to earn fame as a bounty hunter—and how many lives you would risk in the process."

Zekk shifted uncomfortably, trying not to consider the implications.

Unexpectedly, a loud and unruly fight broke out at the automated musical-selection apparatus on the other side of the bar. A burly, white-furred Talz shoved aside a tusk-faced Whiphid. The Whiphid roared, lowered his cliff-sized head, and butted the Talz in the chest. The white slothlike creature squealed in high-pitched alarm and began pounding the Whiphid in turn.

Tables crashed over. The music machine toppled with a jangle of synthesized squawks. The murmuring conversation in Shanko's Hive changed to resounding gasps and cheers as friends of the combatants and other enthusiastic patrons hurled themselves into the fray.

Shanko gestured with one pair of multijointed arms, and his three-armed bartender lumbered into the brawl with a loud bellow. Droq'l grasped the Talz and the Whiphid with his outer two hands, forcefully separating them. At the same time, his central hand balled into a battering-ram fist and punched each creature in an extremely sensitive area particular to their species.

Both fighters dropped like stones, and Droq'l glared down at them as their supporters backed away to slink into the shadows. The bartender righted the music machine, kicked it once to start it working again, then glowered at the two groggy aliens.

"Your bar tab will reflect a surcharge for the necessary repairs," he growled, then stalked back to the bar. There the insectoid Shanko, who had watched the entire altercation without comment, rewarded his bartender with a full tankard of Osskorn Stout.

Zekk shook his head and turned back to Bornan Thul—but the man was gone. He looked around in alarm, but saw no sign of the fugitive. Thul had vanished completely, just as he had last time. . . .

Zekk decided there was no point in pursuing his employer. It would do no good. Instead, he would finish his stew, and then head for Mechis III straightaway.

17

WHEN THE YOUNG Jedi Knights returned to the administrative offices, Tyko hurried off to arrange for a meal to be brought in. Now that he had let them in on his plan, he seemed determined to be the attentive host.

But something still bothered Jaina. "I'm not sure quite what it is," she said, "but something about your uncle's story doesn't add up, Raynar."

Raynar frowned, as troubled as she was. "You don't think he was lying, do you?"

"We would have sensed that, I think," Jacen said. "He was telling the truth."

Tenel Ka arched an eyebrow. "I found several logical flaws in his scheme."

"Well, for one thing," Raynar said, "he's assuming my father is pulling a scam. He doesn't seem to believe my family is in any real danger."

"Yeah, that doesn't make any sense," Jacen piped

up. "Your uncle may have faked his *own* kidnapping, but Boba Fett was sure serious enough in the shards of Alderaan."

Jaina added, "Yes, and the bounty hunter Kusk and his brother who tried to get you and your mother away from the *Tradewyn* were no hoax. I'd say they were pretty *real*—not to mention dangerous."

"We need to tell my mother that Uncle Tyko is safe," Raynar said. "That'll be one less thing for her to worry about." Looking around the spacious administrative office, his eyes glinted with determination. "We should get these targeted defensive lasers working again before we leave—just in case Uncle Tyko gets any unwanted visitors."

"I'm certain that the gesture would be greatly appreciated," Em Teedee said. "If Mistress Jaina would be so kind as to link me to the defense control systems, I believe I might be of some assistance."

Jaina grinned and pulled her multitool from the pocket of her jumpsuit. "I'm always prepared."

She rapidly removed the access plates on the ruined weapons systems. By the time Tyko returned, followed by IG-88 and a serving droid that carried the midday meal, the young Jedi Knights had managed to repair two of the four targeting lasers.

"I don't believe it!" Tyko beamed. He patted

Raynar on the back. "But then, of course, we Thuls have always been resourceful."

"I didn't do this alone," Raynar objected. "Everyone helped—even Em Teedee."

"Yes, of course, my boy," Tyko answered. He glanced over at the console to which the translating unit had been wired. "Ah, Em Teedee, how kind of you to lend, um . . . to lend a wire. You are the one droid in the galaxy I truly trust—with the exception of my own IG-88, of course."

"Why, thank you, Master Tyko. I do try," Em Teedee said, almost preening. The compliment seemed to make no impression on IG-88, however.

Working and tinkering always helped Jaina to concentrate, to let her subconscious work out things that were bothering her. Something clicked now in her mind, and she turned from her work to stare directly at the red-eyed assassin droid.

"Now, children, what may I offer you to eat?" Tyko asked. "We have kebroot stew, dried ossberries, a fine—"

"Wait," Jaina said, her eyes still on IG-88. "I have a few questions first."

"Very well, my dear, but don't dawdle. Our meal is waiting."

Jaina worded her question carefully. "Didn't you say that those new assassin droids were programmed *not* to kill?"

"Why, of course, my child. I programmed them

myself," Tyko answered. "Nothing at all to worry about. Now, can I offer you some sparkling ale or would you prefer—"

"But," Jaina interrupted again, "on Kuar your assassin droids blasted several combat arachnids into dripping chunks."

Tenel Ka nodded suspiciously. "This is a fact. It certainly qualifies as killing."

"Hey, that's right," Jacen said. "Combat arachnids are very rare creatures."

"No! Combat arachnids don't really qualify, of course," the round-faced man spluttered. "The droids were protecting you. Besides—it's not as if those things were *human*."

Jaina's stomach clenched as the implications of his words sank in. Raynar had also gone as pale as stormtrooper armor. "Are you saying," the young man asked in a strangled voice, "that your droids have no compunctions against killing anything—or anyone—that isn't human?"

"An assassin droid wouldn't be much of a bodyguard if it couldn't protect me from an attack by those combat arachnids, would it?" Tyko said.

"Our Wookiee friend Lowbacca was with us on Kuar as well," Tenel Ka said in a dangerous voice.

"And he's *not human*," Jacen said. "Neither is Raaba."

"Neither am I, I might add," Em Teedee chimed

in. "And I am completely without defenses of my own."

Jaina swallowed to loosen the tightness in her throat. "Does that mean, then, that Lowie could have been killed in your little staged attack?"

Tyko looked distinctly uncomfortable. "Well, I suppose it *might* have happened. In theory, at least." He held up his hands in a placating gesture. "But it's hardly an issue anymore. It *didn't* happen, and that's what's important."

Raynar's hands squeezed into tight fists, and his jaw clenched. Jaina had never before seen such an angry expression on his face. "In that case, Uncle, I'd say it was a very good thing that all of your assassin droids were destroyed on Kuar."

"Yes," Jaina said, turning her attention back to IG-88. "All but one."

"Well, well, well," Raynar said. His eyes narrowed, and a shrewd expression stole over his face. "That gives me an idea."

Though Jaina missed Lowie's expertise in programming, she set to work on IG-88 as soon as they had finished their meal. Annoyed over what she intended to do, but unable to argue against it, Tyko Thul left in a huff to check on more assembly lines.

With Em Teedee's assistance, Jaina decided to use the broad administrative desk as an "operating" table. The sinister configuration of IG-88 still caused her to shiver as she pondered all the beings this machine must have killed over the decades. But Tyko Thul had flushed its murderous program and replaced its processors. Now, the menacing droid awaited its revised instructions—and Jaina obliged.

"This was an excellent idea, Raynar," Tenel Ka said, clapping an approving hand on the blond boy's shoulder.

While Jaina completed her special "modifications," the rest of the young Jedi Knights finished the repairs to the targeting-laser defensive systems.

Jacen peered into the open durasteel casing of IG-88's torso where Jaina was working. "I think it just may work."

"There, that ought to do it," Jaina said. She triggered a test switch. The assassin droid raised his gun arm, but did not fire. She smiled and flicked the switch off again. "All systems function perfectly, but there's no way this droid could ever intentionally kill someone—human or alien. He's programmed to serve and protect." She closed IG-88's casing and disconnected Em Teedee's diagnostic leads.

Raynar smiled. "I doubt my uncle could have programmed him any better than you did. Now he's the perfect bodyguard."

At this Em Teedee piped up. "In light of your uncle's expertise, I wonder if I might make a special request? . . ."

18

STEAM HISSED ON the primary droid assembly line. The pungent smells of molten plasteel, lubricants, and hot machinery filled the air.

"Best droid enhancements anywhere in the galaxy," Tyko Thul said with obvious pride, gesturing toward the rows of conveyor belts. "Manufactured right here and subjected to the most rigorous quality control you'll find anywhere. I'm sure you can find anything you need."

Flustered, Jaina continued to tinker with Em Teedee, wondering what parts she might "need." She turned the little droid around in her hands so he could better view the dozens of assembly lines that stretched for kilometers down the length of the utilitarian facility.

"Why, it's breathtaking, isn't it?" Em Teedee said in a reverent voice. "I *am* dreadfully sorry to be so much trouble. I never meant to impose. I'm certain you all have more urgent matters to attend to."

Jaina raised the silvery oval to her eye level and looked earnestly into his yellow optical sensors. "It's all right. You're important to us too, you know."

"Come now, my dear little droid," Tyko said. "You must allow me to give you a gift as thanks for all you've done to help protect the Thul family. Besides, I'm delighted at the opportunity to demonstrate our workmanship in such a practical way. Go ahead, feel free to select any enhancements that interest you."

"That's a terribly gracious offer," Em Teedee said in a warbling voice. "I can't help but think that if I'd had a few more enhancements—if I were a bit more *useful*—Master Lowbacca might not have left me behind."

"Take your pick, Em Teedee," Jacen said. "Plenty to choose from."

"Do you not *wish* to be enhanced?" Tenel Ka asked. "Consider the question well." After the warrior girl's arm had been severed in a lightsaber training accident, Tenel Ka had struggled with whether or not to use a synthetic arm. In the end, she had decided against it.

"Perhaps I should start by showing you what's available?" Tyko suggested with a broad gesture.

For the next two hours Em Teedee was as happy

as a child in a plaything emporium. Jaina could understand the feeling, since she was almost as fascinated by the endless possibilities as the little droid was. They considered enhanced optical sensors, motion detectors, new remote analysis routines.

"Dear me! I've always been a simple translating droid," Em Teedee said. "Whatever would I *do* with so many capabilities?"

"Ah, then you might be interested in our linguistic upgrades." Tyko held up a new traced-circuit crystal. "Here on Mechis III we produce a variety of modules containing anywhere from ten languages to ten million, depending on what a particular droid is required to know."

"I'm afraid Em Teedee's processor wasn't designed to handle a million languages," Jaina said. "He just doesn't have that kind of capacity."

"No," Tyko agreed. "But a few—say, ten—additional languages shouldn't strain his capacity."

Unaccustomed to being the center of attention, Em Teedee listened to each opinion before making his choice. In the end, he selected a secondary protocol module that added ten of the most frequently used languages in the galaxy to those he already had.

When the installation process was finished, Jaina closed the silvery casing. "Well, Em Teedee, how does it feel?"

"Why, it feels absolutely . . . *ops'nyzh!* That is an expression that means 'approaching euphoric' in the Bothan language. Oh—I didn't *know* that word before. Now I am fluent in over sixteen forms of communication!"

Em Teedee decided against adding an obscure idiom analysis chip, but at the next assembly line, he discovered an unexpected enhancement opportunity that was too enticing to turn down: his own repulsor unit. "Just think of it," the droid said, "complete mobility for the first time since I was activated!"

"Hey, yeah. We wouldn't have to carry you around all the time when Lowie's not here," Jacen said.

That clinched it. The companions needed to offer no further encouragement for Em Teedee to accept the enhancement.

Jaina brought out her multitool and commandeered a set of specialized instruments from one of the assembly lines. She fitted a narrow circular collar with a hundred mircorepulsorjets to the base of Em Teedee's oblong head.

"There," she said, tightening the last tiny bolt into place. Em Teedee's optical sensors gleamed with curiosity. "The controls are wired directly into your processor. By selecting the number, strength, and location of the repulsors operating at a given time, you should be able to maneuver in any direction."

"Oh, thank you, Mistress Jaina. This is even more exciting than the waterproofing gaskets you outfitted me with."

"Well, try it out," Raynar said. "Let's see you move."

The repulsorjets whispered, and the ovular miniaturized droid lifted from the table like a levitating ball. "This seems simple enough," Em Teedee said. "I think I'll try going a little higher."

The little droid rocketed toward the far distant ceiling like a projectile fired from a cannon. His speaker grille sounded in alarm, and the next thing Jaina heard was a metallic clang as Em Teedee struck one of the overhead support girders.

"Em Teedee, be careful up there!" she called.

Next the silvery oval came down, only to streak past them, moving sideways down the long corridor, out of control. "Help! Please help! Dear me!"

"The lateral thrusters seem to be working well," Tyko said calmly.

"Dampen the output!" Jaina cried. "Use your collision-avoidance routines."

Em Teedee managed to reverse himself and shot back toward them. Flying upside down, the translating droid circled the table where Jaina had performed her modifications. "How very odd! Everything seems to have changed. What have I done?

Were my optical sensors damaged when I hit the ceiling? I'm doomed! Now I shall be dismantled for scrap metal—"

Jaina reached out and twisted the little droid in the air, righting him. "There. *Now* take a look around."

Em Teedee hovered, wobbling as he adjusted repulsors to maintain his balance. "Oh my, this is quite disorienting. I never realized how challenging mobility could be."

"Just think of it as your baby steps." Jacen grinned as they gathered around the upgraded droid. "You just need a little more practice."

Em Teedee's golden optical sensors flickered. "Ah, that's better. My gyroscopes and coordinate sensors needed to be recalibrated. I'm certain I'll be much more stable now—so long as I proceed with caution. Just let me get my bearings and—oh! Look out behind you!" he wailed.

Suddenly a compelling voice rang out through the echoing lower levels. "Stop right there! I've got blasters aimed at you. No one moves—no one gets hurt."

Raynar knew the voice, though he couldn't place it in the flash of adrenaline that surged through his bloodstream. Surprisingly, his Jedi senses told him that this voice brought no threat, no danger, despite the words.

"No fast moves now. Everyone, raise your hands and turn toward me."

Raynar turned to face a pair of blasters pointing at their little group, but the intruder lurked in shadow behind the assembly line machinery. Then a young man stepped forward, emerald-green eyes wide with amazement. His long dark hair had come loose from the thong at the base of his neck.

"Why, Master Zekk, what a great pleasure it is to see you again!" Em Teedee caroled from somewhere over Raynar's head.

"Zekk!" Jaina cried out, her face suddenly turning a flattering shade of pink.

The young bounty hunter looked tired. Smudges of filthy lubricants stained his cheeks and forehead, and one sleeve of his tight-fitting uniform was scorched through. "Jaina! Jacen!" He gaped at the others around him. "What are you all doing here?"

"Hey, Zekk," Jacen replied with a welcoming grin. "Kind of a rough way to say hello, isn't it?"

"Greetings," Tenel Ka said.

As Zekk lowered his weapons, Jaina launched herself into his arms and twirled him in a happy hug. "It's so good to see you again! Did you get my holomessages? Hey, how did you make it past the targeted lasers?"

Zekk indicated the singed place on his arm. "It wasn't easy."

Tyko chose this moment to break up the reunion.

"More to the point, my young hoodlum, what are *you* doing here? What business do you have threatening us? You're lucky IG-88 didn't blast you to cinders."

Zekk took a moment to holster his weapons and give Jaina a real hug before looking directly into Tyko's eyes. "I take it you're Tyko Thul? I was hired to rescue you. But it looks like I'm a bit late for that."

Tyko stared skeptically at Zekk. "Do you really expect me to believe *you* were hired to help me? A scruffy-looking bounty hunter like you? Aryn Dro Thul would hardly have contracted with some disreputable juvenile to come to my rescue. She could afford the most famous names in the business."

Raynar considered this with surprise. *Would* his mother have hired Zekk? Remembering how the dark-haired young man had dumped him into the river mud during the Second Imperium's attack, he still felt some resentment toward Zekk.

"First of all," Zekk answered in a stern tone, "the 'most famous names in the business' are already out hunting for your brother. Second, it was Bornan Thul himself, not Aryn Dro, who hired me. He wore a disguise, but still risked his life to enlist my help. Just to find you. He attempted to remain anonymous, but I discovered his identity anyway."

This news changed everything. Raynar's face lit

up. "You saw my father? Is he all right? Where is he? Can I go to him?"

Compassion showed in Zekk's emerald eyes when he looked at the blond-haired boy. "He's alive and healthy, at least—but he had to go back into hiding. Everyone is after him."

"Why didn't you simply bring him in, you fool?" Tyko snapped. "Aren't you a bounty hunter? Our family would have rewarded you with more than enough credits to make it worth your while."

"It was tempting," Zekk admitted. "But that wouldn't have been honorable. I can't betray my employer."

"Honor," Tyko sneered. "Who ever heard of a bounty hunter concerned with his *honor*? Besides, Bornan left his entire family to think him kidnapped or dead, for who knows what reason. How honorable is that?"

Raynar rounded on his uncle. "All right, let's discuss honor. Aren't you the one who arranged to have *yourself* kidnapped, Uncle Tyko? You let *us* believe you were in great danger. How honorable is *that*?"

"I had only the best of intentions, my dear boy," Tyko blustered. "I just wanted to help my brother to—"

"Help? You tried to trick my father into revealing himself, without even knowing what he was hiding from. And you succeeded! If someone other than

Zekk had found him, my father could be dead right now."

"He's right," Zekk said. "I believe Bornan Thul is in hiding for a good reason. I can tell you for certain that his life is in danger. There were only two things he hired me for: to locate *you*"—this with an accusing glance at Tyko—"and to send a message to his family."

Zekk reached into a pocket of his vest and pulled out a message packet. He tossed it to Raynar, who, though surprised, easily caught it. "Now I've fulfilled both parts of my job for him. If he's smart, Bornan Thul won't come out of hiding again without expert protection."

"At least we know my father's not hurt," Raynar said. "Yet."

"It is also fortunate no one was hurt by coming to Mechis III," Tenel Ka said pointedly.

"Not hurt much, at least," Jaina said, examining the burn on Zekk's arm. She grinned at him and gave him another hug. "I'm glad you're here. At least this time you didn't show up in the middle of a bounty hunter attack, like you did at Alderaan!"

19

AS RAABA GUIDED her star skimmer toward Ryloth, she proudly shared details about her adventures in procuring the syren fiber for her belt. Then she added some history of the homeworld Nolaa Tarkona had reformed. In the cramped *Rising Star,* Lowbacca and his sister Sirra listened with interest.

Tarkona had chosen Ryloth as the headquarters of her ever-expanding Diversity Alliance. With its slightly irregular shape, the planet was tide-locked in orbit: one side always faced the sun, while the opposite hemisphere remained perpetually in shadow. This made the climate inhospitable, except for a narrow band of twilight between the baking day and the freezing night.

In this thin habitable zone and on the cold side, the Twi'leks had dug mountain warrens, honeycombing the rock with chambers and passages as they mined the addictive mineral ryll, which was sometimes sold as spice.

When Old Republic representatives had stumbled upon their world, many Twi'leks chose to leave and see the vast galaxy. Some had been trained as Jedi Knights, including the legendary Tott Doneeta, who had fought during the great Sith War four thousand years ago. In recent times, the lawyer and X-wing pilot Nawara Ven had been a talented member of Rogue Squadron.

But not all Twi'leks were so revered, Raaba went on. The reviled scientist administrator Tol Sivron had served the Empire by running a hidden super-weapons lab. The traitorous Bib Fortuna had profited from the misery of his own species, selling Twi'lek women as slaves—including Nolaa's beautiful half-sister Oola. The talented dancers were in great demand among wealthy thugs such as Jabba the Hutt. But Nolaa had done her best to quash that trade.

Raaba had no doubt that Nolaa Tarkona marked a new high point in the history of her people. She had founded a political movement that would achieve widespread social acceptance and equality for all alien species. The New Republic, with all of its sweet-sounding promises, would finally be forced to live up to its commitments.

As he listened to Raaba's speech, Lowie rumbled uneasily. He had spent a great deal of time with the

New Republic. Although he had observed some continuing difficulties, most could be explained by ill-mannered *individuals,* not by any overarching human policy of discrimination and repression.

Still, Raaba seemed so passionate about her new calling that Lowbacca decided not to argue. He would hear with an open mind what her friends had to say. His sister Sirra viewed this trip away from home as a great adventure, and he did not want to ruin her enjoyment by making hasty judgments about Raaba's beliefs.

As soon as the *Rising Star* entered orbit around Ryloth, a string of defensive satellites sounded their alerts, demanding that Raaba identify herself. A harsh voice forbade her to proceed until she had been cleared or her skimmer would be destroyed instantly.

Unflustered, Raaba transmitted her identification code, furry fingers dancing over the keypad. With Wookiee growls she announced herself as a loyal member of the Diversity Alliance, bringing two new members to meet Nolaa Tarkona. She was immediately authorized to enter the atmosphere and approach the mountain stronghold. Raaba's dark lips peeled back in a grin, exposing her fangs.

As the skimmer cruised toward the blackened crags, Lowie saw that all entrances to the warrens had been covered and textured to be almost indistinguishable from the rippling rock. Towering blast doors in the naked cliffside ground open for the *Rising Star*.

Without hesitation, the chocolate-furred Wookiee barreled into the passage, swooping down into the lower warrens. Sirra gave a squeal of delight, and Lowie recalled his sister's own practice flying back at the treetop city.

Raaba clearly knew where she was going. She easily followed a path of lights that lit the curving rock walls like colonies of phosphorescent creatures in a dark cave. Paying scant attention, she skimmed around corners, apparently selecting appropriate passages by instinct alone.

Finally, they reached an underground docking area where supply ships, passenger shuttles, and courier drones lay in various stages of preparation. Mixed groups of aliens bustled back and forth, carrying out the business of the Diversity Alliance. They scrutinized maps on electronic wallboards and hauled supplies to storage grottoes. Droids moved about, alert for spies or sabotage from enemies of the political movement and at the same time recording everything for later victorious documentaries.

As the three Wookiees climbed out of the *Rising Star,* Lowie stretched his lanky, ginger-furred arms and sniffed the air. His sensitive nostrils detected volatile hyperdrive fuels and coolants, as well as the body odors and pheromones from a host of different species. Beside him, Raaba seemed proud to be an integral part of such great work. She tugged on her glossy syren-fiber belt, reveling in her newly acquired badge of honor.

A Shistavanen wolfman in an impressive military uniform marched up to greet them. "Welcome back, Raabakyysh—we are pleased that you have brought new recruits to us." He brushed his dark fur back and bowed, baring his fangs in a gesture of respect. "I am Adjutant Advisor Hovrak."

The wolfman made a deep bow toward Lowie and raised his eyebrows, letting an interrogative growl escape his throat. "The fame of Lowbacca and his work as a Jedi Knight reached our ears some time ago. The Diversity Alliance welcomes you." He gestured with one fiercely clawed hand. "Come. Nolaa Tarkona will see you right away."

Inside her grand receiving chamber, Nolaa Tarkona stood from her massive seat and smiled to show sharply filed teeth. Her tattooed head-tail squirmed with pleasure. Lowie noted a glint from the optical sensor implanted in the scarred stump of the other head-tail.

Raaba marched forward with Hovrak, while Lowie and Sirra remained respectfully behind, waiting to be introduced. Lowie was impressed that the political workers were making such a grand gesture to welcome them. Surely, not all potential recruits received this kind of treatment?

Still, something about the Diversity Alliance made him uneasy. He couldn't quite identify what it was . . . but he reassured himself by thinking that Raaba would not have allowed herself to become involved in anything unsavory.

"I am very pleased to have you among our members, my Wookiee friends," Tarkona said. Her voice was powerful, flowing with rich currents of charisma. "Raabakyysh has been one of our most loyal supporters, and I am sure that you will also do your species proud." She strode across the dais, her black robes sweeping around her.

"I am especially honored to have a Jedi among us," Tarkona continued. "The Diversity Alliance has great work to do, and you possess crucial skills." She stepped down to floor level. Raaba smiled, her furry face crinkling with pleasure.

"Raabakyysh tells me that you were also searching for Bornan Thul, Lowbacca. I certainly hope he is found soon. He betrayed my trust in him and . . . stole a precious treasure, a critical key to our work." Tarkona's head-tail thrashed with agitation. "Humans have always found our weak spots and exploited them, uncovering whatever means the most to us—and then taking it! It was my own foolishness to put my faith in a human in the first place."

As she paced the floor, her feet whispered against the polished stone. "Not all humans are so unworthy, of course," she amended when she saw Lowie bristle at the sweeping censure. Her tone was conciliatory. "Some humans have even accepted our assignment to hunt down this unworthy man who has so greatly wronged me. Of course, their reasons are purely mercenary, rather than honorable—but the end result is all that matters."

At that moment Corrsk, the Trandoshan, strode into the chamber, carrying an electronic datapad and a sheaf of documents. He clearly meant to deliver them to Nolaa Tarkona, but when the giant reptilian alien saw the three Wookiees standing in the grotto, he stopped short. Instinct drew his muscles taut, and he dropped the datapad to the floor. Documents fluttered down as Corrsk raised his clawed hands to an attack position. A simmering growl bubbled like a geyser out of his throat.

Outraged and betrayed, Lowie roared defensively at seeing the Wookiees' natural enemy. Bristling, he stepped close to Sirra, so that he and his sister could fight together. Trandoshan bounty hunters were famous for killing Wookiees, and Lowie had no intention of losing his pelt.

Sirra growled, also ready to fight with tooth and claw—but Raaba intervened, holding up her dark brown arms to prevent them from doing anything foolish. She cinched her red headband tighter, and her biceps bulged, holding her metal armlets in place.

"Corrsk, control yourself! Enough posturing," Tarkona said impatiently. "Raabakyysh, thank you for deflecting this battle." She turned to Lowie and Sirra. "Perhaps the concept has not yet sunk in, but here in the Diversity Alliance we've put aside our differences. Ancient rivalries and blood feuds are erased. We agree to surrender interracial hatreds to focus on the most pernicious enemy, our most important foes: *humans everywhere*. Wookiees and Trandoshans can only triumph if they fight side by side as comrades. We must!"

Shamefaced, the Trandoshan lowered his clawed hands and retrieved the items he had dropped. Lowie and Sirra watched the reptilian predator cautiously as he slunk forward to place the datapad and documents on the table beside Tarkona's chair. Without a word, Corrsk vanished down a long dim tunnel.

Only then did Lowie allow himself to relax. Raaba chuffed with laughter, treating the entire incident as a joke.

Lowie didn't find the experience terribly amusing, but he vowed to do his best to accept other species and to fit in with the ways of the Diversity Alliance.

20

THE ASSAULT ON Mechis III came with such sudden force and devastation that Jacen could hardly believe only one bounty hunter was responsible.

The attacking vessel pummeled its way through the atmosphere, throwing off sonic booms like obscuring veils. The ship thundered overhead, crashing through the roiling clouds, pausing only briefly to loose a volley of concussion torpedoes.

Smokestacks crumbled, dropping like felled trees. Secondary detonations ignited combustible gases that rose from the industrial sections in an inferno that blasted through the underground tunnels. A line of factory buildings toppled in a devastating chain reaction as the spreading shock front ripped out their foundations.

Alarms screeched through the administration building. Lights flashed, sirens wailed.

Tyko Thul ran to the diagnostic screens inside his

office. His skin had gone a pasty gray, and his eyes widened in terror. Beside him stood Raynar, his simple Jedi robes contrasting with his uncle's garish display of noble heritage.

The young Jedi Knights scrambled to defensive positions. Tenel Ka took her place beside Jacen, cool and ready to fight, her hand on the hilt of her lightsaber. Even in the midst of such confusion, it made Jacen glad to see how quickly the warrior girl came over to fight next to him.

"Why bother with all the sirens?" Jaina said, pressing her palms to her temples. "The whole planet's *automated*. Do droids care about that stuff?"

Jacen looked out the window across the smoky landscape. Another building erupted into flames. "Good thing there aren't any people out there."

"But think of all the droids!" Em Teedee wailed. "They're doomed!"

Zekk stood near Jaina with his arms crossed over his chest. He squinted into the soot-stained sky as the attacker swung around for another furious pass. A cargo-load of concussion bombs dropped again, blowing up another thermal exhaust port. Zekk's face turned grim as he recognized the ship. "That's Dengar," he said. "How did he know to come here?"

Targeting rooftop-cannons tracked Dengar across the sky and fired long blasts of crackling blue ion bolts or sharp green turbolasers. But the cybernetically enhanced bounty hunter reacted too quickly— flying, dodging, skipping left and right. The clumsy automated defensive systems could not keep up.

A gruff voice came over the citywide intercom system, echoing from a thousand amplification speakers. "This is Dengar. I know the bounty hunter Zekk is down there—I have followed him here to the hiding place of Bornan Thul."

"Why does everybody *make* that assumption?" Zekk said.

"I intend to cause much more damage unless you surrender my bounty." After a pause, Dengar's deep voice continued, "Further negotiation is . . . not acceptable."

An army of scurrying machines spread out through the factory city. Fire-response droids and disaster-mitigation crews pumped flame-suppressant chemicals onto the burning wreckage. Salvage crews set to work cleaning up portions of the assembly lines and strove to keep them running at all costs.

Dengar's ship cruised overhead, banked, then came back toward the administration building. With calculated malice, he dropped another bomb directly onto a droid fire-response fleet, obliterating them.

Tyko gazed around in confusion and horror. "What are we going to do?"

Tenel Ka turned toward him skeptically. "First

we must know if you staged this attack. The timing would appear somewhat . . . convenient. Is this a new hoax—like your assassin droids on Kuar?"

"Certainly not!" Tyko looked at her, the picture of appalled innocence. "My dear girl, that terrorist is destroying my factories!"

Raynar studied his uncle for a second. "I believe him. He'd never damage his own facilities like this."

"No, Dengar doesn't work for Tyko," Zekk agreed. "He's after Tarkona's bounty. He intends to bring in Bornan Thul, dead or alive—it doesn't matter which." He frowned, his green eyes hard as emeralds. "I outwitted him once, but I wouldn't count on it again. Dengar's one of the best."

The broad windows rattled with the thunder of Dengar's passage as he swooped past the administrative headquarters. As if to taunt them, the bounty hunter loosed another explosive . . . but detonated it in midair, so that the walls of the office buildings merely shuddered.

Jacen looked at Raynar with concern. "Hey, we promised to keep Raynar safe on this trip—and it's not very safe just to sit here in an office while we get bombed. I think we should head for the *Rock Dragon* and get out of here. If we all leave Mechis III, Dengar won't have any reason to stay and cause more damage."

Zekk looked over at Jaina. "The *Lightning Rod* is

closer. We could get to my ship and harass him, create a diversion so the others can escape." He raised an eyebrow hopefully. "I could use a good copilot, Jaina . . . if you wouldn't mind coming with me."

She hurried to Zekk's side. "What are we waiting for? Em Teedee, you go with Jacen—he's a fair pilot himself, but he and Tenel Ka may need your assistance getting the *Rock Dragon* out of here."

The little droid floated upward in his excitement, barely managing to keep his new microrepulsors under control. "Oh my! This is a sobering responsibility—I will do my utmost not to let you down, Mistress Jaina."

Jaina grabbed Zekk's hand and they raced out of the offices together, toward where he had docked the *Lightning Rod*. Jacen, Tenel Ka, and Raynar headed for the door as well.

Tyko Thul stood all alone, looking sickened. "But . . . but I can't leave here. This is *my* factory planet! I got Mechis III up and running when all the systems had fallen into disrepair. I won't abandon it just because some . . . some *vandal* comes in shooting."

Raynar spluttered, "But you can't stay here, Uncle Tyko—you'll be killed. You've got to come with us."

"No! I'm going down into the reinforced lower levels. I'll be perfectly safe there. You children go on now." Leaving his office, Tyko turned and jogged out of sight down the corridor.

Jacen looked after him, but Tenel Ka gestured for them to hurry. "Jacen, we must get to the roof or our plans will be wasted."

The three ran toward the nearest turbolift. Em Teedee floated after them, still working to control his new repulsorjets. "Wait! Wait for me!"

Breathing hard, Jaina secured her crash webbing as Zekk lurched the *Lightning Rod* into the air, roaring out of the overhang-covered shipping area where he had landed. She glanced at the dark-haired young man as he worked, his gaze intent on the controls.

"Sure is good to fly with you, Zekk," she said.

"You seem to be making this a habit—getting into situations where I have to come rescue you," he said, smiling slightly.

"Hah! I'm not half-bad at rescues either, you know. Watch it, or I might just turn the tables on you one of these days."

"I don't suppose I'd mind that so much." Zekk punched the engines for a new surge of acceleration. They streaked up between tall manufacturing centers and into the open air. Jaina leaned forward to the cockpit windows, trying to see through the thick curls of smoke.

Dengar dropped a thermal shock-wave generator

onto the roof of the building adjacent to Tyko's administrative headquarters. The weapon burned its way downward like a luminous diving bell, incinerating floor after floor after floor until it impacted the building's foundations.

"I'll concentrate on flying," Zekk said. "You take the weapons controls."

"Sounds like a plan. Let's go," Jaina said.

As if out of nowhere, they soared in. Jaina fired the laser cannons without mercy, targeting the hull of the bounty hunter's ship. They skimmed past so close that Jaina could have kicked Dengar's craft if the *Lightning Rod*'s access hatch had been open.

Zekk sped onward, and Dengar launched after them in hot pursuit. Wrestling with the piloting controls, Zekk rolled the battered old ship. He took them into a downward loop and flew beneath his enemy, jerking sideways and up. Jaina could see that subconscious instincts made Zekk use his Force skills to dodge, but she said nothing to interrupt his concentration.

Dengar followed, blasting away furiously with his ship's weapons.

"Think he'd hold a grudge against me for what I did to him on Ziost?" Zekk said.

With a touch of irony, Jaina said, "At least he's stopped damaging the buildings. Our goal was to distract him so the others could get away to safety."

"Of course, *I'd* like to get away, as well," Zekk

said. "Hang on." He headed in the direction of the smoldering buildings Dengar had already blasted. "That looks like a good prospect."

Sagging and ready to collapse, twin skyscrapers blazed side by side in parallel infernos. With the bounty hunter still clinging to their afterburners, Zekk arrowed the ship directly toward the blazing columns.

"I've got a bad feeling about this," Jaina muttered.

The *Lightning Rod* shot into the gap between the burning towers as a network of connecting girders broke loose. Damaged beyond repair, the skyscrapers began to topple. . . .

Up on the rooftop, the smell of fire saturated the air. Jacen and Tenel Ka ran side by side, with Raynar close behind them. "There they are!" the Alderaanian boy said, pointing. The polluted wind rippled the sleeve of his Jedi robe.

With Dengar's ship perilously close behind them, firing its blasters, the *Lightning Rod* plunged recklessly between two collapsing buildings. Fire and smoke raged upward as the towers crashed together, and Zekk's ship vanished into the inferno.

Dengar broke off his pursuit at the last instant, hauling his ship around and up, away from certain death. He left the wreckage behind and came about.

Tenel Ka drew a breath of dismay as the *Light-*

ning Rod vanished into the billows of smoke and debris. But Jacen shook his head. "I'm sure they made it, somehow. Zekk's too good a pilot—and I'd sense it if Jaina got hurt."

"This is a fact," the warrior girl said.

Jacen looked over his shoulder toward the stairwell, trying to locate Em Teedee. The little floating droid had not managed to keep up with them. When Dengar spotted them and soared toward the rooftop, Jacen forgot about Em Teedee and thought instead about their own survival. "To the *Rock Dragon*—quick!"

The Hapan passenger cruiser sat where they had landed it on the opposite side of the roof. Tenel Ka sprinted along to the sheer edge, running as if she were simply doing her morning workout. Tossing her red-gold braids behind her shoulders, she glanced down, observing the extreme height with interest. "Lowbacca would have enjoyed being up here."

"Yeah, I'd rather he was here to pilot the ship, too. Em Teedee!" Jacen called. "Where can he be?"

Dengar's inelegant ship circled low. Before they could reach the safety of the *Rock Dragon,* the bounty hunter landed defiantly at the edge of the roof, blocking the way.

Jacen, Tenel Ka, and Raynar staggered to a stop, looking grimly at each other.

The bounty hunter opened the hatch and leapt

out. His shoulders were broad, and he carried two massive blaster cannons—each of which usually required two arms to lift, though Dengar easily held one in each hand. The mouth on the bounty hunter's bandage-wrapped face sagged like his loose-fitting clothes, which were dirty and stained from a thousand fights and a thousand quick repair jobs on his ship.

Dengar's sunken eyes flicked from side to side as he scanned the three young Jedi Knights like a targeting computer assessing damage potential. He aimed both blaster cannons at the companions. "Hostages. Expendable." He scowled. "Where is Bornan Thul? Tell me."

Raynar crossed his brown-robed arms and put on a brave face. "I am Raynar, son of Bornan Thul. My father isn't *on* Mechis III. He never was."

Dengar's expression did not change. "Then you will tell me how to find him, or I will begin eliminating hostages." His sallow face showed no sign of regret or anticipation. "I hope one of you cooperates before all three of you are dead."

Around the metropolis, emergency-response droids cruised through the damaged areas. Smoke poured into the sky, blacker and more noxious than the pollution belched out by the manufacturing centers.

Jacen and Tenel Ka exchanged glances, but no one spoke.

Dengar waited precisely five seconds. Then he raised his blaster cannons, both pointing at a single target—Jacen.

The young man's heart thudded, and his hand groped for his lightsaber. He wondered if he could possibly use its blade to deflect such high-powered explosive bolts. He was sure his uncle, Luke Skywalker, could have done it.

"You will not kill my friend," Tenel Ka said, stepping in front of Jacen to shield him with her body. She drew her own rancor-tooth lightsaber and flashed its turquoise blade. Jacen saw her lips part in a feral grin, filled with challenge and menace toward anyone who would threaten him.

Jacen glanced over at Raynar, who stood concentrating, his gaze fixed on Dengar's ship. Jacen felt a ripple in the Force and instantly knew what the blond boy was trying to do.

"Doesn't matter to me who I start with," Dengar answered coldly. He readjusted his aim toward Tenel Ka. She didn't flinch.

Jacen added his own Jedi abilities to Raynar's, concentrating on the bounty hunter's ship. The craft had landed close to the edge of the rooftop, and its rear support pad rested . . .

"Let this first one be a lesson to you," Dengar said. The bounty hunter's finger tightened on the firing stud. Defiant and fearless, Tenel Ka held up her lightsaber, ready to block the shot.

Jacen squeezed his eyes shut and focused. He had to help her! With every ounce of his concentration, Jacen drew on the Force to nudge, push, *shove*.

Dengar fired both blaster cannons.

Using the Force, Jacen jostled the weapons. Both shots went wide, missing Tenel Ka. Behind him, Raynar was still focused on one goal.

"And let this be a lesson to *you*, Dengar," Tenel Ka said. Sensing that she was joining her efforts to Raynar's, Jacen lent his assistance as well.

Dengar's ship slid backward, scraping across the rooftop. Its rear support pad dropped over the side of the building. The craft tipped and lurched, its hull grating against the rough edge of the roof.

The bounty hunter whirled in alarm. "What—?"

Suddenly the rooftop door burst open. The towering bulk of IG-88 strode out, arms extended, weapons powered up.

Em Teedee, hovering above the assassin droid's body frame, amplified his normally tiny voice to a commanding boom. "I suggest you leave our friends alone, you arrogant bully!"

Tyko Thul in his colorful robes confidently followed the two droids out onto the rooftop. "IG-88, I order you to protect us!" The assassin droid aimed his built-in weapons.

Dengar reacted with lightning speed, whirling away from Tenel Ka and letting loose a volley of blaster bolts. Most ricocheted harmlessly off the assassin droid's durasteel torso, leaving cherry-red spots of absorbed energy.

However, one bolt glanced off IG-88's skeletal frame and hit Em Teedee's outer casing. The little translating droid shrieked as sparks flew from his side; his optical sensors flickered wildly. Spinning in the air like an asteroid after a collision, he let out an electronic wail.

IG-88 opened fire again and again, but with such precision that instead of blasting the bandage-wrapped human off the rooftop, his weapon discharges turned one of Dengar's heavy blaster cannons to slag in his fist.

Jacen remembered that the assassin droid's new programming prevented him from shooting down the bounty hunter outright, even to protect his masters. But IG-88 was resourceful enough to find alternatives.

Behind him, Dengar's ship teetered precariously on the edge of the roof.

Still expressionless, Dengar tossed the smoldering firearm away and grabbed his remaining cannon with both hands. But IG-88 targeted carefully with a volley of shots that blew away the muzzle of the second blaster, leaving Dengar unarmed.

Then the droid bombarded the roof plates at the bounty hunter's feet.

Seeing that the situation was hopeless, Dengar dove for his ship. Off balance, it groaned and tilted toward an inevitable crash between the buildings. IG-88 fired once more just as the bandage-wrapped bounty hunter scrambled through the hatch. Blaster bolts sizzled off the frame as Dengar sealed himself in.

With a final shriek of protest, the ship fell from the rooftop. Jacen gasped, and Raynar raced to the edge of the building to look down. The ship plunged and spun, like a paving stone dropped off a cliff.

At the last instant, Dengar managed to power up his engines and wrench the ship out of gravity's clutches. Spinning the craft sideways, the bounty hunter thundered through the narrow gaps between buildings. From the rooftop IG-88 launched grenades toward the stern of Dengar's ship in an attempt to disable the engines as he departed. The explosives fell short as the bounty hunter whirled and dipped, zigzagging skillfully along a random course.

"No more grenades," Tyko yelled at the assassin droid. "If you can't bring yourself to actually destroy his ship, at least wait until he comes back into range, or you'll damage my buildings."

Before Dengar could circle around and come back again, though, the *Lightning Rod* shot up out of an alleyway, gaining speed as Jaina blasted volley after volley of laser fire into Dengar's already damaged craft.

"All right, Jaina!" Jacen cried. "Go!"

Facing Zekk's unexpected and relentless pursuit, Dengar made a logical choice. He set course for escape, and with an angry roar, his ship careened into the sky.

Standing beside Tenel Ka, Jacen watched the bounty hunter's craft jet upward at high speed until it was swallowed by the swirling black smoke. Dengar disappeared into orbit, leaving behind the smoldering wreckage of his devastating attack.

Planting one fist on each of his hips, Raynar observed the bounty hunter's departure with defiant satisfaction. "That'll teach him not to tangle with young Jedi Knights!"

21

IN THE AFTERMATH of Dengar's attack, Zekk brooded, trying to find answers to the question that now haunted him: how had the bounty hunter found him? Despite this worry, Zekk was delighted when Jaina offered to spend two days helping him recalibrate the *Lightning Rod*'s systems. As they worked, he told Jaina about his encounter with Dengar on Ziost, and mentioned his subsequent stops on Mos Eisley, Kuar, and Borgo Prime before coming to Mechis III. Zekk didn't give her many details, but hoped she could help him figure out how the other bounty hunter had found him.

"Odd. Why would Dengar think you were *here*?" Jaina mused aloud.

"I guess it's possible that he discovered the droid debris on Kuar and made the same assumptions I did about the CPU chips. The trail would've led him to Mechis III. . . ." Zekk shook his head. "But I just can't swallow that much of a coincidence. Dengar *knew* I was here."

"You think maybe he managed to mark the *Lightning Rod*, assuming you'd eventually lead him to Bornan Thul?" Jaina asked. "He might've thought you worked for Raynar's father. After all, you were sending messages to the Bornaryn fleet."

Zekk smiled at the irony. "If Dengar was tracking me, then he followed me to the wrong Thul. If he'd gone to Borgo Prime instead, he might have caught Bornan."

Jaina frowned at the thought. "He probably figured you were just stopping for messages or supplies and he didn't want you to suspect that he was on your trail," she guessed.

"If there's some sort of tracer on my ship, I want to know about it," Zekk said through gritted teeth. It gave him the creeps to think that someone could have been tracking his every movement.

Jaina grinned. "Well, then, what are we waiting for?"

Together, Zekk and Jaina carefully inspected the outer hull of the battered transport ship. Zekk couldn't imagine how many times his old friend Peckhum had been in tight situations with this craft. After the Second Imperium's attack on the Jedi academy, when the brutal TIE pilot Norys had nearly destroyed the *Lightning Rod*, Peckhum had made certain the ship got a complete overhaul.

Noting the carbon scoring, Zekk thought back on some of the skirmishes he himself had been through. Dengar had fired on him at the ice world of Ziost, and before that Boba Fett had fought him in the rubble field of Alderaan. It was a good thing that Jaina could help him check the ship over. They found countless patches, spot-welded armor plates, and external systems that had been jury-rigged so many times Zekk couldn't fathom how they managed to remain functional.

As soon as Zekk spotted it, he knew what was wrong. Surrounded by a starburst of slag, a small object had attached itself to the *Lightning Rod*'s hull. He showed it to Jaina.

"Limpet mine," she said. "Perfect for planting a tracer."

"So . . . that 'concussion grenade' Dengar fired at me wasn't a dud, after all," Zekk said, tapping it with a fingertip. "A tracer, huh?"

He pried off the limpet mine and held it in his hand, considering what to do with it. Finally, a sly grin crossed his face. . . .

At one of Mechis III's shipping platforms, Zekk and Jaina found a tiny courier pod. The high-speed drone was only large enough to carry small emergency-repair parts or hardcopy messages that were too sensitive to be transmitted with normal encoding over hyperwaves.

Jaina gleefully assured Zekk the limpet's transmitting beacon still functioned properly before they sealed it inside the courier pod. Next, he programmed a course that would take the drone high above the galactic plane—far away from any inhabited star systems. The tracer's journey would take it on a one-way trip to nowhere, still winking its insidious message . . . luring Dengar to follow.

They launched the courier pod out of the receiving bay and watched it dwindle to a pinprick and vanish into the vast gulf of distance.

Zekk stared after it with a fiery satisfaction burning in his emerald-green eyes. "Happy hunting, Dengar," he murmured.

Tyko Thul kept himself busy by programming armies of construction droids and cleanup crews to work on the damaged towers. He had reluctantly accepted Raynar's offer of temporary assistance, and together the two discussed the damage.

"You know, those structures have needed upgrading for some time now, anyway," Tyko said. "Never got around to it." Somewhat disheartened, he called up the intricate designs for the facilities.

Raynar studied the diagrams. Then, letting his eyes fall half closed, he said, "I think I might have a few modifications to suggest." With calm assurance, he began altering the schematics. He worked for nearly an hour before stopping.

Perplexed, Tyko stared at the screen. "I don't

understand. Why should I want to make these changes?"

Raynar shrugged. "By combining those two operations, you can run the systems in parallel. If one assembly line breaks down, you have the capacity to speed up production on the first line, make your repairs to the second one, and still meet delivery schedules."

"Yes!" Tyko crowed. "I see it now. It's nothing short of brilliant!"

Raynar blinked in bemusement and blushed at the praise. "I wonder if there's such a thing as a merchant Jedi," he mumbled.

Jaina, taking a break from her repairs to the *Lightning Rod*, turned back to her work on the assassin droid IG-88, while Em Teedee hovered overhead like a practice remote. "This is most interesting," he said. After repairing a few scrambled circuits, the modified translating droid now functioned like a new machine. Dangling diagnostic leads hung down, connecting the translating droid to IG-88's main memory core.

Tenel Ka, Jacen, and Raynar crowded around Jaina, watching the additional alterations with interest. Jaina glanced over at Raynar. "You're *sure* your uncle's going to let us do this?"

"He will," Raynar answered. "In return for his cooperation, I promised not to reveal his 'little hoax' to my mother. My message to her will just say that we rescued Uncle Tyko and he's unharmed." The young man smiled.

Scrutinizing the inner mechanisms of the once-lethal droid, Jaina nodded. "All right. When I'm finished here, we'll be able to turn IG-88 loose to continue the search for your father."

"It is a good idea," Tenel Ka said. "This droid was built to track down people who do not wish to be found. We could not ask for a better ally."

"Yeah," Jacen said, "and we've got the perfect job for him."

Em Teedee piped up. "I've tapped directly into IG-88's memory area reserved for storing information about current bounty assignments."

"And you input all of the data about my father?" Raynar prodded.

"Just as you requested, Master Raynar," Em Teedee said. "Everything from the file. IG-88 knows all about Bornan Thul's business affiliations, old friends, favorite haunts, familial connections—"

"Thanks, Em Teedee," Raynar broke in. "There's not another bounty hunter in the galaxy who knows as much about my father as IG-88 does now."

"He will be a fine seeker—relentless," Tenel Ka said, clapping a hand on Raynar's back. Her rustic warrior appearance made an interesting contrast with the gleaming mechanized facility populated by droids. But Tenel Ka seemed perfectly at ease. She was who she was, regardless of her location, and she never let circumstances diminish her self-confidence.

"Are we finished, then, Em Teedee?" Jaina said.

"Yes, indeed, Mistress Jaina," the little droid answered brightly. "IG-88 is now wholly dedicated to finding Bornan Thul and keeping him safe." He paused to consider. "In theory, at least, IG-88's superior design and capabilities make him more likely to succeed than the numerous other bounty hunters attempting to find Raynar's father. Why, perhaps with my additional assistance—"

Jaina disconnected the leads from the translating droid and let the silvery oval float free. "He probably doesn't want your company, Em Teedee. You'd only distract him."

"I'm certain you're right, Mistress Jaina," the droid said wistfully. "It isn't my primary function, after all. Though at the moment, I'm not certain just what my primary function is."

"We need you, Em Teedee," Jaina said.

"Thank you, Mistress Jaina," the little droid replied. "I do miss Master Lowbacca though. I certainly hope he's all right."

"So do we, Em Teedee," Jaina said, struggling against worry as thoughts of her Wookiee friend came again to the front of her mind.

"This is a fact," Tenel Ka agreed.

• • • •

Zekk and the young Jedi Knights accompanied IG-88 to the upper launch platform to see him off on his quest. Raynar looked at the dark-haired young man, remembering how Zekk—the Shadow Academy's darkest Knight—had used the Force to hurl him into the river mud.

Although it had taken Raynar a long time to recover his pride, he realized now that Zekk had in effect saved his life by doing so, humiliating him in front of the other dark Jedi attackers to dissuade them from killing Raynar outright with their burning red lightsabers.

And now the assassin droid had also been precluded from taking fatal actions. "I'm glad IG-88 can't kill anymore," Raynar said.

"Not even aliens," Tenel Ka affirmed.

Jacen tapped the droid on one arm. "Hey, hear that?" he said. "Try not to think of yourself as an assassin droid anymore."

"He can still cause plenty of damage, though," Jaina said. "Especially if it looks as if they're going to be dangerous to your father."

Uncle Tyko hurried up, wringing his hands and looking flustered. "Sorry I'm late," he said. "So much to do. I solve one problem and it leads to two others. But I'll get this place running smoothly sooner or later."

He stopped as the looming assassin droid rotated

its cylindrical head. The blinking red sensors showed no sign of recognition, no memory of its past. Without a word, the droid swiveled its body core and clomped toward a needlelike ship that was identical in design to the *IG-2000,* the droid's original craft. Because the durable assassin droid had no need for life-support systems or acceleration dampers, the vessel had an incredible bank of engines and superior power efficiency.

"Please find my father, IG-88," Raynar said.

The assassin droid climbed into his ship and fired up the engines. The gathered spectators watched as the sleek vessel stabbed up into the atmosphere like a dagger slicing cloth.

Jacen turned to Raynar and clasped his shoulder. "Things are looking up, you know," he said. "Zekk gave us the news that your father is alive, and IG-88 is on the chase."

"And now that we've 'rescued' your Uncle Tyko," Jaina said, "we can hope that it's just a matter of time until your entire family is together again."

Raynar swallowed hard. "My father must have a good reason for hiding. I just wish I knew what it was."

Zekk nodded grimly. "He seems to think that something terrible is going to happen to the human race if he's caught."

Raynar nervously straightened his Jedi robe and ran a hand over his spiky hair. He seemed embarrassed at his friends' efforts to encourage him. "That doesn't mean *we're* going to stop searching for him, does it?"

"Not a chance," Jacen said. Then, in a moment of sadness, he added, "I just wish Lowie was here to help us out."

22

JAINA STOOD NEXT to Zekk, desperately searching for the right words, as he stood on the boarding ramp of the *Lightning Rod*. She had to say something before he left.

"I'll see you soon, I promise," Zekk said. "But right now I'd better be on my way. Maybe I'll even find Bornan Thul before IG-88 does. The least I can do is take him a message from Raynar."

Jaina swallowed. "Remember, Zekk, we're always willing to help you—to talk or listen, if you need us."

"I know, Jaina." He smiled at her, and before she knew it, she found herself caught up in a fierce hug, right there on the rooftop. She returned the hug for a long moment. Then Zekk backed into his ship, waving in farewell. "Maybe I'll drop in to rescue you again sometime soon."

"Unless I rescue you first," Jaina countered. She

stood with stinging eyes on the rooftop as he sealed the hatch of the old freighter. "Don't fly through any black holes, Zekk," she said in a hoarse whisper.

The *Lightning Rod* soared off into the sky, doubling back in a complex loop as Zekk showed off his flying prowess before taking the ship up into the atmosphere, and deep space.

Jacen sat frustrated in the comm center of Mechis III, while Em Teedee hovered and bobbed in the air over his shoulder, practicing with his new microrepulsorjets.

Tenel Ka entered and stood in the doorway, her hand on her hip as she waited for Jacen to finish. With a sigh, he swiveled to look at the warrior girl, and flashed her a smile.

"I've left three messages at Lowie's home on Kashyyyk, but I haven't gotten any response," he said. "Lowie should be there, or at least his parents, or his sister Sirra. I sure hope nothing's wrong."

Tenel Ka's face remained expressionless. "Lowbacca is a good fighter and a talented Jedi. I am certain he can take care of himself."

"I do hope so," Em Teedee interjected, "but there is still sufficient cause for concern."

Jacen gave up his seat at the comm controls, since he knew Tenel Ka had been wanting to contact her parents in the Fountain Palace on Hapes. The warrior girl sat down and, even with only one hand, her fingers flew over the controls, setting up the hyperwave link.

"I am taking the added precaution of using the royal family's encryption codes," she told Jacen, and waited for an answer.

When Isolder and Teneniel Djo appeared on-screen, she told them about the Diversity Alliance, describing it as an antihuman conspiracy that masqueraded as a benevolent political movement. Her parents took Tenel Ka's concern seriously and agreed to put their best counterconspiracy operatives into action; they would find out whatever they could about the group.

Privately, Tenel Ka hoped—no, Tenel Ka *knew*—that her grandmother would intercept this message and feel compelled to investigate the Diversity Alliance. With her own brand of ironic humor, the warrior girl asked her parents to convey her greetings to her father's mother—realizing that Ta'a Chume would probably hear her words even before the communications link between Hapes and Mechis III was broken. Her grandmother would no doubt put her best spies to work immediately.

So much the better, Tenel Ka thought. The Diversity Alliance would find Ta'a Chume a formidable enemy.

• • •

As soon as Tenel Ka had ended the transmission, an override signal winked on the panel. Jacen rushed forward to accept the transmission. "Busy day," he remarked.

"Oh my," Em Teedee said, hovering over the panel, "according to the designators, that message is coming from Kashyyyk. I do hope it's Master Lowbacca."

Jacen was rewarded by the on-screen images of Lowie's parents Mahraccor and Kallabow. "You'd better help translate, Em Teedee," he said.

"At last, my primary function!" the little droid said. "I *am* fluent in over sixteen forms of communication, you know."

After a brief greeting and message, Jacen learned from the slow Wookiee growls that Lowie was no longer on Kashyyyk, that he had left the planet days ago.

"What?" Jacen said. He and Tenel Ka exchanged a concerned glance. "Where did they go?"

He and Sirra had gone with Raaba to meet Nolaa Tarkona in person and learn more about the Diversity Alliance. Many other Wookiees had expressed a similar interest, after the fine speech Raaba had given.

"They have gone to the headquarters—on Ryloth?" Tenel Ka asked, and both older Wookiees nodded.

Jacen felt the blood drain from his face, but he forced a cheerful expression and thanked Kallabow and Mahraccor—no need to trouble them unnecessarily until he knew more.

"Dear me," said Em Teedee from where he hovered just above Jacen's right shoulder. "After what we've learned of the Diversity Alliance, I fear Master Lowbacca has fallen in with an unsavory lot. I do hope he's safe."

Jaina gave the little droid a sympathetic pat. "Don't we all, Em Teedee," she said. "Don't we all."

A trio of young Wookiees stood at a tunnel entrance that faced the cold night side of Ryloth. Together, they gazed up into the star-studded sky. Sparkling white glaciers and ice fields covered the rugged landscape beyond the twilight boundary. The chill wind was harsh enough that it penetrated even their thick pelts.

Chocolate-furred Raaba stood between Lowie and Sirra, an arm across each of their shoulders.

Lowie was glad he had found his old friend again and that Raaba and Sirra were reunited, but he often thought about his companions Jacen and Jaina and Tenel Ka. And he couldn't break himself of the habit of touching the empty spot on his fiber belt where Em Teedee should have been clipped. . . .

As if sensing the flow of his thoughts, Raaba spoke in firm and cheerful tones to reassure him.

He was among *true* friends now, she said. Lowie was where he belonged.

They watched the stars for a while, then went back into the winding tunnels.

The only thing they can trust is the Force . . .

STAR WARS YOUNG JEDI KNIGHTS

JEDI BOUNTY

Lowbacca has left the Jedi academy and traveled to the planet Ryloth, headquarters of the Diversity Alliance, to see what the Diversity Alliance is really all about.

On Yavin 4, Jacen, Jaina, and the other young Jedi Knights have already discovered one truth about the Alliance–once you go to Ryloth, you either join, or you die. Lowie is in great danger, and they must rescue him. But what can a small group of humans do against a planet full of hostile aliens?

JACEN SOLO ADDED another branch to the small campfire. He inhaled the jungle scents that mingled with the spicy smell of burning wood. Yavin 4 was alive and wild and mysterious around them.

His twin sister Jaina stared pensively into the flames, while Tenel Ka, dressed in her usual lizard-hide armor and boots, paced in restless circles around the small clearing. Raynar fidgeted beside Jacen, picking up twigs and tossing them into the embers. His moon-round face had a fretful, haunted look, as if he wasn't at all enjoying their night out camping in the jungle.

Jacen leaned back and lay down with his hands behind his head. Oblivious to the bits of forest debris that distributed themselves through his curly brown hair, he looked up into the star-filled sky and reached out with the Force. He tried to sense small creatures hiding in the jungle around them, but tonight his usual ability eluded him. He sighed. Unfortunately, his Jedi senses picked up mostly his sister's worry, Raynar's anxiety, and Tenel Ka's frustration.

"It's just not the same without Lowie here," Jaina said.

"I should certainly say not," Em Teedee, the miniaturized translating droid, agreed. The little droid hovered with the newfound freedom of the microrepulsorjets he had installed on Mechis III. He followed just behind

Tenel Ka as she made each restless circuit of the clearing.

Jacen gave up trying to sense small animals. "It's been weeks since Lowie left. He hasn't even tried to contact us." He sat up and looked at his sister. "Hey, you don't suppose Lowie decided to *join* the Diversity Alliance, do you?"

"I hope not. They're the ones who put out a bounty on my father, after all," Raynar said. "I'll bet there isn't a bounty hunter in the whole sector who's not trying to track down the infamous Bornan Thul and collect the reward Nolaa Tarkona offered."

Jaina bit her lower lip. Reflections of the flames danced in her brandy-brown dyes. "Zekk's out there with all those bounty hunters—but at least he's on our side. He's taking a big risk, too. If the Diversity Alliance finds out he worked for your father and helped your uncle Tyko, Zekk could be in trouble."

Jacen thought about their dark-haired friend. Zekk had been trained by the Shadow Academy to use the dark side of the Force, but Zekk had turned from the dark side. Deciding to start a new life, he chose to become a bounty hunter. With his piercing emerald eyes, excellent fighting skills, and knowledge of the Force, Zekk would be a formidable opponent to anyone who crossed him.

"Don't worry about Zekk, Jaina. I have a feeling he can take care of himself. I'm more worried that Lowie might be pressured to stay on Ryloth and work for the Diversity Alliance. You heard what they did to Lusa."

Jaina scowled. "Lowie'd never join a political group that despises humans. He's our friend."

Jacen tried to imagine the lanky Wookiee hating anyone simply because he'd been ordered to. The idea seemed ridiculous. "No, I can't believe he'd go along with that. But why hasn't he at least tried to send us a message?"

"Perhaps he has," Tenel Ka said. "He may have been unsuccessful."

Jacen glanced up at the statuesque warrior girl as she

broke into a trot. Her red-gold hair, half of which was caught up in Dathomiran warrior braids, flowed out behind her like the tail of a comet.

Em Teedee kept pace with her. "Surely you're not suggesting that poor Master Lowbacca might have been *prevented* from making contact with us!" the translating droid wailed.

"It is possible. If so, he could also have been prevented from returning here," Tenel Ka said.

Jaina groaned. "That would explain a lot—like why the communications center on Ryloth never lets us speak to Lowie when we get a connection through to them."

"Hey, if Lowie's in trouble, then I think we ought to do something about it," Jacen said.

"Agreed," Tenel Ka said, still jogging along the perimeter of the clearing.

Jaina shrugged. "No argument here. If we can't talk to Lowie any other way, we'll go to Ryloth in person."

"Oh my! We could be doomed!" Em Teedee said. "But I *would* gladly sacrifice my last circuit if it would help Master Lowbacca. Going to Ryloth may be an excellent opportunity for me to use my translating skills: I *am* fluent in over sixteen forms of communication, you know. Well, I suppose that's all settled, then."

"I guess you should count me in too," Raynar added.

Jacen looked at Raynar. The lightly freckled youth with the spiky blond hair seemed tense and edgy. Raynar's blue eyes followed Tenel Ka and Em Teedee around the circle. Around and around and around. "Do you really *have* to do that, Tenel Ka?" Raynar blurted out at last.

"The jungles are dangerous at night," Tenel Ka replied without slowing. Her voice was steady and she didn't gasp or pant as she spoke. "Tionne advised us to post a watch. Therefore, I am ensuring the safety of our campsite by patrolling its perimeter."

"I knew *that*," Raynar said in exasperation.

Jacen gave a lopsided grin. "We know you offered to

take the first watch, Tenel Ka. I think Raynar was just wondering why you're practically running. If you wear yourself out, you'll be too tired to fight against any real threat."

Tenel Ka raised an eyebrow skeptically. "I have found that when I combine physical exercise with my other duties, I am able to think more clearly. It is also an excellent way to release tension."

Jaina chuckled. "In that case, maybe we could all use a good run."

Just as his sister spoke, Jacen sensed it: something out in the jungle was watching them. Tenel Ka noticed it too, for she stopped dead in her tracks. Em Teedee narrowly avoided colliding with her shoulder. A split second later the warrior girl dove to the ground and rolled as a snarling, fang-filled ball of fur sprang through the air where she had been standing.

Jacen and Jaina were both on their feet, lightsabers in their hands, before the furry creature touched the ground. "It's a rakhmar," Jacen yelled. "Probably hoping to catch a quick meal."

The meter-long beast sprang into the air again, a dynamo of black-swirled fur and snapping teeth. This time, the rakhmar struck at the only person who had no weapon.

"Raynar, look out!" Jaina cried, leaping after the vicious creature, but Raynar was already moving to dodge the sweeping claws. He launched himself forward, narrowly missing the campfire. Menacing yellow eyes glittered in the firelight. The rakhmar overshot its target and grazed Raynar's leg with its razor-sharp rear claws.

The jungle predator spun around as Raynar snatched a burning branch from the fire, ready to defend himself. The rakhmar crouched on its back legs, its muscles coiled, ready to lunge again.

Raynar held his torch high. A strong arm yanked him backward just as the predator sprang—and a pair of lightsabers slashed past him in a parallel glare of emerald green and electric violet. The energy blades sliced the vicious rakhmar into three even pieces that fell to the ground with wet thumps.

With their lightsabers still blazing, Jacen and Jaina inspected the clearing for any other would-be predators.

"I do not believe you will need this," Tenel Ka said, taking the firebrand from Raynar and tossing it back into the campfire. "Your instincts and reactions were commendable."

"Oh, yes. Excellently well done, everyone!" Em Teedee's silver oval floated over to Raynar. "I scarcely had time to be frightened—although I do believe Master Raynar has sustained some injury."

"It's not too bad." Raynar pulled aside his brown Jedi robe to examine his thigh where the rakhmar had clawed it. Dark blood ran from a pair of gashes just below his right hip.

Jaina knelt beside Raynar and examined the leg. "What do you think?" she asked her brother.

Jacen winced. It looked worse than he had expected. "I think we shouldn't have walked all the way here. Maybe we should've borrowed Lowie's T-23 instead. It's a long hike back to the Great Temple."

Tenel Ka pressed her hand against the wounds to slow the bleeding. "Raynar should not walk with this injury," she agreed. "We must bind the leg."

By the light of the campfire, Jaina tore strips of cloth from the bottom of Raynar's Jedi robe. Em Teedee brightened his optical sensors to provide lighting from above while Jaina and Tenel Ka bandaged Raynar's wound. Unperturbed by all the blood, Tenel Ka wiped her hand on the ground.

"I think I'll be able to walk now," Raynar said bravely, though his voice wavered. When Jacen and Jaina helped him stand, however, all color drained from his face and his knees buckled. Jacen caught him before he fell.

"Dear me! Perhaps Master Raynar would be better advised to rest while one of us returns to the Jedi academy to summon assistance," Em Teedee said. "I believe I would make an appropriate messenger. Therefore, I volunteer to serve in that capacity."

But before the little droid even finished speaking, Jacen heard something approaching through the jungle. "We've got company," he said.

Tenel Ka had already assumed a fighting stance, lightsaber drawn, before they identified the sound as hoofbeats.

"Lusa?" Raynar murmured. "Is it Lusa?"

At first Jacen thought his friend must be delirious, but he quickly discovered that Raynar was right. Her rich cinnamon hair and mane flying, Lusa galloped out of the trees. Only when she reached the center of the clearing did she come to an abrupt stop.

In the firelight sweat glistened on the centaur girl's bare torso and flanks. Her face seemed to go almost as pale as Raynar's when she looked at him. "You're hurt!" she gasped.

Color flooded into Raynar's face. "Yeah, I . . . noticed."

"Hey, how'd you find us?" Jacen asked.

Still watching Raynar with concern, Lusa answered distractedly. "Before you left, Raynar gave me a general idea where you would be camping. When I got the message, I just headed in this direction and hoped to find you."

"Message? What message?" Jaina asked.

"Oh." Lusa stamped a hoof. Her eyes sought out Tenel Ka. "I believe you have a grandmother who used to be queen of the Hapes Cluster?"

"This is a fact," Tenel Ka said.

"Well, she's wreaking havoc with the protective forces stationed in orbit. She asked for Master Skywalker, and when she found out he wasn't here she demanded to see you immediately. Tionne told her that you were out—and the New Republic forces wanted to detain her ship while they ran a background check—but your grandmother wouldn't listen. She must have intimidated the guards, because she'll be at the landing field in half an hour."

Jacen chuckled. "That sounds like Ta'a Chume all right."

Tenel Ka quirked an eyebrow at him. "It would seem we all have business back at the Jedi academy." She turned her cool gray eyes back toward Lusa. "Raynar requires immediate medical attention. He should not walk."

"I . . . I *could* carry him," Lusa said. She sounded rather uncertain.

Jacen knew the idea must be difficult for the centaur girl. For years the Diversity Alliance had taught her to loathe humans. She was just beginning to unlearn her distaste for physical contact with them.

"I couldn't ask you to—" Raynar began.

"You do not need to ask," Lusa interrupted. She folded her legs to kneel beside him and she spoke gently. "I am . . . offering."

Jacen breathed a sigh of relief.

"Well then," Jaina said, "what are we waiting for?"

It took the companions nearly two hours to get back through the jungles to the Jedi academy. Jaina and Lusa took Raynar into the Great Temple so that the medical droids could examine him, while Tenel Ka and Jacen headed directly toward the landing field.

An armored Hapan vessel hovered overhead. A couple of New Republic guardian ships had apparently accompanied the cruiser down from orbit, and the guards stood awkwardly on the stubbly grass, gazing up at it.

At Tenel Ka and Jacen's approach, the ship finally touched down on the field. When the exit hatch opened, two dozen armored Hapan soldiers scrambled down the ramp and arrayed themselves around the vessel to form a barrier against anyone who might try to come close to the former Queen of Hapes. Only then did Ta'a Chume appear. The aristocratic old woman glided down the ramp, waved an imperious hand to summon Jacen and Tenel Ka, and disappeared again into the ship.

Jacen felt nervous as he and Tenel Ka walked toward the ring of guards, who parted to let them pass. The warrior girl did not hesitate as she led the way into the ship.

In the centermost chamber, Ta'a Chume waited for them. She perched regally on a repulsor bench, looking every centimeter the queen that she had once been.

Tenel Ka stopped directly in front of her grandmother. "I assume you have brought information about the Diversity Alliance," she said without preamble.

Ta'a Chume sighed. "Such a beautiful child. And such a shame about the loss of your arm in that lightsaber accident. If you would only reconsider that prosthetic limb—"

Jacen saw Tenel Ka stiffen. "Grandmother, you did not come to Yavin 4 to discuss my arm."

Jacen was surprised that the former queen did not seem offended by her granddaughter's abrupt answer. In fact, she shrugged and smiled faintly. "No, but you can't blame a grandmother for trying."

Tenel Ka nodded. "What have you learned about Nolaa Tarkona?"

Her grandmother's smile grew warmer. "Your instincts about the Diversity Alliance are quite correct. It's more than a simple political movement. The conspiracies and intrigues are almost worthy of the Hapan government."

Tenel Ka scowled. This was not good news. Jacen leaned forward to hear what Ta'a Chume would say next.

"My spies have only begun to uncover a particular truth that the Diversity Alliance hides, even from some of its most dedicated followers. In fact, although they preach unity and equality for all alien species, the Alliance itself is as intolerant—in its way—as the Empire ever was. I'd even venture to say that the Diversity Alliance was founded more on hatred of humans than on the ideal of unity."

"Yeah, we kind of got that impression, too," Jacen said.

Tenel Ka's grandmother nodded and continued. "You also know that the Diversity Alliance's headquarters are on Ryloth, homeworld of the Twi'lek race."

Tenel Ka nodded impatiently. "Yes, their leader is a Twi'lek. It was only logical that she would base her headquarters—"

"But what you don't know," Ta'a Chume interrupted, "is that all of the profits from ryll spice—the most lucrative of all Ryloth's exports—have for the past two years been siphoned off to fund the Diversity Alliance."

Jacen listened with interest. His father, Han Solo, had told him about his adventures with glitterstim spice from the planet Kessel, but Jacen knew relatively little about ryll.

"And," Ta'a Chume went on, "those profits have built the Diversity Alliance into a formidable power indeed. The funds have been used to purchase weapons—both legal and illegal—to hire bounty hunters to track down enemies, and to hire assassins to ensure the silence of . . . former friends."

Jacen gave a low whistle.

The erstwhile queen's expression turned frosty. "Apparently, this Nolaa Tarkona is rather more tolerant of her enemies than she is of friends who decide to go their own way. Leaving the Diversity Alliance is a dangerous proposition. That is what we have learned so far, but I think we'll find there is much more."

Jacen and Tenel Ka exchanged worried glances.

"Your information is most useful," Tenel Ka said. "We may need to do further research. Thank you, Grandmother."

"We'd better have a talk with Lusa," Jacen said.

Vicki Lewis Thompson

Cowboy All Night

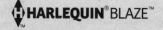 HARLEQUIN® BLAZE™

Recycling programs
for this product may
not exist in your area.

ISBN-13: 978-0-373-79899-5

Cowboy All Night

Printed in U.S.A.

www.Harlequin.com

Dear Reader,

We're riding straight into summer, and you know what that means...cowboys! A summer filled with cowboys has become a habit with me and I'm thrilled that so many of you have made it a habit, too! Thank you for your warm enthusiasm for the Thunder Mountain Brotherhood series. Get ready for three more books!

First of all, let's mosey on out to the barn at Thunder Mountain Ranch, where a foal is about to be born. Brant Ellison, one of the foster boys sheltered at the ranch years ago, has a talent for training foals, and his foster mom, Rosie, has asked him to help with this one. Rosie is always looking for an excuse to bring her boys back home for a visit and if she can play Cupid in the process, so much the better!

She can't wait for easygoing Brant to meet the foal's owner, Aria Danes. In Rosie's opinion, Aria needs to loosen up and who better to teach her than Brant? Aria can't possibly resist the gentle giant of a cowboy who knows all the tricks for winning over a sweet little colt...or an extremely stubborn woman!

Have fun watching sparks fly, and don't forget that two more books will follow this one! *Cowboy After Dark* is Liam and Hope's story, while *Cowboy Untamed* is all about Grady and Sapphire. You won't want to miss them! Oh, and please do come chat with me on Facebook.com/vickilewisthompson or on Twitter, @vickilthompson. I'd love to hear from you!

Warmly,

Vicki Lewis Thompson

A passion for travel has taken *New York Times* bestselling author **Vicki Lewis Thompson** to Europe, Great Britain, the Greek isles, Australia and New Zealand. She's visited most of North America and has her eye on South America's rain forests. Africa, India and China beckon. But her first love is her home state of Arizona, with its deserts, mountains, sunsets and—last but not least—cowboys! The wide-open spaces and heroes on horseback influence everything she writes. Connect with her at vickilewisthompson.com, Facebook.com/vickilewisthompson and Twitter.com/vickilthompson.

Books by Vicki Lewis Thompson

Harlequin Blaze

Thunder Mountain Brotherhood

Midnight Thunder
Thunderstruck
Rolling Like Thunder
A Cowboy Under the Mistletoe

Sons of Chance

I Cross My Heart
Wild at Heart
The Heart Won't Lie
Cowboys & Angels
Riding High
Riding Hard
Riding Home
A Last Chance Christmas

To get the inside scoop on Harlequin Blaze and its talented writers, be sure to check out BlazeAuthors.com.

All backlist available in ebook format.

Visit the Author Profile page at Harlequin.com for more titles.

For Jess Michaels. You've got a friend in me.

Prologue

"BRANT ELLISON. That's a good, strong name. It suits you."

"Yes, ma'am. I like it." He gave the blonde lady driving the pickup truck a smile. Her name was Mrs. Padgett. So far she seemed nice.

"I don't know what you've been told about Thunder Mountain Ranch."

"Not much, ma'am. My aunt Susie found out about it and said it'd be the best place for me 'cause I was eating her out of house and home. But don't worry. I've got that problem handled. I hadn't thought of it before, but you know what? I can fill up on cereal instead of the more expensive stuff."

Mrs. Padgett made a noise in the back of her throat as if she didn't like hearing that.

"I'm talking about cheap cereal." He said it real fast so she wouldn't turn around and take him back to his aunt's. Living on this ranch for a while could be awesome. "Corn flakes."

"I promise you won't need to fill up on any kind of cereal. I enjoy feeding growing boys. The food's not fancy, but there's plenty of it."

Okay, that sounded great—he began to salivate at the thought of all that good food. Eating was one of his favorite things. Even if this place only lasted a month or two, he'd enjoy it while he could. "I appreciate that, ma'am. I'm grateful that you can put me up for a little while."

She glanced at him in surprise. "I guess you didn't get much information, after all. The office is understaffed right now, so I understand how certain procedures get lost in the shuffle. But this isn't a temporary situation. You can stay as long as you want."

"Even though I'm a foster kid now? I thought foster kids got moved around. Which is okay. I'm used to that."

"I'm sure you are." They stopped at a light and Mrs. Padgett gazed at him with her kind blue eyes.

He recognized that look. It meant the person, usually one of his teachers at school, had read his file and knew that his dad was dead and his mother had flown the coop. At least she'd left him with Aunt Jane, and yeah, that hadn't worked out, so Aunt Susie had taken a shot, which also hadn't worked out. But that was life, wasn't it?

The light changed and Mrs. Padgett went back to her driving. "Brant, you don't have to leave Thunder Mountain unless you hate it there. And I don't think you will. The other boys seem happy."

"Oh, I can guarantee I won't hate it, ma'am."

"Why?"

"Because I'm happy anywhere I go. There's no point in feeling miserable all the time, so I just don't."

1

Fifteen years later...

"KEEP COOL, LUCY. I'm almost there." Brant turned down the dirt road leading to Thunder Mountain Ranch. He hadn't been back since Christmas, but the scenery was so familiar it felt as if he'd left only a week ago. Spring rains must have been good this year judging from the abundance of yellow and purple wildflowers lining the road. Wyoming was tuning up for summer, his favorite season.

The phone lying on the passenger seat of his truck remained silent, which was a good sign. Rosie, his foster mom, had promised to text if the mare gave birth. It looked as if he might make it in time.

Herb, his foster father and a crackerjack veterinarian, would be down at the barn monitoring the situation. Cade Gallagher, one of his many foster brothers, would probably be there, too. With those two in charge, he didn't absolutely have to be on hand for the birth.

He just liked it better when he was. Aside from the thrill of watching a new life enter the world, the training process worked better if he could bond with the foal immediately.

Herb was a mild-mannered guy, but sometimes Brant had encountered tense owners and vets.

He didn't like any nervous energy in the birthing stall and he always did what he could to calm things down. By lowering the anxiety level, he could begin socializing a foal immediately. Not a single one he'd worked with from birth had turned into a skittish horse.

His business grew along with his reputation for successfully starting foals, which gave him work he loved and the personal freedom he craved. He would have done this particular job for free in return for the safe haven his foster parents had provided when he'd been a homeless teen. But Rosie and Herb had insisted on paying so he'd gone along with that.

They weren't hurting for money anymore, thank God. The serious financial issues they'd had a year ago had been resolved with the formation of Thunder Mountain Academy, a residential program in all things horse related. Sixteen high school juniors and seniors had attended the spring semester, which had ended a week ago. Another sixteen were enrolled for the summer session starting in three days.

Rosie and Herb had hoped Lucy would stick to her due date of mid-June so the summer session kids could watch a foal being born. But, like her *Peanuts* namesake, Lucy had a mind of her own. He'd left for Sheridan on a hunch this morning. Sure enough, Rosie had called him while he was on the road to say the mare was in labor.

Personally he was glad that Lucy had jumped the gun. He'd wondered if having sixteen kids grouped around the birthing stall would have made his job tougher. He could have handled it, but now he wouldn't have to.

The students would still get to watch him work with the foal as part of their summer curriculum. He'd have three days to establish a routine before they arrived, though, which suited him. He'd never considered trying to pass on his knowledge before, but the more he thought about this gig, the more he liked it.

The sun had begun its descent behind the Big Horn Mountains by the time he arrived at the ranch. He drove straight to the barn and parked next to a cherry-red van with a wheelchair mount on the back and a vanity plate that read COOKIN. The van was empty but the driver's door was wide-open.

The van probably belonged to the mare's owner, Aria Danes. According to Rosie, Aria had been three years behind him in school, so he didn't remember her, but now she worked at the bank where Rosie and Herb had an account. Weird license plate for someone who was in banking, but maybe the lady had a dark sense of humor. If so, he'd enjoy that.

The foal was intended to be a morale booster for Aria's older brother, Josh, who'd taken a bad fall during a riding event and had mobility issues. Brant vaguely remembered the guy although they'd never been friends. Rosie had heard about Aria's plan and had offered to board Lucy in exchange for the educational value a pregnant mare and her foal would bring to the curriculum. Rosie loved win-win situations like that.

Brant walked over and closed the van's door. Aria had left her keys in the ignition and her purse lying on the passenger seat, but that was no problem around here. She and her brother were probably too excited to think about the van.

He understood that. He'd begged to go along every time his foster father had been called out to deliver a foal. Watching the process had convinced him that his future would involve helping those vulnerable babies get a good start in life.

The sound of low-pitched voices drifted through the open barn door. According to Rosie they'd created a birthing stall by taking down the partition between two regular stalls at the far end of the barn. That was where everyone was gathered, including Rosie, Cade and Cade's girlfriend, Lexi. Herb was probably inside the stall with Lucy.

Brant spotted Cade's easygoing gray cat sleeping on a blanket thrown across a hay bale. There was no sign of a guy in a wheelchair, but a young woman paced the width of the aisle, head down and arms folded against her stomach. Because he was a guy, he noticed the curve of her breasts and hips.

But he was also a horse trainer who recognized the tension eddying around her. Unwelcome tension. If she had a sense of humor, dark or otherwise, it wasn't showing.

The skirt of her purple-flowered sundress swirled around her knees with each impatient step. Wavy dark hair that hung to the middle of her back rippled as she moved. Aria Danes was wound tight and that was not good for this impending birth.

Rosie started toward him, followed by Cade and Lexi, but just then the woman glanced up, unfolded her arms and marched in his direction. Rosie paused and motioned Cade and Lexi to do the same.

"You're Brant. I remember you now. You look the same, only bigger." Her eyes, an unusual shade of violet, reflected her agitation.

Time to diffuse this bomb. He touched the brim of his Stetson and smiled. "Bigger and I hope better. Pleased to meet you, Aria."

"Thank God you're here." She didn't return his smile as

she tilted her chin to meet his gaze. "Rosie says you have a magic touch with newborns."

"Now that's a fact." He lifted his hat slightly and settled it back on his head. "I can make them appear and disappear, float three feet in the air, change color—"

"Rosie also warned me you like to kid around."

"On occasion." And that obviously wasn't working for her, although he'd heard a muffled snort from Cade.

"I'm not in the mood for jokes."

"I can see that." He snuck a quick glance over Aria's shoulder and his three railbirds were still there taking in the show.

She folded her arms again and frowned. "It's very important to me and to…to my brother that this foal gets a good start in life."

"I promise to give it my all, ma'am." He adopted the soothing tones he used with a nervous horse. "But with all due respect, things will go a lot smoother if everyone stays calm and relaxed."

She blinked. Then her cheeks turned pink. "Oh, um, I didn't mean to sound so…" She trailed off with a sigh. "I'm sorry. I've been on edge ever since Rosie called me at the bank this afternoon. She said you were on your way, but when I got off work and found out you weren't here…"

"Well, I made it." From the corner of his eye he caught Rosie giving him a thumbs-up.

"Yes, you did." Some of the strain eased from Aria's expression.

He counted that a small victory. "What about Josh? Couldn't he come with you?"

Disappointment flickered in her eyes. "No, he… I couldn't convince him to come. And, to be fair, there's no set timetable for this, is there? It could be awkward for him if it goes on all night."

"I suppose it could." But he wished she'd been able to talk her brother into coming out to be a part of this. It might have done him a world of good. "What do you say we go on down there and check on Lucy's progress?"

"Absolutely." She clapped her hand to her forehead. "And I just realized I've been keeping you from your family. Not nice."

"I'm sure they understand that you're stressed."

"That's no excuse." Straightening her shoulders, she turned, but by that time Rosie and company had resumed their stations right outside the stall, as if they hadn't been lined up behind her listening to every word. "Rosie, I apologize for intercepting him." She walked toward the group and Brant followed. "I was just...glad to see that he'd made it."

"We're all glad." Rosie came forward and gave him a fierce mom hug. Usually she dolled herself up when one of her boys was headed home, but today she'd been helping with Lucy and wore practical clothes—an old shirt and faded jeans. Her blond hair was in disarray and her usual red lipstick was AWOL.

As he wrapped his arms around one of the two most important people in his life, he breathed in the cherished floral scent that he associated with comfort and security. The top of her head didn't reach his shoulder, but she was a bigger person than anyone he knew besides Herb. "Love you, Mom."

"Love you, too, son." Then she stepped back and winked at him. "Good thing you made it."

He grinned back at her. "You ain't seen nuthin' yet, little lady. Wait'll I show you my floating foal trick."

Cade stepped forward and grasped his hand before pulling him into a quick dude hug. "I can hardly wait, bro."

"I'll bet." Brant was glad to see Cade looking so good—tanned, fit and happy.

"Yeah, I haven't seen that trick in ages." Lexi, one of the main reasons for Cade's happiness, moved in for her hug. A bundle of energy with a curly mop of brown hair, she was the daughter of Rosie and Herb's closest friends and had been part of Thunder Mountain life for years. "Every ranch needs a resident magician."

Aria's frown had reappeared. "Can you really lift that foal in the air? I thought you were making that up."

"I was." He'd never come across a more serious woman than Aria Danes.

Her smile was faint, but at least she knew how to create one. "Just wanted to make sure. I don't want this foal floating anywhere."

"No floating, I promise." He felt a tug of sympathy for her. Everyone else knew him well. They could separate jokes from fact.

Lexi stepped into the breach. "You have to take everything Brant says with a grain of salt, but on the plus side, you don't have to worry that he'll ever get mad at you. You can't rile this cowboy. Believe me, I've tried."

Cade laughed. "We've all tried. My specialty was rubber snakes tucked into a guy's bunk. I got a rise out of everyone but Brant. He named that rubber snake Elmer and treated it like a beloved pet. Then he—"

"Hate to interrupt." Herb's gentle voice from the depths of the stall brought them all back to the matter at hand. "But it's show time." His comment was punctuated with a loud groan from the mare.

Brant walked to the stall door and looked in. Lucy, a golden palomino the color of the setting sun, lay on her side with her flanks heaving. Herb moved with the brisk efficiency of a man twenty years younger as he crouched behind the mare. He'd put on his glasses, always a sign the birth was imminent.

Opening the unlatched stall door, Brant slipped inside. "Hey, Dad."

He glanced up. "Good to see you, son."

"You're looking chipper. Teaching must agree with you."

"I had no idea I'd love it so much." He smiled at Brant. "Like old times being together like this, huh?"

"Sure is. Nice feeling."

"Yep." Herb held his gaze for a moment before clearing his throat. "All righty, then. You take her head and I'll handle the business end, just like we've always done."

"Got it." Nudging his hat back, Brant dropped to his knees in the straw and began stroking Lucy's sweaty neck. "Easy does it, sweetheart," he crooned. "Just relax and let nature take its course."

Lucy snuffled in response.

He laid his hand against the vein pulsing in her neck and held it there. "You'll be fine," he murmured, "and your baby will be fine. Just go with it. No worries, Lucy."

She groaned again and quieted.

"Good," Herb said. "I just felt her relax. Keep talking."

Brant settled into the rhythm he'd developed over the years. Moving his hand in slow circles, he congratulated Lucy on the beautiful baby she was about to bring into the world. He praised her bravery and talked about what a good mother she would be.

What joy he felt during these moments. Every time he watched a birth, he felt like a kid on Christmas morning. Or rather, the way he imagined a kid who'd had a typical childhood might feel. His type-A dad had always been on the phone or his computer, even on Christmas morning. Probably why he'd died so young.

With luck and good care, the foal would live thirty or even forty years. It would bring happiness to many people and would be trustworthy because he would teach it not to be afraid. He couldn't guarantee that every foal's life would be perfect, but he only accepted jobs when he knew the people in charge were kind.

If Rosie approved of Aria, that was good enough for him. The brother was an unknown, but Rosie must have faith that Aria could handle that situation, too. He believed horses could work miracles with people, so he'd do his part to help this plan along.

"I see the forelegs." Herb's voice vibrated with excitement.

Love for his foster father gripped him in a warm embrace. The guy had been delivering foals for many years, yet he still felt the thrill. Herb and Rosie Padgett had been wonderful role models for all their foster boys.

Lucy shifted beneath his hand and her flanks heaved. "Doing great, Lucy," he said softly. "A few more minutes and we'll meet your little one."

"There's the nose." Herb nearly chortled with glee.

Someone sucked in a breath. Brant glanced up to see Aria white-knuckling the stall door as she stared at the emerging foal with wide eyes. Rosie, Lexi and Cade had given her the front-row view.

"It's going well, Aria," Brant said quietly. He willed her to bring it down a notch.

She nodded without taking her attention from the foal. Then she took a deep breath and her shoulders relaxed a little. She was trying.

"And there you go," Herb said. "Just like that. All done. Lucy, you have a beautiful little colt." He reached for a bucket and began cleaning the glistening membrane away.

Brant glanced up at Aria and smiled. "Congratulations."

"Thanks." Her response was shaky and she blinked away tears as she continued to hold on to the stall door for support. Behind her the others kept up a happy little buzz of conversation. Their camera phones clicked many times, but Aria didn't move.

"Yep, he looks great," said Herb. "Brant, ready to switch with me while I check Lucy's vitals?"

"You bet." Brant traded places with Herb and sank to his knees next to the peach-colored colt. This little guy might turn out to be a palomino like his mom. "Pleased to meet you, buddy." He picked up a clean towel from the stack Herb had brought in and began slowly wiping the colt's damp coat while he murmured every compliment he could think of.

When the foal was reasonably dry, he discarded the towel and used his bare hands to massage the tiny body. Then he raised his voice enough that Aria would be able to hear him. "Does this fellow have a name?"

"Linus," came the whispered reply.

That made him smile. Linus had been his favorite *Peanuts* character.

"Can I…can I come in?"

He mentally crossed his fingers. "Sure." He kept his focus on the baby, who seemed relaxed. "Just do it slowly. No quick movements."

Her flowery perfume was subtle, but he registered it as she knelt in the straw beside him. The straw must be rough on her bare knees, but she didn't seem to notice. Her breathing was steady and he didn't feel tension coming from her. For a moment she didn't say anything.

He wasn't surprised. Miracles had a tendency to rob people of speech. He would have been disappointed if she'd started chattering away, oblivious to the wonder of watching a life begin.

At last she spoke, awe in her voice. "He has a blaze."

"Yep."

"And blue eyes."

"For now. They'll darken later."

"He's...perfect."

"Yes, he is." The emotion in her voice matched what he felt every time he attended a birth. He didn't know much about her, but judging from her reaction to this foal, he would get along with her. If she could manage to relax a little more, they'd get along even better.

2

As they all headed back to the house for a celebratory dinner, Aria was still puzzling over this exceedingly tall and muscular cowboy with the gentle voice. Her high school memories of him were vague, although she'd recognized him the minute he'd walked into the barn. But she hadn't spent any time with him before today and hadn't been prepared for his laid-back attitude.

When it came to this foal, she wanted a trainer who had laser-like focus. Rosie had said Brant was the best, but Rosie was prejudiced. She thought all her foster boys were the best.

Aria couldn't deny that Brant had concentrated on the task during Linus's birth. He'd been calmer than Herb. Although she didn't fully trust his relaxed manner, she'd felt it settle over her like a soft blanket when she'd dropped to her knees to pet the foal.

Slowly her agitation had been replaced by awareness of Brant, the man. How unnecessary. How inappropriate. In spite of that, she'd noticed the ripple of muscles in his tanned forearms. She'd glanced at his profile and admired his strong nose and well-defined chin.

As if he'd felt her gaze on him, he'd looked her way. The

warmth in his hazel eyes had stolen her breath. He loved animals. She could trust him with Linus. That might be all she needed to know.

On the way to the house, Cade, Lexi and Brant walked ahead with Cade's gray cat, Ringo, trotting behind them. At one point Brant stopped, scooped up the cat and carried him. Ringo wore a blissed-out expression as he perched on Brant's wide shoulder.

She couldn't hear the cat purring at this distance, but with Brant stroking him, he must be. Brant made some remark about being a certified cat whisperer. Then he started whispering to Ringo and whatever he said sent Lexi and Cade into hysterics.

What a happy soul, this Brant Ellison. She wondered what it felt like to be that relaxed. She wouldn't know.

Whether due to nature or nurture, both she and her brother had been high-energy kids who'd thrived on competition. She'd always known she'd run her own business someday and Josh had expected to ride his way to fame and fortune. Although fate had knocked him down, she was determined he'd get back up.

Brant must have been knocked down, too, or he wouldn't have landed in foster care as a teenager. But if he'd been emotionally traumatized, he hid the damage well.

Rosie and Herb walked on either side of her on the way back to the house. "I'm sorry Josh wasn't here." Rosie's voice was filled with compassion. "I know how much you wanted him to be a part of it."

"He'd said he would come, but then he changed his mind. He must have had a bad day."

"I'm sure it's tough." Herb took off his glasses and tucked them in his shirt pocket. "I've never had to use a wheelchair, thank God. Is he making any progress with his physical therapy?"

This was a recent development Aria hated talking about. "He's stopped going. Says it's no use."

"Huh." Herb tugged on the brim of his hat, a gesture that usually meant a cowboy was buying some thinking time. "He'd have an easier time working with Linus if he could get out of that chair."

"I know. I thought he'd be motivated by Lucy's impending due date. Instead he seemed to get more depressed."

Rosie put her arm around Aria's shoulders and gave her a quick hug of support. "Linus is a handsome colt. Wait'll Josh gets a look at him. He won't be able to resist that sweet baby."

"He is handsome." Aria's throat tightened with gratitude. "Thank you both for making this possible. I didn't have a clue what I was getting into."

Rosie chuckled. "I could tell. I'm glad you went for the idea of boarding Lucy here."

"So am I," Herb said. "I haven't delivered a foal since I retired. That was a blast."

"You did a fabulous job, Herb. So did Brant."

"He has the touch," Herb said. "I knew that the first time I took him along on a call and watched him with a pregnant mare. Then he went nuts over the foal and he's been in love with the process ever since."

"So why didn't he become a vet like you?"

"I can't say for sure, but he never expressed any interest in the other parts of the job. He only wanted to come with me when a mare was foaling. Besides, he doesn't like being tied down, and a vet needs to live in one place and establish a practice."

"Yeah, that wouldn't fit Brant," Rosie said. "He likes to stay loose, take life as it comes."

The exact opposite of her, Aria thought. She required routine, stability and concrete goals. Her brother's uncertain future coupled with his lack of focus had worn her to a frazzle. "Thank goodness he was available today."

"It was meant to be." Rosie looked pleased with herself. "Did you get pictures? I didn't see you taking any."

"I didn't have my phone. I left my purse and my phone in the van and didn't even think about pictures until it was too late." And that was unlike her. She was usually a details person, but having Lucy go into labor early had thrown her off her game.

"That's okay. We all took some. We'll text them to you. That will light a fire under that Gloomy Gus of yours."

Aria smiled as she followed Rosie up the porch steps. Rosie's confidence boosted her own. "I'm sure you're right. By the way, are you going to let me cook tonight? I really want to, after all you've done today."

She'd discovered her passion for cooking through sharing meals with her best friend Camille's large Italian family. Her bank job allowed her to save money toward her goal of opening a cooking school. In the meantime she made deliveries for Camille's restaurant in exchange for using the kitchen to give classes on Monday nights. She lived for those classes.

Rosie paused before going inside. "You sure don't have to. I thawed some chicken and planned to bread and fry it like usual."

"Do you have mushrooms?"

"I think so. Yes, I'm pretty sure I do."

"I saw a package of mushrooms in the fridge," Herb said as he joined them on the porch.

"Okay, good. How about bacon and pearl onions?"

"I always have bacon, and I still have some pearl onions left over from the last time you cooked for us. What are you leading up to?"

"Coq au vin! It's one of my new specialties. I taught

the recipe to my cooking students last Monday night and everyone loved it."

"Coq au vin?" Herb's eyes widened. "Really?"

"Wait a minute," Rosie said. "I just remembered it's Friday night. What about your deliveries for Camille? Can you even stick around, let alone cook dinner?"

"Absolutely. I called her after I heard from you. For all I knew Lucy could have been in labor all night and I wasn't going to leave to make deliveries. Camille asked her sister to fill in for me." She let out a breath. "So I actually have the night off."

"What a concept," Herb said. "Nobody works harder than you."

"I don't mind. I like staying busy." Especially when going back to her apartment meant dealing with her brother. She'd optimistically encouraged him to move into a first-floor apartment in her complex so she'd be available for anything he needed during his recovery.

But instead of helping him get better, she was forced to watch him giving up. He'd found an IT job that allowed him to work from home and set his own hours, so theoretically he didn't need to learn to walk again.

"There's such a thing as being too busy," Rosie said. "Why not let us fix *you* dinner while you relax on the porch with a glass of something refreshing?"

"That's very sweet, but cooking is fun for me, and doing it for people I care about is even more fun. Your kitchen is one of my favorite places in the world, especially when everybody hangs out while I'm fixing the meal."

Herb looked at Rosie. "Then it looks like we'll be feasting on coq au vin tonight."

Aria saw a subtle message pass between them. "Is that a problem? I didn't think to ask if you hated it. I can make something else with the chicken. I don't have to—"

"We both love it," Rosie said. "We had it on our honeymoon in Jackson Hole at the fanciest restaurant we've been in before or since. I briefly considered trying to make it, but one look at the complicated recipe took care of that."

Aria began having misgivings. "Was it a five-star restaurant?"

"Probably." Herb chuckled. "There were no prices on the menu, so the bill was a bit of a shocker, but…" He shrugged and gave Rosie a fond glance. "It was worth it."

"Hey, slowpokes!" Brant opened the front door and came out holding two frosty champagne bottles with vapor coming from the uncorked necks. "We fed the cat and then I found these hiding in the rec room fridge with a bunch of their buddies. Looks like we're all champagned up for this occasion."

"I knew we'd be celebrating," Rosie said, "so I stocked in plenty."

"Excellent." Brant nodded in satisfaction. "So are we going to toast Linus or stand around gabbing all night?"

"I'm ready to toast." Lexi walked out on the porch, clutching four champagne flutes by the stems. Cade followed with two more.

Aria was charmed by their enthusiasm. Although she wished Josh had come with her, she couldn't predict his moods anymore and he might have been a sourpuss. Maybe it was just as well he'd stayed home. She took the flute Lexi handed her.

After everyone had glasses, Lexi turned to Brant. "Okay, do your thing." She moved over next to Aria. "Hold your flute next to mine and be amazed by the two-fisted pourer."

"Aw, shucks, Lexi." Brant ducked his head. "You'll make me blush."

Lexi snorted. "As if. You're too cool to blush."

"When you're right, you're right." Grinning, Brant lifted both bottles and filled their glasses without spilling a drop.

Cade rolled his eyes. "You are such a show-off, Ellison."

"Just honoring the lady's request for a demonstration of my unique skill." He turned the bottles upright with a flourish and glanced at Aria. "You're in charge of the toast, so make it good."

Aha. A challenge. Anticipation fizzed within her like the champagne bubbles in her glass. "Oh, I see. No pressure."

"None at all." He used the same dramatic pouring routine for Rosie and Herb. "Just be aware that some excellent toasts have been made on this porch, so the bar's pretty high." He winked at her before continuing over to Cade.

"Way to go, Ellison," Cade said. "Intimidate our special guest."

"I'm not intimidated." A task she could handle got her blood pumping, but Cade and Brant might not know that. She waited until everyone had champagne before raising her glass. "To everyone who's a part of Thunder Mountain Academy. Today a handsome colt named Linus became linked with its history and I thank you all for giving him that honor."

Cheers and whistles of approval followed. Before taking a sip, Aria looked over and caught Brant's smile. She was ridiculously pleased that he seemed to like her toast.

"Now that we all have champagne," Rosie said, "we should move this party into the kitchen. Aria's going to make coq au vin."

Brant's eyebrows lifted. "That sounds sexy and possibly illegal. I'm in."

"Down boy." Lexi patted his chest. "It's chicken cooked in wine."

"It's way more than that." Herb moved to the door and

held it open as they all trouped inside. "It's a dish fit for the gods."

Although Aria had faith in her cooking skills, she'd never put her work up against that of a highly paid chef. "I can't promise a dish fit for the gods. Your chef in Jackson Hole probably studied in Paris."

"What chef are we talking about?" Once they were in the kitchen Brant emptied the rest of the champagne into Rosie's and Lexi's glasses.

"The one who cooked their most memorable honeymoon dinner, which happened to be coq au vin," Aria said.

"No kidding? This is new information." Dropping the empty bottles into a recycling bin, Brant turned to Cade. "Do you remember hearing anything about this?"

"No, but they got married, so it stands to reason they'd have a honeymoon."

"Of course we had a honeymoon." Herb leaned against the kitchen counter. "Three days in Jackson Hole."

Cade nodded. "There you go. So, logically, you had honeymoon food, and it stands to reason it would be fancy and pricey."

"Huh." Brant polished off the last of his champagne. "I always figured honeymoon food would be booze and munchies."

Aria spoke without thinking. "Remind me never to go on a honeymoon with you." Then she realized what she'd said and felt her cheeks warm. When Cade grinned at her, she braced herself for some teasing.

But then he surprised her by turning to Brant. "I would never go on a honeymoon with you, either, Ellison."

Brant's deep laughter filled the kitchen. "And here I was all set to propose, bro. Way to shoot a guy down."

"Seriously, Aria." Cade gestured toward Brant with his champagne flute. "This guy may be able to double-fist a couple of champagne bottles, but after that, it's nothing but chips and peanuts. Maybe some cheese. He has no concept of honeymoon-worthy dining. Keep that in mind."

"I will."

Brant shrugged. "I like things to be simple and straightforward. Nothing wrong with that."

"There is if you're talking about that special time after the ceremony when you pull out all the stops," Cade said. "Obviously, Dad knew that." He set down his empty glass on the kitchen table. "But if we're going to continue this discussion, we need more bubbly and I know where to find it. Be right back."

"We can drop the subject of our honeymoon." Rosie opened the refrigerator and began pulling out ingredients. "It was a long time ago and I'm sure customs have changed."

"Have not!" Cade called out from the rec room.

Rosie chuckled. "He's really looking forward to having one, Lexi."

"I know. He probably will, eventually. Hey, Aria, Rosie and I can be your sous chefs, or whatever they're called."

"No, you can't." Brant put aside his empty glass. "You've both worked hard all day while I've been sitting on my butt driving. Allow me to help Aria. The rest of you have a seat. We've got this."

Cade walked back into the kitchen with an unopened bottle of champagne. "Did I hear that right? Is Ellison, the chips and peanuts king, going to help prepare this fancy dish?"

"I actually don't need anyone to help." Aria wasn't sure she'd be able to concentrate with Brant standing right next to her at the stove. Earlier she'd thought of him as a calming presence, but he wasn't having that effect on her now.

"I promise not to get in your way." His smile was endearingly genuine. "And I'm very good at taking direction."

"I'll vouch for that." Herb pulled out a chair for Rosie and motioned her over to it. "The guy knows how to listen."

"I reluctantly admit that's true," Cade said. "He may turn out to be good at this, after all. Mom, more champagne?"

"Love some." Rosie sat and allowed Cade to refill her glass. "If I'm not going to help cook, then maybe we should talk about what needs to be accomplished this weekend. I haven't allowed myself to think about that today because Linus took priority, but those kids will be here before we know it."

"Even more reason I should be the one to help, so you guys can discuss academy stuff." Brant turned to Aria, his expression hopeful. "Right?"

"Right." Dear God, what had she gotten herself into? First she'd offered to cook a dish that was loaded with significance for Rosie and Herb, and now she'd be working with a sexy cowboy. She relished a challenge, but this might be a bigger one than she'd anticipated.

The four people sitting at the table obviously assumed she had the meal under control. Herb rounded up a pen and pad of paper while Rosie began outlining the weekend's projects. Ringo snoozed in his bed tucked into a corner of the kitchen.

Aria glanced over at Brant.

He laced his fingers together and turned his palms out as he stretched both arms in front of him. Then he jogged in place. "Put me in coach. I'm ready to play."

She couldn't help laughing. "All right. While I prepare the onions, you can cut the bacon into one-inch pieces, cover the pieces with water and boil them." She pulled a saucepan out of the cupboard and handed it to him.

"I'm boiling the bacon." He sounded amused. "Can't say I've ever done that before."

"You're probably used to pan-frying it."

"To be honest, bacon isn't my long suit."

"Well, this part is easy. Once you have it cut up and in the pan of water, turn the heat to high. When it starts boiling, turn the heat to low and let it simmer for ten minutes."

"I can do that."

"So what's your long suit?"

"I'm a pretty fair hand with toast."

"I see." She wasn't sure how he could be funny and sexy at the same time, but he pulled it off.

"Okay, I'll come clean. I don't know anything about cooking."

"Then why did you volunteer to help me?"

"Because I want to get to know you better." He turned away and started cutting up the bacon as if he hadn't just dropped a conversational bombshell.

Her heart rate picked up. "Why?" Trying to be nonchalant, she filled another saucepan with water, set it on a burner and switched the heat to high.

"I'm about to work with your foal. I want him to suit you."

So maybe his gesture had been strictly business-related. "But actually he needs to suit my brother, not me."

"I suppose that's true. Then I'll try this answer on for size. You intrigue me."

"Oh?" Maybe his motives weren't strictly business-related. Maybe he was interested in her as a person. He even might be interested in her as a woman. She didn't need that kind of complication in her life, so why was her pulse racing?

"Is that other pan of water supposed to be boiling, too?"

Startled, she glanced at the bubbling water. "Yes. Yes, it is." She dumped the onions in. "How's that bacon coming along?"

"Just scooped the pieces into the water and turned on the heat. Am I good or what?" He did a little victory dance.

"Yes, you're amazing." Although he made her laugh, he was horribly distracting. At this rate she'd ruin the meal. "But you know what? I can handle it from here if you want to hang out with the others."

He grinned. "Trying to get rid of me?"

"No, of course not."

"Tell the truth, Aria."

She hesitated. But Lexi had claimed nothing bothered him. "I admit you're destroying my concentration."

"Damn. And here I promised not to get in your way."

"You're not getting in my way. It's my fault. I'm not paying attention to what I'm doing and that could be a problem, especially when I set fire to the brandy."

"You're going to set fire to it on purpose?"

"Yes, and I—"

"So this is one of those flaming dishes?"

"Yep."

"Hot damn. I've always wanted to see how that's done. Look, I won't make any attempt at conversation. I won't say a word unless it's required. I'll just stand here and do what I'm told. Can I stay?"

She couldn't very well admit that he could turn her brain to mush simply by his existence. She took great pride in her cooking. Sending him back to the table would be the smart thing to do. But that wasn't what came out of her mouth. "Sure."

"Thanks."

She prayed that she wouldn't burn down the house.

3

BRANT KNEW HE made Aria nervous, but backing off wouldn't solve the problem. So he'd moved in closer and joked around with her, which had worked better. He couldn't say for sure if her skittish behavior was a sexual thing, but he suspected she might be unwillingly attracted to him.

He was definitely interested in her, but he could dial that back if she wasn't in the market. A boyfriend didn't seem likely unless he wasn't in town. She'd put her heart and soul into Linus's birth so any guy worth her time would have been here for the event.

She could be hesitant to encourage a new relationship for any number of reasons, and he'd respect that. Her uptight attitude in the beginning had put him off a little, but after they'd shared a special moment while admiring the newborn colt, he'd found himself liking her, after all. He'd looked forward to being around her a little more. Then she'd proudly given her champagne toast.

He hadn't been prepared for the visceral punch of desire as she'd stood on the porch in her flirty little dress, glass raised and sincerity ringing in her voice. Despite not knowing her very well, he'd been swamped with lust.

He'd desperately wanted to kiss her. He'd wanted to do a lot more than that.

So he'd volunteered to help her fix the meal to see how she reacted to working closely with him. She'd admitted he was a distraction, which probably meant she was interested in him, too. But he couldn't shake the feeling that she was resisting that attraction.

If so, they should have a frank discussion about it. That little colt would pick up on either positive or negative tension between them and he wanted Aria to be part of the training process. That way she could continue using his methods after he'd left.

Ideally her brother would participate, but no telling how that would turn out. Aria already loved the colt. Brant had seen it in her eyes. If her brother lost interest, she would take full responsibility for Linus's welfare, which meant she needed to be included in the early stages of his socialization.

Right now, though, wasn't the time for that discussion. He didn't plan to talk at all unless necessary. Following her instructions, he cut up the mushrooms while she cooked the onions and bacon in a heavy skillet. He concentrated on being totally nonthreatening as they worked silently side-by-side.

Gradually her shoulders lowered and her breathing evened out. He matched that rhythm and she seemed to loosen up a little more. She was getting used to having him close by. She might not be flattered to discover he was using a horse training technique to settle her down, but she'd never hear that from him.

Unfortunately, watching a beautiful woman prepare food was like foreplay. Her breasts shifted gently beneath her flowered dress as she stirred the onions and bacon.

Heat from the skillet created a flush on her skin. Or maybe his presence did that.

If they'd been alone, he would have reached out to stroke a finger along the dewy curve of her cheek. He would have been able to judge where they stood from her reaction. But they weren't alone, which left him with an ache that wouldn't be satisfied now and might never be.

She was good at this cooking stuff, which probably explained her vanity plate. He'd never watched someone prepare a fancy dish like this, but Aria knew what she was doing.

Her obvious mastery impressed him and her calm instruction struck a chord. After all, that was how he worked. Under her watchful eye, he took the onions and bacon out of the pan and put them on a plate while she got the chicken ready.

"When the chicken's browned," she said, "that's when the flaming brandy comes into play."

"Do you mean brown like a buckskin or brown like a bay?" He'd spent all his adult life on ranches where someone else had done the cooking and he'd done the eating. Although he'd helped Rosie in the kitchen because she'd required all the boys to take a turn, she'd never attempted something this complicated. He found the process almost as fascinating as the cook.

"Somewhere in between those two. It'll take about ten minutes." She carefully flipped the pieces of chicken in the pan as she glanced over at him. "Do you want to pour the brandy or light it?"

His macho instincts kicked in. "Light it, of course. Even though I can't cook, I know my way around matches."

"I'll just bet you do. And we should probably warn everybody what's about to happen. They won't be expecting flames."

"I thought Rosie and Herb had this once before."

"They did, but the flaming part was probably done in the kitchen. Rosie might know because she checked out the recipe years ago, but I can picture Herb dousing it with the fire extinguisher."

Brant laughed. "That would be—" Then he caught Aria's thunderous expression. "Terrible. Absolutely terrible."

"Exactly." She met his gaze and gave him a sunny smile. "Why don't you tell them?"

"Okay." One look into those violet eyes and he was a goner. No point in fooling himself. He wanted her. But if she didn't want him, or did want him but wasn't happy about that, he'd recalibrate.

"I'd suggest you explain it to them now, though," she added. "We're minutes away."

"Right." He reluctantly stopped gazing into her eyes and walked over to the kitchen table.

Herb glanced up. "Don't tell me it's done already."

"Not yet." He realized he had incomplete info and turned back toward Aria. "How much longer before it's ready to eat?"

"After the flaming part, it needs to simmer at least another forty-five minutes."

Cade got out of his chair. "Then how about some more champagne and maybe some munchies?"

"Just don't spoil your appetite, hotshot." Brant had become protective of this meal prepared by a woman he admired. "The food will be primo."

"I have no doubt," Rosie said. "But cheese is very French." She left the table and in moments was back with a cutting board, a knife and a block of cheddar.

She offered some to Brant but he shook his head. "No, thanks. I'm saving my taste buds for the main event. But we're about to pour brandy over the chicken and light it. When flames shoot up, we don't want anybody to panic."

"Flames?" Herb straightened in his chair. "Is that absolutely necessary?"

"It is if you want the real deal," Aria called over.

"She's right." Rosie passed the cheese board around. "The torched brandy was the reason I never tried it. That's not in my repertoire."

Lexi stood. "I don't know about the rest of you, but I want to watch this flaming chicken trick."

"Me, too." Cade put down the champagne bottle he'd been about to open.

Herb scooted back his chair. "I should probably get the fire extinguisher."

"No, you will not." Rosie gave him a look. "Aria knows what she's doing."

"She absolutely does," Brant said. "She'll pour the brandy and I'll light it. Easy peasy."

Cade gazed at him. "You've done this before?"

"No, but how hard can it be?"

"Like I was saying." Herb headed for the pantry. "Nothing wrong with having the fire extinguisher handy."

Brant joined Aria at the stove while the rest of them gathered in a semicircle behind them. If his foster father tried to use the extinguisher, Brant was prepared to stop him. Whether Aria wanted one or not, she had a knight in shining armor. "Nothing like cooking with an audience, huh?"

She sprinkled some flour on the chicken and continued to turn it in the pan. "I do it once a week. My friend Camille lets me use her restaurant kitchen to give cooking classes every Monday night."

"No kidding? That's great." And it explained her teaching skills.

"Aria's a busy lady," Rosie said. "Works forty hours a week at the bank, teaches the class on Mondays and makes deliveries for Camille's restaurant on the weekend."

"Wow." Having her participate in Linus's training might not be easy to arrange. Maybe that explained her hesitation where he was concerned. She was too damned busy. "When do you have fun?"

"Having fun isn't a priority."

He noticed that she didn't sound resentful. Apparently she liked being under pressure, whereas he avoided it like the plague. He might want her, but they were a total mismatch. The next couple of weeks could be interesting.

She studied the pieces of chicken as they gradually turned a golden brown. "I'm ready to pour the brandy. Do you have the match?"

"Right here." He held up the long match he'd found in a can by the fireplace. "And some extras, although I won't need them."

"And something to strike it on?"

"I'll use my thumbnail." When she frowned at him he felt the need to defend the practice. "It's something my brothers and I taught ourselves when we lived here. I'm good at it. We all are."

"And let me add that I disapproved back then and I still do," Rosie said. "But they're convinced it makes them manly."

"Which it absolutely does," Brant said. "Whenever I strike a match with my thumbnail, I grow extra chest hair." He glanced over his shoulder at Cade. "Right, bro?"

"Yep, and my pecs get bigger, not to mention my—"

"That's enough," Rosie said. "We don't need to hear about that."

"I do," Lexi said. "I had no idea. Cade, strike those

matches any time you get the urge. I'll buy you a few extra boxes."

Brant laughed. "Let's just say that a cowboy who can strike a match with his thumbnail gets respect. Ask anyone." He paused. "Except Mom. She doesn't get it."

"Neither do I," Aria said. "But strike that match however you care to." She doused the chicken with brandy. "Just do it now."

Naturally the first match wouldn't cooperate. The second one wasn't any better. "Guess I'm out of practice. Hang on a sec—"

"Here you go." Herb appeared at his side with a butane lighter.

"Uh, no." Aria looked panicked. "Just a match, please."

"Then light the match with the butane," Herb said.

Brant hesitated. "Let me have one more try." From the corner of his eye he saw Cade smirking. There would be payback for this.

"Do it this way, son. The brandy's waiting."

"I guess you're right." He lit the match with the butane and eased it toward the chicken. The brandy caught with a whoosh and fire leaped from the frying pan.

Everyone gave a little gasp—everyone except Aria and Herb. She watched the flames with a smile of satisfaction.

Herb picked up the fire extinguisher. "Shouldn't you put the lid on the pan to smother that?"

"It'll burn down in a minute," Aria said.

Rosie gestured toward the flames. "See, Herb? This is why I never tried to make coq au vin."

"For which I'm grateful." He lowered the fire extinguisher as the fire gradually died.

Lexi stepped closer and peered into the frying pan. "That was cool."

"I like a little drama in my cooking. Keeps things interesting."

Brant filed that statement away as another clue to her personality. So far he'd pegged her as somewhat driven, a trait that he associated with his dad's workaholic behavior. But unlike his father, she wasn't a martyr. She'd found a creative outlet that gave her a joyful purpose.

That still didn't leave room for him to approach her other than as the owner of the foal he'd agreed to train. He hadn't come here expecting anything else. But he hadn't pictured working with Aria, either. She was damn near irresistible and he'd have to resist. Somehow.

"That's the showiest part." Aria added the cooked onions and bacon to the pan. Then she poured some red wine over everything.

"I was wondering where the wine came in," Lexi said. "Have you taught your students to make this?"

"Last Monday."

"I didn't realize a cooking class could be so exciting." Lexi turned to Cade. "How about you and me signing up for some classes?"

"Sure, I'm game."

"I'd love to have you." Aria sprinkled in some herbs and more wine. "But just so you know, there's no class this Monday. Camille always stays open on Memorial Day, so I'll be making deliveries for her." She put the lid on the frying pan. "That needs to simmer for about thirty minutes before I put in the mushrooms."

"Hallelujah! Time to head for the watering hole." Brant gestured toward the table. "After you, ma'am."

"You go ahead. I need to sauté the mushrooms."

"I'd offer to do it for you but sauté sounds like a square-dance move to me."

"I could do it," Lexi said, "but I hesitate to meddle with such an elaborate concoction."

Rosie nodded. "Same here."

"I'll be done in a few minutes." Aria dropped some butter into another frying pan.

Her comment had a familiar ring. His dad used to promise that the business call he had to make would only take a few minutes and then he'd be available to play catch, or go to a movie, or take a hike. Those promises had rarely panned out.

Maybe he should douse this flame of lust before it got him into trouble. "Your bubbly will be waiting for you." He picked up her champagne flute along with his and walked over to the table.

"'Bout time you showed up." Cade slid open a box of kitchen matches and dumped it in the middle of the table.

Rosie groaned. "Here we go."

"Brant Ellison?" Cade looked up, his green eyes sparkling.

"Dear God, you've gone senile. You don't recognize me anymore."

"I recognize you just fine, and I hereby challenge you to an official Battle of the Sacred Flame."

"A Battle of the Sacred Flame." Lexi grinned. "I haven't heard those fateful words in years. Takes me back."

"Doesn't it, though?" Rosie shook her head. "Ah, for the good old days filled with testosterone and the smell of sulfur. I'd love to know what bonehead started this activity but nobody will say."

As Brant sat at the table and reached for the champagne bottle, he avoided looking at Herb. Rumor had it that Herb had taught Cade how to light a match this way. Then Cade had taught Damon Harrison, the second boy to arrive, and so on. The trick had spread like…well, wildfire. "What's on the line?"

"I would say your reputation." Cade folded his arms and smiled. "But you obviously don't give a damn about that if you'd surrender to a butane lighter, so let's make it interesting. First guy who fails to light a match will wash the other guy's truck in the morning."

Brant thought of his mud-spattered vehicle. Old Bessie hadn't been near a hose and a bucket for at least a month. "Have you seen my truck?"

"Not up close, but it doesn't matter. Judging from your recent performance, you'll be washing my truck."

"And if it's a tie," Lexi said, "you can both wash *my* truck."

"My van could use a wash," Aria said as she stirred the mushrooms. "I planned on driving out here in the morning, anyway, so I can see Linus."

Brant perked up at that announcement. Logically she should have tomorrow morning free and he'd planned to ask her if she'd come to the ranch. Instead she'd volunteered to come back, so she was making the foal a priority. Good news for Linus.

"That works," Lexi said. "I'll share."

"I like this bet now." Rosie sipped her champagne. "Puts a different spin on things. Too bad Herb just washed our truck or I'd get in on it."

Herb leaned forward. "I won't tell you not to have this contest, but that's a full box. I'd advise you to set a limit on the number of matches per contestant. You can't be lighting matches while we eat."

"Might be sort of festive," Brant said. "Take a bite, light a match. Take a bite, light a match."

"Might be sort of stupid." Cade gazed across the table at him. "What do you think? Thirty?"

"Thirty it is." Brant dug a quarter out of his jeans pocket and flipped it in the air. "Call it."

"Heads."

"And it's tails, my friend. Which is a sign that my luck has turned." Brant counted out thirty matches and leaned back in his chair. "Light 'er up, loser."

"Wait." Aria hurried over to the table. "I want to see this Battle of the Sacred Flame."

"Then allow me to be your champion." Brant stood and pulled out her chair.

"Hang on." Cade paused, a match in his hand. "She only said she wanted to watch. She didn't say anything about making you her champion."

Brant shrugged. "Seems only right. You have a fair maiden rooting for you, so I should be able to—"

"I'm actually rooting for a tie," Lexi said. "I want my truck washed."

"That's my stake in this, too." Aria took her seat.

Oh, really? Brant reevaluated the situation. A woman who didn't want to have anything to do with a man wouldn't jump into a contest that might cause that man to wash her vehicle. Would she?

"Right on, girlfriend." Lexi exchanged a high-five with her.

Brant decided to go with it. "Looks like we're on our own, bro. No fair maidens cheering us on like in the good old days."

"Just as well. This won't take long." Cade leaned forward and locked his gaze with Brant's as he flicked the match with this thumbnail. It ignited. "And that's how it's done." He blew it out and tossed it on the plate he'd been using for cheese. "You're up."

Brant didn't care if he won or not. He never had cared. But early on he'd figured out that winning mattered to most guys, especially when it came to things like championship basketball games. So he'd pretended to be competitive as hell. Besides, Aria was sitting at the table, and while he didn't personally mind if he lost, winning might be better with her watching.

So he concentrated more than he would have normally and lit match after match. Cade kept pace with him and eventually they each had only one left. Brant held his up. "Let's go for the big finish. On the count of three, we'll both light our match...or not."

"Just so you both end up with the same result," Lexi said.

"My thoughts exactly." Aria finished off her champagne. "Matilda is filthy."

Brant glanced away from the match in his hand. "You named your van?"

"Yep. I always name my ride."

"Me, too." He liked knowing they had that in common. Somehow there had been a subtle shift and Aria was no longer quite so resistant to...what? He wasn't sure, but the situation was more promising than it had been.

"Are you counting or conversing?" Cade waved his match in the air.

"Counting." Brant dragged out the process because at this stage of the game dignity was gone, anyway. On three he scratched the head of the match with his thumbnail. Nothing. He looked over at Cade.

His brother held an unlit match and had a goofy smile on his face. He tossed his match on the table. "Looks as if we'll be washing vehicles for the ladies." He didn't seem particularly upset about it, either. Brant had the distinct impression Cade hadn't tried to light his match.

"Excellent!" Aria clapped her hands together. "How early do you want me here?"

"Early." He couldn't remember when he'd anticipated anything more. Between washing Aria's van and working with her foal, he'd spend the bulk of his morning with her. He wondered if Cade had figured that out and had decided to play Cupid.

"Everybody be sure to forward your pictures to my phone," Aria said. "I'm going to show them to Josh so I can convince him to come with me."

"Yeah, I hope he does," Brant said immediately. He'd forgotten about her brother, and he couldn't let himself do that.

Linus was supposed to be Josh's colt and if a wheelchair would be part of the mix, that should be introduced early. Yeah, the prospect of seeing her tomorrow had lost a little of its shine because Josh might be there. So what? He'd comfort himself by picturing how happy she'd be if Josh fell in love with the foal the way she had.

4

ARIA PRESENTED THE meal in the traditional way, placing the skillet in the middle of the table on a hot pad. Once she'd served everyone, Rosie raised her glass. "To Aria."

"To Aria!" everyone chorused.

She believed it was good, but their expectations were high thanks to Herb's extravagant comments. "Maybe you should taste it first."

"Don't have to," Herb said. "It looks and smells exactly like what we had on our honeymoon."

"Must have been quite a meal," Brant said. "I can't remember what I ate yesterday, let alone years ago."

"Because you don't seek out gourmet food." Cade waved a hand toward his plate. "Aria's cooking classes are gonna turn Lexi and me into adventurous eaters. We'll set stuff on fire and everything."

"Sometimes even on purpose," Lexi said.

"You're all welcome to talk about food for as long as you like, but I'm ready to eat it." Herb took a bite of his chicken.

Aria held her breath as Herb closed his eyes and made a little sound of pleasure deep in his throat. At least she hoped it was pleasure and not distress. Come to think of it, those sounds might be similar.

He chewed and swallowed. Then he looked at her and smiled. "Absolutely delicious, even better than I remembered. Thank you."

"You're welcome." She relaxed and picked up her fork. As everyone else dug in, she was bombarded with praise. The meal was a hit.

When Ringo sat expectantly beside his bowl, Cade put a small bite of chicken in it. After a curious sniff, the cat polished it off and fixed Cade with a demanding stare. "That's all you get, buddy," Cade said. "I'm being selfish tonight."

Aria considered that high praise. During the months she'd been visiting her mare and sharing meals with the family she'd noticed that Cade normally shared generously with his cat.

Herb glanced over at Rosie. "This tastes so much like the meal we had in Jackson Hole that I feel as if I'm on my honeymoon again."

"Uh-oh." Brant looked at Cade and lifted his eyebrows. "Maybe we should all clear out of here after dinner, hmm?"

"Sounds like it to me."

Rosie blushed bright red. "Oh, for pity's sake. Nobody has to run off."

"It's fine with me if they go home early." Herb's eyes twinkled.

"Herbert!" Rosie hid her face in her napkin.

Aria had never seen anything so adorable. "I should make this for you two more often."

"Just warn me when you do," Cade said, "so I don't accidentally drop by some evening and find them making out on the sofa."

"Stop!" Rosie waved her napkin in the air. "Just stop!"

"Speaking of interrupting things," Brant said. "I should probably sleep in my old cabin tonight. I figured Rosie would put me in one of the guest rooms, but under the circumstances…"

Rosie groaned. "This has gotten so out of hand." She turned to her husband. "And it's your fault."

He looked unrepentant. "I know."

"Ellison, you don't have to settle for your old cabin," Cade said. "I've decided to offer you my new one."

"You have a new one?"

"Yes," Lexi said, "because he's very important."

Cade grinned at her. "Yes, I am. Because I'm the guy supervising the students after hours, I now have my own cabin on the property within walking distance of what are now the student cabins. You can have my place while you're here and I'll stay at Lexi's."

Brant folded his arms across his chest. "And who's supposed to ride herd on these teenagers while you're kicking back in Lexi's apartment?"

Cade pretended surprise. "You know, I hadn't thought of that!"

"Uh-huh."

"I guess it would be you." Cade's attempt to look innocent failed completely when he started to laugh. "Is that a problem?"

"Hell, no. I can sleep through anything. Enjoy your mini-vacation."

"They won't act up," Rosie said. "You've never quite understood how much your size intimidates people who don't know you."

Brant laughed. "Are you saying I'm scary?"

"Don't knock it," Cade said. "Last semester's kids were pretty good, but they tested me. You look like a nightclub bouncer. Once they meet you, they'll behave."

"I'm not crazy about playing the role of enforcer, but

if it helps you out, brother of mine, I'll do it. Is this cabin within walking distance of the bathhouse?"

"No need. It has plumbing."

"Why didn't you say that in the first place? For a cabin with plumbing I'll gladly flex my muscles and look forbidding."

"Thought so."

"But I trust you didn't mess with tradition and install plumbing in the old cabins."

"Of course they didn't," Lexi said. "I think it's ridiculous, but the guys all insist that walking to the bathhouse in the dead of winter builds character."

Aria made a face. "And did all sixteen students from last semester agree?"

"Most did," Cade said. "We had a couple of whiney pants in the beginning, but peer pressure is a wonderful thing. After the first week the spoiled babies realized they were losing points with the others and shut up about it."

Lexi skewered him with a glance. "If trudging to the bathhouse is such a character-builder, how come you have a full bath with a tub and shower, *plus* a towel warmer and a heat lamp?"

"Oh, man." Brant shook his head. "You're getting soft, Gallagher. I'll take the high road and not use those particular amenities while I'm here."

"It's almost June, bozo. You don't need them in the summer. Besides, those extras aren't for me. They're for Lexi when she stays over."

"Oh, no, they're for him," Lexi said. "I made some surprise visits this past winter and if I happened to catch him in the shower, he'd have them both cooking."

"Just testing them out to make sure they were up and running for you, sweetheart." Cade pushed back his chair. "And now that we've taken that subject and stomped it to death, let's clean up these dishes so I can escort Brant over to the cabin he'll call home."

"I need to scoot on down to the barn and check on Linus and Lucy." Herb glanced over at Rosie. "Shouldn't be long." Then he winked at her and left the kitchen.

"Ooo-wee!" Lexi gave Rosie a thumbs-up. "Your man is feeling frisky tonight!"

Rosie seemed genuinely flustered. "I had no idea coq au vin would have such an effect on him."

"Want to learn how to make it yourself?" Aria picked up the empty skillet and carried it to the sink. The meal had turned out better than she could have imagined. Thank goodness she'd suggested it, even if the evening had created complications regarding one Brant Ellison. She'd let down her guard and now she'd have to deal with the consequences.

"You know, maybe I should." Rosie's color was still high, but there was a gleam of anticipation in her blue eyes. She looked years younger.

With extra motivation to get the job done, everyone had the kitchen shipshape in no time. Giving Rosie hugs, they all left the house and headed for the barn. Ringo was on mice duty every night, so he trotted along beside Cade.

They met Herb on his way back. "Both mama and baby are doing fine," he said. "Linus is fast asleep and Lucy's dozing."

"Would it be okay to look in on them?" Aria didn't want to leave without seeing them one more time.

"Sure thing."

"Thank you, Herb, for all you've done." Aria gave him a hug.

Herb hugged her back. "You're more than welcome. That meal was amazing."

"Rosie wants to learn how to make it." She considered that a professional victory.

He looked surprised. "She does? Even with the flaming brandy?"

"She does," Lexi said. "I heard her say it. Listen, I have an idea. Since we all loved it so much, how about a private lesson here at the ranch? I'm thinking this coming Tuesday night if you're available, Aria. On Wednesday the students will arrive, so it's now or never."

Aria nodded, happy that her cooking skills were valued. "I could absolutely do that."

"Great! Just figure out what you need to charge us and we'll divide up the—"

"Hey, I wouldn't dream of charging you guys. If you decide to take my regular lessons on Monday nights, I'll accept payment for that. But this is special. You were all here for Linus. Let me give something back."

"That's very generous of you," Herb said. "After all Rosie and I have been through lately, I'm getting much better at accepting the generosity of others. Thank you."

She smiled at him. "Then it's settled. Tuesday night it is."

"I look forward to it. And on that note, I'll bid you all good-night." Herb set off toward the house, his pace brisk.

Lexi sighed as the four of them continued on toward the barn. "They're still in love after all these years. That's inspiring."

"Yeah." Cade wrapped an arm around her shoulders.

"Apparently the coq au vin was inspiring, too." Brant fell into step beside Aria. "Good job."

"Just a lucky coincidence. When I suggested fixing it tonight I had no idea I'd stir up honeymoon memories. But that's the thing about food. There's often an emotional connection to it."

"You're right," Lexi said. "Assuming I learn how to make it, I'll always think of Linus being born and all of us enjoying a great meal together afterward."

"Me, too." Cade gestured toward Brant's truck. "And I'll remember our epic Battle of the Sacred Flame. Too bad you didn't win, though, Ellison. That sucker needs a wash bad."

"You know what? I like it that way. The mud covers up the dents and scratches. Besides, I'd rather wash a pretty red van named Matilda any day."

Cade laughed. "I figured."

Aria tingled with awareness. Brant was flirting and Cade had just acknowledged it. She liked feeling sexy and carefree for a change. Ever since Josh's accident she'd focused most of her attention on his recovery, and the process hadn't been a lot of laughs. But guilt followed soon after with thoughts about Josh. How could she enjoy herself when he was stuck in that wheelchair?

"Since my truck's parked at the cabin," Cade said, "I planned to hitch a ride over there with Brant and then drive back and pick up Lex." He looked at her. "Unless you want to come along?"

"I'd rather stay with Aria and check out the baby."

"I thought as much. I'll take a quick look when I get back."

Aria turned to Brant. "I should say good-night. You'll probably want to turn in."

"Not yet. After I dump my stuff in the cabin, I need to see how mama and baby are doing. I'll ride back with Cade."

"Then we shall return, ladies." Cade gave Lexi a quick kiss before climbing into Brant's truck.

"Cade's a great guy," Aria said as she and Lexi started toward the barn.

"He is a great guy and I love him to death, but I want to make absolutely sure we're ready before we take the big step. It's a huge commitment."

"Definitely."

"I didn't realize that at twenty, but I do now." She slid aside the bar holding the doors closed and swung open the right-hand side. Ringo dashed through it. "Plus Damon and Philomena are getting married at the end of this month. That's enough wedding hoopla for the time being."

"Their relationship seems solid." Aria followed Lexi into the dimly lit barn. Damon and Phil had fallen in love last summer while working together to build a fourth cabin for the students. They were bank customers, and every time she saw them together they looked very happy.

"They're perfect for each other," Lexi said. "Cade and I are, too, but our relationship still needs some seasoning."

"I can't even think in terms of marriage right now." Aria lowered her voice as they drew closer to the back of the barn so she wouldn't disturb the mare and foal. "There's Josh to think about in the immediate future, and once he's better, I'll concentrate on getting my cooking school up and running. That'll take years."

"I understand." Lexi kept her voice down, too. "I built my riding clinic business myself, and you get really protective after putting in all that time and effort. Any guy you're involved with has to realize that you won't be the little wifey who caters to his every whim."

"Does Cade expect that?"

"Not really. Once in a while he'll say something that comes from outdated thinking. But I'm tough to please. I've been making my own decisions for quite a few years."

Aria nodded. "I'm pretty much the same. I know what I want and I'm not looking for some guy to provide it. On the other hand…"

"Brant Ellison is pretty to look at?"

"Yeah." Aria glanced over at Lexi and smiled. "Yeah, he is."

They both stopped talking as they reached the birthing stall. Standing side-by-side, they gazed silently at the newborn curled up beside his mother. Aria felt a tug of love so strong it was almost painful. Surely, Josh would soften once he met this little guy.

Lucy's head was up but her eyes were closed. When Aria turned sixteen and was allowed to have her own horse, she'd chosen the mare for her golden coat. Dramatic color had been important to her at that age, but Lucy was a great deal more than a beautiful horse. Gentle and sweet, she'd become a cherished companion.

Three years ago Aria's mom and dad had sold their small ranch and moved to Texas, which had meant boarding Lucy. Aria had vowed that someday she'd buy horse property and have both Lucy and her cooking school on site. Maybe Linus, too.

"I hear Cade's truck," Lexi murmured.

Male laughter drifted in through the open barn door, but once inside, the guys toned it down. They even managed to walk quietly on the wooden floor, which had to take skill since they were wearing boots.

As they drew closer, Aria and Lexi moved away from the stall door and motioned them forward. Aria was blessed with a tantalizing view of Brant's wide shoulders and tight buns. He had the slight bow-legged stance of most cowboys who spent time on horseback, and Aria found that endearing.

Lexi was right—he was pretty to look at. Feelings she hadn't entertained for quite a while warmed her. Even if nothing could come of those feelings, she was glad to know they weren't hopelessly buried.

The men stepped back from the stall door and gestured for Aria and Lexi to walk out ahead of them. Aria held up her hand so she could go over for one last look.

"Lexi and I will just head out, then," Cade murmured.

She wondered if Brant would go with them, but instead he joined her at the stall door. They stood very still, not quite touching, but she inhaled his earthy, masculine scent with pleasure. No designer fragrance for this guy.

Desire uncurled and stretched within her, creating a sweet ache that made her shift her position. She accidentally brushed against him. "Sorry."

"No worries." His low voice worked as effectively as a caress.

As heat shot through her body, she shivered.

"Cold?"

"A little," she lied.

"Let's go."

She nodded and walked beside him down the wooden aisle. The air seemed to crackle between them, but maybe she was the only one who could feel it. She wished he would take her hand. No, she really didn't. That would be the beginning of something she shouldn't want.

He chuckled softly.

"What?"

"I thought they'd be gone by now, but apparently they're having a little tiff."

She'd been concentrating so hard on Brant that she'd missed the sound of voices. The argument didn't sound serious, though. Lexi and Cade were both laughing.

"Okay, here's the guy who can settle this," Cade said when they walked outside.

"Settle what?" Brant closed the door and slid the bar across.

"Lexi seems to think washing her truck includes detailing it. I don't recall a word about detailing, do you?"

Brant gazed at him with a smile. "I was planning to detail Aria's van. Otherwise it's not a complete job, and I know how you hate doing something half-assed."

"Ah, I see how things are." Cade clapped him on the shoulder. "Okay. I guess keeping the women happy is worth it."

Lexi glanced at Aria. "Like that remark, for instance."

"Oh." She pressed her lips together to keep from laughing.

"What remark? I was only—"

"Quit while you're ahead, bro," Brant said. "Although I think you might be behind. In any event, you need to shut the hell up."

"Listen to your brother." Lexi linked her arm through Cade's. "Let's call it a night, shall we?"

"All righty." Cade touched the brim of his hat. "Good night, all. See you in the mornin'."

As they drove away, Brant started laughing. "I swear to God, if he doesn't quit making those bonehead comments, Lexi's never gonna propose. 'Keeping the women happy.' What a moronic thing to say."

"Lexi's supposed to propose to him?"

"Yep. Last summer he popped the question a few days after he'd come back to town. It was way too soon. After she turned him down, he decided she'd better choose the timing. At this rate they might tie the knot in their golden years."

"She's an independent woman."

"Which is the best kind, in my opinion." Brant nudged back his Stetson. "Speaking of that, on the way over to the cabin Cade told me you plan to open a cooking school."

"Eventually." The glow of the barn's dusk-to-dawn light

gave her a better chance to admire his handsome self. Coming upon Cade and Lexi had momentarily interrupted the buzz she'd had going on, but once she looked at him she got it back.

"So that's why you're working so hard."

"It is, although I've become sidetracked with Josh's accident."

"I'm sure." His gaze warmed. "It's a generous thing you're doing for him."

She shrugged. "He's my brother. Anyone would do the same."

"Not necessarily." He shoved his hands into his pockets. "I'm trying to say I admire you, and making a poor job of it."

Her heartbeat sped up. "Thank you."

"Let me make it a little plainer." He looked into her eyes. "I like you."

"I like you, too." She swallowed. "Quite a bit."

"I had a hunch. So…?"

"We should probably leave it at that." Damn it.

"Why?"

"I'm really busy."

"Okay." He sounded skeptical.

"I don't blame you for questioning that tired old excuse. Plenty of busy people find the time to indulge in…stuff." Her cheeks grew warm.

"So I've heard." His lazy smile ramped up his sex appeal several more notches.

"But there's also Josh to think about."

"I'm not following you."

"He's stuck in a wheelchair with not much of a life. Working to change that has to be my focus."

"Ah." He rocked back on his heels. "And indulging in

stuff with me might cause you to forget about Josh's situation."

"Yes." Guaranteed. Just talking about indulging in *stuff* with this gorgeous cowboy had short-circuited her brain.

"Temporarily, anyway."

"Right but—"

"Is that such a bad idea?"

"You're suggesting I need a break."

He shrugged. "Only you know if that's true."

"I hadn't thought about it that way." Her pulse began to race.

"We could try a kiss and see how that works out."

She could barely breathe. This was the moment that would either stop him dead in his tracks or invite him to go further. Although she shouldn't, she yearned for Option Two. Someday she might regret this, but she wanted him so much. "I suppose we could."

Slowly he took his hands out of his pockets and stepped closer, his breathing uneven. "You get to me."

Excitement coursed through her. "You get to me, too."

He cradled her face in his big hands and looked into her eyes. "One kiss. Just enough to see if we suit."

She slid both palms up the soft, warm material of his shirt and felt the rapid thump of his heart. "Maybe we won't."

"I'm guessing we will." Angling his head, he settled his mouth over hers.

5

IMMEDIATELY BRANT KNEW he was in trouble. One kiss from
Aria would make him want a hundred. But he'd announced
that he'd only claim one, so he'd better make it count.

He started slowly, learning the contours of her lips as he
listened to her breathing change. When he connected more
fully and began to explore the sweet depths of her mouth
with his tongue, she moaned and curled her fingers into
the fabric of his shirt. That moan traveled straight through
him, firing his blood and sending it south.

He desperately wanted her lush body pressed tight
against his rigid cock. But that would lead to more than
they'd bargained for. He thought they'd get there eventually, but not tonight.

Savoring Aria's plump lips would feel like a party no
matter what, but the flavor of champagne added to the celebration. She cooperated with each move he made, giving
him access to every delicious part of her mouth. She obviously liked kissing him and, oh, man, did he like kissing her.

He was so involved in the sensuous feel of her tongue
sliding against his that he almost missed the fact that she'd
wound her arms around his neck. He didn't miss her next

maneuver, though. When she molded her hot body to his, it was like touching a match to brandy.

If this was a test of his restraint, he was failing miserably. Before he realized it, he'd cupped her bottom and pulled her hard against his straining erection. He'd meant for their kiss to be subtle and classy. Somehow it had morphed into a demonstration of primal lust.

Ah, but how encouraging that she wanted him. He didn't need more than that to figure out the next step. Consoling himself that there would be a next step, he slowly ended the kiss and lifted his head. A breeze ruffling his hair indicated his hat was now on the ground. Small matter.

He gazed down at her, and slowly she lifted her lashes to reveal eyes darkened with the same urgency he felt. He took a shaky breath. "I need to stop while I still can."

His comment seemed to take a while to penetrate, but at last she gave him a slight nod. "Me, too."

"Were you about to take advantage of me?"

"I thought about it. Would you have gone willingly?"

"Probably, God help me. You pack a punch."

"You, too."

Looking into her eyes, he fought the urge to start kissing her again. Not tonight. "But you need to get home and talk to your brother about tomorrow."

"I do."

"It's lucky that you'll have your next three days free so you can hang out with Linus."

"Yes, but the restaurant will be busy over the holiday weekend, so my nights…"

"You have a full schedule."

"Unfortunately." She reached up and traced his mouth with her finger. "But you'd think I could make room for a top-notch kisser."

"I surely hope so, because if you liked that kiss, you're gonna love the rest of the program."

"Can you make me float in the air?"

"You bet."

She smiled, but then her expression turned serious. "It's just that I'm not sure of the logistics."

"Usually folks start by taking their clothes off— at least I've found that it works better that way. But the floating part is a professional secret and I'm honor-bound not to reveal it." He was gratified when her smile reappeared.

"I meant the logistics of when we'd get together."

"I know. I just saw you getting serious all of a sudden, as if you needed to plan it all out. You don't. Let's see how it goes."

"I want to spend time with you. But it's complicated."

"No worries." As much as he wanted her, he wasn't going to push. "If it's supposed to happen then it will."

She gazed up at him. "You really do take life as it comes, don't you?"

"Yes, ma'am." He wondered if she had the power to mess with his usual approach. He combed her hair back from her face. "And now, much as I hate to do it, it's time to say good-night."

She sighed. "Okay."

After scooping up his hat, he draped his arm lightly over her shoulders and walked her to her van.

As he opened the door for her, she turned to him. "I don't want to leave."

He searched her expression and found desire mixed with confusion. For one brief moment he imagined tipping the scales in his favor and asking her to stay. She might do it, and then she'd miss her chance to convince Josh he needed to visit Linus.

So he didn't say anything.

"But I have to."

"See, you won't forget about your brother. It's not in your nature."

"I can't forget about him. Nobody understands him as well as I do, not even Mom and Dad."

"Then go."

She accepted his outstretched hand and stepped into the van, then gave him a sad smile. "In spite of needing to talk with Josh, I was sort of hoping you'd beg me to stay."

"Don't think I didn't consider it."

"But that's not you."

"Not normally, no." The fact that he'd even thought about it was significant, though. "You've done all this to help Josh. I don't want to sabotage your efforts."

She studied him for several seconds. "I'll figure something out for us."

The determination in her voice made him smile. It also gave him hope. He had a feeling she followed through on whatever she'd set her mind to.

"Good night, Brant."

"Good night, Aria." He closed her door, which created something of a separation between them although her window was open. He could have reached in to touch her. Instead he patted the van. "Take her home safely, Matilda."

"You remembered her name."

"Yeah, well, I was the goofy kid who named his rubber snake Elmer."

"What's your truck's name?"

"Bessie, after my grandmother. I never knew her, but I'll bet she was reliable like my truck."

"That's sweet."

"I'm a sweet guy."

"I have no doubt." She put the van in gear.

He stepped back and watched until she reached the

curve that would take her out of sight. He didn't know if she was looking in her rearview mirror or not, but he lifted his hand to wave goodbye. She blinked her lights.

He continued to think about her as he walked through the cool night toward Cade's cabin. He hadn't counted on meeting a beautiful woman today, let alone sharing a hot kiss with her. But he understood her feelings of guilt whenever she started thinking of herself instead of Josh. He didn't want to add to her burden so he'd back off if necessary.

But judging from her words, she wouldn't let him back off. Oh, yeah, he could imagine how much fun they could have in a bed, but he wouldn't push her into something that would cause her stress. He'd go with the flow, as he always did.

HE WAS WORKING in the barn early the next morning when he heard her drive up. After telling himself to go with the flow last night, he discovered that his breathing was suddenly affected by the prospect of seeing her again. He pulled in air and let it out slowly.

That he was here waiting for her was another troubling sign that he wasn't as cool as he pretended. Rosie had tried to talk him into having a big breakfast up at the house with Herb, Lexi and Cade, but instead he'd grabbed coffee and toast so he could be down here when Aria arrived.

He'd told himself that he needed more interaction with the mare and foal before Aria showed up. That was true to a point, but he'd seen the look that had passed between Rosie and Lexi. Cade had grinned at him in a knowing way, too.

No wonder they weren't buying his story. Food was important to him, and passing up one of Rosie's excellent ranch breakfasts so he could wait for a woman was totally out of character. As he walked out to meet Aria he saw that she'd come alone. He berated himself for being glad about it. Spending a good part of the day at the ranch without Josh wouldn't move her any closer to her objective.

But you might get another chance to kiss her. And that was all he could think about as he rounded the van to the driver's side and helped her out. Her hand was as silky-soft as he remembered, and her scent teased him with the possibilities he'd dreamed of while he'd slept.

She wore sunglasses, which was probably just as well. If he couldn't see into her eyes he might not be so tempted to kiss her. Besides, after last night's supercharged encounter he didn't trust himself to keep things PG-rated, and now was not the time or place.

"As you can see, Josh didn't come." Her smile was tight and the tension he remembered from their first meeting was back.

"His loss."

"I know. I just wish…"

"Do you mind if I ask how he was injured?"

"He was riding in an eventing competition and a jump went bad."

He winced. "Eventing is a dangerous sport. People and horses die going over those hurdles."

"I know. We used to do much tamer cross-country riding competitions as teenagers. But Josh craved a bigger challenge. I think he became an adrenaline junkie and paid the price."

"I'm sorry. That sucks." He hesitated. "And the horse?"

"By some miracle Pegasus wasn't seriously injured."

"Thank God for that, at least."

"It could have been so much worse. When my folks visited last month they told Josh he was lucky, but he didn't want to hear it. They offered to move him down to Texas and find him a different physical therapist, but he refused. I think he gave up when he realized his eventing days were over. That's when he stopped going to physical therapy. And he sold Pegasus."

Brant winced. "Too bad." He pitied the animal. After years of devoted companionship, Pegasus had been shipped away.

"I tried to talk him out of it, but his horse represented a lifestyle that was gone forever."

He let out a breath. Hearing about such situations always tested his resolve to stay positive. "I can see why you wanted to breed Lucy and give him something new and exciting to think about. A foal is not the same as the horse he rode in competition."

"That was my reasoning. The thing is, I'm desperate. I feel as if I've lost my brother and I want him back. You're about the same age. Did you know him in high school?"

"Not really. I think we had a couple of classes together but he had his crowd and I had mine."

"You were with the Thunder Mountain boys. As I recall, they were a unit."

"Yeah, we did tend to stick together. Probably didn't mingle as much as we should have." He searched his memory to dredge up something for her sake. "But I seem to remember your brother was a pretty happy guy."

"He was, and that's what I want to see again. Somehow."

If Josh had stopped going to therapy then Brant had less hope for him. But he wouldn't say that to her. "I'll do what I can to make the training smooth for both Josh and Linus."

"I know you will. I never thought to ask how long it generally takes."

"Anywhere from one week to several. It's impossible to predict, but I've never tried teaching a foal to be comfortable around a wheelchair. That'll be an interesting challenge, something new. I look forward to it." He chose his words with care. She was already jacked up about the situation so he didn't want her to worry that the wheelchair would be a stumbling block.

"And the sooner we get started on that, the better, right?"

"Right."

"I'm determined to bring Josh out here tomorrow, then."

"Well, sooner is better, but I wouldn't force it. We don't need someone hanging around who doesn't want to be here. Horses, even very young ones like Linus, pick up on that."

"Understood."

"Eventually he'll come around." On impulse he gave her shoulder a light squeeze. He let go immediately, though.

"You're probably right." Her voice sounded breathy.

"Curiosity will get the best of Josh." He was a little short of breath, too. Touching her aroused all the emotions he'd felt the night before. He'd have to watch himself today because she looked more beautiful than ever.

She'd put her dark hair in a single braid down her back, which made him want to undo it. Her jeans, purple T-shirt and boots reminded him that she was an accomplished rider as well as a talented cook. He noticed a Western hat sitting on the passenger seat.

He couldn't remember the last time he'd gone for a pleasure ride, one that involved a blanket on the ground and making love to a beautiful woman in the great outdoors. They didn't have time now, but that didn't stop him from fantasizing. He liked sunset rides best, but she'd be delivering meals for the restaurant by then.

"I've promised myself to make better use of this today." She held up her phone. "The still pictures might not be dynamic enough for Josh to grasp how adorable Linus is, so I'll take some videos, too."

"Good idea." But he was growing impatient with her brother. She'd put a lot of effort into her plan and Josh should get his ass out here and at least take a look. "You'll have a chance for some great stuff. Once Lucy finishes breakfast, we'll head on out to the pasture."

"Really?" Her delighted laughter chased away the last evidence of tension in her expression.

"I wouldn't kid about a thing like that."

She smiled at him. "No, you wouldn't."

He longed to reach for her, but instead he leaned into the van and snagged her hat. "You'll need this."

"Thanks." She took off her sunglasses, tossed them on the seat and closed the door. Then she settled the hat on her head. Instant sexy cowgirl. She glanced up at him, anticipation glowing in her eyes. "Let's go."

Somehow he managed to stop looking at her long enough to put his feet in motion. No doubt about it, he was hooked on her, and they'd only met yesterday. He wasn't sure what to make of that.

If she was aware of his infatuation, she didn't let on as they walked into the barn. "I'm excited that we'll be taking him out today. I thought he might have to stay inside a little longer."

"Only if the weather had been nasty. But it's gorgeous." *Like you.* He'd almost said that out loud. Talk about cheesy compliments. "Cade and I already turned the other horses out in the far pasture, but we kept these two in the barn. We figured you should be here for Linus's big moment."

"Thank goodness you waited for me. I would have been crushed if I'd missed this."

"I wouldn't have let that happen." Okay, he was grandstanding a little, but it was true. Nobody at the ranch would have allowed Aria to miss watching Linus experience his first time outside.

"How about Rosie and Herb? Will they come and watch?"

"You couldn't keep them away. A foal's first day in the pasture is special. Lexi and Cade are up at the house having breakfast with them, so they'll all come down in a bit." And he'd text them so they'd know she was here.

But not yet. He didn't foresee a lot of opportunities to be alone with her unless he created them. He wanted to savor their privacy for a little while longer.

"Brant, can I ask a favor?" She paused and turned to him.

"Sure." He stopped walking.

Taking off her hat, she stepped toward him. "Would you please kiss me?"

With a groan he swept her up in his arms so fast she squeaked in surprise and his hat fell off...again. His mouth found hers and he thrust his tongue deep. His hands slid unerringly to her sweet ass and when he lifted her up, she gave a little hop and wrapped her legs around his hips.

Dear God, it felt good to wedge himself between her thighs. He continued to devour her mouth and she gave as good as she got, parrying each thrust of his tongue with one of her own. Her little whimpers of need drove him beyond reason.

Backing her up against an empty stall, he supported her with one forearm while he reached beneath her shirt and cupped her breast. She arched into his caress with a soft moan.

He pressed his aching cock between her thighs. So damn good. Wrenching his mouth from hers, he gasped for breath. "I swear I could take you right here."

Her eyes glittered. "And I'd let you."

"We can't." But he found the front catch of her bra and flipped it open.

"I *know.*" Her fingers dug into his shoulders as he stroked her breasts. She swept her tongue over her moist lips. "I've… I've been…thinking."

"Good." He sucked in more air as he brushed his thumb over her erect nipple. "I can't think at all right now. All I want to do is—"

"Me, too." She closed her eyes and shivered. "That feels so good."

"Aria, *when*?"

"Tonight, after I'm finished with deliveries."

"You'll call me? Because I can be at your apartment in—"

"I'll come over."

"Oh, thank God."

"Leave your door unlocked."

"I won't be asleep." He couldn't imagine falling asleep when he knew she'd show up.

"Maybe not, but…go to bed. I could be late."

"And I could be naked."

She smiled. "Saves time."

"I'm all for that. Okay, one more for the road." He delved into her luscious mouth and feasted for as long as he dared. But they were taking an enormous chance that someone would come into the barn, so he eased her back to her feet. "Someone's probably noticed your van by now. They'll wonder."

"Will they really?"

He looked into her eyes. "No. I skipped breakfast so I could be down here when you drove in. And I never skip breakfast. As they say in poker, that was a tell."

She reached under her shirt and fastened her bra. "I

thought you were the cool guy who never let anything rattle him."

He watched her breasts shift under the purple material and another jolt of lust shot through him. "Yeah, I thought so, too."

6

ARIA MADE A quick trip to her van and repaired her lipstick while Brant texted Rosie. She was a little shocked by her forward behavior but not the least bit sorry. She was used to guys who latched on to every opportunity to get physical, but Brant wasn't like that, so she'd had to make the first move this morning.

Once they'd walked into the privacy of the barn, she'd expected him to kiss her. When he hadn't, she'd realized a more direct approach was required. As he'd said the night before, he wasn't out to wreck her carefully laid plans.

She knew how much he wanted her, but he'd focused on Josh. She appreciated that, but Josh wasn't here. Dealing with her brother had become increasingly frustrating, and in contrast here was Brant, willing to go along with… whatever.

Brant offered the perfect gift for these trying times—a chance to take a break, have fun and relieve some of her tension. She remembered what Rosie and Herb had said—he liked to move around and keep his options open. They hadn't spelled it out but she'd gotten the distinct impression that Brant wasn't a good prospect for a committed relationship.

No problem there. She wasn't in the market for a forever guy. Her cooking school plans were already delayed because of Josh, but she would dedicate every spare moment to them once he recovered. Although she wouldn't have gone looking for someone like Brant, he'd dropped into her lap. She'd be a foolish woman to let a busy schedule and guilt over her uncooperative brother keep them apart.

He was waiting where she'd left him, halfway down the aisle of the barn. He leaned casually against the side of a stall, his thumbs hooked through his belt loops. His lazy smile sent her hormones into overdrive. Thanks to their enthusiastic kisses and the promise of more later, her irritation with Josh had been replaced with lust for Brant. Not a bad trade-off.

She had her phone in one hand and would have loved a picture of his casual pose. He was pure cowboy yumminess. Somehow she didn't think he'd go for a photo shoot right now, though. It could destroy the mood.

He watched her approach with a masculine gleam of appreciation in his eyes. She didn't have to guess what he was thinking about. She was thinking about it, too. The question of whether they'd have sex had been decided. It was only a matter of time.

A very long time. Their rendezvous was hours away and he was right there. She pictured stripping off his shirt and smoothing her palms over his muscled chest. Then she'd unbuckle his belt and unzip his jeans…that image sent moisture between her thighs.

"You're going to have to stop ogling me like that."

She lifted her gaze from his crotch and looked into his eyes. "You started it."

"That's not my fault. You have a sexy walk."

"I don't, either. No one's ever said that before."

"I can't help it if other guys are blind. Watching you walk toward me was like foreplay."

"Seeing your hot self leaning against the stall was like the opening scene of a porn movie."

"Except in the movie they get to do it." He grimaced as he pushed away from the wall. "Lady, you are tough on my package."

"They say anticipation is half the fun."

"Somehow I doubt that's true in this case." His smile was strained. "Speaking for myself, I could ditch the wait."

"Me, too." She gazed at him. "Maybe I shouldn't have asked you to kiss me, huh?"

"Are you kidding?"

"If I hadn't started something you wouldn't be in pain right now."

He chuckled. "Worth it. Totally worth it. But the gang will be here any minute so let's proceed to Linus and Lucy's stall while I do my level best to calm down and not grab you." He turned and ambled away.

"If you're worried about accidentally grabbing me, you could put your hands in your pockets for safekeeping."

"Ordinarily that's a great idea, but at the moment the front of my jeans is stretched to capacity."

"I noticed."

"I'm sure you did, you saucy wench."

"Brant, can I say something?"

"Sure. Just don't touch my privates. Something might detonate."

"I'm really glad we met."

"Not half as glad as you'll be when you're floating around the cabin tonight." He paused in front of the stall door and peered in. "Aw, look at that. Cuteness to the rescue. If we concentrate on that we'll be fine."

Aria smothered a laugh. "Oh, my God." While Lucy

nosed in the grain bucket searching for any stray alfalfa pellets, Linus strutted around the stall, neck arched and stumpy tail in the air as if he owned the place. "Has he got attitude or what?"

"I guess all the compliments I've given him have gone straight to his head. Now he thinks he's all that and a bag of chips."

"Which he most certainly is. Can we go in?"

"Absolutely." He opened the stall door.

Linus paused and eyed the new development with curiosity. "Hey, Linus, you handsome devil," Aria crooned as she stepped inside.

Linus snorted and tossed his head.

"FYI, Linus." Brant came in behind her and closed the door. "The ladies usually prefer a more modest sort of fellow. Just sayin'."

"Not me," Aria said. "I like me a little attitude."

Brant chuckled. "Duly noted."

"Would you please hold my phone? I'm going to need both hands."

"Want me to take some video in here?"

"Sure, why not?" About that time Lucy glanced up and started toward her. Aria had tucked a few carrot pieces in her jeans pocket before leaving home and she pulled one out. "Hey, Luce. You did good, girlfriend." She gave the mare a chunk of carrot and scratched under her cream-colored mane.

To Aria's delight, Linus edged up close to his mom as if he wanted to find out what was going on. "Lucy, sweetheart, is it okay if I make friends with your baby boy?"

"Nice technique," Brant murmured.

"Hope so. I'm making it up as I go along."

"Following your instincts is always a good idea."

She smiled. "Guess so." She gave Lucy another piece of

carrot and spoke softly while gradually transferring her attention to the foal. Crouching down, she held out her hand with her fingers curled under. The colt nuzzled the back of her hand, which tickled. She swallowed her laughter so she wouldn't startle him.

Moving slowly and talking to both mare and foal, she eased her hand around until she could scratch Linus's neck. He gazed at her with his baby blues and she fell even more in love than she had the night before. "His coat is like mink."

"I know. It won't be like that forever."

"But it is, now, and I'm so lucky to be here on his first day of life. I've never experienced that before."

"It's special."

"I can see why you love your job." She glanced over at Brant and noticed his wide smile as he kept the video running. "You look pretty happy right now."

"I am. This is a great beginning. Linus seems to like people. He shows every indication of being an easy colt to train."

"That would be fabulous." She turned back to Linus. "You're going to be awesome, aren't you? I love your white blaze. So handsome."

"See if he'll let you rub his face." Brant kept filming. "He let me do it earlier this morning."

"I'll bet you'll let me, won't you, Linus? That's a good boy. What pretty blue eyes you have." She stroked up the length of his blaze and back down. "Doesn't that feel nice? Now I'll massage your cheeks, and now scratch your forehead. What a beautiful colt you are."

Lucy bumped her on the shoulder in an obvious bid for more carrots and almost knocked her over. "Easy, Luce. Easy does it." Aria gave Linus one last gentle scratch. "Your mom wants more treats, kid."

She stood and looped an arm over the mare's neck. "She probably deserves it after producing such a fine son." Hauling out another piece of carrot, she held it on her open palm so Lucy could curl her lips around it.

"Perfect ending to the segment. Turning off the video."

"Thanks. Whether Josh is interested or not, my folks will love having a copy."

"I'm sure they will. It went really well."

"Didn't it? Not that I was the reason. You hung around with him before I got here. You laid the groundwork."

"And you could have obliterated that groundwork."

"So why did you let me go right in?"

He smiled. "Following my instincts."

"Oh." Pleasure warmed her cheeks. "Thank you." After giving Lucy one more pat she stepped toward him and held out her hand for the phone. "I'll send this to my folks right now. They bought Lucy for me and they'll love seeing the three of us together." They'd love seeing Josh as part of the happy group, too, and they would, eventually. Typing quickly, she sent off the video.

"I just realized something. You're the only client I've had who's a first-timer with the birth process."

She smiled at him. "Do I get an award for that?"

"Yeah." His chuckle was low and extremely sexy. "I'll have one waiting for you at the cabin."

Before she could respond, Herb, Rosie, Cade and Lexi walked into the barn. "Can't wait," she said under her breath.

"You and me both." And he left the stall to greet his family.

Moments later Aria had the honor of leading Lucy out of the barn. "I wish this horse had a rearview mirror," she said to the group walking ahead of her.

"Linus is following right along," Brant said as he monitored the colt from behind. "Head up, ears forward. It's like he knows something good is coming."

Aria wondered if that comment had been a veiled reference to tonight's rendezvous. She wouldn't put it past him.

Rosie looked over her shoulder and grinned at Aria. "I've never seen a colt more perky than this one. I can tell from your expression how happy you are with him."

"I am. He's a beauty." She hoped that Rosie and the others attributed her extra sparkle to her excitement about Linus's first day in the pasture. She *was* excited, but not only about Linus. A certain tall cowboy vied for the top spot in her thoughts.

Thank goodness for that. Otherwise she might be feeling sad about Josh not being here for this big moment. Brant gave her something else to think about.

For example, he'd taken a moment when nobody else was paying attention to inform her that he'd be at the back of the parade with an excellent view of her cute little fanny. Naturally she thought of that the whole time she was leading her mare out to the pasture. When she heard his singsong comment of "lookin' good," she didn't think he was referring to Linus.

And that was okay with her. She hadn't been in a relationship in a while, and she'd never been in one with a man as fun-loving as Brant. He could tease her all he wanted. She was soaking it up like a sponge.

No one had mentioned Josh's absence, and that was fine with her, too. The others had probably sensed she was uncomfortable with his lack of participation and didn't want to make a point of it. She hadn't realized how much Josh had consumed her every thought until Brant had suggested she might need a break.

Last semester's academy students had helped modify the pasture in anticipation of Linus's birth. The other four horses were on the far side of a new fence, which gave Lucy and Linus their own private section. Aria was relieved that Herb and Rosie had taken that precaution.

Cade opened the gate for Aria and flashed her a smile as she led the mare through. "This is a treat. Thanks for sharing Linus with all of us."

"I'm the one who's grateful. You guys have been terrific."

"And we're about to get our reward." He glanced behind her. "The star of the show looks ready for his debut."

As Aria led both horses in, the four on the other side of the new fence glanced up, surveyed the newcomers and went back to their grazing. Aria turned around to watch Linus as he stepped gingerly through the gate and into his first experience with grass.

Brant walked in behind him and Cade closed the gate. "Turn mom loose," Brant said. "Let's see what happens."

She unclipped the lead rope and moved away. At first neither horse moved. Then Lucy snorted and trotted a few yards away. Linus followed, picking up his hooves as if he'd stepped in something icky.

"He doesn't know what to make of it," Aria said.

"He'll figure it out." Brant walked over to stand beside her.

She had the oddest parental feeling, as if she and Brant were watching their child head off to school on the first day. "What if he doesn't? What if he hates being out here?"

Brant laughed softly. "He won't."

"But what if—" She forgot whatever she'd meant to say as Lucy took off and Linus was forced to follow or be left behind. In seconds he had the hang of it. Before long he was the one leading the romp and racing around his mother.

His stubby tail wagged as he ran on his impossibly slender legs. He bucked and whirled in ecstasy as the horses in the far pasture eyed his antics with apparent disdain. He took a couple of pratfalls, but he bounced right up again and bounded off.

"Oh, Brant." Her throat clogged with emotion and she clutched his arm. "He's so…happy."

"Yeah." He covered her hand with his and squeezed. "This is something you'll never forget."

"I should be filming it."

"Give me your phone. I'll do it. You just enjoy."

She handed over her phone and let go of him so he could be the videographer for this moment. She didn't want to view it on a screen. Tears of joy blurred her vision and she wiped them away so she wouldn't miss a thing.

Linus cavorted as if his hooves were on springs. Lucy clearly grew weary of it after a few minutes, but the colt seemed oblivious. He tore around the pasture in a frenzy of happiness.

"He's so excited," Aria said. "He looks as if he could go on like this for hours."

"His battery will run down pretty soon. This is a sprint, not a marathon."

Sure enough, Linus began to tire. At last he stopped in his tracks and looked around for his mother. When he spied her grazing nearby, he trotted over and began to nurse.

"Should we take them back into the barn now?"

"Not yet." Brant turned off the video. "The grass will be good for Lucy and I'm sure she likes being outside again."

"Great show," Lexi called out.

Aria turned around to find everyone sporting big smiles as they leaned on the rail fence. "I know!" she said. "It was *awesome*."

"I have video." Rosie waved her phone. "Is it okay if I put it on the Thunder Mountain Academy website?"

"Of course! Spread it around online as much as you want." Aria hadn't thought of that, but pictures and videos of Linus would draw plenty of attention to the school. Rosie and Herb had done her a huge favor by offering free boarding and Brant's training, but the resulting publicity could be huge. She felt better about the arrangement when she thought of that.

"I'll go do it." Rosie hurried toward the house.

Herb chuckled. "She won't stop with the website. She'll have Linus on YouTube before you can turn around."

"Actually that's a cute idea," Lexi said. "Any past or future students will be interested."

"Then maybe you'd better go tell her, just to make sure." Herb pushed away from the fence. "I would, but I have to run some errands in town. I'll see you all at lunch."

"Wish I could hang around some more, too," Cade said. "But I have a truck to wash and detail."

"Aw, poor baby." Lexi pretended to look sympathetic. "I'll stop by after I make sure Rosie plans to upload that video to YouTube."

Cade brightened. "You'll help?"

"No, I'll supervise."

"I knew that."

"I'll work on Aria's van when you're done." Brant glanced at Aria. "If that's okay with you?"

"Sure." After Cade left she turned to Brant. "You know, honestly, I don't care if you wash Matilda or not. After all you've done with Linus, making you wash my van seems kind of obnoxious."

"If you want, you can supervise, just like Lexi plans to do."

"Or I could help, which makes a lot more sense. But it's really not necessary. I'll run it through a car wash next week."

"But my honor's on the line."

She couldn't tell if he meant that or not. "Really?"

He laughed. "No, not really. If Lexi's truck is sparkling and your van's a mess, I can take the abuse from Cade."

"Then let's forget it."

"I'm thinking you've never had a guy wash your vehicle before. All sorts of fun things can happen when a hose and water are involved." Mischief danced in his hazel eyes.

She began to grasp the potential in the activity, although it seemed risky to make out in broad daylight when she wasn't ready to go public with their mutual attraction. But he was right. She'd never had a boyfriend wash her car. "We won't be alone, though."

"We'll be sort of alone. I won't start until Cade's finished." He paused and gave her a teasing smile. "Also, whenever I wash a vehicle, I generally remove my shirt."

The guy made it impossible to be serious, so she gave up the effort. "You think I want to see your manly chest?"

"After the way you were ogling me back in the barn, I'd say that's a distinct possibility. So do you want me to wash Matilda or not?"

She heard the slap of an invisible gauntlet being thrown down. Apparently he was offering more of an adventure than she'd anticipated. She hesitated as her normally cautious nature told her to nix the idea. They'd managed to get away with a stolen kiss in the barn, but this could be pushing their luck.

He waited.

She imagined him shirtless and sweaty. He'd implied that there would be water play and sensuous, slick body contact. Lots of kissing. As her body began to tingle, she lost the battle to be sensible. "Wash and detail, cowboy."

He grinned. "You've got it, lady."

7

BRANT LOOKED FORWARD to the van-washing experience more than ever. Obviously, Aria had never fooled around with a guy in the process of cleaning up a vehicle. She also didn't realize that the cement slab behind the barn where the ranch trucks and sometimes the ranch horses were washed was a notorious make-out spot.

During Brant's high school years he and his foster brothers had taken full advantage of it. Offering to wash a girlfriend's truck during the summer months meant getting them alone behind the barn and hopefully soaked to the skin. Wet T-shirts never went out of style.

On a warm summer day they'd dry fast, too, which meant that theoretically the adults remained ignorant of what went on back there. Or so the guys had imagined. Rosie and Herb had probably known exactly what was going on and had quietly monitored the situation to make sure things didn't get out of hand.

Cade didn't need that kind of setup anymore now that he and Lexi were essentially living together, but Brant had hours to wait before he and Aria would be alone and naked. Washing her van and playing games with her in the water would tide him over until then.

A teenage make-out maneuver was in keeping with his frame of mind at the moment. Whenever he looked at Aria he felt the same reckless desire he'd experienced at seventeen.

Like a roller coaster at the county fair, the thrill would be over eventually and life would settle back into its normal routine. She seemed ready to let off some steam, too, after months of worrying about Josh. But she wasn't the type to abandon her plans completely.

That made this temporary relationship almost perfect for both of them. Sure, he knew perfect didn't exist. And nothing lasted forever. Dads could suddenly die of a heart attack and mothers could decide they were sick of taking care of a kid. But leaning against a rail fence next to Aria while he watched a day-old foal expand his horizons was good stuff.

Having her as a client was a new experience. He'd worked with women before, but never sexy and single women. That was probably just as well. He could combine work and pleasure this time, but making it a regular thing would be too distracting.

She let out a contented sigh. "This is so nice. I don't get outside enough. That's a disadvantage of my bank job."

"So what's the advantage?"

"Isn't it obvious?"

"Nope."

"A steady paycheck, of course."

"Oh, that."

"Yeah, that. I like my customers, some more than others, but the stable income is the big draw."

He shook his head. "If I had to work indoors five days a week I'd have to keep a bottle of whiskey in a desk drawer."

"Good thing you don't have to do that, then."

"True." He pulled his hat a little lower to shade his eyes.

"I doubt people would trust their money to someone who keeps nipping from a flask."

She laughed. "Probably not."

"But if you crave a steady income, aren't you worried about starting a cooking school? I can testify that once you're self-employed, the concept of a regular paycheck disappears."

"I've considered that, and it scares me a little, but I like being in charge. The alternative is working as a chef in a restaurant. Camille's offered me a job but I can't see myself taking it."

"Why not?"

"I'd have to follow a set menu over and over, cook the same dishes night after night. When I'm cooking I like to innovate constantly. I'm afraid working at Camille's would start feeling as repetitious as working at the bank."

He glanced over at her. "You did say you like drama in your cooking."

"I do. Camille has a great little restaurant, but her customers are vocal about keeping the menu the same. Last fall I suggested changing up the barbecue sauce recipe and it was a disaster. People pitched a fit, not because it was bad, but because it was different."

"But there are other restaurants where they love putting new stuff on the menu. You could go to an area like Jackson Hole where movie stars hang out. They'd be all about variety in their food."

She met his gaze. "You're right, but I like living in Sheridan."

"Because Josh is here?"

"That's a big part of it. The other part is I grew up in this town. Camille and I became best friends in second grade, but I've made other good friends here, too. I know the countryside and the best riding trails. If I'm going to

build a business, I want to build it in Sheridan." She took
a deep breath. "I belong here."

He nodded slowly. "It's good that you know that about
yourself." They were so different. He felt a deep connection to Thunder Mountain Ranch, but he didn't need to
make it his permanent home. Permanence was an illusion, anyway, although that wasn't how she related to life.
"Ready to lead your mare back in so I can get started on
your van?"

"Sure. But if you're determined to wash Matilda, then
I'm determined to help you."

He smiled. "Suit yourself."

They had Lucy and Linus tucked into the stall in short
order. Brant checked that the automatic watering system
was working and gave Lucy more alfalfa pellets while Aria
loved on Linus some more. Once they left, mom and baby
would likely take a nice long nap.

"The wash area is behind the barn." He worked hard
not to smile as he said it. "I'll go out there and make sure
Cade's left the bucket and towels while you drive around."

"I didn't know it was behind the barn." Judging from
her expression the location made a difference. "I thought
we'd do it in the gravel driveway by the house."

"This is way more efficient."

"And way more private?"

"Well, yeah." Finally he couldn't hold back a smile.
"Why do you suppose I've been so dead set on washing
your van?"

"Despite what you said before, I still thought it was a
point of honor."

"Nope. I wasn't kidding. I don't give a damn about my
reputation."

"I see." She looked him up and down. "Then maybe I
should worry about mine."

That slow perusal flipped a switch and he was suddenly ready to rock and roll. "Now your reputation is something I do care about. I would never—"

"You wouldn't? What a shame." Turning, she sauntered down the aisle.

He groaned softly. "Sexiest walk ever."

"I should hope so," she said over her shoulder. "Since I'm putting some effort into it this time for your benefit."

He groaned. "Better be careful. I feel like something's going to break."

"No, it won't. I'm very sure-footed."

"I wasn't talking about you."

She laughed. "See you around back."

Taking a deep breath, he willed his bad boy to calm down. Soaking her shirt and stealing a few kisses were all he'd had in mind for this episode. Chances were slim that someone could show up, but it wasn't impossible.

Yeah, too risky. He picked up the old canister vac from its spot near the back door and walked outside. Cade had left the bucket, a couple of sponges and the chamois for him. Some old towels were draped over the faucet and the hose was coiled and ready to go.

A rock was sitting on the edge of the cement for no good reason. But when he moved it, he found a scrap of paper with "Have fun" scribbled on it. He'd suspected Cade had engineered this van washing by not lighting his last match. This somewhat confirmed it.

Lexi wouldn't interrupt them, either. She knew the score. Herb was in town running errands and Rosie would be busy in the house posting pictures online and getting lunch underway. That should give him a good half hour alone with Aria, maybe longer. As a teenager he'd learned that a lot could happen in thirty minutes.

Just then, Aria drove around the end of the barn and parked on the cement. "How's that?"

"Perfect." He unsnapped his shirt.

"I'm taking off my boots," she called from the driver's seat. "I don't want to get them wet."

"Take off whatever you want." He hooked his shirt on a nail that had been put there for the purpose years ago. "I won't complain."

"Considering we're out here where anyone could see us, I think just the boots and socks are all I'm willing to strip off." She hopped out and closed the door. "What about you? You don't want your boots getting wet, do you?" She walked around the van and stopped short.

Her wide-eyed stare and audible swallow did wonders for his ego. Usually he didn't care what a woman thought of his body, but apparently with Aria he did.

"You took off your shirt."

"I said I would." He picked up the end of the hose and tightened the nozzle so it wouldn't go everywhere…yet.

"You did say that. I just wasn't—"

"Prepared for all this male beauty?"

Her laughter made him feel great. Her dedication to her brother's cause was admirable, but he sensed she'd let it rule her world for too long.

"I'm worried about your boots, though," she said.

"Don't be." Maybe worrying about stuff was a habit with her. He hoped not. "They're my work boots. They're old and have been through all kinds of weather." He turned on the water.

"If you say so. What do you want me to do?"

"Stand there and admire my manly chest while I hose down Matilda."

"Am I required to say ooh and aah at the same time?"

Teasing was a good sign. "Wouldn't hurt." He activated the spray and moved it over the roof of her vehicle.

"Ooh, ooh, you big strong man, you. Little ol' me can't reach the top of my van. I don't know what I'd do if I didn't have someone tall and handsome to hose it down."

He flashed her a grin. "You'd get a stepladder."

"A stepladder wouldn't look like you, though, would it? A stepladder wouldn't have bulging biceps and an impressive six-pack. It wouldn't have back muscles that ripple whenever you—"

"That's enough." Yeah, she was teasing, but his libido didn't seem to know that.

"I don't think so. I haven't praised your sculpted pecs or the cute line of blond hair that leads a woman's eye straight down to your—"

"No, really. You can stop, now."

"Why? Are you getting uncomfortable?"

"You might say so." He ignored the pressure building behind his fly as he wrangled the hose so he could rinse off the hood and the other side.

"I hate it when that happens, don't you?"

"I'm not sure you can even understand the concept, given your different setup."

"Sure I can. I—" She rounded the back of the van just as he directed the spray there. "Oh!"

He'd soaked her unintentionally. The intentional part was supposed to come later, after they'd accomplished most of the task. "I'm sorry! I didn't realize you were in motion!"

"It's okay." She stood there smiling at him, drops of water sliding down her cheeks and chin. Her T-shirt was transparent and her nipples jutted forward, clearly outlined through the fabric of what must be a thin bra and shirt. "Isn't this supposed to be part of it?"

He twisted the nozzle and shut off the water. She looked so sexy standing there that he could barely breathe. If he ditched the hose and picked her up, he could prop her against the van and repeat that amazing kiss they'd shared in the barn. He could fondle those tempting breasts, maybe even taste them.

But the van might never get washed. "Um, yeah, but I figured we'd at least get the van mostly—"

"How likely is it that somebody will show up back here in the next few minutes?"

He cleared the hoarseness from his throat. "Not very likely."

"Maybe later?"

"It's possible."

"Then give me that." She grabbed the hose, twisted the nozzle and turned it on him.

"Hey!"

"Fair is fair!" She shut off the water before lowering the hose to the cement.

He wiped his face. "Okay, we're even."

"Yeah, but I don't want to be even. I want to be ahead." She grabbed his belt. "Come here, cowboy." Pulling him closer, she began licking the drops of water from his chest.

He groaned. "Aria…"

She paused in mid-lap. "You don't like it?"

"I didn't say that."

"Good." She didn't stop.

Belatedly he remembered that a grown woman might have more moves than the teenaged girls he'd played the car-wash game with years earlier. The unexpected blast of cold water followed by the warmth of her lips and tongue created a sensation he'd never experienced before, and despite his halfhearted protest, he didn't want her to quit.

"You can't strip off your shirt and not expect a woman

to want this," she murmured. Hanging on to his belt, she sank lower, lapping and kissing, nibbling and sucking.

Naturally he began imagining how her mouth would feel on another part of his anatomy, and before long he was hard as a fence post. He figured she could tell when she dropped to her knees. He shouldn't allow her to continue.

He opened his mouth to tell her to stop and nothing came out. He blamed it on the erotic feel of her tonguing his navel. No guy could think of the right words to say when a woman did that. She kept it up while she unbuckled his belt and worked down the zipper on his damp jeans.

After that, he had no choice. His cock was doing all the thinking. He braced both hands against her van because otherwise he might fall.

And then…oh, dear God. His fantasy of how this car wash situation might turn out hadn't gone nearly far enough. She took her time at first and he understood that. He was a little intimidating. But she didn't stay intimidated for long. Eventually she took in most of what he had to offer and drove him right out of his mind.

He fought against coming too fast, but it was a losing battle with Aria in charge. From the beginning he'd pegged her as a goal-oriented person, and apparently her goal at the moment was to make him come.

Although he wanted to believe he'd held out for minutes, the actual time might have been seconds. He climaxed spectacularly but quietly because sound carried. His breath hissed out between his teeth when she swallowed. As he stood there gasping for breath, he knew this moment would stay with him forever. He would never forget Aria. Maybe that had been a foregone conclusion all along.

Gently she tucked his extremely happy cock inside his damp briefs, tugged up his zipper and buckled his belt. Although he watched her do it and understood intellectually that this must have been real, he still thought it could have been an outstanding dream and he'd wake up any minute.

Dream or not, he leaned down and offered her a hand up, the gentlemanly thing to do. He remained at a loss for words, though.

She smiled at him as he lifted her to her feet.

Searching his dazed brain, he tried to come up with something cool to say. "I...that was very..."

"Nice?"

He shook his head.

"It *wasn't* nice? From the way you reacted, I thought—"

"Way more than nice." He drew her into his arms. Her wet T-shirt was refreshingly cool against his overheated skin. "I can't think of any word that applies."

Her eyes sparkled with new awareness. "I wanted a preview of tonight."

"Oh, God." He squeezed his eyes shut. "Please don't judge my staying power on what just happened."

"I wasn't talking about that."

"No?" He opened his eyes. "What then?"

"Length and girth." She wrapped her arms around his neck. "You're pretty big, but I think I can handle you."

"I think you just did." Dipping his head, he gave her a quick kiss. "And now it's my turn to get even."

8

ARIA WASN'T USED to someone with Brant's strength. He picked her up with ease and, when she automatically wrapped her legs around his waist, he carried her to the side of the van as if she weighed nothing. Supporting her with one arm, he pushed open the sliding door and lowered her to the seat so she was facing him.

"What about washing my van?"

"Don't worry, lady." He leaned in and cupped the back of her head. "I'll wash Matilda. Right after this." His mouth claimed hers as he deftly unsnapped her jeans.

Her pulse rate shot into the red zone. The zipper came down next, adding fuel to a fire that was already raging. The hose had soaked her jeans, but her panties were wet for a totally different reason.

He raised his head to gaze into her eyes. "The jeans need to come off."

"Are you sure?" Much as she longed for whatever he had in mind, she wasn't happy about taking off her jeans. "What if somebody comes?"

He smiled. "I'm counting on it."

"Brant! I mean—"

When he stopped her protest with a kiss, his mouth was

very persuasive, almost as persuasive as his fingers sliding in through the open zipper and stroking whatever he could reach. He breached the barrier of her panties just enough to taunt her with the possibilities.

Like a magician, he dissolved her misgivings. She broke away from his kiss and dragged in air. "Okay, okay. Get rid of the jeans."

"Lie back and lift up."

The three-passenger seat gave her room to lie down and lift her hips. As luck would have it, her panties came off at the same time.

"Perfect."

She thought he was referring to the maneuver that had left her completely accessible. But when she propped herself up on her elbows, she noticed his rapt expression and the focus of his attention. Self-consciousness started to take hold.

He drew in a deep breath and let it out. "You're so beautiful…everywhere."

The awe in his voice was exactly what she needed to claim this moment. He'd given her the power to excite and arouse him and she decided to use it. Sitting up again, she peeled off her T-shirt. Next she unhooked her bra and tossed that away, too.

He swallowed. "My God."

"Come here."

He didn't have to be told twice. Ducking his head, he leaned inside and cradled her face in both hands. "Maybe I won't wash your van, after all," he murmured. Then he guided her back down to the seat and kissed her so thoroughly that she wondered if she'd have an orgasm just from that.

She didn't, but she trembled on the edge of one as he moved his attention from her mouth to her throat and finally to her breasts. Gripping his shoulders, she arched upward, straining toward the sweet suction, the swirl of his tongue and the nip of his teeth.

He swept a hand over her belly and between her thighs. One deep thrust of his finger and she came, pressing a hand to her mouth to keep from crying out. But he wasn't finished. Sliding down her body, he wedged his shoulders under her thighs.

While she was still quivering from her first climax, he settled his mouth over her slick entrance. The stroke of his tongue made her moan. "I can't."

He kissed the tight bud nestled in her sensitive folds. His breath was hot against her moist skin. "Sure you can." He raked the same spot lightly with his teeth. "Relax and let it happen."

She couldn't imagine relaxing when every nerve was vibrating. Then he began massaging her thighs with his gentle hands while he pressed lazy kisses in a circle around that trigger point. Gradually the tenseness left her body except for the growing ache right where he was kissing her.

And she wanted…more. Clutching his head in both hands, she surrendered to needs she'd never acknowledged before. She wanted to be taken, possessed, ravished. *"Now."*

"Yes, now." His cupped hands supported her, holding her steady for his assault.

She thought he would turn her inside out, so intense was the pleasure. He burrowed deep and the connection became so intimate that had she not been writhing in ecstasy she might have been shocked. Instead she abandoned herself to loving more passionate than she'd ever known. She came quickly and almost forgot to muffle her cries.

In an endearing display of tenderness, he stayed where he was, kissing her damp thighs and pressing his hand where his mouth had been as if to steady her descent. Earlier she'd been worried that someone might discover them like this. Now she didn't give a damn. Some things were worth risking embarrassment.

Gradually the chirping of birds and the rustle of wind through the nearby pines reminded her that a whole world existed beyond the confines of the van. Someone might eventually show up and wonder why it was parked here with two comatose people inside, including one who was completely naked.

The outrageous nature of what they'd just done began to penetrate her lust-fogged brain. She'd never had sex in a semipublic place in the middle of the day. She'd never had sex in a semipublic place in the middle of the night, either.

Brant lay with his cheek against her thigh and his eyes closed.

She stroked his hair. "That was wonderful."

"Mmm."

"But we should probably move." The precarious nature of their situation had finally dawned on her.

He snuggled closer.

She patted the top of his head. "Really. We can't stay like this."

No answer.

"Are you *asleep*?"

"No." His eyes remained closed. "But I've found my favorite place and I don't want to leave it."

"Sorry, but your favorite place is about to go. I'm getting dressed." She tried to extricate herself.

"Wait." His big hand closed over her thigh, pinning her down.

"I really think we need to make ourselves presentable."

"We will, but let's not rush it." He opened his eyes and looked up at her. "Man, I love this view. And, FYI, you may think you're done with the program, but your nipples say otherwise."

As usual, he made her laugh. "They don't speak for me. I say it's time to put some clothes on."

"Promise me this. Once you're inside the cabin tonight, you won't wear clothes until you're ready to leave in the morning."

"Easy promise. I like being naked with you. It's the rest of the population I'd rather not face."

"Actually, I'm okay with that reservation." He pushed himself up on his forearms. "Having an exclusive sounds excellent to me. Let's get you covered up."

She breathed a sigh of relief. The heat they'd generated had burned away all her inhibitions, but now they came surging back. "I'll need some help finding things. I have no idea where you put my panties."

"I do. Be right back." He slid out of the van and plucked something from the door handle. "Hey, they're dry. They were really wet before." He waggled his eyebrows at her.

"Because you hit me with the hose." She shimmied into them and was aware that he watched her do it.

"I don't think it was the hose." He handed her the jeans he'd draped over the door. "I think somebody was turned on."

"Maybe." She struggled into her jeans, which hadn't dried as thoroughly as her panties. She found her bra and T-shirt on the floor where she'd tossed them. Both were still damp.

"So you're dressed."

She glanced down at her wrinkled shirt. "But not very presentable. We're supposed to have lunch with Rosie and Herb."

"Okay, I have an idea. There's a compact washer and dryer in Cade's cabin."

"Wow, it really is fitted out well."

"It is. So let's quickly get the outside of this van looking good and then head on up there. I can at least dry your
clothes and you can fix your hair."

She hadn't even thought about her hair, but when she
ran her hand over it she discovered the braid was coming
loose. Not surprising. Everything had come loose a few
minutes ago.

She hopped down from the van. "Great idea. Matilda
doesn't need more than another quick rinse and a toweling off. That's good enough."

"Got it. Stand back."

Moving to the edge of the slab, she watched him hose
down the van. He was poetry in motion, his back muscles
shifting invitingly as he worked. Normally cowboys wore
shirts, long-sleeved ones at that. The fabric protected their
arms from thorny bushes and rough fence posts.

She understood the need for shirts most of the time,
but it seemed a shame that Brant stayed dressed. Washing vehicles might be one of the few times he could go
bare-chested. Well, that and jumping into bed with a willing woman.

She looked forward to spending an entire night with
him. He'd seen every naked inch of her today, but she still
had uncharted territory to explore when it came to Brant
Ellison. She couldn't wait.

After he turned off the hose he threw her a towel. "You
take the lower half and I'll take the upper."

"Makes sense. I'll follow you."

"No, I should follow you so I can see where you left off
and dry from there on up."

"Brant, that's crazy. I can just as easily see where you
left off and dry from there on down."

He started laughing. "I know. I just wondered if you'd buy it. I want to ogle your ass."

"And I want to ogle yours! I thought of it first, so move it, cowboy."

"That's why you said you'd follow me?"

"You think you're the only one with sex on the brain?"

His eyes gleamed. "Obviously not." Turning toward the van, he slapped the towel on the roof. "Enjoy the show." He started humming and gyrating his hips as he worked.

She lost it. The harder she laughed, the more he exaggerated his movements.

"This van won't dry itself, you know," he called out. "Better hop to it, Danes."

"I can't!" She gasped and held her aching sides. "Not with you dancing around like a stripper!"

He paused long enough to grin at her. "Then maybe *I* should follow *you*."

"That won't work anymore. You're way ahead of me."

"Oh." He walked over, turned on the hose and sprayed the side of the van again. "Problem solved. Over to you."

"All right." She wondered if they'd make it back to the cabin before lunch. But her clothes were nearly dry and she could redo her hair easily enough, so maybe it didn't matter how long the job took. Besides, payback would be sweet.

Positioning herself beside the van, she began toweling it dry at shoulder height. Normally she would have crouched to get the lower section. Instead she moved her feet apart and bent slowly at the waist.

His sharp intake of breath told her she'd achieved her goal. She pretended not to notice as she moved to the next section and repeated the maneuver. Halfway down she glanced over her shoulder and discovered him staring fixedly at her ass. The fly of his jeans was stretched as tight as it had been earlier that day. "This van won't dry itself, you know. Better hop to it, Ellison."

"You win." His voice was husky. "But let the record show that you fight dirty."

"So do you." Walking over to him, she looped the towel around the back of his neck and tugged. "Now come down here and kiss me."

"I'd like to do a hell of a lot more than that."

"I know." She wiggled against the bulge in his jeans.

"Stop." He cupped her bottom and held it still. "I'm going to kiss you and then I'm going to finish drying your van while you sit quietly on your sexy tush."

"If that's what you want."

"It doesn't begin to describe what I want." His fingers flexed in a slow massage. "You know exactly what I want, but I can't have that now. So I'll settle for this." His lips came down and he kissed her most thoroughly while his fingers continued their rhythmic kneading motion.

She clutched the ends of the towel and hung on for dear life. When he finally lifted his head, she was gasping and her panties were damp once again. She gulped for air. "I guess I should learn not to mess with you."

He took a shaky breath. "On the contrary. I love it when you mess with me. Keep it up."

"I'll bet we're running out of time, though."

He glanced up at the sun. Typical cowboy, checking the position of the sun instead of a smartphone. "Yeah, we are."

"We don't have to go back to the cabin. My clothes are dry and I can tidy up my hair right here."

His eyes brightened. "Let me undo it for you." Reaching behind her back, he deftly unwound the elastic holding the end of her braid, then combed his fingers through the strands, gradually loosening the braid until her hair fell in waves down her back. "Here you go." He handed the elastic to her.

"Where'd you learn how to unfasten a braid?"

"Horses. I've braided and unbraided plenty of manes and tails."

Some women might have been insulted but she wasn't. "I used to do that all the time with Lucy. Pegasus, too. I'd forgotten that." She closed her eyes as he massaged her scalp and combed the last tangles from her hair. She marveled that his fingers could both arouse and soothe. Versatile guy. "That feels good."

"Hope so. I've been wanting to take your hair down ever since you arrived."

Keeping her eyes closed, she basked in the feeling of being cared for. "Do you treat the horses this nicely?"

"Not quite. Their hair isn't as silky." His breath warmed her mouth. "And I didn't feel like doing this, either." His lips touched hers in a feather-light kiss. Then he changed angles and increased the pressure, but not by much.

So sweet. She let go of the towel and cradled his head with the same easy touch. But soft kisses, she discovered, could get her just as hot as demanding ones. Her grip tightened and she thrust her tongue into his mouth.

With a deep groan he responded and in seconds they were plastered together again and breathing hard. He was the one to end it. Grasping her by the shoulders, he set her gently away from him. As his chest heaved and his hands trembled, he gazed into her eyes. "Damn, Aria."

"Damn, Brant." Looking up at him, she fought the urge to launch herself into his arms.

He chuckled and rubbed the back of his neck. "Last night I was thinking we needed to get comfortable with this attraction so we wouldn't have any tension when we worked with Linus. Do you think we're comfortable with each other yet?"

"I'm not sure. Maybe you should kiss me some more."

"I didn't mean to kiss you that time, let alone kiss you some more. But when you closed your eyes and sighed, I couldn't help it."

"Did I sigh?" She didn't remember, but she might have. She'd felt so…cherished.

"Yep. It was this teeny, tiny exhale, as if you were surrendering to the moment."

"That's exactly how I felt." She met his gaze. "You have that kind of effect on me."

"I think we both know the effect you have on me. Once we're in polite company I'll have to lock that down."

"Speaking of polite company, I think I hear a truck out front."

He blew out a breath. "Me, too. Probably Herb. How about you go sit on that old stool beside the barn and re-braid your hair while I do a half-assed job on your van? Lunch will be served soon."

"Okay." She located the stool and brought it over closer. "Really, don't worry about the van. At least the dust has been washed off."

"And it's covered in water spots. I don't want it looking worse than when we started." He picked up the hose and sprayed the van for the third time.

"I thought you didn't care about your rep?"

"I don't, but when Cade and Lexi see those water spots, they'll have a fair idea why it looks like that. Rosie and Herb probably will, too."

"So it's my rep you're protecting."

"Yes, ma'am."

"Thank you." Feeling like a princess, she sat and finger-combed her hair while she watched him dry the van quickly. Man, he was beautiful to look at. She forced herself to concentrate on her braid when she'd much rather focus on that gorgeous cowboy.

By the time she finished with her hair, he was almost done with the van. Then she heard another vehicle out front. "Somebody else is here."

"Yeah, I heard them pull in. Rosie tells people to drop by for lunch whenever they feel like it, so they do. She always has plenty of food." He gave the fender one last wipe. "That'll have to do."

"It looks fabulous."

"No, it doesn't. I failed to wash your vehicle properly, sweet lady." He grinned at her. "Can't say I'm sorry."

She laughed. "Neither am I."

"Go ahead and drive it back around." He coiled the hose. "I'll gather up this stuff and join you there."

"How about I meet you in front of Lucy and Linus's stall? I'd like to touch base with them before lunch."

He smiled and walked over to bracket her face with both hands. "I like that you're still focused on them, even after all this."

"Everything sort of goes together, don't you think?" She captured his hands and pressed them to her cheeks.

"I do." He looked into her eyes.

She could see the soft glow building there and knew where it would lead. "Don't kiss me."

With a heavy sigh he released her and stepped back. "See you in the barn."

"You can't kiss me in there, either."

"That's what you think." He walked away and began gathering up towels.

"Seriously, you can't. We need to chill."

He glanced at her with a wicked grin.

"I'm leaving." Adrenaline pumping through her, she

hopped in the van and managed to get it started even though she was quivering with excitement. Brant was becoming a little too hot to handle. But that wouldn't stop her from meeting him in the barn in five minutes.

9

BRANT PUT ON his shirt and tucked it into his jeans before walking through the back door of the barn. Good thing he did, because he stepped right into a crowd of folks standing in front of Lucy and Linus's stall. They'd been keeping their voices down in deference to the mother and foal or he would have heard them earlier.

Or maybe not. He was still dazed by what had happened. They were moving way too fast but he couldn't seem to slow down and obviously neither could she.

Herb was standing by the stall with Aria, along with his foster brother and best bud, Ty Slater, who worked for a law firm in Cheyenne. "Hey." He clasped Ty's outstretched hand and pulled him into a bear hug. "Why didn't you tell me you were driving up?"

"Rosie called and said you'd come earlier than you'd planned. I told her I wanted to surprise you." Ty was all smiles as he stepped back and slipped his arm around the waist of a tall blonde. "This is Whitney."

"Ah." Brant took both of her hands in his and looked into her steady blue gaze. As he'd suspected from listening to Ty back in December, she was perfect for him. On Christmas Eve, Ty had been a disaster zone, but since then he'd worked everything out with the love of his life. They'd bought a house in Cheyenne and wedding bells should be ringing soon.

Brant gave her hands a friendly squeeze and released them. "I've heard a lot about you, ma'am."

"I could say the same. It's good to finally meet you."

"Well, just so you know, Tyrone has a vivid imagination. You can believe about fifty percent of what he puts out there."

She smiled. "Funny, but that's exactly what he says about you. And I've been talking with Aria, who seems to agree with his assessment."

"Floating foals," Aria said. "Ty and Whitney got a charge out of that one."

"Don't go picking on my boy." Herb came over to clap a hand on Brant's shoulder. "He kids around when he wants to ease a tense situation. Isn't that right?"

"That's exactly right." He chose not to look at Aria. They'd managed to ease a tense situation in a completely different manner, but what happened behind the barn stayed behind the barn.

"You never know for sure how things will go during a birth," Herb said. "Fortunately this one was easy, but then again, having Brant there to soothe Lucy might have had something to do with it."

"I'm sure it did," Aria said, all teasing gone from her voice. "Plus, I give him credit for how confident Linus is already."

"Hey, it's not all me. I'm convinced he was born with a sunny disposition. Confidence may be his normal setting, which means we lucked out."

"Whatever the reason, he's adorable." Whitney gazed at the colt. "I've never seen a day-old colt before, but I'm already a fan."

"He should be a good one." During the conversation, Brant had watched Linus's reaction to having unfamiliar visitors. Although the foal had kept tabs on his mother, he'd also pranced around a good bit as if the company didn't bother him. But it was probably time to get everyone out of the barn and let mother and baby rest. "Herb, how soon is lunch?"

"I'll bet it's ready, so we should get a move on." Herb caught his signal. "Lexi and Cade are up there helping, and I can guarantee Rosie's excited to see Ty and Whitney."

Brant knew that was true. When Rosie's boys came home it was always cause for celebration. Ten minutes later, as all eight people crowded around the kitchen table, Rosie had never looked happier. She and Herb had intended to have a big family but that hadn't worked out. Instead they'd taken in a whole passel of foster boys over the years and had created a different kind of family.

Inevitably talk at the table focused on those days. He knew it was only a matter of time before someone brought up the day Ty had challenged him to a fight. Chances were good that Aria hadn't heard about the incident and everyone else at the table would feel she needed to.

Ty ended up being the one to broach the subject. He glanced across the table at Aria. "Has anyone told you about the time I tried to pick a fight with this guy?" He motioned toward Brant with his fork.

She sat forward. "Nope, but it sounds like a good story."

The energy in the room spiked and Brant sighed. He was sick to death of this tale, but everyone else at Thunder Mountain Ranch seemed to think it was an epic event that had to be relived on a regular basis. Aria represented another opportunity to dust it off.

Cade leaned back in his chair. "Rock on. This is a classic Thunder Mountain legend."

"Absolutely." Lexi nodded. "One of my favorites."

"It's growing moss," Brant said. "Aria really doesn't need to be put through it."

"Oh, but I want to be put through it." She gave him a sidelong glance. "I've heard vague references, but never the nitty-gritty."

"Then here goes." Ty looked over at Brant. "You can all see the size of this cowboy. He was almost that large at fifteen."

"I was not." Brant rolled his eyes. "You make me sound like Paul Bunyan."

"Great comparison!" Lexi gave him a thumbs-up. "That's how the other guys thought of him, right, Cade?"

"Sure did." Cade folded his arms and smiled, obviously enjoying having Brant on the hot seat. "I'm pretty sure we had you chop down the Christmas tree every year with your mighty ax."

"I did it once my senior year. That's it."

"Doesn't matter." Ty waved the issue away. "The point is, Brant was the biggest guy at the ranch when I arrived. I was mad at the world and spoiling for a fight."

"In other words, a PITA," Cade said.

"I admit I was a pain in the ass, but damn it, there was Brant, smiling at everyone, making jokes, acting as if the world was just a bowl of cherries, and it pissed me off."

Brant groaned. "You make me sound like Little Orphan Annie. I wasn't like that."

"Yeah, you were," Cade said. "A cross between Paul Bunyan and Little Orphan Annie."

Lexi made a face. "That's a disturbing image."

"My point is that if Brant hadn't been so big, guys would've picked on him for being so damned cheerful all the time. But we weren't about to needle somebody who could smash us flat." Cade looked over at Aria. "Ty, however, had no more sense than a horsefly and decided to take him on."

"Aw, he wasn't serious." Brant appealed to Ty. "You were just fooling around, right? Let's set the record straight once and for all."

"Sorry, but they're right. I wanted to be David to your Goliath. I wanted to wipe that irritating grin off your face."

"So he went for the big guy," Cade said, "throwing punch after punch, and Brant just stood there taking it until Ty ran out of steam."

Brant shifted uncomfortably in his chair. "I wasn't in the mood."

"Exactly." Ty gazed at him. "You're never in the mood to pound on someone. Eventually, I got that through my thick head and stopped hitting you." He glanced over at Aria. "I worked out the worst of my anger thanks to him, and we've been best friends ever since."

"That's a great story." Aria's expression was soft as she turned to Brant. "Why wouldn't you want him to tell it?"

"I was okay with hearing it the first twenty or thirty times."

"We don't tell it that often," Rosie said. "Just when someone new shows up."

He suddenly had a horrible thought. "Promise me you won't tell it to the summer session kids."

Cade laughed. "No worries, bro. We want them to tremble in their boots at the sight of you. That story's going back under the bed while you're the nighttime chaperone."

"Good." But now he wished he hadn't accepted that responsibility. It could seriously interfere with his plans regarding Aria. "They're arriving Wednesday, right?"

Rosie nodded. "The last one comes in around five, so they'll all be here for the welcome dinner."

Ty drained his glass of lemonade. "Are you ready for them?"

"Somewhat."

"Everything's pretty much under control," Herb said. "Don't you think so, Cade?"

"Sure." Cade leaned back in his chair. "We're good."

Brant knew from personal observation that wasn't exactly true. He'd planned to offer his services this afternoon while Lucy and Linus enjoyed quiet time.

Ty didn't look convinced, either. "So the cabins are all cleaned, everything's working in the bathhouse, the fences are all repaired, the barn roof's in good shape, the—"

"Maybe not *all* of that's done," Cade said. "But Damon and Phil are due back from her dad's tomorrow night and they'll come out Monday to tackle some of those things. You guys are on vacation this weekend. Go have fun."

"We'll have fun helping," Whitney said. "We talked about it on the way up and figured you'd all be rushing around getting ready. Let us pitch in. It'll make us feel more like we've contributed to the cause."

Rosie looked relieved. "I'd be so grateful. We didn't notice until after Damon and Phil left that we have some dripping showerheads in the bathhouse. They're old and might need to be replaced. And Cabin Two has a leak in the roof and a crack in one of the windowpanes."

"I'll leave the roof and the window to Damon and Phil," Ty said. "But I might be able to fix the showerheads. You with me, Whitney?"

"I'm no plumber, but I can replace a showerhead."

"That's more than I can do," Cade said. "You got anything that doesn't involve hammers and wrenches?"

"Actually, I do." Rosie looked at him. "My cleaning crew, Sister Mary Meticulous and Sister Mary Methodical can't make it."

Brant grinned. "You're joking."

"Actually, she isn't," Cade said. "They're new in town and they're biological sisters, not nuns. Their slogan is Make Us a Habit. So what happened? I thought we'd nailed that down."

"They emailed late last night and they have a family emergency in Billings. I didn't see the email until this morning, and I tried a couple of other places, but no luck. It's short notice on a holiday weekend."

"Don't worry about it," Lexi said. "Cade and I can start on the cabins this afternoon."

Rosie beamed at her. "You're a gem. I could handle it myself except that I haven't finished planning the menus for the first couple of weeks and obviously they'll be different from the winter menu. I—"

"I'll help you with that," Aria said. "And I promise it won't be too fancy. I could do it this afternoon, except I'm not sure if Brant needs me to spend more time with Linus."

He shook his head. "They could use a siesta. I was planning to leave them alone for the next couple of hours. Unfortunately, about the time they're ready for more interaction you'll probably have to leave."

"Yeah, I should take off around three-thirty so I can change clothes and talk with Josh. No worries. I'll see them in the morning." But she looked sad.

He wasn't sure if that was because she was worried that her brother would still be uncooperative, if she was disappointed that she wouldn't get to pet Linus and Lucy, or if she felt guilty for having fun while Josh languished in a wheelchair. Could be all of that, but he could only fix one of those issues. "Fifteen minutes earlier won't hurt anything. Come on down to the barn about three-fifteen. I'm sure they'll be rested by then."

"All right." Her smile banished the sadness from her eyes. "Thanks."

"Hey, they're your horses. If you ever disagree with what I'm doing, you have the right to question it."

"That wouldn't be very smart of me. I'm not the expert here."

"You know a lot more than you think you do." If they'd been alone he would have followed that comment with a hug or a kiss. Instead he turned to Rosie. "What can I help with? I can clean or work in the showers, too, if you need me."

"Just don't let him plan the menu," Cade said. "I think we established last night that he has no imagination when it comes to food choices."

Brant gave him the stink-eye. "Kids don't want imaginative food choices."

"You're right about that," Rosie said with a laugh. "So you're welcome to sit in on the menu discussion if you want."

He was tempted because it would mean spending time with Aria, but he wasn't really needed there. "I wouldn't mind, but I noticed that some fence posts in the pasture look a little wonky."

"Yeah, that's on the list," Herb said. "The oldest ones out there have rotted. I picked up replacements at the lumberyard today. I thought I'd start this afternoon, if you want to help."

"Be glad to." He knew his foster father could still operate a posthole digger as well as the next guy, but the work would go faster with two people and they'd always enjoyed sharing a job whether it was delivering foals or digging holes in the ground.

As was the tradition at Thunder Mountain, everyone worked to clean up the kitchen before heading off in different directions to accomplish their chores. When Brant was ready to leave with Herb, he glanced toward the table where Rosie's and Aria's heads were bent over a couple of well-worn cookbooks. He resisted the urge to give Aria's shoulder a squeeze before walking out the door.

"See you ladies later," Herb said.

"Three-fifteen." Brant knew Aria didn't need reminding, but it allowed him to add a comment and maybe get her to look up.

She did and, bonus, she smiled at him. "I'll be there."

He felt unexpected warmth in his chest. It was different from the lust he'd experienced this morning, which had settled mainly in his groin. "See you then." He walked out with Herb.

The warm feeling remained as he pictured meeting her in front of the birthing stall. And it wasn't because he planned to seduce her, either. She needed to spend time with her horses and he'd have the privilege of sharing the experience. That was special.

He helped his foster father gather up tools and gloves and stow them in the back of the truck. Herb put on one of the battered straw hats he kept in the barn for this kind of job. Brant decided to do the same and leave his Stetson in the tack room. Those straw hats had seen a lot of use and wearing one reminded him of the old days.

Pulling the brim down to shade his eyes, he walked ahead of the truck and opened the pasture gate so Herb could drive through. Then he hopped back in.

"I'm glad you like her," Herb said.

"Me, too. Makes things easier." He didn't need to ask who they were talking about.

"I wasn't sure you two would get along. She's got her life planned out and I pity the person who throws a monkey wrench into those plans."

"Like her brother?"

Herb sighed. "You know, in the beginning, I was all for this idea of hers. I've seen how horses can heal a person. Raising a foal to maturity is a privilege I've never had, but I can imagine the deep bond such a project would create. But Josh isn't buying in."

"Have you met him?"

"Not that I know of. I wasn't his horse's vet. Sheridan's a small town, so I've probably run across him somewhere or other, but I don't remember him. You must have known him, though."

"Not really. I hate that Aria's gone through all this for his sake and he doesn't seem to give a damn."

"Doesn't sit well with me, either." Herb stopped the truck next to the first rotted post and turned off the engine. "She's a nice girl—I mean a nice *woman*. Rosie's warned me about calling adult women girls. But at my age, Aria seems like a girl."

"I'm well aware that she's a girl."

Herb chuckled. "I thought so. There's a vibe between you two."

"I admire what she's attempting to do."

"I'm guessing that's not all you admire."

"Yeah, I like her."

"Is that so?" Herb nudged back his hat and gave him a long look. "She's not your type."

"Actually, she is my type. Like you said, she has her life all mapped out and doesn't want anybody disturbing her plan. I won't."

Herb was quiet for a while and Brant had learned to respect those silences. Finally he spoke. "I don't pretend to understand how things are these days. All I wanted at your age was to find the right girl—*woman*—settle down

FREE Merchandise is 'in the Cards' for you!

Dear Reader,

We're giving away FREE MERCHANDISE!

Seriously, we'd like to reward you for reading this novel by giving you **FREE MERCHANDISE** worth over $20 retail. And no purchase is necessary!

It's easy! All you have to do is look inside for your Free Merchandise Voucher. Return the Voucher promptly...and we'll send you valuable Free Merchandise!

Thanks again for reading one of our novels—and enjoy your Free Merchandise with our compliments!

Pam Powers

Pam Powers

P.S. Look inside to see what Free Merchandise is **"in the cards"** for you!

W

e'd like to send you two free books like the one you are enjoying now. Your two books have a combined price of over $10 retail, but they are yours to keep absolutely FREE! We'll even send you 2 wonderful surprise gifts. You can't lose!

REMEMBER: Your Free Merchandise, consisting of **2 Free Books** and **2 Free Gifts**, is worth over $20 retail! No purchase is necessary, so please send for your Free Merchandise today.

Get TWO FREE GIFTS!
We'll also send you 2 wonderful FREE GIFTS (worth about $10 retail), in addition to your 2 Free books!

Visit us at:
www.ReaderService.com

Books received may not be as shown.

FREE MERCHANDISE VOUCHER

☐ Please send my Free Merchandise, consisting of
2 Free Books and **2 Free Mystery Gifts**.
I understand that I am under no obligation to buy
anything, as explained on the back of this card.

150/350 HDL GKAW

Please Print

FIRST NAME

LAST NAME

ADDRESS

APT.#   CITY

STATE/PROV.   ZIP/POSTAL CODE

NO PURCHASE NECESSARY!

HB-516-FMH16

with her and have babies. I met Rosie and that was it. We didn't have the babies, but that worked out okay."

"Speaking from my own selfish viewpoint, it worked out great."

"It did work out great. I wouldn't change a thing." He looked over at Brant. "But you don't want what I wanted, do you?"

He considered his answer because he'd rather not insult his foster father's choices. "I'm like a Plains Indian, moving from place to place dragging my possessions behind me on one of those contraptions they used."

"A travois."

"You're so damned smart, Dad. I swear you could go on a game show and clean up."

"That doesn't interest me at all, but I get what you're saying. You and Aria are two ships passing in the night."

"Guess so, but that's hard to do in a landlocked state like Wyoming. Maybe we should be eighteen-wheelers passing in the night."

Herb apparently got a kick out of that one. He couldn't seem to stop chuckling. "I wouldn't use that analogy when you're speaking to the lady. Women don't appreciate being compared to a semi."

"I'll keep that in mind." Making his foster father laugh was one of his favorite things to do. "You think the ship comment works any better though? Those ocean liners are *huge*."

"Good point. Don't say anything like that." He smiled. "I know what kind of man you are, son. You'll treat her with respect for whatever time you spend together. I'm not too worried about either of you. You've always been self-sufficient and she seems to be, too. Whatever happens with her brother, she'll have that foal to love. I wonder if Linus was always supposed to be for her."

"You could be right. She adores that little guy." He hadn't envisioned maintaining contact with Aria after the training was finished. Usually he made himself scarce once he'd socialized a foal. They needed to bond with the people who would be caring for them every day.

Logically he should treat the situation with Linus the same. He never wanted to give a woman the wrong impression, so he'd make sure Aria didn't expect him to hang around.

Herb reached for the door handle. "Ready to tackle those ornery fence posts?"

"You bet." He was smiling as he climbed out of the truck. Having the trust of a man like Herb Padgett was pure gold. He wouldn't trade places with anyone.

10

ARIA WALKED DOWN to the barn energized by all that had happened today—Linus's first experience in the pasture followed by a scandalous hour with Brant behind the barn. Then she'd met his best friend.

Learning how they'd become close had been an eye-opener. Not too many teenaged boys would have stood there and allowed themselves to be pounded on. Brant was even more unusual than she'd thought, and she'd been impressed from the moment he'd stepped into Lucy's stall the night before.

Impressed and fascinated. She'd never met anyone quite like him. And when they were together she didn't obsess about Josh.

Instantly she felt guilty. If she didn't figure out how to help her brother, nobody would. He might be his own worst enemy, but she was his very best friend. She mustn't lose sight of the goal—getting Josh on his feet.

When she stepped into the cool recesses of the barn, Brant was waiting for her at the far end. He'd propped his back and one booted foot against the side of the stall. He'd also traded his Stetson for an old straw cowboy hat. Seeing him wearing it reminded her that he was a hardworking cowhand who didn't care about fashion and wasn't afraid to get his hands dirty.

His smile told her that he was happy to see her. His eyes told her he'd like nothing better than to pull her into his arms. God, help her, she wanted him to.

But instead of closing the gap between them, he stepped back and shoved his hands in his pockets. "I promised myself I wouldn't kiss you, so you'd better stop looking at me like that."

"How am I looking at you?"

"Like a chocoholic eyeing a plate of fudge."

She laughed. "Is that so?"

"Yeah." His voice was husky. "And I guarantee if you start sampling the fudge we'll use up all of your fifteen minutes."

She'd always been proud of her willpower. Then she'd kissed Brant Ellison. The prospect of feeling his mouth on hers drove every other thought from her mind.

"They need you more." Taking a deep breath, he turned and opened the stall door. "They're waitin' on you."

Humbled by his selfless gesture, she nodded and walked inside. Both Lucy and Linus came over, which made her heart squeeze. "Hey, there, my sweetie pies." She took a piece of the carrot Rosie had given her and fed it to Lucy while stroking Linus's coat. "I can't believe how soft he is."

"I know." Brant stood in the open doorway. "Another good reason to get him used to being handled. The kids will all want to pet him."

She glanced in his direction. "I'm glad you'll be around to monitor the interaction so they don't overdo it. Please tell me you didn't have to wake them up just for this."

"Nah, they were moving around when Herb and I got back from setting fence posts. Lucy was looking for more food. We have to keep it coming while she's nursing Linus."

"I'll bet." She returned her gaze to the horses and managed to rub Lucy's nose and scratch Linus's neck at the same time. "This project would have cost me a small fortune if Rosie and Herb hadn't stepped in."

"I can tell you feel obligated to them and I won't minimize the gesture, but they love having a foal around and I'm sure putting his pictures online has brought loads of publicity to the academy."

"I hope so. I'm sorry the birth didn't happen when the students could see it." She thought of how that would have changed things, specifically her relationship with him. "But not real sorry, to be honest."

"I'm not, either."

She gave Lucy another piece of carrot and a pat before crouching and using both hands to caress the foal. "He seems to like being stroked."

"That's a guy for you. Loves that stroking part."

Lust gave her insides a tweak. "No fair making comments like that."

"Sorry. When I'm watching you fondling him it's tough to keep my mind from going there."

"Did you get the postholes all dug?"

He chuckled. "Holes dug and posts in. Until this minute I hadn't thought of that as a sexual image, either. Ah." He blew out a breath. "I know a safe topic. The menu. Did you and Rosie get it figured out?"

"We did. I think it's workable and won't break the budget."

"Good. What about Josephine Talley, the woman she hired to help cook for the first semester kids? Is she still on board?"

"She should be back from visiting her daughter before

the students get here." Aria ran her hands over Linus's chest and laughed when he tried to nibble on her shirt.

"Don't let him eat your clothes. They can pick up bad habits really fast."

"I won't let him." She gently moved his nose away. "That's not for you, kid."

Linus gave her a long, blue-eyed stare. Then he turned toward his mother and soon was completely involved in nursing.

Aria stood. "I've been replaced. I think that's it for now." She gave Lucy the last piece of carrot and left the stall.

"And look at that." He closed and latched the door before turning toward her. "You have five minutes to spare."

Stepping closer, she smoothed her hands up his broad chest. "Must be your turn, then."

He pulled her in tight. "I should warn you I worked up a sweat digging postholes."

"Ask me if I mind." She took off his hat and held it while she ran her fingers through his hair. It was still slightly damp.

"Do you mind?"

"That you work hard enough to sweat?" She breathed in the scent of earth and healthy male. "As it happens, I like that about you."

He gazed down at her. "You know what I like about you?"

"What?"

"Everything."

She flushed with pleasure. "Thank you."

"But I can be more specific. For one thing you're smart." He kissed her forehead. "And you have amazing eyes." He kissed the bridge of her nose. "And cheeks like satin." He placed a kiss on each one. "I'd kiss your other cheeks, too, but I only have five minutes so I'll save that for tonight."

How easily he turned her on. Her heart pounded with excitement and their rendezvous was still hours away. "I'll try to get there early, but I can't promise that I'll—"

"Shh." He pressed a finger to her lips. "It doesn't matter when you get there. The second you arrive I'll be as hard as a tire iron."

"Oh." Enthralled by that potent image, she gazed up at him in breathless anticipation.

"You may not realize what an impression you've made on me." Lazily he brushed his thumb over her lower lip. "I don't just like you, Aria. I crave you." And he kissed her, thrusting his tongue deep.

Her surrender was complete. She held nothing back as she melted against him, everything forgotten except this— a connection so powerful that her nipples tightened and her body trembled.

Slowly he lifted his mouth from hers. "You need to go."

"Mmm." She kept her eyes closed as she tried to remember where and why. Her legs felt rubbery. She didn't want to wobble as she walked away from him. "Give me a sec."

"Sure." He rubbed her back.

Taking a deep breath, she opened her eyes and met his gaze.

He swallowed. "I swear, when you look at me like that, it's all I can do not to haul you into the tack room and bolt the door."

And she would go with him despite knowing she had to get home and talk to Josh. Her cherished self-control disappeared when she was in the grip of this intense longing. The realization alarmed her.

"It's a bad idea to head to the tack room, though. For a lot of reasons."

"Yes." Good thing at least one of them was exercising restraint. She unwound her arms from his neck and discovered she was still clutching the straw hat. "I might have dented this some."

He grinned. "Don't know how you can tell. That's one disreputable hat."

"I like it on you." Stepping back, she handed it to him. "Makes you look rough and ready."

"I'm never rough." He settled the hat back on his head. "But when it comes to you, I'm always ready."

Damn, he was intoxicating! She fought the urge to throw herself into his arms and beg him to make love to her. Instead she smiled as she backed away. "See you tonight."

"Can't wait."

"Me, either." Understatement of the century, she thought as she turned and hurried out of the barn. But she couldn't think about that now. Time to switch gears and focus on her top priority. Ideally, Josh should get acquainted with Linus before the students arrived.

That meant getting him out here tomorrow. Having Brant to herself might be tons of fun, but her decision to breed Lucy made no sense if she couldn't get Josh involved. Linus was adorable and she loved knowing he existed, but he was supposed to serve a purpose. So far he wasn't doing that.

Once she was in the van she checked the time on her phone. She wasn't nearly as late as she'd feared, but she kept the needle slightly above the speed limit all the way back to her apartment complex. With luck she wouldn't catch Josh working, which would give him the perfect excuse to blow her off.

He billed the tech company by the hour and by calculating how much he needed to live on, he'd left himself plenty of time for computer games. Apparently his competitive nature had to find another outlet so now he fought digital fire-breathing dragons.

When he answered the door, he looked annoyed. "Can it wait? I'm in the middle of something."

"Are you working?"

"No."

"Then it can't wait." Her patience was nearly gone. "I need to talk to you. Please shut off the TV." She walked in without being invited and he had no choice but to roll his wheelchair out of her way unless he wanted her to run into it.

Fortunately he hadn't become that belligerent. He clicked off the TV and she closed the door. Forcing herself to ignore the apartment littered with trash from the junk food he ate these days, she cleared a space on his couch and sat.

She'd had visions of cooking nourishing meals for him at least five nights a week, but he'd brushed aside that offer. The apartment's stale odor made her wonder how long since he'd cleaned. She'd attempted to do that for him and he'd told her he could operate a vacuum and mop from his wheelchair.

"I suppose this is about Lucy's foal." He shoved his fingers through his dark hair, the same shade as hers. He needed a haircut, but claimed that he didn't.

"Yes, it's about Linus." She pulled her phone out of her purse. "He went into the pasture today. It was awesome. Rosie took a video and I want you to see it."

He sighed. "Look, I'd rather not, okay?"

"Why?" She gazed at her brother, someone she loved with all her heart despite the fact that he'd turned into a moody, unpredictable man. "He's amazing!"

"I'm sure he is, Aria. I've seen foals before and they're

cute as shit. But I'm over the horse thing. I tried to tell you that but you didn't listen. You charged ahead with this idea of breeding Lucy. I wish you hadn't." He'd inherited the brown eyes that ran in the family and they gleamed with frustration.

She put the phone away. Then she took inventory of their surroundings before focusing on her brother. He used to be fit but now he looked soft and doughy. "Is this what you want for the rest of your life?"

"It's not what I *want*." His eyes flashed in defiance. "It's what I can have."

"That's not true. The doctors said you could walk again, ride again, live a normal life."

"Oh, sure. But I might have to use a damned cane. I can ride if someone helps me up on the damned horse. I can drive if I order a special plate and buy a specially equipped vehicle! No, thank you!"

She got it, then, for the first time since his accident. He'd rather live as a disabled person cut off from nearly everything and everyone he'd ever known than risk humiliation in the world he used to inhabit. As an eventer, he'd thought of himself as a warrior. That image had been permanently destroyed, so now he'd chosen to hide and be a warrior in the anonymous world of gamers.

But just because she understood didn't mean she had to accept his decision. He was resigning himself to a half life, and she wouldn't let him do that, not if she had a chance in hell of rescuing him.

"All right." She faced the despair in his expression and vowed to replace it with hope. "Maybe I shouldn't have bred Lucy in some misguided attempt to cheer you up."

"You shouldn't have, but once you get going, you're unstoppable. You've been like that ever since I can remember."

"And you've been my hero ever since I can remember."

"Don't say that." He looked away. "I don't need to hear it right now."

"I think you do. Josh, there's this little foal out at Thunder Mountain Ranch. He's only one day old, but he has gumption. I didn't know he'd turn out like that, but he seems to have been born with attitude. You were, too."

"Yeah, well, things happen that can knock the attitude right out of you."

"Watching Linus would make you laugh. You never laugh anymore."

He gazed at her. "You're not going to let up on me, are you?"

"It's not in my nature." She shrugged. "You said so just now."

"Let me think about it."

"Come with me tomorrow. Thunder Mountain Academy starts up again on Wednesday. Until then, it's fairly quiet at the ranch."

"I'm not making any promises."

"Want to watch the video?"

He shook his head. "You know I'm a sucker for cute baby animals. It's emotional blackmail."

"I'm not above that."

"You don't have to tell me. I'm your brother." A hint of a smile touched his mouth. "You've been using emotional blackmail on me for years. I broke up with Clara Simpson because of you."

"She was horrible! You should never have gone out with that skank!"

"I agree she was horrible, but she had a great body."

"Don't remind me. I saw every naked inch of it."

"Yes, you did." This time he gave her a real smile, almost a grin like the old Josh. "Those pictures were awe-

some. You could have sold them to every guy in school.
I'm surprised you didn't blackmail *her*."

"I didn't care about her. I just wanted evidence that she
was two-timing you with Jerry Hauserman in the back of
his pickup. I was thirteen, for God's sake! I'd never seen
people having sex before. I was traumatized."

"I know. That's why I had to break up with her."

"Good thing you did, too, because…wait. Are you saying you broke up with her because I was traumatized?"

"Yep."

"I thought you broke up with her because I presented
you with the damning evidence of her betrayal." She remembered saying those exact words when she'd handed
over the pictures. It had been one of her finer moments.

"Not quite. I had a pretty good idea she was getting it
on with Jerry but I pretended not to know."

"You knew already?" She stared at him in confusion.
"Why didn't you dump her?"

"Because the sex was *really* good. But after what you
put yourself through, not to mention how outraged you
were on my behalf…" He shrugged. "I had no choice."

"I can't believe you didn't care that she was boinking
someone else. You're just saying that."

"Actually, it's the truth. At seventeen, a guy doesn't always make those fine distinctions, especially if he's having sex for the first time in his life and it's the best thing
ever. I never wanted it to end."

She was stunned. All these years she'd congratulated
herself on rescuing him from the bad girl's clutches. "And
I ended it for you."

"Yeah, but you meant well."

"That's humbling." She thought about it while she
rubbed a spot on her jeans where Linus had nuzzled her.

Then she glanced up. "You probably think I'm doing it again, huh? Butting in when I should leave you alone."

"In a way, yes. But this isn't kid's stuff anymore. I loved eventing more than I ever loved Clara."

"I know."

"That's gone forever."

"I know that, too, but that doesn't mean—"

"It means the man I thought I was died."

She sucked in a breath. "Oh, Josh."

"I'm sorry, Aria, but playing around with a cute little foal isn't going to change that."

11

THANKS TO A lively poker game suggested by Cade, Brant managed to get through the time between dinner and Aria's arrival. He'd texted her directions for reaching the cabin by a back road so she wouldn't have to drive past the house. She'd said not to expect her before ten.

But he didn't want to take the chance she'd beat him there, so he cashed in his chips at nine thirty. Everybody except Herb gave him a hard time about getting too old to stay up late.

"Hey, ease up," Brant said. "Ringo left an hour ago and I didn't notice anybody razzing him about it."

"Ringo went to hunt mice in the barn, not catch extra shut-eye," Cade said.

"Yeah, but Ringo's been snoozing all day whereas I've put in long hours of manual labor, right, Dad?"

"Right, son." Herb concentrated on shuffling the cards and didn't look his way, for which he was grateful.

Ty pushed back his chair. "Deal me out for the next hand. I'll walk the tired old man out the door."

That produced more laughter and teasing, but Brant was grateful for Ty's help in moving out. "Great. Glad to have the company at my age." He figured Ty had something on his mind.

Sure enough, once they'd ambled down the porch steps, Ty came out with it. "What's going on with you, bro? You've been watching the clock all night and that's not typical of the laid-back guy I know."

"Aria's coming out to the cabin sometime after ten."

That brought Ty to a complete stop. "She *is*?"

Brant met his gaze. "Yeah."

"So that's how the wind blows. I wondered after seeing you two together. Did you know her before this?"

"Nope. She was just some kid I passed in the halls at school. She was three years behind me. Do you remember her?"

Ty shrugged. "Not really. The name's familiar, and I sort of remember her brother Josh." He paused and rubbed his chin. "Are you saying this all developed since yesterday?"

"I know how it sounds but—"

"It sounds like you've been blindsided." He smiled. "I wondered if that would ever happen."

"It's not what you're thinking. The chemistry's off the charts but she has her life and I have mine. Once Linus's training is over, I'm gone."

"Yeah, right." Ty gave him an irritatingly know-it-all smile.

"You always were a smartass and I see that having Whitney around hasn't changed that particular aspect of your personality."

"Good thing you love that about me, huh?"

"Sure is."

"Whitney has changed me, bro. I'm a better man because of her." He was quiet for a minute. "Can I give you some advice?"

"Are you asking my permission? Because if you are, I'm gonna pass."

"Judging from your behavior, you think a lot of this woman. If I were you, I'd make sure she understands that you're not planning to stick around." He peered at him. "Unless you are."

"Nope. Not hanging around. Not my style."

"Then she deserves to know that. She might misunderstand your eagerness."

"She won't. It's not that kind of relationship."

"Tell that to somebody who hasn't known you for fifteen years. You don't leave a hot poker game with your nearest and dearest unless it's important. She'll pick up on that."

"It's sex, bro. Plain and simple." Brant knew that was a lie the second the words were out of his mouth. "Well, it's more than sex and we get along great, but you know me. I don't make a long-term commitment with any woman."

"I saw the way she looked at you during lunch. You might want to give her some background on that decision."

"I see no reason to drag that out. It has nothing to do with what's between Aria and me. We're both focused on having a good time with each other in the here and now."

"Are you absolutely sure about that?"

"Look, Whitney's terrific and I understand that you two share everything. I haven't given Aria any reason to think we're headed in that direction and she hasn't implied it, either."

Ty studied him for several long seconds. "Okay. Obviously you're not ready to hear my words of wisdom." He punched him lightly on the arm. "I'd better get back in there and continue my complete domination of the game. Have fun."

"Thanks, I will." The trek to the cabin took a while, which gave him time to think about what Ty had said.

Back in tenth grade, the school psychologist had tried to get him to admit he was upset about his mother taking off after his father's death.

Not really. He'd accepted that relationships didn't last and he'd simply enjoy them when he could. Tonight he was about to do that very thing.

After switching on a few lights in the cabin, he went out to the small front porch and sat in one of the two rockers. By ten twenty she still wasn't there. Although he considered himself a patient man, he couldn't make that claim tonight. He'd kept his chair in such constant motion that he'd probably worn grooves in the porch floor.

He'd left the porch light off because he didn't relish sitting in a spotlight waiting for her. Entertaining a woman at his place was a new experience and so far he liked the concept. The washer and dryer had come in handy. This afternoon he'd changed the sheets on the bed and turned them back. He'd washed the towels in the bathroom, too.

In moving from ranch to ranch, he'd always bedded down in the bunkhouse. Consequently any night spent with a lady had been at her place. While that was fine, this was better.

He'd felt right at home from the moment Cade had brought him here. He wouldn't mind having his own cabin someday, but he couldn't imagine how that would fit into his lifestyle. He'd just appreciate this one while he had it.

After Aria had left this afternoon he'd made a quick trip to town on the pretext of buying some snacks for the cabin. He didn't really need them. Cade had left him stuff like bread and crackers, plus some cheese, peanut butter, jelly, a six-pack of beer and some milk. He had not, however, left a box of condoms, because he wasn't a mind reader.

Now the bedside table drawer had that item tucked inside, and there was red wine on the kitchen counter and white in the refrigerator. He didn't figure Aria for a beer drinker. She was a gourmet cook and they were all about wine. He'd seen that demonstrated while they'd made coq au vin.

He was ready. He couldn't be any more ready, in fact. And still no headlights had appeared on the dirt road. He should just relax and listen to the sounds of the night—an owl hooting, the distant yipping of a pack of coyotes chasing a rabbit, the wind sifting through the branches of nearby pines, *the muted growl of an engine.*

He stood, as if being upright would allow him to hear it better. Yep, the vehicle was coming closer. His pulse rate accelerated. Had to be her. Then he saw the headlights bobbing along and his chest tightened.

Watching the lights approach, he clattered down the steps. He'd originally planned to wait for her on the porch, envisioning himself in the rocker, looking relaxed. Eager anticipation of a woman's visit was so unlike him. That thought came and went and he no longer cared if it was like him or not. She was here.

He had her door open before she'd shut off the engine. Gathering her into his arms, he lifted her from the seat and nudged the door closed with his shoulder. Then he started toward the cabin.

"Wait! I brought something."

He paused. "What?"

"Pie! I brought us pie!"

"Later." He started off again.

"But it's still hot!"

"I'm a hell of a lot hotter than that pie."

She laughed and wound her arms around his neck. "You're a crazy man."

"You know what? I am and I can't seem to do anything about it. Only one thing is going to make me sane again."

"I may know what that is."

"I suspect you do." He climbed the porch steps.

"Cute cabin."

"It's cuter inside. Can you open the screen door?"

"Sure."

Shouldering his way in, he carried her across the wooden floor of the main room.

"Nice."

"The bedroom's nicer." He strode quickly down the hall. Once inside the room he crossed to the bed and sat her on the end of it. He was breathing hard, but that had nothing to do with the effort of carrying her.

Kneeling down, he undid her ponytail and tossed the scrunchie away. Then he buried his fingers in her hair. "I apologize in advance. I'm feeling like an animal right now. The next time we do this, I promise to take my time."

Her hands locked around his neck and she gazed into his eyes. "I've waited all day. Behaving like an animal sounds perfect to me."

"But you brought pie." He massaged her scalp.

"In case you were hungry."

"I'm desperately hungry."

Her eyes glittered. "Me, too. Go for it, cowboy."

That was all he needed to send him into overdrive. While he jerked off her boots, she pulled her Camille's Restaurant polo shirt over her head. Next he went for the snap on her jeans.

She quickly caught his hands. "Never mind. I'll do it." She sounded as desperate as he felt. "Work on your own clothes."

She had a good point. No sense getting her naked if he wasn't. He leaned against the wall and took off his boots. Then he opened the bedside table drawer and took out a condom. He didn't want to be groping for it at the zero hour and he wanted her to know he'd remembered.

She noticed and smiled. "I wondered about that."

"Went shopping after you left."

"Thank you." She wiggled out of her jeans. "I thought you might be lying in bed naked when I showed up."

"I needed to watch for you." He left his shirt mostly fastened and pulled it over his head.

"Were you afraid I wouldn't make it?" She reached for the clasp of her bra.

"I knew you would. I just…needed to be there when you drove in."

"So you could sweep me up and carry me off to your lair?"

"Something like that." He hadn't planned on scooping her out of the van and hauling her inside, but apparently instinct had taken over.

"For the record, I thought it was fun." She tossed her bra aside. When she leaned toward the nightstand and picked up the condom packet, her breasts swayed enticingly. "Ready when you are."

For a moment he couldn't do anything but stare at her. The rosy flush of her skin and her taut nipples told him that she wanted him and the fierce glow of desire in her violet eyes sent a surge of heat straight to his groin. He almost came.

Fingers trembling with anticipation, he peeled off his jeans and briefs. His cock leaped free, ready for action. A drop of moisture gathered on the tip. He was so damned close to losing control.

Her gaze lowered to his pride and joy. When she looked up, her intent was there in her eyes. "We could play a little first."

He hesitated, his balls tightening. "I love having your

mouth on me." Lust strummed his vocal cords and deepened his pitch. "I love it too much. If you touch me now, I'll come."

"Let me try." Her voice became a silky purr. "I'll be careful. When it's too much, I'll put this on." She laid the packet beside her on the bed.

He wanted what she offered. His cock twitched at the memory of her lips drawing him in and her tongue swirling over every sensitive inch. He stepped toward her.

"Just a taste. Then we'll go for the main event." Wrapping her fingers around his shaft, she leaned forward and kissed the tip.

He groaned. "I don't think I can—"

"I do." She took him in slowly.

Watching her do it was heaven but trying to hold back was hell. His cock touched the back of her throat. He clenched his jaw against the climax that hammered at the door. But, oh, God, this felt amazing.

She hollowed her cheeks, sucking gently as she rose. She finished by pressing a kiss to the tip once more. Her lashes lifted and she looked into his eyes. "You're magnificent. I love taking your measure."

He groaned. She was incredible, the most perfect lover he'd ever had.

"Besides, these go on easier when you're wet."

He'd somehow missed the part where she'd opened the packet. She rolled on the condom with a minimum of fuss, but he had to brace himself against coming. He'd spent too much time imagining this next step. Finally he'd experience that ultimate connection.

Once she had the condom on, she scooted back on the bed, giving him room to climb in after her. His heart pounded like a jackhammer as he crawled onto the mattress and straight into her waiting arms. It was all so easy, so right.

One moment he was kissing her ripe mouth and the next he'd eased his hips between her thighs. She welcomed him by wrapping her legs around his and then…he thrust deep and was there, all of him.

She moaned and he lifted his mouth from hers. "You okay?"

"I've never been more okay in my life." Her fingers dug into his backside. "We fit."

He brushed his lips over hers. "I guess you were worried."

"You're a big guy." She wiggled against him. "I like that, but I wasn't sure if we'd…but we do."

"So it's okay to move?"

"God, yes. Move. And move some more."

That worked for him. He needed to move, to ease back and slide home again. He craved the sweet friction of her tight channel, but now that he was there, he'd regained some control. He fit, but just barely, and that made every thrust a very happy occasion indeed.

Apparently it was for her, too. She rose to meet each stroke and began to make small, whimpering cries of joy. She tightened around him and he bore down. "Can you come?"

"Yes." She began to pant. "Oh, yes."

He pumped faster and she arched upward with a cry of release that thrilled his soul. Next time she came he'd let himself go, but he'd wanted to guarantee her pleasure first. Turned out she was easy to please.

Slipping both hands beneath her bottom, he lifted her so he could shift the angle.

"Ohhhhh."

"Like that?" He kept rocking into her.

"Yes, oh, yes."

"Look at me, Aria."

She met his gaze and took a shaky breath. "I'm looking."

"We're going to come together this time."

"Okay."

He couldn't help smiling. She was so sweet, so sexy, so willing. "Tell me when you're there." He was poised on the edge of his climax, ready to launch himself over.

She trembled beneath him. "Nearly there."

He thrust up and in. "How's that?"

"Yes, more."

He held her gaze and gave her what she asked for. Her eyes darkened and her body hummed as he thrust in again and again and—

"Now!"

He pushed hard and she exploded. The tremors set off a chain reaction and his cock responded with a climax that seemed to go on forever. Gasping, he buried his cock in her pulsing body and rested his forehead against her shoulder.

So good. So damned good. He'd known loving her would be special, but he'd never imagined a sensation like this. As she came and he came, the world sparkled and fizzed like a million bottles of champagne all opened at once.

She held him tight and he loved that. She wasn't off on some private rocket ship enjoying the show all by her lonesome. She was sharing this experience with him. That was a gift he didn't take lightly.

When their breathing eventually slowed, he propped himself up on his forearms and looked down to see how she was making out.

She gazed up at him and grinned. "I'm gonna want to do that again."

He laughed, but he felt some pride, too. She'd enjoyed the experience he'd helped create. Apparently she'd enjoyed it a lot. "Maybe we should take a break and eat some of that pie you brought."

"I had to guess at what you liked."

"What'd you bring?"

"Cherry."

He smiled down at her. "You have just become the most amazing woman I've ever met. Cherry pie is my absolute favorite. How did you guess that?"

"I used my psychic powers."

"Apparently." He leaned down and kissed her softly. "Be right back."

When he returned from the bathroom she was out of bed and wearing his shirt. It hung to mid-thigh so he couldn't tell if she'd put on her panties or not. But a quick glance at the clothes they'd both tossed on the floor gave him the answer. Not.

She glanced at him with a cute little smile. "Do you mind?"

"Do I mind that you're standing there looking sexy as hell wearing my shirt and nothing else? Yeah, I hate that."

"I know you said I shouldn't wear clothes at all, but this works better for me and it still makes everything…easy." She rolled back the sleeves.

He pretended not to understand. "Like for eating pie?" He pulled on his briefs and jeans because somebody had to go fetch it and he wasn't expecting her to.

She laughed. "Yeah, like for eating pie." She gathered up her clothes and began folding them.

"Might be even easier if you took off the shirt, though." He zipped his pants and decided he'd walk outside barefoot. The fewer things he had to put on and take off the better. "Then you wouldn't have to worry about spillage."

"I'm a very neat eater."

"That's too bad." He watched as she set the folded pile of clothes on the dresser and the boots beside it. He wasn't surprised that she liked things tidy. They were alike in that. He would have picked up his clothes except he was wearing half and she was wearing the other half.

She turned to him. "You like messy eaters?"

"Under certain circumstances."

"Such as?"

"Eating cherry pie naked."

12

WHILE BRANT HOBBLED outside in his bare feet to get the pie, Aria explored her surroundings. Damon Harrison, one of the original Thunder Mountain boys and a master carpenter, had joined forces with his equally competent fiancée, Philomena Turner, to build the place for Cade. Damon's and Phil's combined talents with tools had created a beautiful little cabin.

The bedroom had a rustic look with an elegantly carved headboard depicting the Big Horn Mountains. The lamps on the bedside tables were frosted glass globes on wooden bases, a modern replica of an old-fashioned gas lamp design. She'd been rushed in here so fast she'd barely noticed the headboard or the lamps.

Heading down the hall toward the main part of the cabin, she discovered that the floor plan was simple. Living and dining areas were combined and a waist-high counter sectioned off the kitchen. Honey-colored wood was everywhere, from the walls themselves to the sturdy wooden furniture.

Aria decided on the spot that when she bought land for her home and cooking school, she wanted a house like this. She walked into the kitchen first and admired the gleaming

appliances, all top quality, and the butcher-block counter-
tops. She could have a blast cooking here.

The living area was basic and classy. Thick cushions
upholstered in a forest pattern covered all the furniture. A
large rag rug anchored the living room, but the hardwood
floor was left bare under the oval dining table.

But no one had added personal touches like plants or
framed photos. The walls were bare of art, too. As she
wondered if Cade had been too busy to choose those
things, Brant came through the screen door with the bakery box containing the cherry pie.

"It's still a little warm on the bottom," he said. "We
could stick it in the oven for a few minutes and heat it
back up."

"Okay." Aria opened the built-in oven and peered at
the immaculate surfaces. "I don't think this has ever been
used. We'd better put some foil or a cookie sheet underneath so it won't drip all over this pristine oven."

"Cade wouldn't care."

"I'd care." She searched the cupboards until she found
aluminum foil. Judging from the scarcity of pots and pans,
she wouldn't come upon a cookie sheet. "He doesn't use
this kitchen, does he?"

"Doesn't look like it. He's never been what you call
domestic."

"Then it's a good thing he's planning to take my cooking class with Lexi." She tore off some foil, placed the pie
plate on it and rolled up the edges to keep any overflow
from escaping.

"How come?" Brant leaned against the counter, watching her.

"I get the impression she's looking for an equal part-
ner who'll share the housekeeping chores. And that usually includes fixing meals." She slid the pie into the oven

and turned it on. "She'd probably be thrilled if he learned to cook and made her dinner here."

"You know what, I'll bet you're right. Maybe I should mention that to him, see what he says."

"If he's never thought to do it, and from the looks of this kitchen he hasn't, that helps explain why Lexi thinks he's not ready for marriage."

"Then why doesn't she just tell him that? Something subtle like 'You need to learn to cook, bozo.'"

That made her laugh. "I can picture her saying that, too. Maybe she's hoping he'll come up with it on his own."

"Oh. Then I won't suggest it to him. I might muck it up."

She sighed. "Who knows? Maybe saying something is a good idea. I shouldn't be giving out advice."

His gaze sharpened. "Why is that?"

Shoot. She'd promised herself that her frustrating conversation with Josh wouldn't spoil tonight. Then she'd gone and made that dumb comment. "Oh, just because I'm no expert." Her throat tightened unexpectedly and she searched for a distraction. "Let's see what we have in the way of dishes around here." She turned and opened a cupboard.

Brant's response came a beat late, as if he'd taken a moment to assess her mood. "Sounds as if we're going to get all prissy and civilized when we eat this pie. Next you'll tell me we need forks."

She dredged up a smile as she found plates and took them out of the cupboard. "And how were you planning to eat it? With your fingers?"

He closed the distance between them and took the plates from her. Then he set them on the counter and drew her into his arms. "Yes, ma'am. I was hoping you'd serve it to me on your naked body."

She slid her hands up his muscled chest and laced her fingers together behind his neck. "Goodness, that's—"

"Right after you tell me what happened with Josh today."

She met his gaze. "Let's not get into it."

"Let's do." Holding her gently, he reached up and brushed her hair back from her face. "He's the reason for Linus being born and the reason I met you. It's no use pretending that he's not a player in this drama. I know you were planning to talk to him after you left the ranch this afternoon."

"I did talk to him." She pushed the words past the lump in her throat. "But it's not a cheerful subject."

"Want to tell me about it?"

"No."

"You sure?" His solid warmth was reassuring as he continued to look at her in that patient way that was so Brant.

She sighed, uncertain. "No."

"Then tell me."

"It's a long story."

"I have time."

She blew out a breath. "Okay, but you should probably know the dynamic." As she told him about Clara Simpson, she watched his mouth twitch. "You can laugh if you want."

He cleared his throat. "I'm sorry, but the image of you hiding in the bushes taking pictures…" He grinned and shook his head. "It wasn't funny to you, though."

"Actually it was funny after I got older. Then today Josh admitted he'd known about her and hadn't cared, but because of me he'd felt obliged to end it."

"I see." He massaged the small of her back.

"I ruined his first sexual adventure. I feel terrible about

messing that up for him. I thought I was doing the right thing."

"And you meant well." He studied her with his kind eyes.

"That's what he said today. He knows I mean well this time, too." She took a shaky breath. "I think he wanted to make the point that I butt in when I shouldn't and here I am doing it again." Frustration tightened a knot in her stomach. "Damn it, Brant, this is a *totally* different situation." She hesitated. "Isn't it?"

"Definitely. A cute foal prancing around the pasture looks nothing like naked people having sex in the back of a pickup."

"Okay, so pictures were involved both times, but—" She heard his soft chuckle and peered up at him. "You're teasing me, aren't you?"

"Just a little." He smiled. "Aria, you're a loving sister who wants the best for your brother. He's not responding the way you wish he would, but that doesn't mean he won't ever come around. Maybe it's time to back off and see if he'll come to you."

"But you said the sooner Linus gets used to the wheelchair the better."

"I did, but—"

"Besides, if he'd come out to the ranch before the students get here, it would be easier all the way around." Thank goodness she'd found out he didn't want to advertise his disabled status to the world. That insight was important.

"But it's not any good if he comes out reluctantly."

"Even if he's reluctant, he'll change his mind once he sees Linus. I know he will."

Brant opened his mouth as if to say something. Then he closed it again.

"What?"

"He's your brother. You know that better than I do."

"You were going to make a comment, though. I'd like to hear it."

"Just that we don't know yet how it will go and if Linus balks at the sight of the wheelchair...that could affect Josh's reaction."

"It could." She understood that much better after Josh's outburst today. He'd be humiliated if Linus turned out to be afraid of his chair.

"I've been wondering if I should rent a wheelchair and introduce Linus to it before Josh shows up. That might be smarter."

"But what if it's all for nothing?" The words slipped out and she hated the way they sounded, the way *she* sounded—fearful and despairing. "Forget I said that. I didn't mean to be negative." She went into planning mode. "Renting a wheelchair's a great idea. I'll see if I can get one in the morning."

"It's Sunday."

"I know the people at the medical supply place and the owner is an early riser. If I send him a text first thing in the morning, he might let me pick one up before I drive out to the ranch."

"That would be great." He continued to rub her back.

"I'm glad you had the idea. It's one more hurdle we can eliminate so that if... I mean *when* Josh comes out, it'll be smooth. Or smoother. I promise the wheelchair training won't be for nothing."

"But for the sake of argument, let's say I go to the trouble of teaching Linus about wheelchairs and Josh still doesn't want anything to do with him. I know how much that would upset you, but—"

"It won't happen. I'll get him out here."

"I'm sure you will, but don't worry that I'll be upset if he refuses to cooperate."

She stared at him. "How could you not be upset after putting so much thought and effort into the project?"

"That's not how I roll. I'd hate to see you get disappointed because I know how much you want this to work out. For me, though, it's just…life. Linus will have a good start, no matter what."

She gazed at him, unsure how to respond to an attitude so different from hers. "Don't you let *anything* get to you?"

"I saw someone mistreating a puppy a few months ago. That got to me, but it was easily settled. I took the puppy."

"The person just let you do that?"

"As a matter of fact, they did." He grinned. "That's where being big as a house comes in handy."

"Did you keep the puppy?" She imagined this big guy cradling a little puppy and wished she'd been there.

"I move around too much. But I happened to know of a little girl on another ranch whose dog had just died. I checked with her parents to get the okay and now she has him."

"So you rescued a puppy and consoled a sad little girl." It was a touching story. As if she needed one more reason to like him.

He shrugged. "You asked if anything got to me and that came to mind."

"Okay, puppy rescuer, you can eat cherry pie off my naked body."

"I can? Hot damn! What will you let me do if I saved a kitten from a tall tree?"

"When was this?"

"Never happened. But if that kind of story gives me special treatment, I'm sure I can dredge up another one for more points. Let's see, there was the time—"

"Save it for later, Sir Galahad." Laughing, she wiggled out of his arms. "That was the oven timer you just heard. The pie's ready."

"You're right. I should wait until after I claim my first good-guy reward before I hit you up for another one."

"Smart man." She found a couple of pot holders in a drawer and took the steaming dessert from the oven. "Incidentally, I'm not clear on how you planned to do this, but I'm not letting you smear pie on me until it cools a little."

"Gotcha."

She glanced around for a place to put the pie. She didn't want to damage either the butcher-block counter or the round wooden table. "Could you grab one of those plates and put it on the table so I don't scorch the finish?"

"Sure." He picked up one of the blue pottery plates and set it on the table. "These look brand-new. Not a scratch or a chip."

"Too bad everything's going to waste." She set the pie down.

"Seems like it to me, too. I can't cook, but when I look at that kitchen, I almost think I can."

She smiled at him. "Of course you can. You just never had a reason to figure out how."

"Still don't."

"True." If she'd had a sudden impulse to teach him, she could forget about it. His jobs came with room and board.

He pulled out a chair and gestured toward it. "Have a seat, ma'am."

"I'm curious as to how you plan to work this without making a god-awful mess." She took the chair and he scooted her in.

"I'm not sure yet. I'm making it up as I go along." He sat in the seat next to her. "But that pie smells mighty good." He broke off a piece of the sugary crust and offered it to her.

"You're really going to eat it with your fingers?"

"It can be done, you know. Want this piece of crust?"

"You're welcome to it."

"Okay." He popped it in his mouth and chewed. "Mmm-mmm."

"How do you know it can be done? Wait. I don't want to hear about you licking cherry pie off some other woman."

"I've never done that before. But a few times the brothers and I raided the kitchen and made off with some left-over pie, which we'd eat with our fingers." He broke off another section of crust and this time red cherry filling oozed from the jagged opening he'd made. "Now that's sexy." He dipped the crust in the filling. "Want this?"

"You go right ahead. This is your fantasy."

"When we're done, it'll be yours, too." He winked at her. Then he ate the gooey crust with relish and licked his fingers. "Now I'm getting inspired."

She wasn't ready to admit it, but so was she. The sight of a half-naked, muscular cowboy eating with his fingers was erotic as hell.

He turned to her. "Let's take off your shirt."

"Technically your shirt."

"Whatever." He began unfastening the snaps.

"There's a faster way." She lifted up so she wasn't sitting on the shirttails and pulled it over her head. "How's that?"

"Oh, lady." His gaze raked over her as she sat beside him. "You have cherry pie written all over you."

The anticipation in his eyes fired her blood. "When I brought you a pie, I never expected to be wearing it." Then she had another thought. "If this is such a great idea, why can't I eat my dessert from your naked body?"

"Want to?"

"Yes, I believe I do. Strip down, cowboy."

"Okay, I'm game." Taking off his jeans and briefs revealed that he was more than a little interested in this plan.

She glanced at his rigid cock. "I see a place that needs to be decorated with some cherry pie filling."

"Hey, this is my idea. I get first dibs."

"Then you'll have to tell me what you have in mind, because I have no clue."

"Like I said, it's a work in progress." Pulling out his chair, he turned it sideways, facing her before sitting down. "You need to come over here and sit on my lap."

She eyed the situation. "Your lap already has a lot going on there."

"There's room. I have long legs." He patted his thighs. "Right here."

So she perched on his warm and extremely solid thighs. His pride and joy was within easy reach.

He caught her wrists before she could act on that impulse. "Wait your turn."

"But you like being touched. I know you do."

"I do, but so do you." He dipped his fingers into the pie and brought them to her mouth. "See how it tastes."

She grasped his hand and licked his fingers clean. It was unbelievably arousing.

"I think you liked that." His gaze fell to her nipples. "A lot."

"It wasn't bad."

"Then let's try this on for size." He scooped up a glob of filling and let it drip over her breasts.

She gasped as warm syrup spread over her sensitized skin and bits of cherry clung to her nipples.

"Now arch your back a little."

She gave him room to maneuver and he lowered his head so he could lap at the red juice and the cherry bits.

The suction of his mouth combined with the swipe of his tongue was enough to drive her crazy, but his soft murmurs of pleasure threatened to snap her control.

She clutched his head and eased him away. "That's enough for you. Let me have a turn."

"You like my idea?"

"Yes. Now let me play."

Laughing, he leaned back in his chair. "I'm all yours."

The moment she plunged her fingers into the warm pie filling, she understood the sensual appeal. She'd baked hundreds of pies but she'd never eaten a single one with her fingers. Which made sense—it wouldn't be nearly as much fun alone.

She started with his mouth, covering it with filling and then licking it away. Next she dripped cherries and thick juice on his chest. He moaned and his big body shook as she cleaned him up. She dipped her fingers into the pie again, intending to smooth it over his cock.

Eyes glittering, he grasped her wrist. "Once you do that, the game will be over. I'll haul you into the bedroom and have you flat on your back in five seconds."

"And that's a problem because?"

"There's a lot more pie left."

That made some kind of crazy sense.

"Don't worry. I won't let this go to waste." He proceeded to suck on her fingers.

As he slowly drove her insane with that maneuver, she moved restlessly in his lap. "Okay," she murmured. "You can stop now."

He lifted his head. "I don't think so."

Before she understood his intent, he'd dipped her fingers into the pie filling again. He licked and sucked her fingers some more, and while she was still reeling from that sensation, he lowered her hand between her thighs and coaxed her to touch herself.

"Add a little flavor for me," he murmured, "and make yourself feel good."

Dazed by the eroticism of the moment, she instinctively followed his directions. Oh, yes. So good. She didn't utter a word of protest when he lifted her onto the table and parted her legs.

He slowly spread warm cherry pie filling at the entrance to her most secret place. When he began tasting and sipping and suckling, she quickly lost her mind.

She came once, and he reapplied more filling. She came again. The pleasure was so intense that she made a lot of noise. Good thing no one was around to hear.

After her second orgasm he carried her into the bedroom, snapped on a condom and buried himself inside her. She came again, and finally, so did he.

At last her breathing returned to normal and she regained a slight grasp of reality. She noticed that he'd readjusted their position so they lay side by side. Maybe he'd worried that his weight would crush her. She could imagine him having that thought.

She hugged him close. "I didn't get to put any more on you," she murmured.

"It's okay." He gathered her close. "There's plenty left."

13

WHEN BRANT EASED out of bed to take care of the condom and clean up a bit, he left Aria dozing. She must have been exhausted from a long day followed by explosive sex. He was grateful that she'd driven out there, but maybe next time he should go to her place. That might be easier on her.

He assumed there would be a next time. She seemed as eager to take advantage of this unexpected attraction as he was. No telling how often they'd be able to see each other once the students arrived, but until then they had late evenings to themselves.

Still, she obviously was tired, so he quietly slipped back into bed and turned off the light so she could sleep.

"Brant?"

"I thought you were off to dreamland."

She rolled toward him. "Just for a few minutes. I took a power nap, which is something I learned to do years ago. You get so much more done."

"Guess so." He'd never believed in power naps, but she did, so he kept his mouth shut.

"Do you think there's cherry pie filling on the sheets? Maybe we should turn the light on and look. That red might stain."

He chuckled and pulled her close. She might be the most compulsive woman he'd ever been to bed with, but she felt amazing nestled against him, her head tucked under his chin, as if the two of them were meant to fit this way.

"Seriously, I don't want to leave things a mess." Her breath tickled his skin.

"I'll wash the sheets tomorrow. I may not be much of a cook, but I'm a heck of a linens wrangler. I know about bleach and everything."

"I'll bet you do. It's just that I'm not usually this wild. I've never climbed into a bed after being covered with cherry pie filling."

"I'm shocked to hear it."

She pinched his butt. "Be nice."

"Sorry." They should sleep, but he couldn't help caressing her. Getting acquainted with her curves and the satin texture of her skin was such a treat. "Am I a bad influence on you?"

"I wouldn't say bad. I'd say different." She was quiet for a moment. "I know that I take things too seriously a good bit of the time. For instance, I used to think every guy I had sex with should be a potential husband."

"Oh?" His hand stilled as he thought of what Ty had said. This might be his opening. "Speaking of that, I—"

"Settle down. I don't think that anymore. I'm not looking for a husband at all, actually."

"Oh."

She laughed softly. "I just felt your whole body relax. Don't worry, Brant. You're like the guy in that old song. You want to leave your sleeping bag behind my couch."

"I'm not even that guy, Aria." He began stroking her again because it calmed him. "I don't have long-term relationships. I just don't."

"No problem. I have zero expectations."

"That's good." Maybe he'd be off the hook just that easy.

"But now that we're talking about it, are you saying you've never had a long-term relationship?"

"That's right."

"I understand that you move around because of your job, but the guy in the song moved around, too. He just kept coming back to one woman."

So maybe they weren't on the same page, after all. "That's not for me." He waited to see if she'd ask why.

He felt a shift in the mood and that bothered him. Obviously she didn't want to keep pestering him, but he hadn't given her much of an answer. He took a deep breath. "It's not for me because I don't believe in it."

Her breath caught. "Wow."

"Ty said I should explain my history to you and he could be right."

"Ty said that?"

"He thinks I'm different around you than I usually am with women."

"Are you?"

"Yeah." He massaged the small of her back. "I've never let myself get this involved in such a short time." He placed a soft kiss on her forehead. "I'm nuts about you, Aria, but that doesn't change anything."

"I wouldn't want it to."

"Good." He should be overjoyed with the way this conversation was progressing. Instead it depressed him a little.

She slid her arm around him and nestled closer. "But I wouldn't mind having you tell me your history."

"There's not much to say." He let out a slow breath. "My dad died of a heart attack when I was twelve and my mom left me with her sister. That's the last I saw of her."

"Oh, no." She hugged him tight. "That must have been—"

"I know it sounds terrible, but it really wasn't so bad."

He continued to rub her back. "Neither of them spent much time with me, anyway. I'm good at being on my own. It's the way I like to live."

"And you don't get lonely?"

"Nope."

She was quiet for a moment. Then she lifted her head and wiggled up higher so she could cup his face in both hands. "I believe you. I've felt your strength from the beginning." Then she kissed him.

It wasn't a sweet, I-feel-sorry-for-you kiss. She went all-out and one hand strayed south to fondle his very stiff cock. So he began a little fondling action of his own and in no time thoughts of their conversation were replaced by thoughts of sex. Much better.

She was panting by the time she wrenched her mouth from his. "You have more of those raincoats, I hope."

"I bought a box." He gulped for air. "If necessary, I'll buy another one."

"Tonight?"

He laughed and moved away from her long enough to open the drawer and take out the box in question. He plopped it down between them. "If we go through all these…" He paused to suck in a lungful of air. "I'll contact the *Guinness World Records*."

She took the box and opened it. "You never know." She pulled out a packet and put the box on the pillow above her head. "We might set some records."

"Here's the problem with that. We'd have to go for quantity, not quality." He rolled her to her back and feathered a kiss over her mouth. "I'm in the mood for some quality."

She laid the foil packet next to them and wrapped her arms around his back. "Sounds good to me."

"Your mouth still tastes like cherry pie. It really is my

favorite. I think we need some more." Yeah, cherry pie was exactly what they needed right now. He started to get up.

She tightened her grip. "Not in here. It'll be too messy."

"It won't if I'm careful. Plus I'll bring in one of those huge green towels from the bathroom." He nuzzled behind her ear. "Come on. It'll be great."

Laughing, she squirmed beneath him. "That tickles."

"I promise not to tickle you with cherry pie." He kept nuzzling.

She laughed harder. "Brant, we don't need pie!"

"Are you sure about that?" Whispering in her ear, he reminded her in vivid detail how he'd used the syrup before and how many times he'd made her come. All the while he ran his tongue around the delicate curve of her earlobe. She was breathing faster and she let him go without another word of protest.

By the time he walked back into the bedroom with the towel and the pie, she'd turned on the light and climbed out of bed.

"I'll take this." She pulled the towel off his shoulder and spread it out on the mattress. "Now lie down."

"I was thinking you'd be the one lying down and I'd be the one applying pie to your sweet body."

"You got to do that already. I, on the other hand, only got half a turn. So lie down, cowboy, and let me juice you up where it counts."

He stood there grinning at the transformation. Her tendency to be bossy was no different. She'd been like that from their first conversation. Her spirit of play was new, though, at least to him.

"I'll take the pie, too." She plucked it out of his hands. "And be sure to lie in the middle of that towel so I don't have to worry about the sheets."

"Yes, ma'am." He stretched out on the nubby material

and stuffed a pillow behind his head so he could see. Anticipation of what lay ahead had his cock standing as straight as a lodgepole pine. "What did you do with the condom?"

"Let me worry about that."

"Okay." Considering her cautious nature, he knew she wouldn't forget.

Setting the pie plate on the towel, she lifted her arms and gathered her hair behind her neck. Then she looped it into a soft knot. Judging from how easily she did it, she'd gone through that routine a thousand times when she needed to quickly get her hair away from her face. She probably thought nothing of it, but he was entranced by the simple gesture.

She picked up the pie plate before easing onto the bed. "I believe I'll go straight to the main event."

"You won't get an argument from me."

She dipped her fingers into the pie. "And you've never had a woman smear cherry pie filling on your manly self before?"

"Nope."

"Any kind of pie?"

"Nope."

"Cake?"

"Nope."

"Whipped cream?"

"Um, well, there was—"

"That's okay. You don't have to elaborate. I'm glad to be the first one in the pie and cake category, at any rate."

He couldn't help smiling at that. Her brother wasn't the only competitive one in the family. Even in something like this, she wanted to be first.

"Where to start, where to start." She licked her fingers absently as she surveyed him.

His breath caught. "You may not realize it, but when you lick your fingers, that's…arousing."

"Is it?" She dipped two fingers into the filling again. As they dripped with scarlet juice, she held them over the pie plate. Then she slowly sucked each one clean.

A surge of lust made his cock twitch. "You realize it."

"Mmm-hmm." Her violet eyes sparkled. "I learned from the best."

"You've managed to outdo your teacher. I'm a wreck."

"Thanks for the compliment. Maybe it's time to do my teacher."

"That would be very—" He gasped as her juice-covered fingers began to stroke up and down, around and around. Sticky, slippery and incredibly erotic.

But that was nothing compared to the sensation of her tongue licking him clean. She was thorough, oh, so very thorough. This morning's episode out behind the barn had been a mere preview of what that tongue of hers could accomplish. He moaned and shifted on the towel.

"Don't thrash around too much." Her breath was cool against his wet shaft. "You'll move the towel."

"I'm the laundry guy," he said through gritted teeth as she continued to drive him insane. "I'll take care of… Oh, God…when you do that…"

"Glad you like it. There's more."

He watched in fascination as she located a whole cherry and placed it on the very tip of his cock. Then she took the tip in her mouth and rolled that soft cherry around. He clenched his fists and prayed that he wouldn't come.

She seemed to enjoy that maneuver, since she repeated it a couple more times. Then she went back to licking, nipping and dripping juice, letting drops slide from the tip downward until she caught it on her tongue. His breathing was out of control and soon he would be, too.

He dragged in air. "Better get the condom."

"Nope."

"I'm going to come."

"So do it." With that she stopped playing and got serious.

He didn't stand a chance. He came within seconds, yelling and cussing. He felt as if he might never stop coming. He thought his balls would explode. He was absolutely certain his eyes had rolled back in his head.

But he did stop coming eventually. He still couldn't breathe well, but he could focus again.

She sat on the bed, facing him, with the pie plate in her lap. She smiled. "That was fun."

"Mmm." It was the only sound he could manage, especially in his bedazzled state. She was stunning. Her hair was coming loose from the soft knot she'd made and her mouth was stained red from all the cherry juice. She had some on her chin, too.

He loved looking at the juice stains and remembering the intense pleasure she'd given him, more than he could have imagined. But her eyes captivated him most of all. He could bask in the glow of their violet depths for hours.

"You look happy," she said.

He cleared his throat. "Take happy multiplied times a million and you'll be close."

That seemed to please her. Her smile widened as she tightened her grip on the pie plate and climbed off the bed. "I'll get a washcloth. Just lie still."

"I don't think I could move if a grizzly walked through the bedroom door."

"I doubt that's going to happen, but if it does, I'll protect you."

"I don't doubt it. You're mighty." After she left the room, he lay there thinking about her strong protective instincts. Her campaign to save her brother from sinking into despair was fueled by that. In the unlikely event a grizzly walked into the bedroom, she probably would try to save him.

She came back in with a washcloth and a hand towel. Obviously she'd made a detour and had left the pie plate in the kitchen. "I need to clarify something."

"What's that?"

"I should probably tell you that I haven't the faintest idea how to deal with a grizzly. I've only seen one in the wild and that was from a long distance. So if you want me to protect you, you'll need to tell me how."

She was absolutely adorable. He cleared his throat. "Well, now, some experts advise standing as tall as possible and making lots of noise. Others say curl up in a ball and play dead. But everybody agrees you don't run away. They're way faster than you are."

She sat on the bed. "I'm not the type to play dead."

"I believe you. So you'd better stay true to character and go with the loud noises and standing tall—ahhh." He closed his eyes in ecstasy as she began sliding the warm, moist washcloth over his privates. "I should probably do that for myself, huh?"

"You could, but isn't this nicer?" She finished with the washcloth and began rubbing him gently with the hand towel. Once again, she was extremely thorough.

"Definitely nicer." He would have said she'd finished him off with the last episode, but apparently not. The warm washcloth had awakened his sleeping giant and the hand towel made it rise and shine. He gestured toward her work area. "Was that what you had in mind?"

"I wasn't sure what would happen." She nodded toward the bedside table as she continued to massage him with the towel. "But the condom is lying right there, and I got a little excited while I was having fun with pie filling."

"Say no more." He reached over for the condom before sitting up and capturing her wrist. "I'm well and truly dried off. So here's an idea. You lie down, I'll put this on, and we'll see what happens next." He slid over to make room for her.

"I should take the washcloth back to the—"

"How about this?" He snatched it away and tossed it over the glass lampshade. "It'll dry in a jiffy, and we have instant mood lighting."

She glanced around the room. "Everything looks sort of greenish."

"You don't like greenish?" He ripped open the packet and rolled on the condom.

"As it turns out, I love greenish." She stretched out beside him. "I'll pretend you're the frog prince."

"You can pretend I'm the King of England for all I care." He moved between her thighs. "Choose whatever royalty makes you happy." He leaned down and kissed her sweet mouth.

"I don't need royalty," she murmured against his lips. "I just need you."

14

ARIA LEFT BEFORE DAWN, promising to be back at the ranch after breakfast with a rented wheelchair. She longed to head down to the barn to peek in on Lucy and Linus, but she wasn't ready to advertise her overnight stay at the cabin. Brant had said he'd mentioned it to Ty, and Herb had probably guessed, so it wasn't exactly a secret.

But having them know and meeting Herb in the early morning at the barn were two very different things. Brant understood that, thank goodness. He understood so many things without being told.

The drive back to Sheridan gave her a chance to think about this complicated man. He might be the kindest person she'd ever known, and yet he'd been given such a rotten start in life. Her heart ached when she thought about a twelve-year-old who'd essentially lost both parents, although his mother must not have been much of a parent. That Brant had retained his sunny disposition was a testament to his inborn optimism.

At one point during the night she'd gently asked about his dad. Apparently the guy had been so engrossed in his work that he'd been oblivious to both his wife's and his son's needs. Rosie and Herb had been a godsend, but that couldn't have made up for having two neglectful parents for twelve years.

Brant had been conditioned to keep his connections with people loose and cheerful and she understood why. Despite the great sex and the bond of friendship they seemed to be developing, he wasn't interested in maintaining contact after he'd finished with Linus. She'd suspected that from the beginning and at first she'd liked the idea because she didn't want to be tied down any more than he did.

She didn't like it so much anymore. The thought of losing contact with him in a few weeks filled her with sadness. He was becoming important to her and she couldn't believe the reverse wasn't true.

That didn't mean she wanted a forever commitment from him. She had things to do and so did he. But if he'd consider keeping his sleeping bag stashed behind her couch, she'd be fine with that. And she would be there for him. He might not believe in that kind of relationship now, but if he'd give her a chance, she'd prove that it was possible.

At her apartment she showered and changed clothes. Before leaving the complex she glanced at Josh's door and wished things were different with him. But they weren't and taking a wheelchair out to the ranch today was actually more important than convincing Josh to go.

Getting the wheelchair had been easy. The owner of the medical supply place had taken several of her cooking classes. He let her in and handled the paperwork even though the sun had barely peeked over the horizon.

On her way out of town she stopped at her favorite bakery for a half dozen doughnuts. Then she picked up a latte at Rangeland Roasters, Sheridan's newest coffee shop. It wasn't the kind of healthy breakfast she usually had, which made it more fun.

Eating her sugary treat and drinking her coffee on the way out to the ranch, she smiled in anticipation of the day ahead. She looked forward to being with Linus and Lucy again, but she had to be honest with herself. Brant was the big draw.

And he really might leave after he finished training Linus. Her smile wobbled as she made herself face the possibility. He'd given her every reason to believe that he would end their relationship once his job was done.

Then why imagine that he might change his pattern for her? That kind of thinking led to heartache and disillusionment, which wouldn't help her bolster Josh's spirits. She'd be better off assuming he wouldn't remain in her life.

He came out to meet her when she pulled up to the barn just as he had the morning before. But this time he nudged back his hat and kissed her the minute she climbed out of the van. Holding her close, he gazed into her eyes. "Missed you."

"Missed you, too." He seemed to be quite attached for a guy who didn't do commitment. But until he announced a change in attitude she'd be a fool to place importance on the fact that he'd missed her.

"I see you got the wheelchair."

"Yep. Told you I would. Are we okay with kissing in public?" She knew that ranch people were out and about at dawn. "Where is everybody?"

"Ty and Whitney are down at the bathhouse working on the showerheads. They had some issues yesterday and had to go back twice to the hardware store. They're determined to finish today. Herb and Rosie are up at the house having breakfast. Cade and Lexi aren't here yet. So I get to kiss you again."

"Sounds like fun." Wrapping her arms around his neck, she vowed to enjoy the kiss for the temporary pleasure that it was and not read anything more into it. That worked for about two seconds. Nothing about his kiss felt temporary and in no time she'd resurrected her fantasy that he would stay.

He eased back. "Gotta stop now."

"I know." Good thing she was having trouble breathing or she might have asked him straight-out if he expected to leave her in a few weeks.

"You taste like doughnuts."

"I have doughnuts." It was a welcome change of subject. "Want some?"

He smiled. "It's a poor substitute, but I'll take it."

"Turn me loose and I'll get the box."

"I'll get it." Releasing her, he leaned through the open driver's door and picked up the box from the passenger seat. "If you keep bringing treats I'm gonna get fat."

"Not if you stay active."

He straightened. "What sort of activity did you have in mind, as if I didn't know?"

"Laundry."

He laughed. "It's done, so you can relax."

"Were the sheets a mess? They were, right?"

"Let's just say that every cherry juice stain reminded me of you. If I had my way, I wouldn't have bleached them out, but the sheets don't belong to me."

"Thanks for doing the laundry." So he would have liked a permanent reminder of making love to her? That didn't sound like a man who planned to ride off into the sunset.

"You're welcome. Thanks for bringing doughnuts." He opened the box. "Well, if it isn't raised glazed. My favorite."

"Are you sure you don't just automatically say that about everything?"

"I don't, I swear! I'm a real traditionalist when it comes to doughnuts. You can have all your frosting and jelly-filled and sprinkles. I like this kind best." He pulled one out and took a generous bite. "Mmm." He chewed and swallowed. "Super fresh. They must have just come out of the oven."

"They did. My timing at the bakery was perfect." She gestured at the two that were left. "You can have those. I had all I wanted on the drive out here."

"You ate nine doughnuts all by yourself? Go, you!"

"No, I bought six and ate three."

His hazel eyes gleamed. "Aw, come on. Nobody goes into a bakery and buys six doughnuts, especially on Sunday morning. You get a dozen. That's how it's done. It's okay if you ate nine. I won't judge."

"But I didn't! I only... You're teasing me, aren't you?"

"Would I do that?" He licked the glaze from his fingers.

"Here, let me." She took his big hand in both of hers and swiped her tongue over his thumb. Then she sucked on it.

"Oh, I see how it is." His voice grew husky. "You're a lady who believes in payback."

"Mmm-hmm."

"Very effective."

"Mmm."

"But you'll need to stop now."

She wasn't about to. She didn't care if his jeans were getting tight. Nine doughnuts, indeed. Moving from his thumb to his forefinger, she resumed her licking routine.

"Really, you'll want to quit."

"Why?" She drew his finger slowly into her mouth.

"Because my dad's coming down from the house."

She pulled his finger out so fast it made a popping

sound. Her cheeks burned as she scrambled away from him. "Do you think he saw me doing that?"

"If he did, he won't say a word. If it had been Cade, we'd never hear the end of it, so count yourself lucky."

She gulped. "Let's go get the wheelchair."

Chuckling, he put the doughnut box back on the passenger seat and shut the door before following her to the back of the van. "Want me to make up a story about having a splinter? I could do that."

"No stories. We'll just pretend he didn't see a thing." She unfastened the brackets holding the wheelchair in place.

"Here, let me get it." He stepped in and lifted the wheelchair down. "Could have been worse. You were really into that sucking business. No telling what you might have done next."

"Nothing," she said in an undertone. "We're going to forget all about it, okay?"

"Easy for you to say. You weren't the one being sucked on."

"Brant." She started to giggle, which was so unlike her. She wasn't the giggling type.

"I see you have a wheelchair," Herb said as he approached. "Is your brother here?"

Maybe he hadn't noticed anything since she obviously wouldn't leave her brother sitting in the van while she sucked on Brant's finger. Another wave of giggles threatened as she turned to face Herb. "I rented this from the medical supply place." She managed not to laugh but she couldn't erase the grin.

Herb smiled back. "Must be a jolly group down at the medical supply place."

"It's not them. It's him." She pointed to Brant.

"Ah." Herb nodded as if that explained everything. "So if your brother's not here, what's with the wheelchair?"

"We came up with the concept yesterday," Brant said.

"It was Brant's idea." Aria thought he should get credit for it. "He figured if we can get Linus used to it before Josh shows up, their first meeting would go a lot smoother."

"But I didn't know if we could get one on a Sunday morning. Aria pulled that off."

Herb glanced at her. "I have a feeling you can do about anything you set your mind to."

"Thanks, Herb." She was grateful for that kind of support. "I hope you're right. I didn't anticipate Josh being so stubborn."

"Don't worry about it." Herb waved his hand as if dismissing the problem as unimportant. "Sometimes people react just like horses. Leave them alone, give them time to think about the situation, and they might become more cooperative."

"That's pretty much what Brant said." *Maybe it would work with that cowboy, too.*

"Mind if I watch and see how it goes? I'm kind of curious, myself."

"Of course you can. You and Rosie have been so supportive through all this. I can't thank you enough."

"Just teach Rosie to make coq au vin and you can board Lucy and Linus here as long as you want."

"Okay." She loved seeing the twinkle in his eyes.

He turned back to Brant. "This wheelchair won't roll worth a damn on gravel, will it?"

"I was just going to carry it into the barn." He paused. "But I see what you mean."

"I hadn't thought that through, either," Aria said. "When Josh comes out here, I'll need to drive the van right up to the door." She'd wanted him to watch Linus run in the pasture, too. Navigating over there could be tricky.

Herb rubbed his chin and looked around. "We're not exactly wheelchair accessible at Thunder Mountain Academy."

"Please don't worry about it on Josh's account."

"He's the reason I'm thinking about the issue," Herb said, "but there's more to it than that. What if we had a visiting parent who uses a wheelchair to get around? Or maybe even an instructor who needs one?"

"It wouldn't be that tough to figure out." Brant lifted his hat and set it more firmly on his head. "You might have to pave some walkways and have Damon and Phil build a few ramps. A long weekend would be enough time to finish everything."

Herb nodded. "I'll talk to Rosie. I'm surprised she hasn't thought of it."

"If you need to retrofit the area for wheelchair access, that's fine," Aria said. "But please don't rush into it because of Josh. For one thing, he might assume you'd done it for him." She shuddered to think what Josh's reaction would be to freshly poured asphalt paths and recently constructed ramps.

"I agree that seeing new ramps could make him self-conscious, no matter how we explained it."

She sighed in relief. "Thanks."

"But thinking about Josh's visit was a good thing. We have an issue that should be addressed. In fact, I wouldn't mind talking to Josh about it when he comes out. He might be able to offer some suggestions."

"Um, maybe." Her brother had a long way to go mentally before he'd be willing to consult with Herb on making Thunder Mountain wheelchair accessible.

"Enough about that." Herb's smile told her he understood her misgivings. "Let's get this experiment with Linus underway." He glanced at Brant. "I'm guessing you have a procedure in mind."

"I do." Brant hoisted the folded wheelchair under one arm and they all started toward the barn. "We want Lucy and Linus to accept the wheelchair, but we also want them to understand its function. I'd like Aria to be sitting in it when I roll it into the stall. That way they can see it's a method for carrying people around."

"I can do that," Aria said.

"Then we might as well start here, at the entrance." He unfolded the wheelchair and placed it on the barn floor. "Hop in."

"Okay." The footrests were in the upright position, so she stepped past them before turning and sitting.

"Lift up your feet." He adjusted the footrests so she could prop her boots on them.

Settling her feet on the metal footrests disoriented her in a way she hadn't anticipated. No part of her was touching the ground. That also was true when she was driving a car, but there she felt more in control. "I've never sat in one of these before."

"You never tried out your brother's?"

"No." And she hadn't wanted to, either. Sitting in his chair would mean looking at the world from his perspective. She'd resisted that, maybe because she was so determined to get him out of that chair. "I should have, though, to find out what it's like for him. It feels weird."

Brant crouched in front of her, his hat tipped back and his expression gentle. "How so?"

"I just had this flash of 'what if this was the only way I could get around?' I take up more floor space, but I'm low to the ground. I have the view of an eight-year-old."

He nodded. "I've had people tell me that you get dismissed when you're in a wheelchair. Maybe it's because you're the same height as a kid."

Herb made a sound of impatience. "People shouldn't dismiss a kid, either."

"They shouldn't," Brant said. "But they do." He put his big hand on her knee and squeezed gently. "Are you freaked out by being in this chair?

"Not freaked out. But…" She met his gaze. "I'm learning some things."

"That's always a plus." He squeezed her knee again. "Ready for me to push you down to the stall?"

"Shouldn't I roll myself?"

"This is just an experiment to see how Linus reacts to a person he knows while she's sitting in a wheelchair. You'd only have to push yourself if you needed to build up your muscles."

She had a sudden image of Josh's biceps. The rest of him was getting soft, but his arms were worthy of a body-builder. He had handle grips on his wheels and he used them to spin himself across the room.

Glancing down at the wheels on this one, she saw the same grips. "I want to roll myself."

"Okay." Brant stood and moved away from the chair. "Off you go."

She wasn't very efficient at it. Now she appreciated how effortlessly Josh zipped around his little apartment without crashing into the furniture. "Sorry I'm a slowpoke." She glanced up at Brant, who seemed ten feet tall from this angle. "Would you rather just push me?"

"I'm not in any hurry." He looked over at Herb walking on the other side of her. "You got any pressing engagements, Dad?"

"Not at the moment. Rosie and I are heading to the grocery store in a little while, but right now I'm free. And by the way, Aria, she really appreciated your help with the menu."

"Glad I could do it."

"I think knowing that these kids' parents are paying for their meals puts a different spin on things for Rosie. Back when she was feeding the boys, she relied on simple recipes and made sure to cook plenty of everything."

"Like tuna casserole," Brant said. "One of my absolute favorites."

Herb laughed. "They were all your favorites, son. You just plain love food. Rosie got the biggest charge out of your enthusiasm at the table."

Aria started to say that Brant was still enthusiastic at the table but decided that was a comment best not made.

"I do enjoy my food."

She looked up and caught his cute little smile. Maybe he was thinking about cherry pie. So was she, but she also realized how much she wanted to cook for him. Given her passion for feeding people and his for being fed, they should really carve out some time to make that happen.

While Herb and Brant reminisced about Rosie's old standbys and who had been partial to which one, Aria began planning what she could fix for him if she ever got the chance. It might work out that she could do that some evening, even if the students were here. Potential menus scrolled through her mind.

She was so involved in dreaming about food that she was surprised to discover they'd arrived at Linus and Lucy's stall. Without thinking, she started to get out of the wheelchair.

Brant put a hand on her shoulder. "It'll be better if you stay there."

"Oh, right. I forgot for a minute." She wondered how many times Josh had forgotten, tried to get up and then realized he couldn't do it. The next time she saw him she'd be much more understanding about the difficult adjustments he'd had to make.

"The straw is going to keep the wheelchair from rolling easily," Brant said, "so why don't I push you in?"

"Good idea. That way you can decide how fast or slow to do it. I don't want to go lurching in there and scare them because I'm clumsy." She felt in her pockets. "Shoot, I forgot carrots."

"I'll go get some," Herb said. "Carrots for Lucy would be helpful in this situation in case she starts thinking she has to protect her foal from the scary wheelchair."

"We'll wait for you," Brant said.

"Be right back." Herb started down the aisle at a fast clip.

Brant crouched in front of her again. "How're you doing with this contraption now?"

"Better. But I don't have to stay in it, which makes a huge difference. And what really bothers me is that Josh doesn't, either. Some people have no choice and they have to adapt, but he could go back to PT, work harder, get out of this thing and walk again."

"Steady." He rubbed his hand back and forth over her thigh. "You're shaking."

She hadn't realized it. She closed her eyes, took a deep breath and blew it out. "Sorry." She opened her eyes again. "Me getting upset won't help Linus adjust to the wheelchair."

"No."

She looked into his eyes and soaked up the kindness and understanding she found there. "I wish I had your patience."

"He's not my brother."

"He needs to get out of that wheelchair. I can't help

thinking that the longer he's in it, the harder getting out will be for him."

"Maybe he's just not motivated yet."

"That's where Linus was supposed to come in."

Brant smiled. "Give that little foal a chance. He's only two days old."

"You're right." She smiled back. "But Josh needs to visit Linus before Herb and Rosie start making the place wheelchair accessible. If I bring him after, he'll be mortified. He won't even let me get the special plate for my van."

"But with the setup as it is, he'll be pretty much confined to the barn."

"I know. If I could coax him out of that thing, even if he has a walker, he could maneuver around the area and watch Linus romp in the pasture."

"Considering what you've told me about Josh, I can't imagine him going for the walker."

"Yeah, he announced months ago that was a nonstarter. I've brought it up a few times since then and he gives me the stink-eye." She sighed. "But he simply can't stay in that chair. It's unacceptable."

"For you or for him?"

She understood the subtext. Long ago she'd admitted to herself that extricating Josh from the wheelchair was partly for her sake. As long as he was in that chair, her world would feel out of balance.

She was okay with knowing her motivation had selfish overtones. Achieving her goal would be a win-win situation. "For both of us."

15

BRANT DIDN'T THINK pushing Josh to visit the ranch was a good plan, but he admired the heck out of Aria's dedication to her brother's welfare. Even though Josh had rejected her efforts, she wasn't about to give up on him. Still, a more measured approach might get better results.

As he debated whether to say anything more, Herb came back with Rosie. Turned out she wanted to watch, too. Everyone chatted while Aria stuffed the carrot pieces in her pockets.

Brant chatted, but his mind wasn't on the conversation. Instead he thought about the steely determination in Aria's expression when she'd said, "It's unacceptable." If she took that attitude with Josh, chances were good he'd dig in his heels. Her motives were pure, but her methods could cause everything to blow up.

Last night he'd slipped in a comment about backing off to see if Josh came to her. She'd sounded interested in that option. Herb had said essentially the same thing this morning and she'd seemed receptive.

But that was before she'd spent time in the wheelchair. Hindsight was twenty-twenty. He should have put himself in the chair because he wouldn't have had an emotional reaction to it. He'd also assumed she would have been curious enough to try out her brother's months ago, but she hadn't.

He'd been going on his own experience. In his junior year a basketball teammate had been temporarily confined to a wheelchair following a skiing accident that broke both his ankles. But Steve had attended every practice, so afterward they'd transferred him to the bleachers and taken turns rolling around the gym in his chair for the hell of it. Next season Steve had been back on the floor.

Putting Aria in the wheelchair today had seemed like a no-brainer. Linus was her colt so he'd thought she'd want to be the person who taught him that the strange object wasn't scary. In making that decision, he'd apparently increased her feeling of desperation right when she needed to simmer down.

Maybe it would be okay. He hoped so. But the first step was to find out if the metal apparatus would freak out the mare and colt. Grasping the handles of the chair, he pushed it slowly through the open stall door as he watched the horses' reaction.

Lucy and Linus eyed the chair and backed away, but Aria began talking to them in a soothing voice. "It's just a silly old wheelchair. Nothing to be worried about."

Brant wasn't too concerned about the wariness shown by both horses. Lucy was smart to be alert to any potential dangers now that she had a foal to protect. Linus picked up on her caution and peeked out from behind her.

"I brought carrots, Lucy." Aria placed one on her palm and held it toward the palomino mare. "I know how much you like carrots, girlfriend."

Lucy gazed at it and snorted.

"You have to come over here if you want some. And bring that little guy with you, okay? He can't have carrots yet, but I'd love to give him a scratch." Aria continued to talk softly to both the mare and foal.

Lucy held out a little longer, but eventually she walked over, stretched out her neck and took the carrot.

"Next time you'll have to come closer." Aria rested her arm on the wheelchair. "It's okay, Linus. I know you're curious. Look, your mom's fine with this shiny thing. You should investigate it."

Brant stood very still as both mare and foal came up to be scratched and petted. Then Linus surprised the hell out of him by walking past the wheelchair toward him to get some attention. Crouching, he rubbed and stroked the colt's soft coat. "You're brave, Linus," he murmured. "I kinda figured you would be, kiddo."

"I'm out of carrots," Aria said. "What next?"

"Let's hang here a little longer. Then I'll pull you back out. That might startle them, but I hope not." He continued to caress the foal. Linus didn't seem to mind the wheelchair at all.

Lucy was more concerned about it. Now that the carrots were gone, she'd edged away. Soon Linus noticed and followed her to the other side of the stall.

"That's good enough for now." Brant stood. "I'll wheel you out slowly, but they still might react now that it's moving."

They didn't, though. He was gratified to see that they stayed where they were and merely watched as he wheeled the chair back out the stall door. "Excellent."

Herb latched the door. "I think they'll be fine."

"Me, too," Rosie said. "How long did you rent that for, Aria?"

"A week." She reached down, flipped up the footrests and got out as if eager to escape the chair. "I wasn't sure how long it'd take."

"I wonder if we should see how the other horses do with it if we plan on making the academy wheelchair accessible." Rosie glanced at Brant. "What do you think?"

"Good idea. We could start by taking it out to the pasture right now. The surface won't be great, but we'd have more room to maneuver it and see how they react to that."

"Now would be a good time since we've been dry for a few days." Herb glanced at his watch. He had a phone, but he never used it to check the time. "I wish we could stick around to see how that goes, but we should take off if we expect to be back for lunch. That shopping list's longer than my arm."

"We have a lot of mouths to feed." Rosie squeezed Aria's shoulder. "Thanks again for helping plan the menus yesterday. And I won't forget the pearl onions and mushrooms for Tuesday night's cooking lesson."

"I'm not about to let her forget those," Herb said. "In fact, I've decided I should learn to make this meal right along with the rest of you. Cooking together sounds like fun."

Rosie grinned. "He's saying that because he wants to keep an eye on me when I flame the brandy."

"That, too." Herb wrapped his arm around her waist. "Come on, lady. Let me take you out for a big morning on the town."

"Ooo, ooo! Can't wait!" She winked at Brant and Aria before leaving the barn with Herb.

Aria gazed after them. "Is it my imagination, or are they flirting a lot more?"

"They're definitely flirting more than they were before the coq au vin. It's great to see." He never intended to get married, but lately he'd become more aware of how happy his foster parents were after all these years. Unless he changed his trajectory, he'd never know what that was like.

On the other hand, they weren't as free as he was. Yep, he was totally free to move on to the next town, the next job. Whoopee.

"Were you going to include Lucy and Linus in the pasture experiment?"

"I'm sorry. What?" He snapped back to the present.

"I wondered if we're taking Lucy and Linus out and when you want the wheelchair to come into play."

"I'll take the wheelchair first and try it out in the far pasture with the other horses. If that goes well, I'll move it to the smaller one and text you."

"Okay."

"I don't know what these things cost, but I'd hate to have one of them decide to kick the hell out of it. They probably won't, but you can't always predict horse behavior, so I want to take it slow." He folded the wheelchair and started to pick it up.

Then he put it back down and propped it against the stall. Closing the gap between them, he gathered her close. "Whatever you decide to do about Josh, I'll help you as best I can."

She cupped his face in both hands. "You think I should back off, don't you?"

"Yes, ma'am, I do."

"I disagree. Every day that goes by will only make it harder for him. He's getting used to that chair and I can't let that happen. Besides, he needs to become acquainted with Linus before the kids arrive and certainly before Rosie and Herb start pouring asphalt paths and building ramps."

"They won't be doing that for a while. I'm guessing they'll wait until the Fourth of July break at the earliest."

"Maybe, but Herb would like Josh's advice on the project. It would help Thunder Mountain and Josh at the same time. He's an analytical thinker, a strategist. He'd be the perfect consultant, and he could also see that his experiences will benefit others."

She made good points, logical points. But his gut told him she was headed for disaster. "As I've said before, he's your brother, not mine. You have to do what you think best."

"But I also understand why you'd want me to hold off. That's your way, to be patient and let things happen in their own time. That's not my way. In this particular case, I think it's a mistake to procrastinate."

"I wouldn't call it procrastinating. It's more like giving him breathing room."

"He's had *months* of breathing room. He needs a kick in the butt. I'll leave earlier today so I can have a long talk with him before I head off to work."

He looked into her eyes. The glint of determination that was so much a part of her personality and so opposite his was shining brightly. "I hope it goes well."

"It will. I'll make sure of it." She stood on tiptoe and gave him a quick kiss. "See you in fifteen minutes."

"I'll text you." He resisted the urge to pull her close for a real kiss and settled for a hug instead. Then he walked quickly out of the barn before that hug had a chance to work on him. Her warm, soft body called to him more urgently than any woman he'd taken to bed, but he had to stop thinking about sex ASAP.

A couple of deep breaths helped. Concentrating on the job helped even more. The sight of Cade's truck stirring up dust as it came down the ranch road distracted him further.

Cade and Lexi might figure something was going on, but they didn't know for sure. Better to keep it like that, at least for now. As he continued on toward the pasture, he heard Cade's truck rumbling behind him and turned around.

Cade pulled alongside and leaned out his window. "It's not often I see a cowboy hauling a wheelchair out to the pasture. Is Aria's brother here?"

"Nope." Brant shifted the wheelchair to his other arm.

"Is that his chair?"

"Nope."

"Then what the hell are you up to, bro?"

"Thought I'd hook your horse up to it and see if he'd pull me around the pasture. You okay with that?"

"Heck, yeah. I'd pay money to see it. But since I know you're blowing smoke, what's the real story?"

Brant described the wheelchair training for the horses and the resulting plan Herb had come up with to make the academy wheelchair accessible.

Cade let out a low whistle. "That borders on brilliant. Good for Herb."

"It's a fantastic idea." Lexi ducked down so she could make eye contact through the driver's-side window. "I'm amazed nobody thought of it before. We're a public facility and we should be able to accommodate wheelchairs."

Cade glanced around. "How big a project are we talking about?"

"Might not be as much as it seems at first—asphalt paths, ramps, stuff like that. Nothing Damon and Phil couldn't do over Fourth of July."

"Wait a minute," Lexi said. "I hope nobody's asking them to cancel their honeymoon."

"Oh, right." Brant kept forgetting about the wedding at the end of the month. A wedding he'd be attending. Considering Aria's close connection to the family, she'd probably be there, too. He needed to think some more about that.

"Besides, Fourth of July is a little late to help Josh," Cade said. "I've wondered how he'd get around once he showed up."

"Yeah, well, Aria thinks he'd freak if he came out and the place had been freshly renovated for wheelchair users, so she's hoping the changes will be made later on. I guess he's touchy about his disability."

"Then he should go back to PT!" Lexi glanced toward the barn. "And I should lower my voice. But he needs to. Rosie told me he'd quit going. That's crazy."

"I know, but it's his life. Listen, I'd better get going. I told Aria I'd text her once I'd introduced the wheelchair to the other horses. Then she'll bring Lucy and Linus out for their turn."

Cade put the truck in gear. "I want to see how it goes, too. Why don't you haul that chair into the back and we'll drive you over there?"

"Okay. Thanks." He lifted the chair into the truck bed and climbed in after it.

Cade parked beside the main gate and all four horses in the far pasture lifted their heads and flicked their ears forward. "I'll bet they're hoping for a new salt lick," he said as he got out of the truck. "The last one's about gone and Dad's planning to pick one up when he and Mom go into town today." As he said that, the horses moved toward the interior gate that separated the far pasture from the smaller one designated for Linus and Lucy.

Lexi hopped down from the passenger seat. "I'll back them up so you two have plenty of leeway." After opening the first gate, she walked the short distance to the second one and unlatched it. "Sorry, guys and gal." She slapped a few rumps to get them to back off. "This isn't what you think."

Brant lifted the wheelchair down to Cade. "Maybe it's good they all came over. Let's see what they do if I roll this through the gate while they're still milling around."

"I predict they'll do exactly nothing." Cade carried the

wheelchair over to the second gate before unfolding it. "They might not have seen one before, but they might think it's some fancy version of a wheelbarrow."

"That would be great if we get no reaction whatsoever." Brant pushed the chair inside the gate as Lexi held it open. The four horses moved out of his way, but not a one bolted or acted scared. Hematite, Cade's black gelding, pranced a little—not a surprise, since he was the most high-spirited of them all.

"They're a lot calmer than Lucy was." He continued to push the chair here and there. He circled Isabeau, Rosie's horse. She watched him but didn't move away.

"Hematite's the only one who acts the least bit skittish," Cade said. "Then again, he had a lousy childhood."

"I'd say we're good here." Brant pulled his phone from his jeans' pocket. "I'll tell Aria she can bring Lucy and Linus now." He tapped out a message and hit Send.

"So what about Josh?" Lexi stepped inside the gate and latched it. "Is he coming to see Linus or not?"

"Good question." Brant put the phone away and continued to weave among the grazing horses. Even Hematite had settled down. "Aria wants him to come out before the students get here, but so far he's resisting the whole concept."

Cade leaned against the fence and crossed his arms. "That's a shame. She's put a lot of effort into this idea."

"I don't think Aria expected him to be in the chair at this point. But it's not like she can force him to go to PT."

Lexi sighed. "No, she can't. And here they come! Oh, my God, that Linus is the cutest thing *ever*. Josh is missing out. Look at that saucy colt trotting along behind his mom. Adorable."

"Nothing cuter," Brant said, although his attention was on Aria, not the foal. Earlier her hair had been loose around her shoulders and she hadn't been wearing a hat but now she was wearing one, her hair up under it, emphasizing the graceful curve of her slender neck. His gaze roamed hungrily over her hourglass figure showcased by her scoop-necked, yellow T-shirt and snug jeans. Anyone would think he'd never seen a beautiful woman before, but Aria was so…

At that moment he became aware that Lexi and Cade had stopped talking. When he glanced over to check on them, they were both watching him and grinning.

"Seems like you might have enjoyed washing her van," Cade said in an undertone.

"Maybe."

"You owe me one, bro."

"And why's that?"

"I totally took the fall in the Battle of the Sacred Flame."

16

BY THE TIME Aria arrived in the smaller pasture, Cade and Lexi had returned to their truck and Brant stood waiting behind the wheelchair. Lucy ignored it, perhaps because she had more room to move away in case she decided it was a threat to her and her foal. Linus took his cue from his mom.

Once Brant had convinced himself that Linus and Lucy wouldn't shy away if he approached with the wheelchair, he sat in it. Aria was relieved. She would have done it for Josh's sake, but wheelchairs gave her the creeps.

Brant didn't seem to mind, but then again, Brant didn't let very many things upset him. He looked completely at ease in that chair. She wondered if her dislike of it had been one of the reasons Lucy had backed away when they were in the stall.

No matter. Thanks to Brant, the wheelchair wouldn't be a problem if she could get Josh out here tomorrow. He was running out of time, though. Tomorrow would be better than Tuesday, when everyone would be busy preparing for the students' arrival on Wednesday.

Brant was laying a good foundation for Josh's visit and she was grateful. Lounging in the chair, he coaxed Linus over with a series of soothing words and soft clucks of his tongue. Aria watched in fascination and a tinge of envy as the foal walked right up to him for some nose rubs and neck scratches.

Cade and Lexi stayed outside the fence, probably to minimize the number of distractions. "You've done a great job with him already," Cade said. "If Hematite had been started like this, he'd be a different horse."

Lexi reached over and laced her fingers through Cade's. "And you never would have ended up with him."

"That's true. I guess things happen for a reason. But it's fun to see this little guy getting exactly what he needs at a very young age."

"It's fun for me, too." Brant exchanged a glance with his foster brother. "It helps, you know?"

"I do. Between the two of us we have this covered. I work with the ones who're already messed up, and you make sure they don't get messed up in the first place."

Aria realized she'd just been privy to a rare acknowledgment of the challenges both men had faced. On the surface Brant seemed undamaged, but he wasn't. Because of that damage he might choose to walk away and she had to accept that with a smile and gratitude for what he'd given her and Linus.

He continued to rub Linus's soft coat as he looked over at Cade. "Speaking of your business, what's your next project?"

"One of Lexi's riding students just bought a mare with all kinds of problems. Lexi and I are going over there tomorrow to evaluate the situation and decide if she'd be a good teaching opportunity for the academy kids."

"Nice." Brant stroked down the length of Linus's back and the colt shivered in delight. "Good for the mare and good for the kids."

"I have great hopes for that mare," Lexi said. "But if we don't make tracks we won't finish cleaning all the cabins today, which is a more immediate concern."

"Yeah, yeah." Cade smiled at her. "You just want to see me operating the vacuum cleaner. It gets you hot."

"I won't deny it." Lexi winked at Aria. "Nothing sexier than a man wielding a vacuum, right, Aria?"

"Right. Unless it's a man washing dishes."

"But you know the best one of all?" Lexi paused for effect. "A man cleaning a toilet."

"Oh, *yeah*." Aria sighed. "That's the ultimate turn-on."

Cade shook his head. "You two are certifiable. Women like candy and flowers. Every guy knows that. Back me up on this, Ellison."

"Sorry, bro. I've never had much luck with candy and flowers."

"So what's your secret weapon?"

Carried away by the teasing mood, Aria spoke without thinking. "Pie."

Cade looked at her and blinked. "Pie?"

"Yes." She'd started this so she'd have to finish it. From the corner of her eye she noticed Brant struggling not to laugh. "Pie is much more sensual than candy."

Lexi nodded. "You are so right, sister. Candy is a cliché. Pie has infinitely more possibilities."

"Then I guess it's time I brought you a pie." Cade glanced at Lexi. "What kind would you like?"

"I recommend cherry," Brant said, and Aria almost lost it.

"That sounds good." Lexi smiled at him. "I'd ten times rather have a cherry pie than a box of drugstore chocolates."

"Duly noted. Pie it is. And we're off to clean cabins."

As their truck pulled away, Brant's shoulders began

shaking. *"Pie."* He laughed until the tears came. "I can't believe you said that."

"I probably shouldn't have." Now that the moment was over she was having second thoughts.

"It's fine." He took a breath. "They'd already caught me ogling you as you brought Lucy and Linus to the pasture."

"They did?"

"Couldn't help myself." He stopped petting Linus and stood. "You look luscious."

"Thank you, but I didn't do anything special." Not quite true. Her shirt was new and she'd left her hair down today on purpose because she knew he liked it that way.

"You don't have to do anything special to get my attention, but I have to ask, how did you stuff all your hair under your hat?"

"It's easy." She took off her hat and her hair spilled down around her shoulders. "Hold this." She handed him the hat. Then she gathered her hair up and wound it in a circle on top of her head. "Hat, please."

When he gave it to her, she used one hand to hold her hair in place and the other to cram on her hat. "Ta-da!"

He gazed at her in amazement. "That's incredible."

"When you have long hair, you have to figure out how to manage it when it's likely to get in the way."

"Like applying cherry pie to my cock?"

She gasped and looked around for potential eavesdroppers.

"Don't worry. No one heard me except the horses and they won't tell." He drew her into his arms. "When you tied your hair back last night, it was one of the sexiest moves I've ever seen." His eyes darkened. "If I could get away with it, I'd make love to you right here."

The intensity in his gaze stirred her blood. "On the ground?"

"That's one possibility." He cupped her bottom and pulled her in tight. "But I'd rather do it up against the fence so I wouldn't get that pretty yellow shirt dirty." He lifted her to her toes and nestled his bulging fly between her thighs. "Damn, you feel good."

"You, too."

"But we can't scare Linus."

Moisture dampened her panties and she tilted her hips to make a better connection. "Yeah, I'd hate for him to be traumatized at a young age like I was."

"He's the only reason you're still wearing all your clothes." His fingers flexed. "The other horses wouldn't care and nobody's likely to show up for a while."

"You talk big, but I'll bet you're not actually prepared to follow through."

His eyes gleamed. "Wanna bet?"

"You're kidding." Her pulse raced. "You didn't really bring a—"

"Yes, ma'am."

"Is it burning a hole in your pocket?"

"Damn near."

"When did you plan to use it, pray tell?"

"If and when the opportunity presented itself. I wasn't counting on anything, given how many people are roaming around, but I have one, just in case."

"Now I'll be thinking about having sex with you."

He laughed. "Are you saying you wouldn't think about it otherwise?"

"Oh, I would, but knowing you have a condom makes a big difference in my thought process."

"Meaning you'll be looking for opportunities, too?"

She sucked in a breath. "Uh-huh."

Heat flashed in his gaze as he rocked his hips forward. "Lady, you sure get me hot. I'm gonna let you go before I do something I might regret." He released her and stepped back. Then he bowed his head and took several deep breaths before looking at her again. "How about if I take the wheelchair back down to the barn while you stay here and play with Linus? He and Lucy could use more pasture time."

As always, his self-control impressed her. He could have suggested they tuck Lucy and Linus in the birthing stall and go have some fun in the tack room. Instead he put the little foal's needs ahead of his own. "Good idea."

"I need to muck out some stalls, anyway. We want the barn in tip-top shape when the kids arrive." He smiled. "The exercise should help."

"Since I won't be mucking stalls, guess I'll romp with Linus."

"I highly recommend it. Dancing around with a foal is the most fun you can have with your clothes on." He folded up the wheelchair and tucked it under his arm. "I'll come back in a while to check on you."

"Okay."

"See you soon." Touching the brim of his hat in a typical cowboy farewell, he turned and left. She watched him make the long walk back to the barn lugging that wheelchair. She'd been so busy thinking about having sex with him that she'd temporarily forgotten what this morning's activity had been about.

Or more accurately, *who* it had been about. As Brant had said, Josh was the reason behind everything they were doing, yet he wasn't a participant in any of it. She was determined to change that. He simply had to come out with her tomorrow.

Turning around, she located Lucy and Linus. The foal was nursing while Lucy tore at the tender new grass with her strong teeth. Sunlight played over Lucy's golden coat and Linus's soft peach-colored fuzz. They were heart-breakingly beautiful. She pulled out her phone and took picture after picture.

She was still snapping away when Linus finished nursing and turned to look at her. Switching to video, she began talking to both him and Lucy. Mother and son started toward her and she kept filming until their noses were right in front of the screen. She couldn't stop laughing.

She backed away to see if they'd follow. They did. Clicking off the phone, she turned around and began to jog. When she glanced over her shoulder, she saw that Lucy was no longer interested and had gone back to grazing but Linus bounced along behind her. When she swerved he swerved, cavorting and kicking up his heels.

She turned the phone to video again while she jogged slowly backward. He followed, his scrawny tail waving. "We're dancing, Linus!" With a playful snort he bucked and raced past her, his slender legs flashing in the sun.

As she turned and kept filming his race around the pasture, her throat tightened. She loved playing with this sweet baby horse. Josh would love it, too. But before he could truly enjoy the experience, he had to get on his feet.

THE REST OF the day went quickly and Aria had no more time alone with Brant. When he returned to the pasture, he had Whitney and Ty with him. They'd finished installing the new showerheads and had decided to reward themselves by visiting Linus, the ranch's new superstar.

After taking the mare and foal to the barn, they all walked to the bathhouse to admire the new showerheads. Then they checked on the cleaning job Lexi and Cade were doing. Aria got a kick out of watching the foster brothers tease each other even if it did mean she and Brant had constant chaperones.

The number of chaperones increased by two when Rosie and Herb came home loaded with groceries. Everyone gathered for a late lunch and Rosie grabbed the opportunity to get everyone's advice on cabin assignments.

As Aria participated in the lively discussion, she pictured sixteen teenagers on the premises. Josh really should get out here before they arrived and she was the one who had to convince him.

She helped clean up the dishes and then Brant walked her out to the van.

"I can go fetch the wheelchair if you want," he said. "Maybe you could get a partial refund. I don't think we have a problem with any of the horses, including Linus."

"No, we just have a problem with my brother." She paused at the driver's door and turned to him. "But could you stow the wheelchair in the barn for now? I plan to have Josh's wheelchair mounted on the van when I drive out tomorrow morning."

He shoved his hat to the back of his head and gazed at her without saying anything, but his expressive eyes said it all. He didn't want her putting pressure on Josh.

"It'll be fine." She slid her hands up his chest and savored the firm muscles beneath his shirt. "I took more pictures and a video for him while I was out with Linus today."

"Okay." He slipped an arm around her waist and drew her in for a very sweet kiss.

The gentleness of it moved her. It wasn't a kiss of lust, but one of caring. That made it very precious, indeed.

Easing back slowly, he gave her a warm smile of encouragement.

Her heart stalled. She would miss the sex when he was gone, but kisses and smiles like these didn't come along every day. He'd begun to care for her, but he'd cared about that puppy he'd rescued, too. Then he'd given it away.

"Hey." He cupped her cheek. "If that was the worst kiss in the world, just tell me and I'll give you a better one."

"Just the opposite. It was the best kiss in the world."

He shook his head. "Nope. That's impossible."

"I'm the one rating it and I say it's the best."

"And I'm here to tell you that the best kiss in the world hasn't been delivered to your sweet lips...yet."

"Oh? And when should I expect it?"

"No telling. I get more inspired every time. At some point I may peak, but I'm not there yet. When I finally say 'I can't do any better than that,' you'll have experienced the best kiss in the world. But not until then."

Of course he'd made her smile. He was talented that way. "Thanks for clearing it up for me. Sounds as if we have an interesting evening ahead of us."

"I can guaran-damn-tee it. But don't bring pie."

"I won't. Wouldn't want to be redundant."

"You couldn't be if you tried." He gave her a different kiss, a brisk, time-to-get-going kiss. Then he released her and helped her in. "Matilda, get her home safe."

She leaned out the window. "See you tonight."

"You bet. Now go before I have to kiss you again."

"Right." She put the van in Reverse.

Brant occupied her thoughts during the drive home, but when she pulled into the parking lot of her apartment complex, her stomach rolled. If Josh wouldn't agree to go tomorrow...but he would. She wouldn't take no for an answer.

Keeping that thought uppermost in her mind, she knocked on his door with the code tap they'd worked out when they were kids. He opened it and pushed his wheel-chair out of the way so she could come in. He looked as disheveled as he had the day before, but at least he hadn't argued with her about interrupting whatever he'd been doing.

He hadn't been playing video games. Instead he'd been watching television coverage of a riding event, one he would have competed in if he hadn't fallen. He picked up the remote from his lap and clicked off the TV.

She walked immediately over to his couch and sat. After experiencing a wheelchair today, she understood the psychological impact of looking up at people who remained standing. Not pleasant. She gestured toward the screen. "Why torture yourself?"

He shrugged. "Everybody needs a fantasy life."

"Josh, I want you to have a real life."

"Sorry, sis. That's not the hand I was dealt." His matter-of-fact tone was more chilling than if he'd become angry.

"I danced with Linus today."

For a brief moment curiosity flickered in his brown eyes. Then it disappeared. "Now you're making stuff up just to mess with me."

"No, I'm not. Let me show you the video."

"I'd rather not."

"Damn it, Josh! You can look at eventing on TV but you can't look at a two-day-old colt running in a field?"

"Oh, what the hell. You're going to keep bugging me until I see your precious Linus so we might as well get this over with."

She ignored the sarcasm in his voice and pulled up the video on her phone. Leaving the couch, she crouched next to him and held it so they could both see. Yesterday she might have stood and leaned over him, but her perspective had changed.

"That's the first section, when I got them both to come over to me and they put their noses practically on the screen. Is that funny or what? Look at his cute blaze. I wonder if he inherited that from his dad."

Josh didn't comment.

Determined to get a reaction, she clicked to the next video. "Here's the part I meant about dancing with him. I got him to chase me and then I turned around and we sort of...danced together." The video was jerky and her breathing and laughter were really loud, but Linus was adorable.

She became absorbed in the video. "He's bonding with me already and he needs to bond with you. If you come out to the ranch with me tomorrow, things will be fairly quiet. Then you can come again on Tuesday, before the kids get there."

The video stopped and still Josh hadn't said anything.

"Look, I know you're reluctant." She took the phone and returned to the couch. "But I can drive the van right up to the barn door. We'll get you into the wheelchair and then you can roll right down to—"

"Who's *we*?"

"Me and Brant, the guy who's starting the foal. He's doing a terrific job. Linus is already comfortable with people."

"Would he be comfortable with a wheelchair?"

"Yes, he would!" She sensed victory. "I wasn't going to tell you this, but I rented one today and sat in it while Brant pushed me into the stall. Linus is *fine* with it. And I can tell you, I learned a lot about what it's like to be in a wheelchair."

"So you realize that on a place like Thunder Mountain, which I've researched online, by the way, that I'd be confined to the barn. No rolling around the property for this boy."

"That's the other really cool thing, Josh. Herb Padgett wants you to consult with him on making Thunder Mountain wheelchair accessible for future students and visitors. He plans to put in some asphalt paths and ramps, but he would love to have your advice before he does that."

He gazed at her, his expression unreadable. "You've been busy."

"Because I want you to get acquainted with this foal. And I want you to ultimately get out of that chair. Making the ranch wheelchair accessible would be fabulous but you won't really need any of it. I'm betting you'll be walking around the place before summer's end. So what do you say? Want to come with me tomorrow?"

"No."

She drew in a sharp breath as if she'd been slapped. "Why not?"

"Have you noticed how many times you've said 'I want'?"

"I haven't noticed but—"

"This isn't about what you want, Aria. It's about what I want. And don't want. What I don't want is some burly cowboy lifting me from the van into a wheelchair so I can roll myself down the length of the effing barn to see a foal I'll never be able to dance with! Can you get that? Please? And leave me the hell alone?"

"I can't leave you alone because you've given up! You've accepted your *fate* as you call it, and you won't fight any-more. Don't do this to yourself, Josh."

He took a deep breath. "I can do whatever I choose, Aria. This is my life, not yours. As I mentioned before, I never asked you to breed Lucy so that I'd have something to distract me."

"But if you'd just come out to the ranch and look at him, you'd—"

"I'd be even more aware of my limitations. I need you to stop, Aria. Just stop."

"I *won't*." She left the couch and headed for the door. "You could be out of that chair if you wanted to be. I love you and I refuse to stand by while you flush your life down the—"

"It's not up to you, sis."

Despair clawed at her, but she fought it with everything she had. "You're not giving up, Josh. I won't let you!" And she stormed out the door. No brother of hers would languish in a wheelchair when he was perfectly capable of getting out of it.

17

ALTHOUGH BRANT CRAVED Aria's company, having his brothers around was a good second best. The opportunity to become better acquainted with the women in their lives was a bonus. Damon and his redheaded fiancée had returned from their weekend visit with Phil's dad and stepmother and they showed up just in time for dinner.

Without missing a beat, Rosie directed Ty and Brant to convert the pool table in the rec room into a dining table. In minutes plates and utensils had been transferred and two additional places were set for Damon and Phil. Everyone gathered for the meal and discussion began immediately about plans for making the ranch wheelchair accessible.

"But I've realized it can't be done over the Fourth," Herb said. "Our chief builders will be on their honeymoon."

"We will." Damon reached over and took Phil's hand. "But we can work something out before or after, right, sweetheart?"

"Absolutely. It's a terrific idea. Since this has come up, I take it Josh has been out here with his wheelchair."

"Not yet," Herb said.

"Is that because he's worried about the logistics? Damon

and I could rig up something temporary, at least a ramp so he can navigate in and out of the barn."

"I don't think that's the issue," Rosie said. "According to Aria, he's not interested in coming out to see Linus at all."

"Oh, dear." Phil looked upset. "Aria was so excited. She thought for sure he would be, too."

"She's still planning to drive him out here tomorrow," Brant said. "Let's hope she does. Even if there's no ramp, I can help him in and out of the barn."

"Paul Bunyan to the rescue," Cade said with a chuckle.

Damon laughed. "I know, right? But Phil and I could build a ramp if you guys want one."

"Let's wait and see what happens," Herb said. "I'd like Josh to give us advice on the layout of the walkways and the ramps, but first we have to see if he'll show up. Let's not build anything or do anything until we know one way or the other."

"I sure hope he does come out, and soon," Phil said. "Aria's crazy about that brother of hers. This must be breaking her heart."

Rosie sighed. "It probably is."

"Sometimes you have to give a person time to come around, though," Herb said. "I'm willing to do that."

Until this very moment Brant had agreed completely with that sentiment. He'd told Aria as much this afternoon. But Phil's comment stuck with him. This *was* breaking Aria's heart. The longer he thought about it the less willing he was to give Josh time to come around. But he needed to consider his options.

Meanwhile the conversation had shifted to Damon and Phil's wedding at the end of the month and he promised to be there. He wasn't about to miss it.

But he'd be finished training Linus in a couple of weeks. Ending the training theoretically meant ending the affair with Aria, and yet she'd probably be at the wedding. Treating her like a casual friend would be difficult, not to mention insensitive. He'd still want her and he'd bet she would still want him.

Continuing their affair for one short weekend didn't seem right, either. In the past he'd successfully avoided this kind of awkward situation by staying away from any woman connected to Thunder Mountain. He'd conveniently forgotten about that strategy with Aria, probably because his brain cells had been stewing in lust.

Oh, who was he kidding? The relationship had gone way beyond lust and the wedding wasn't the problem. Aria wasn't fitting into the neat little compartment he'd designated for his short-term relationships.

She was supposed to be temporary, like the other women he'd had in his life, but when he looked into her violet eyes, she didn't feel temporary. Thinking back, he had to admit she never had.

Although she didn't want a committed relationship any more than he did, they'd shared some extraordinary moments in the short time they'd been together. He couldn't remember ever feeling so bonded with a woman. Ty had seen it right away. Cade and Lexi had, too.

So now what? He'd noticed Aria looking at him in a way that could mean she was rethinking her independent stance. To be honest, so was he. His cherished pattern didn't look quite so wonderful anymore.

With new eyes he saw the depth of understanding between Rosie and Herb. Part of him longed for that, and it wasn't even the part assigned to make Aria really happy tonight. His heart had become involved. Those emotions were raw and new, but he recognized what was happening. He was falling in love.

He even knew why. Besides being beautiful and sexy,

she was strong, strong enough to go the distance. He'd convinced himself that unconditional love didn't exist, but the evidence was all around that it did—Herb and Rosie, Damon and Phil, Cade and Lexi. Aria's refusal to give up on her brother told him she was made of the same stuff. She kept her promises.

Thinking about his future had never been a priority, but it was now. He wanted Aria to be a part of it. She might reject the idea because of her personal plans, but he'd have to put it out there, and soon.

He'd always imagined that making a commitment was all about him and his decisions, but it wasn't. If he needed and wanted her in his life and she preferred to concentrate on her plans instead…he didn't want to contemplate the pain involved. He had to risk it, though. There was no going back.

Hanging out with loving couples only emphasized his new direction. Damon and Phil exchanged secret smiles and Ty kept his arm draped over the back of Whitney's chair. Lexi and Cade teased each other unmercifully, as always, which was how they showed their love. Herb and Rosie's connection was subtle and always present—his hand lightly brushing her shoulder, her warm glance when he refilled her coffee mug.

Brant had never felt like the odd man out in a group like this, but he did tonight. He joked around with everyone because that was what everyone expected of him. But through the toasts, the stories and the laughter, he missed Aria.

After dessert, which was chocolate cake instead of cherry pie, thank God, Rosie insisted that everyone else could clean up the dishes while he took Damon and Phil down to the barn for a peek at Linus.

"You two go on out to the porch," Phil said. "I'll be right with you."

Brant had noticed that she'd turned down a glass of wine at dinner and that she'd made a trip to the bathroom halfway through the meal. Once they were out the front door, he glanced at Damon. "Is she—?"

"Yeah." He grinned. "But don't say anything, okay?"

"She doesn't want anyone to know before the wedding?"

"She doesn't care about that, but miscarriages run in her family and she's superstitious about announcing it too early."

"I can promise you that Mom's figured it out."

"Of course. When Phil refused the wine, Mom looked at me and I'm sure it was written all over my face. When I helped her bring in dessert and coffee, I told her to keep quiet. She will."

"So will I and I'm sure everything will be fine. Congratulations, Daddy-o."

"Thanks. Sobering, isn't it?"

"It is, but in a good way. Hey, let me ask you something. How long did you know Phil before you figured out it was serious?"

"You mean serious like love?"

"Well, yeah." The word sent shivers up his back. Except for Rosie, he'd never told a woman he loved her. He might be really bad at it.

"Honestly? I was in love with her by Day Two, but I couldn't admit that. I was a rolling stone who gathered neither moss nor maidens. Couldn't possibly be in love, y'know."

Brant sighed. "Right." Damon had resisted the concept just as he had. He felt a little less like an idiot.

"All set!" Phil breezed out the door. "Sorry to keep you waiting."

"No worries." Brant started down the steps. "By the way, that cabin you and Damon built for Cade is great."

"We had fun doing it, although I'd hoped that they'd both have moved in there by now. If Lexi's keeping her place in town, she's not ready to propose."

"Guess not." He considered repeating Aria's theories about why that was, but he decided against it.

"You're looking good," Phil said. "Life must be treating you well."

"Can't complain."

"You never do," Damon said. "You could be sitting in a pile of cow patties and you'd smile and say you were lovin' it."

"Yeah, well, I wonder if I've been a little too easy to get along with."

"Whoa!" Damon clapped a hand to his heart. "I can't believe you just said that. I'm thinking we need to call CNN with this breaking news."

Normally he would have sparred with Damon, but he didn't have the time right now. "It's this business with Josh. Aria's put her heart and soul into her project and he can't even be bothered to come out here and take a look. That's not right."

"I can tell you feel strongly about it," Phil said. "I'm running to keep up with you."

"Oh. Sorry." He slowed his pace.

"So what are you gonna do about it, brother of mine?" Damon shot him a glance. "And for the record, I'd be happy to provide backup. This could be fun to watch."

"I haven't decided, but whatever it is, I can handle it. Thanks for the offer, though."

"Let me know if you change your mind. I've never seen you this worked up, not even when we played for the state basketball championship. Or the football championship, come to think of it." Damon looked over at Phil. "We both double lettered, so be impressed."

"I am. I'd be honored to wear your letterman's jacket."

"Well, um, the thing is, I loaned that jacket to Mary Ann Templeton and I never got it back."

"Because she burned it in a school trash can after you broke up with her." Brant smiled at the memory. "What a stink it made, too. Polyester doesn't burn well." They'd reached the barn and he slid aside the wooden bar so they could go in.

"I need to buy you a drink sometime, Brant," Phil said as she walked inside. "Then you can tell me all about Mary Ann Templeton and any other girlfriends I should know about."

"Just don't invite your fiancé if you want the scoop."

"Don't worry. It'll be just you and me."

"Hey, people. I'm right here." But laughter rippled in Damon's voice.

Brant wasn't surprised at Damon's mellow mood. He was about to be married to a great woman and soon he'd be a father. Good for him. His childhood hadn't been pretty and he deserved his happily-ever-after.

Baseboard lights cast enough of a glow to guide them but not enough to disturb the sleeping horses. They stopped talking as they walked to the far end of the barn. Brant glanced in first. Lucy and Linus were lying curled together in the straw, but Damon and Phil would be able to get a decent view of the new foal. He stepped back and motioned them forward.

"Oh, my goodness," Phil murmured softly. "He's precious."

Damon wrapped an arm around her shoulders. "Yeah, he's cute, all right. Lucy did good."

"You'll get a better view tomorrow when he's out in the pasture."

"I'm sure we will." Phil moved away from the stall. "But I wanted to see him tonight. We've all been waiting so long."

"I know." Until now he hadn't fully grasped the anticipation surrounding this event. He'd come in at the very end, but these two had been watching Lucy's progress for months. So had Lexi, Cade, Rosie and Herb. Then there was the person who'd anticipated it most of all. She deserved better than to have her brother refuse to even see the foal.

Phil waited until they were outside the barn and headed back to the house before she vented her frustration. "I can't *believe* her brother hasn't been out here! How could he be that way? She must have shown him pictures!"

"I'm sure she tried. I don't know if he agreed to look at them."

"I'm ready to go over to his apartment and give him a piece of my mind. Maybe this isn't going to be his salvation, but he should at least have the decency to come and see this sweet baby once, for Aria's sake. I don't think that's too much to ask."

Brant made his decision. "You know, Phil, neither do I."

ARIA WAS CONFUSED by Brant's text. He'd asked her for directions to her apartment and said he'd meet her there instead of having her come out to the cabin. She agreed to the change of plans although she was disappointed. Her apartment wasn't nearly as romantic as that beautiful cabin.

But she'd texted him when she'd finished her last delivery and was headed home. At least she'd get to see him. She'd thought a lot about his comments that she should leave Josh alone and let him decide his own fate. Maybe that was the right thing to do.

She couldn't imagine backing away when Josh had a chance of walking again, but she couldn't make him get out of that chair. She couldn't force him to go see Linus, either. She needed his full cooperation to get him into her van.

She didn't have any power in this situation. Josh had it all, and he'd chosen not to go along with her plan. She could rant and rave all she wanted, but that wouldn't accomplish anything.

So she might as well enjoy Linus and her time with Brant without expecting anything from Josh. Maybe she needed to accept the idea that he'd spend the rest of his life in a wheelchair. The possibility horrified her, but it must not horrify him or he wouldn't have dropped out of physical therapy. She would love him even if he never walked again.

Brant's mud-spattered truck was waiting in the visitor's section of the parking lot when she drove in. She remembered that he'd named it Bessie, which made her smile. She pulled into her assigned slot and climbed out.

His long legs and determined stride brought him over to her before she'd locked the van. She welcomed him with open arms, deliriously glad to nestle against his solid chest and absorb the warmth of his body. "I've missed you."

"I've missed you, too." He held her close, his cheek resting on the top of her head. "But before I can show you how much, there's something we need to do."

"What's that?"

"I'm here to take your brother out to see Linus."

"You're *what*?" She jerked away from him and peered into his face. Surely she'd misunderstood. "Aren't you the one who told me to back off?"

"I am, and I've changed my mind. You've done all this

out of love for him because you want him to get better. Maybe it's a bad idea, or the wrong idea, but he needs to see that foal at least once before rejecting him."

Her breath caught. "But…he doesn't want to go."

"Then let's convince him. It's dark out. We can sneak him in and sneak him out without anyone knowing except the three of us. If he can't manage that, then I find it hard to believe you share the same genetics."

She felt a rush of emotion so strong that it could only be one thing. But now wasn't the time to declare it. Maybe she never would. After all, he hadn't said why he was doing this. To him, it might not be any different than saving a puppy.

Taking his hand, she led him to Josh's apartment. Light shone through the curtains drawn over his living room window and the noise of a video game filtered through the door, so at least he wasn't asleep. She didn't think he slept much, anyway. She tapped their code knock on the door.

It took a while before the sound of the video game ended and Josh opened the door. He did a double-take. "Who the hell is this?"

Brant stepped forward. "My name is Brant Ellison. I'm here to take you out to see Lucy's foal."

"Damned if you are." He backed up the wheelchair and tried to close the door but he was no match for Brant.

Pushing his way in, Brant pulled Aria after him. "We need to have a talk."

"We don't and you're trespassing." Josh glared at him and picked up the phone from a nearby table. "I'm calling 9-1-1."

"You could, but that seems like a piss-poor way to react when your sister is only trying to help you."

Josh shifted his anger to her. "Apparently you decided to bring the muscle to bend me to your will."

"This was Brant's idea and you have no clue how unusual it is for him to take this kind of action. He's the kindest, most gentle—"

"Spare me. And get out of my apartment or I swear I'll call the police."

Brant crouched beside his wheelchair. "Don't do that, Josh. We have a lot in common, you and I. We both love horses. We both love our personal freedom. And…we both love Aria."

She gasped. "Brant!"

But he didn't look back at her. He kept his attention on Josh. "So what do you say? It's the middle of the night. No one will see you come and go. We don't even have to take your wheelchair. There's one out at the ranch."

"So I heard." But the venom had left his voice.

"It'll be a couple hours out of your life, but it will mean the world to your sister."

In the silence that followed, Aria's heart thumped so loud she wondered if they could hear it. She hadn't known what to expect when Brant shoved his way into Josh's apartment, but it certainly hadn't been a declaration of love. Plus, he hadn't even said it directly to her.

Yet barging in here to confront Josh was the most loving and romantic gesture she could imagine. This was the man who believed in giving people space, the man who'd counseled her to back off. But he was right in Josh's face, pressing him for a decision.

Josh gazed at him for several long moments. "You must love her or you wouldn't have tried this stupid stunt. Let's go."

18

BRANT AGREED TO drive Aria's van to the ranch because she asked him to. She looked a little shaky, but the glow of happiness in her eyes would stay with him for the rest of his life. He lifted Josh into the backseat, next to the sliding door, and Aria climbed in front.

As he drove away from the apartment complex he could feel her gaze on him and he debated whether to reach over and take her hand. But with Josh in the back seat, it didn't seem like a good idea. The more they behaved like a cozy couple, the more they'd exclude her brother.

The drive was a silent one. He didn't want to say something wrong after apparently saying something right.

When he'd crouched next to Josh's chair, he hadn't known he was going to say that. The words had flowed from his heart, not his head. He'd scared the bejesus out of Aria, too. Once this was over and they were alone, he'd apologize. That had to have been the lamest declaration of love in the history of romance.

Maybe she'd forgive him if he explained that he'd never said that to any woman besides Rosie. Technically he still hadn't. He'd told her brother, instead. But he had a hunch that without those words, they wouldn't be on their way to Thunder Mountain.

Josh had issues—no doubt about that—but he loved his sister. Apparently he'd needed someone who also loved her to point out the critical nature of paying Linus at least one visit. He might be going under protest, but at least he was going. And he'd behave himself or else.

Brant didn't think there'd be a problem, though, or he wouldn't be doing this in the first place. His money was on Linus. Josh pretended to be a badass, but most guys in his position would do the same. That colt could melt the heart of a seasoned criminal, let alone a fake hard-nose like Josh. He wouldn't stand a chance against Linus's maximum-force cuteness.

All was quiet at the ranch and no lights glowed except for the one on the porch and two dusk-to-dawn lights. Brant swung the van around so Josh's door was next to the barn entrance.

"Be right back with the chair." Good thing Aria had asked him to keep it in the barn. That eliminated the hassle of transporting Josh's wheelchair out here. The quicker this could be accomplished, the more likely it would succeed.

By the time he returned, Aria had opened the van's sliding door and she and Josh were talking in low tones. He was glad to see that the guy hadn't completely zoned out. Not wanting to intrude on the brother-sister conversation, he held back.

But Josh spotted him. "Your boyfriend's here."

Boyfriend. That term grated on his nerves and not only because of the sneer in Josh's voice when he'd said it. Brant didn't want to be Aria's boyfriend. He wanted to be the man she counted on when the going got rough, the one she laughed with and made love to, the one she kissed good-night and woke up with in the morning.

After positioning the chair next to the van, he stepped away. Aria and Josh had accomplished this dozens of times without his help. In fact, they didn't need him at all now that Josh was only a few feet from the barn. He could wait in the van, for that matter.

But he wasn't willing to, so he walked into the barn and joined Ringo, who was sitting on a hay bale near the door. "Keep your toes crossed, Ringo," he murmured as he scratched behind the cat's ears. "This one's for all the marbles."

Josh's upper body strength served him well as he got into the chair and propelled it across the gravel and into the barn. Aria didn't have to do much at all. He might be able to navigate the pasture, after all. Good to know.

Josh didn't look Brant's way as they started down the wooden aisle toward the birthing stall. Aria gave him a quick smile and he responded with a thumbs-up. He resisted the urge to follow. Yes, he was the trainer, but Aria had good instincts and could handle this without his interference.

From his vantage point he'd be able to tell if something went seriously wrong. He wouldn't get to watch Josh's reaction to seeing the foal, but Aria could describe it to him later. He stayed put and continued to pet the cat.

Ringo's loud purr blended with the muted sounds of horses moving in their stalls. They were probably wondering what the hell was going on and if this middle-of-the-night intrusion involved food.

When Aria opened the stall door and eased the wheelchair inside, he was glad they'd already practiced this move. If they hadn't, he wouldn't have been so sure about hauling Josh out here tonight. A horse nickered, but the sound came from a stall close to him, not Lucy's.

He hoped she and Linus were awake, but the colt looked

adorable curled up asleep, too. Either way should do the trick. If it didn't, then Josh was a hopeless case and Aria would have to accept that. If she needed any support as she worked through her disappointment, he would gladly provide it.

He'd also give Josh a piece of his mind, even though that wouldn't accomplish anything. It would make him feel better, though. Funny how his easygoing nature shifted when someone was hurting Aria.

That wasn't all that had shifted, either. If someone had suggested that his world view could change in forty-eight hours, he would have laughed his head off. But it had.

Taking this action for Aria's sake, a move he wouldn't have imagined himself making even last week, showed him that he could change, and damned fast, too. Just because he'd never wanted to commit to a woman in the past didn't mean he wasn't ready to do it now.

She'd said she wasn't in the market for a husband, and that was fine with him. He didn't need a piece of paper to tell him what he knew in his heart. That part they could take a day at a time. No rush, as long as she agreed they should be together. Judging from the way she'd looked at him after he'd confronted Josh, he thought maybe she would agree.

They didn't come out for quite a while. That should be a good sign unless Josh was sitting there in a funk and Aria was knocking herself out trying to spark his interest in the foal. After what seemed like an eternity and likely was only about twenty minutes, the wheelchair reappeared.

While Aria closed and fastened the stall door, Josh rolled himself down the aisle toward Brant. The guy had impressive dexterity. The basketball team hadn't been that coordinated when they'd fooled around with Steve's chair.

Josh came to a stop in front of Brant. His cheeks were damp and he cleared his throat several times.

Brant waited.

Finally, Josh held out his hand. "Thanks, man." His voice shook. "I owe you." In spite of his obvious distress, he had a hell of a grip.

"Don't thank me. Thank your sister."

"I did. And I will, many times over. I told her this afternoon that a cute little foal wouldn't make a difference." He cleared his throat again and met Brant's gaze. "I was wrong. Thanks for insisting I come out here."

"You're welcome." Brant wanted to do a victory dance or at least a fist pump, but he controlled the impulse. "I thought you should at least meet the little guy."

"Yeah, well, I intend to do a hell of a lot more than that. He came right over to me, like he knew me. I'm sure that's because of the way you've socialized him in these first couple of days, but still..." He swallowed. "It was very cool."

"Horses choose who they like just like people do."

"I've always thought so." He took a deep breath and glanced away. "I guess I was worried that he wouldn't like me."

Probably because he didn't like himself much these days. But that could change. Maybe the process had already started.

Aria approached and he realized she'd been waiting until Josh had said his piece. Her quick little sniff told him she'd been crying, too, but he suspected they were happy tears. "Thank you, Brant." Her voice quivered and she paused to take a breath. "We can go back now."

Once again he let Aria and Josh work out the logistics of getting into the van. They seemed to have a system. After he stashed the wheelchair in the tack room he got behind the wheel and started the van.

Aria reached over and squeezed his arm. She let go immediately as if she'd had the same thought about excluding Josh, but he treasured that brief contact. He liked making her happy. He hoped she'd let him do that for a very long time.

In sharp contrast to the silent drive out, the drive back was filled with animated conversation as Josh described Linus's behavior in great detail and Aria added footnotes. Brant joined in with his own anecdotes about Linus and they all agreed that he was the most amazing colt that had ever lived.

"You were right, Aria," Josh said. "I needed motivation to get out of that damned chair and Linus is it. I want to help halter-train him and later on I want to introduce him to a saddle. How cool is it to be there for every stage of his development?"

"I think it'll be great." Aria looked over at Brant. "Do you ever check back to see how your other foals are doing?"

"Not really. I've had reports from the owners, but they're not my foals, so I make myself turn loose of them when the training's over. Better for them, better for me."

"Hmm." She gave him a little smile but didn't say anything more.

Back at the apartment complex, he carried Josh in because it was simpler than bringing his wheelchair out.

"I'll make you a promise," Josh said as Brant settled him in his chair. "This is the very last time you'll have to do that."

"I don't mind."

"Yeah, but I do. I'll be out of this thing in no time. You may know this already, but when someone in our family sets a goal, then that's it. The goal will be accomplished."

Brant glanced at Aria standing in the doorway smiling at him. "I do know that."

"Yes," she said softly. "But sometimes we need a little help from our friends."

"Thanks for being there for Aria." Josh held out his hand again. "Sorry I've been such an a-hole."

Brant shook his hand and smiled. "Hey, any friend of Linus's is a friend of mine."

"Ditto." Josh looked from Brant to Aria. "Okay, get out of here, you two lovebirds. I know you've been keeping your hands off each other for my sake, and I appreciate that. But I'm sure you have business to take care of and I have strengthening exercises to do."

Crossing the room, Aria leaned down to give him a hug. "Will you go out to the ranch with me tomorrow morning?"

"I will." He sighed. "I'm tempted to wait until I'm back on my feet, except I'd miss so much." He glared at Brant. "But don't you dare treat me like a cripple."

"I won't because you're not."

Josh held his gaze. "Thank you for that." Then he waved them off. "Now beat it, both of you."

They'd barely made it out the door before Aria grabbed his face in both hands and kissed him for all she was worth. She knocked off his hat in the process and he let it fall as he gathered her close and delved into her hot mouth. He wanted her with a ferocity that defied all reason.

He lost track of where they were and who might come upon them. He simply had to get as close to her as possible. Their clothes became an unacceptable barrier and he reached under her shirt, searching for the hooks on her bra. No telling what might have happened if she hadn't wiggled against him and nudged the panic button on the keys he'd shoved in his pocket.

They both started laughing and he had a devil of a time silencing the alarm, but eventually he got it turned off.

They hopped in the van so he could park it where it belonged. With that done, she grabbed his hand and tugged him up the outside staircase to her second-floor apartment.

She wasted no time getting in and hurrying him through her living room. But in the hallway outside her bedroom, she suddenly stopped and stared at him in dismay. "We can't. I don't have any—"

"Never mind." He caught her by the shoulders and propelled her through the door. "Your keys weren't all I had in my pocket." After that, clothes flew and he made love to her without pulling back the comforter, without foreplay, without finesse of any kind. She didn't seem to care. Her eagerness matched his and they both came in a noisy, jubilant rush.

At last they quieted, their bodies slick and flushed with pleasure. It was time. Taking a deep breath, he propped himself on his forearms and gazed into her eyes. "I love you, Aria Danes."

"I know. I love you, too."

"I'm sorry I just blurted it out when I was talking to your brother, but—"

"Shh." She placed a finger against his lips. "What you did tonight, including what you said to Josh, was the most romantic thing I can imagine. You blew me away."

"Yeah?" He couldn't help grinning.

"Yeah."

Success made him bold. He had something to say and he might as well say it now. "You know, when we raced through your apartment, I didn't notice whether you had a couch."

"I do." She frowned in confusion. "Why?"

"Is there room to stash a sleeping bag behind it?"

Her eyes widened and then they filled with tears. "Oh, Brant."

Leaning down, he kissed the tears as they dribbled from the corners of her beautiful, violet eyes. "The truth is, I don't have a sleeping bag. What I really want is to lie here with you in your bed every night I'm not on the road."

"You do?" The tears flowed faster.

"I want to be with you, Aria. Just you, for as long as you'll have me."

Her voice was thick with emotion. "I hope you know what you're saying because that could be a really, really long time."

"I know what I'm saying." Lifting his head, he gazed down at her. The sweet ache in his chest told him this was right. "I told you that I didn't believe in this…in love. But now…" His throat tightened. "Now I do."

Epilogue

WHEN LIAM MAGEE delivered his tired but extremely happy rafting clients to their hotel, he popped into the lobby long enough to flirt with Hope, the blonde at the concierge desk. One of these times he'd ask her out, but not today.

He had other things on his mind as he pulled away from the hotel entrance and found a shady parking space. The river always helped him think through a problem and he'd come to a decision. Taking his phone from the waterproof bag in his knapsack, he called his foster brother Damon in Sheridan.

The guy might not be available since he was getting married in two weeks. Plans for that major event at Thunder Mountain Ranch had been in the works since before Christmas, so Damon was probably going crazy with the details.

Luckily he answered his phone. "Hey, Liam! You'd better not be calling to cancel." He sounded a little manic. "I'll personally haul your ass to the ranch if I have to. This is important."

"Damn sure is, bro. Never thought I'd see the day, so I'll be there come hell or high water."

"Grady, too, right? Philomena's excited to meet you, but she's ready to fan-girl all over your little brother."

That was a bonus. He hadn't realized the bride liked Grady's sculptures. Not everyone was into recycled metal art. "He'll be there along with his wedding present. That's what I called about. He's putting the final touches on it this weekend."

"Are you saying we're getting a sculpture?"

"Yep, and—"

"No way! Phil's gonna go ballistic. She's found several she loves but none of them fit our budget. I can't wait to see her face when it shows up."

"Me, either." *Or yours.* "You might not remember, but Grady kind of idolized you when we were living at the ranch."

"He did?"

"Yeah. He went to welding school mostly because you encouraged him to capitalize on his natural talent. I told him the same thing, but I think it meant more coming from you. He was inspired by your determination to become a master carpenter."

"I didn't know that, but it's nice to hear. And he sure has done well for himself."

"He has, and this wedding gift is his way of thanking you. I thought I'd better warn you that it's...substantial."

"Even better! Phil will be over the moon. She'll give it a place of honor."

"Damon, it's not going to fit in your living room."

There was a moment of silence. "Just how big is it?"

"Large."

"How large?"

"Let's put it this way. It won't fit in the back of a pickup so we're using a trailer to haul it up there."

"Wow. What's he building, the Eiffel Tower?"

"Not quite. I promise you it's gorgeous, but I'm not saying anything more because he wants it to be a surprise. I've already spoiled that by calling you, but I thought you should be prepared. I'd appreciate it if we can keep this conversation to ourselves."

"Understood." Damon chuckled. "And you're still watching out for him, I see."

"Guess so."

"Well, don't worry. Doesn't matter what size it is. It'll be a hit and we'll find the perfect place for it."

"Thanks, bro. See you in two weeks." He hung up with a sigh of relief. Grady hadn't stopped to think that not everyone was prepared to display a nine-foot sculpture, but now Damon wouldn't be caught flat-footed when it arrived.

Buoyed by the successful phone call, he almost drove back to the hotel to ask Hope for a date. But instinct kept him from doing that. She seemed special, which meant he should give the matter more attention than a spur-of-the-moment invitation. As soon as he came back from the wedding, he'd concentrate on Hope.

* * * * *

Available June 21, 2016

#899 COWBOY AFTER DARK

Thunder Mountain Brotherhood

by Vicki Lewis Thompson

Liam Magee is at the ranch for a wedding—so is Hope Caldwell, whom he's wanted in his bed for months. Hope craves the sexy cowboy but can she trust him for more than a fling?

#900 MAKE MINE A MARINE

Uniformly Hot!

by Candace Havens

Having recently returned home, Marine Matt Ryan is looking forward to a more peaceful life as a helicopter instructor at the local base...not realizing free-spirited Chelly Richardson is about to rock his world!

#901 THE MIGHTY QUINNS: THOM

The Mighty Quinns

by Kate Hoffmann

Hockey player Thom Quinn has never hesitated to seduce a beautiful woman. But the bad boy has to be good this time, because Malin Pederson controls his fate on the team. And she's the boss's daughter.

#902 NO SURRENDER

by Sara Arden

Fiery Kentucky Lee burns hot enough to warm Special Ops Aviation pilot Sean Dryden's frozen heart—not to mention his bed—but he must NOT fall for his ex-fiancée's best friend...

YOU CAN FIND MORE INFORMATION ON UPCOMING HARLEQUIN® TITLES, FREE EXCERPTS AND MORE AT WWW.HARLEQUIN.COM.

HBCNM0616

REQUEST YOUR FREE BOOKS!
2 FREE NOVELS PLUS 2 FREE GIFTS!

H HARLEQUIN®

Blaze®

red-hot reads!

YES! Please send me 2 FREE Harlequin® Blaze® novels and my 2 FREE gifts (gifts are worth about $10). After receiving them, if I don't wish to receive any more books, I can return the shipping statement marked "cancel." If I don't cancel, I will receive 4 brand-new novels every month and be billed just $4.74 per book in the U.S. or $5.21 per book in Canada. That's a savings of at least 14% off the cover price. It's quite a bargain. Shipping and handling is just 50¢ per book in the U.S. and 75¢ per book in Canada.* I understand that accepting the 2 free books and gifts places me under no obligation to buy anything. I can always return a shipment and cancel at any time. Even if I never buy another book, the two free books and gifts are mine to keep forever.

150/350 HDN GH2D

Name	(PLEASE PRINT)	
Address		Apt. #
City	State/Prov.	Zip/Postal Code

Signature (if under 18, a parent or guardian must sign)

Mail to the **Reader Service:**
IN U.S.A.: P.O. Box 1867, Buffalo, NY 14240-1867
IN CANADA: P.O. Box 609, Fort Erie, Ontario L2A 5X3

Want to try two free books from another line?
Call 1-800-873-8635 or visit www.ReaderService.com.

* Terms and prices subject to change without notice. Prices do not include applicable taxes. Sales tax applicable in N.Y. Canadian residents will be charged applicable taxes. Offer not valid in Quebec. This offer is limited to one order per household. Not valid for current subscribers to Harlequin Blaze books. All orders subject to credit approval. Credit or debit balances in a customer's account(s) may be offset by any other outstanding balance owed by or to the customer. Please allow 4 to 6 weeks for delivery. Offer available while quantities last.

Your Privacy—The Reader Service is committed to protecting your privacy. Our Privacy Policy is available online at www.ReaderService.com or upon request from the Reader Service.

We make a portion of our mailing list available to reputable third parties that offer products we believe may interest you. If you prefer that we not exchange your name with third parties, or if you wish to clarify or modify your communication preferences, please visit us at www.ReaderService.com/consumerchoice or write to us at Reader Service Preference Service, P.O. Box 9062, Buffalo, NY 14240-9062. Include your complete name and address.

HB15

Hope was a puzzle, and he didn't have all the pieces
yet. Something didn't fit the picture she was presenting
to everyone, but he'd figure out the mystery eventually.
Right now they had a soft blanket waiting. He lifted her
down and led her over to it.

He'd ground-tied both Navarre and Isabeau, who were
old and extremely mellow. The horses weren't going
anywhere. Hope sat on the blanket like a person about
to have a picnic, except they hadn't brought anything to
eat or drink.

Liam decided to set the tone. After relaxing beside
her, he took off his Stetson and stretched out on his back.
"You can see the stars a lot better if you lie back."

To his surprise, she laughed. "Is that a maneuver?"

"A maneuver?"

"You know, a move."

"Oh. I guess it's a move, now that you mention it." He
sighed. "The truth is, I want to kiss you, and it'll be easier
if you're down here instead of up there."

"So it has nothing to do with looking at the stars."

"It has everything to do with looking at the stars! First you lie on your back and appreciate how beautiful they are, and then I get to kiss you underneath their brilliant light. It all goes together."

"You sound cranky."

"That's because nobody has ever made me break it down."

"I see." She flopped down onto the blanket. "Beautiful stars. Now kiss me."

"You just completely destroyed the mood."

"Are you sure?" She rolled to her side and reached over to run a finger down his tense jaw. "Last time I checked, we still had a canopy of stars arching over us."

"A canopy of stars." He turned to face her and propped his head on his hand. "Did you write that?"

"None of your beeswax."

Although she'd said it in a teasing way, he got the message. No more questions about her late great writing career. "Let's start over. How about if you lie back and look up at the stars?"

"I did that already, and you didn't pick up your cue."

"Try it again."

She sighed and rolled to her back. "Beautiful stars. Now kiss—"

His mouth covered hers before she could finish.

Reading Has Its Rewards

Earn **FREE BOOKS!**

Register at **Harlequin My Rewards** and submit your Harlequin purchases from wherever you shop to earn points for free books and other exclusive rewards.

Plus submit your purchases from now till May 30th for a chance to win a $500 Visa Card*.

Visit **HarlequinMyRewards.com** today

MYRI6RI

Whatever You're Into… Passionate Reads

Looking for more passionate reads from Harlequin®?
Fear not! Harlequin® Presents, Harlequin® Desire and
Harlequin® Blaze offer you irresistible romance stories
featuring powerful heroes.

✦HARLEQUIN *Presents*

Do you want alpha males, decadent glamour and jet-set
lifestyles? Step into the sensational, sophisticated world of
Harlequin® Presents, where sinfully tempting heroes ignite a
fierce and wickedly irresistible passion!

✦HARLEQUIN *Desire*

Harlequin® Desire novels are powerful, passionate and
provocative contemporary romances set against a backdrop of
wealth, privilege and sweeping family saga. Alpha heroes with
a soft side meet strong-willed but vulnerable heroines amid a
dramatic world of divided loyalties, high-stakes conflict and
intense emotion.

✦HARLEQUIN *Blaze*

Harlequin® Blaze stories sizzle with strong heroines and
irresistible heroes playing the game of modern love and lust.
They're fun, sexy and always steamy.

Be sure to check out our full selection of books
within each series every month!

www.Harlequin.com

HPASSION2016